HIS EVERYTHING

"I'm okay," she whispered.

He sucked in a breath, letting go of the fear that had gnawed on him since hearing that first gunshot.

She placed her hands on his biceps. Her gray eyes pulled him in. She was his focal point. She'd been his everything. And she was okay.

Nikki was *mi cielo*. She'd never stopped, though she'd also never known what she meant to him.

He slid his hands up to cup her face. So many mistakes. So much missed time.

She held perfectly still. Maybe she was still stunned from the attack, or maybe she felt it, too.

Gabriel placed his mouth on hers, mindful of her split lip. An electric-like current shot through him, reviving those deep recesses of himself only she'd touched. Her body jolted against his hands, but only for a second. She remained completely still. He didn't care. What mattered was that she was alive and unhurt.

Her lips parted, maybe to tell him off, but he didn't give her the chance. He suckled the sweet morsel of flesh between his lips and she groaned.

Better than I remembered.

Books by Sidney Bristol

Drive

Shift

Chase

Published by Kensington Publishing Corporation

CHASE

SIDNEY BRISTOL

ZEBRA BOOKS
KENSINGTON PUBLISHING CORP.
http://www.kensingtonbooks.com

ZEBRA BOOKS are published by

Kensington Publishing Corp.
119 West 40th Street
New York, NY 10018

All Kensington titles, imprints, and distributed lines are available at special quantity discounts for bulk purchases for sales promotion, premiums, fund-raising, educational, or institutional use.

Special book excerpts or customized printings can also be created to fit specific needs. For details, write or phone the office of the Kensington Sales Manager: Attn.: Sales Department. Kensington Publishing Corp., 119 West 40th Street, New York, NY 10018. Phone: 1-800-221-2647.

Zebra and the Z logo Reg. U.S. Pat. & TM Off.

First Printing: December 2016
ISBN-13: 978-1-4201-3925-9
ISBN-10: 1-4201-3925-8

eISBN-13: 978-1-4201-3926-6
eISBN-10: 1-4201-3926-6

10 9 8 7 6 5 4 3 2 1

Printed in the United States of America

Chapter One

Identities were like T-shirts, easy to change out until you found one that fit.

Gabriel Ortiz had worn so many identities in his life, sometimes he wasn't sure who he was anymore. At least until he got behind the wheel of a car. It was easier to tap into the parts of himself that were Gabriel and not a made-up persona for a job. When it was just him, his car, and the road, things made sense. Lately he'd spent almost all his spare time behind the wheel of his new ride, a bad little Nissan Skyline he'd rebuilt piece by piece, but instead of feeling more whole, he was restless.

"I cannot believe how badly you smoked them." Roni Chazov, one of his fellow mechanics at Classic Rides, smacked him on the shoulder. She grinned at him, a rare thing these days, and flipped her long, red hair over her shoulder. Men fell over themselves for Roni's attention, but she'd always been one of the guys to him.

"Yeah." He nodded.

"You could at least act like you're having a good time." Roni crossed her arms over her chest and turned to face the line of cars across the street.

Hip-hop thumped from a chrome plated lowrider. Half

a dozen other cars had their hoods popped while drivers and onlookers kicked tires, talked shop or bragged about their fastest time. Several of them were Gabriel's friends and coworkers, people he'd bled with. People he'd die for.

"They're watching us," Roni said, pitching her voice low.

"I know."

Their crew's reputation had always been solid on the streets, but now people were scared of them. Fear didn't sit well with Gabriel. At least not while he was himself. He'd pretended to be men who thrived on that kind of attention, but not Gabriel. Not his real self. He didn't like it at all.

"What do you think they're saying?" she asked.

"Probably wondering where we hid the bodies."

"That's not funny." Roni shot him a glare.

"Hey, you asked what they were saying. I just answered." He shrugged. It wasn't an understatement. Rumors were all over Miami about what their crew had done to a couple of hit men out for the Chazov twins.

"Yeah. I miss the days when they just wanted to know what was under the hood." Roni tapped the Skyline's tire with the toe of her boot.

Gabriel nodded. They'd all known the day was coming when their undercover FBI operation would change the street game. But none of them had anticipated this. Thanks to a friend at the Miami-Dade PD keeping the details of the arrests under wraps, they'd been able to put a spin on the latest exploits to paint themselves as the new street bosses. With their biggest rivals out of the picture, Gabriel and his crew were it. Which was the biggest joke there was. They were the crime kings who didn't do crime.

"Where's your twin?" Gabriel asked.

"Where do you think?" Ice laced Roni's tone.

"Things okay between you two?"

"Yeah."

"Okay." He shrugged.

Unlike most of his crew, Gabriel had experience with long-term, deep-cover missions. They were hell on the body and the soul. That the crew was three years into the operation without any real problems with their people was remarkable. In his book, Roni's sister shacking up with their field tech wasn't all that bad. He was even happy for them, if he could be happy about anything.

Roni leaned toward him. "I was thinking—"

Gabriel's pocket chimed, and an echoing noise emanated from Roni's pocket.

That couldn't be good.

He dug his phone out of his pocket, unlocked the screen, and tapped the message notification from—speak of the devil—their field tech, the Walking Brain, Emery. In Gabriel's peripheral vision he could see the others doing the same thing.

Alarm at Classic Rides. Security offline.

"Shit," Roni said. She glared at him. "Get driving. You're fastest."

Classic Rides was the business they all worked out of, restoring classic muscle cars, and acted as the front for their FBI gigs. They didn't keep anything at the garage except tools and cars, but thanks to current events, they had a huge bull's-eye on their backs. If someone wanted to fuck with them, the garage was a prime target.

Roni jogged toward her new V10 Viper while Gabriel pulled the door open to his Skyline and dropped into the driver's seat. The onlooking pedestrians scattered, jumping onto the sidewalk as Gabriel peeled out in a plume of exhaust and squealing tires. He glanced in his rearview mirror. The closest headlights were over a car length away. Aiden's, if he had to guess. Their fearless leader was the owner and had wrapped up his life's savings in the garage.

The fastest route to Classic Rides this time of night was via I-95, but he had to get to the interstate first. Gabriel ignored a red traffic light, barreling through before the oncoming traffic had even let off their accelerators. Another car turned onto the old two-lane street ahead of him, blocking him. He jerked the Skyline into the left lane, stomped on the accelerator, and shifted. The car lurched forward, the engine barely even working. Yet. There was a discernable lack of vibration as the car coasted over the road as if the tires never really touched the asphalt. This really was the fastest car he'd ever had.

And right now, he needed every second it could buy him.

Being part of the crew at Classic Rides had given him a purpose when he had nothing. After his world crumbled and everything he thought he had walked out the door, the crew had put him back together. They'd given him a mission. Something to live for. The garage might just be a building, but it was more to him. It was his new home, and he wasn't about to let anyone destroy that.

"Come on, come on," he chanted.

He coasted through another intersection, weaving between cars, and passed under the overpass, cutting off a sedan as he changed lanes, ignoring the angry blare of the horn. The speakers began to ring and Emery's name flashed across the display mounted into the dash.

Gabriel pressed a button on his steering wheel, activating the call.

"Talk to me."

"Someone just used CJ's codes to access the garage, but it can't be CJ. He's still in DC. You're the closest. I have no eyes on the facility. Someone had to have taken the security out at the power source—or something else. Fuck. I don't know." Normally Emery was quiet and rather mild mannered. That was a well-constructed front. Right now, Emery cursed and growled with the best of them, and for good reason. They'd lost their direct FBI handler, CJ, after the death of his wife in the line of action. Every one of them suspected someone higher up at the FBI to be setting them up to take a fall. Who knew who was at the garage right now? What were they trying to do?

"I should go in hot, you mean?" Gabriel maneuvered around the slower traffic, making liberal use of the shoulder. There were only two exits to go. He couldn't see Aiden in his rearview mirror. He pushed the car faster, his focus narrowing to the vehicles around him and the way the Skyline handled.

"Yes, but hold up a second and wait for backup. We don't know what's in there yet, and I want them alive."

He could hear the frustration in Emery's voice. Classic Rides had remained as secure a location as they could make it. No doubt Emery would take it personally should the facility ever be breached. Like now.

"No can do, Brain."

He flipped on his blinker as he coasted over the white line, cutting off a red van. The shop was a few streets over from the highway, still a couple lights to go.

"That's not a good idea. Wait for backup."

Emery's voice drifted into the background. Gabriel pulled the hand brake and let the Skyline whip around at a ninety-degree angle. Cars honked and their tires screeched as drivers swerved to avoid him. He gunned the engine and shot forward, the familiar storefronts a blur as he focused on the retro sign of Classic Rides ahead with the purple and indigo night sky behind it. Palm trees waved in a stronger-than-normal breeze.

A single bay door was open and all the lights were on. The parking lot was empty save the cars for sale lined up along the perimeter. Hell, the gate and chain were down, too, almost as if someone had opened the garage for business. It wasn't exactly a covert setup.

Screw it.

Gabriel steered the Skyline into the parking lot and shifted hard into park. He grabbed his primary weapon out of the center console while keeping his gaze on the open doors. His 1967 Pontiac GTO was inside. If whoever thought of hitting them tonight touched the car, he was likely to ignore the directive to take any and all adversaries alive.

He got out of the Skyline and crept toward the closed bay door, keeping his eyes on the storefront windows.

Nothing moved.

In the distance he could hear the rumble and whine of engines. The others would be here any moment. The smart thing to do would be to wait, but this garage, these people, they were his safe haven. His family. When it came to those things, he'd face down a dozen thugs for them.

He took a deep breath and peered around the open door, into the first bay.

Four cars sat ready for the morning. A tune-up, an oil change, Gabriel's ride, and a complete restore job. All the familiar smells filled the air: oil, rubber, and lemon-scented cleaner. Nothing was out of place, except the woman with dark hair wearing a suit standing with her back to him. She appeared to be looking at something on the workbench surface.

Suits meant Feds. And right now he didn't have any love for them.

He took another step, gun trained on the woman.

"Turn around," he barked.

The woman straightened, and for a moment neither moved. Did she have a partner? Someone hiding as her backup? There were easily a dozen places in the garage to take cover. They'd designed it that way for exactly this reason.

She pivoted to face him, and everything froze. He didn't

breathe or blink. The world could have stopped moving for all he cared.

The hair was different and he'd never seen her in drab black before, but the face was still the same. Or similar. She'd always smiled when he'd seen her, but that was before. Now her lips were compressed in a tight line. Pity, she was rather stunning when she smiled.

"Gabriel." She licked her lower lip and he couldn't help but focus on that one action. "I . . . wasn't expecting anyone to be here this late."

"Nikki?" He lowered his gun, frowning. Lights slashed across the garage as one and then another car turned into the parking lot. He stalked toward her, needing to know it was really *his* Nikki before the others arrived and all hell broke loose.

Nikki swallowed and held her ground as six feet of rock-her-world man barreled down on her. The garage was supposed to be closed. She should have had hours—all night even—to get acquainted with this case, her new team. Working with him.

She'd known from the moment this assignment landed on her desk that nothing about it would be easy. The director in charge of this operation wanted her to control Gabriel, and through him this team he'd joined. How the hell was she supposed to do that? She hadn't been able to control him when she'd been his handler and it was her job. The best she could do was give him his orders and nudge him a bit in the right direction, make a suggestion or two. No one controlled Gabriel, least of all her.

His sinful, dark chocolate eyes stabbed her heart. There was no warmth there. No friendliness. She didn't doubt for a second if she made the wrong move, he'd shoot her. His hair was longer, a bit unruly, but she kind of liked it. It suited him better than the close-cropped stubble had. The lines around his mouth were the worst. Frown lines. His smile had unnerved her in the beginning, but that was probably her good sense, knowing that inevitably, he'd charm her out of her panties. The rest of him, well, if memory served her well, it was rock hard, lined with scars, and yet, he'd always held her with such tender care. As if the cruelty of what he had to do, of who he had to be, got all used up and left only the gentler side of him for her.

She had to say something.

They were staring at each other.

This was entirely ridiculous.

They'd broken up. Or really, she'd dumped him after—after the nightmare.

"I realize—"

"Stop." His voice reverberated through the garage, making it sound louder than it really was.

She tensed, which was better than jumping out of her skin. He'd stopped less than a foot away from her. Oh God, was he going to touch her? She could survive this, hell, maybe she could even succeed, but not if he touched her. There was too much history between them to not dredge it all back up once the feel of his hands was involved.

"What are you doing here?" he whispered. While his voice was soft, his features were hard. The only time she'd seen him look this way was in the beginning. When he'd been close to breaking. Yeah, he wanted to see her again about as much as she wanted to be there.

"Gabriel?" a man yelled.

"In here," he called without looking away from her.

More of the team? Shit. This was not her night.

Feet thudded against the concrete outside. Several people running their way at once.

"What are you doing here?" he asked her once more, voice pitched low for her ears only.

She opened her mouth to reply.

"What the—who the fuck is that?" A big, dark-haired man with a gun in his hand was followed by a red-haired woman and a man with lighter-colored hair, somewhere between brown and blond.

Julian, one of the Chazov twins, and Aiden. Her memory supplied the names from their files while her focus remained on Gabriel.

This was a mistake. She should have stayed in DC. Things were going well for her, but she just had to get out in the trenches and get her hands dirty on this case. It wasn't enough to stay in the field office and work it from afar.

"Nikki?" Julian's bloodshot eyes worried her as much as his file had. She'd only worked with Julian on that one job toward the end with Gabriel. Looking at the case file and getting up to date, it was safe to say they'd both been busy.

"Stand down," Gabriel barked to the newcomers.

A man in cowboy boots and a Stetson, of all things, brought up the rear, ushering in a heavily tattooed woman who crossed to the man who'd entered first. The cowboy pressed the button to close the bay doors. Six people stared at her, and there wasn't a friendly one in the bunch.

This was such a bad idea.

"I—Are we free to talk?" she asked Gabriel.

His gaze narrowed.

"I'd say yes, but you took the security offline and—" A phone ding from several pockets made him pause long enough to glance at his cell. "Security's back up. Talk."

"I . . . I'm sorry. I used the code CJ gave me to get to his files." She gestured toward the office.

"What code did you use?" Aiden asked.

She took a deep breath and recited the six-digit code CJ had made her memorize.

"What the fuck are you doing in my garage?" Aiden was almost yelling now.

"Boss," Gabriel barked.

Aiden glanced toward him, none of the anger dissipating.

Gabriel turned and strode away from her, toward an electric purple muscle car. He was both beautiful and deadly when he moved. There was a fluidness to his movements and an understated strength that made it easy for people to dismiss him as just another average Joe. Boy, were they wrong.

She cleared her throat, tore her gaze from him, and slowly took stock of those present. She'd hoped to do this tomorrow, after she'd prepared herself a bit more, but now was as good as ever. They were missing the other twin as well as the field tech, but she'd read the notes on them. Besides, a tech so highly recommended as Emery Martin, she was willing to bet he was listening to them right now.

"I'm Special Agent Nikki Gage—"

"Gage?" Aiden leaned forward, arms crossed.

"Yes." She held her head up a little more. Damn it. She'd have liked to get through the high-level overview before they cracked this nut.

"Any relation to Danny Gage?"

"My father is the deputy director of the FBI, if that's what you're asking."

"This is rich." Aiden wrapped one arm around the woman sticking close to his side while glaring at Nikki. "Madison, would you mind getting some coffee going?"

"I can do that." The tattooed woman glanced from Nikki to Aiden, and the look was not friendly. Awesome. More people who didn't like her. She was making friends today.

"Thank you." She took a deep breath, grounding herself. Yes, her father was one of the most influential men in the FBI. She'd practically grown up in the bureau, and she'd still had to work her ass off to get where she was. No one had handed her anything, contrary to rumor and public opinion. "CJ gave me his access codes so I could come here after I landed. Familiarize myself a bit more before we met—officially—tomorrow. Director Scott—I'm getting ahead of myself. I apologize. I'm part of a new task force geared toward handling homegrown security threats."

"What? Like the Unabomber?" the man with the Stetson asked. John. They called him John Wayne, but the man was no joke. Behind that country-boy façade was a dangerous and decorated war hero who'd walked away from a promotion to come work on cars.

"Exactly like the Unabomber." She clasped her hands in front of her. "Today we face more threats from Americans on our own soil than we do from foreigners."

"What's the job?" Gabriel asked from across the garage. He'd retreated almost as far as he could go and still be in the same space as her. Did he hate her? She couldn't blame him. She had walked out on him, but he'd left her long before she removed herself physically.

"Director Scott is supposed to call you," she glanced at Aiden, then Julian, "tomorrow morning and notify you that until further notice, I am your FBI handler, and your mission is changing. Only for a little while. There's a man by the name of Bradley Wilson. He's a charismatic guy that has been involved in a number of militant cells. Until now he's been a footnote in a file tracking their movements, but not as anyone with any kind of clout." She picked up her satchel and set it on a red metal set of drawers. It was surprisingly clean, with little grease or gunk. Settling into her role helped. This she was used to. She could focus on Gabriel less.

"Why is this our problem? We've already got enough on our plates." Aiden was closer now, but he still regarded her warily.

Nikki knew Aiden was going to be the one to win over.

From all accounts, since the arrest of their prime target he'd become increasingly belligerent toward FBI involvement. "I did not request you, if that's what you're asking. I was assigned to this, and Director Scott told me this team was at my disposal."

"Look, lady, you can tell Emery and Julian what to do, but the rest of us? We're contract employees. We don't have to say yes to anything you're trying to sell us." The way Aiden stared at her, she didn't doubt he'd tell her to leave for the fun of it.

"Aiden." Gabriel nodded, motioning the other man over.

Aiden strode over to the purple car, abruptly pausing their conversation. If it could be called that. Julian, John, and the redhead joined them, putting their heads together and closing her out.

While they were otherwise occupied, Nikki pulled out her cell phone and shot off a text to CJ. What kind of game was the man playing at?

Setting me up?

His reply was almost instantaneous. As if he'd been waiting to hear from her.

You needed the Band-Aid ripped off.

He'd set her up. Figured.

Nikki pocketed the phone without another glance and tried to act naturally. As if she came face-to-face with her past every day.

She tried to not stare either, to not feel like the kid looking through the window, but this was what her relationship with Gabe had always been like. She was the professional, kept on the outside, while he did the messy business. Every day she'd fought against the divide in his life, wanting to be let in, and he'd just kept her at a distance. He was the most infuriating man, so why hadn't she been able to shake him? She still slept in his shirt on really bad days, ordered his pizza, drank his beer.

God, she was pathetic.

Coming here, accepting this case, was the biggest mistake she'd made since . . . since leaving him.

Chapter Two

Gabriel stared at Aiden's forehead to keep from looking over his shoulder at Nikki. She had the carved-from-stone look down to an art. She'd wait them out all night if they tried, and they'd get nowhere with her. The FBI was literally bred into her. If they were going to outplay her on this, they had to get their shit together.

"She's your ex. What do you think?" Julian asked Gabriel.

"She's your what?" Aiden asked, his gaze ping-ponging back and forth between Gabriel and Julian.

Gabriel wasn't ready to have that conversation with Aiden now. Or ever.

"I think you and Emery have no choice, and we can all say we won't be part of whatever she's here to do, but when Julian's ass is on the line we'll all be there for him, doing exactly what she needs us to do." He tilted his head toward Julian slightly before catching himself and halting the gesture. Nikki saw everything.

"How can we spin this?" Aiden asked him.

Usually, Aiden and Julian made the decisions, called the shots, and that was it. Now everyone's gaze centered on Gabriel, as if he knew what he was doing. It was a strange place to be. Especially with this group. He'd shed the mantle of responsibility when he left the FBI. Stretching his decision-making skills felt good. Once, he'd been the one to set up operations, direct units, but not anymore.

"Nikki is honest," he said.

"For a Hoover," Aiden threw in, using their private term for the FBI. Most of the agents they worked with just sucked the time and life right out of them.

"She's as honest as she can be." Gabriel stared Aiden in the eyes now. "Let's make her a deal. See what we can make happen."

"You do the talking," Julian said.

"What?" Aiden scowled, his brows drawn down into a hard line.

"Trust me." Julian slapped his best friend's chest.

"Fine. Go." Aiden's mouth twisted into a scowl. No matter how this went down, he wasn't going to like it.

Everyone stepped back, facing Nikki with a unified front, not that he expected her to back down. The woman had a backbone stronger than steel.

She hadn't moved from where she stood at Aiden's workbench except to pull out a thin manila folder. The black suit was severe, yet well tailored. He knew from experience the prude clothing hid a banging body. Of course she had to cover up those curves, or else her fellow agents would hound her, a lot like he had, but that was before he'd laid eyes on her.

His last handler got himself fired in the middle of Gabriel's deep-cover gig. Nikki had been introduced to him over the phone. He'd liked her immediately—because of her honesty. She'd treated him like a person, not a tool to be used. She wasn't like the other suits. From there, they'd been two lonely souls sharing about their day, what kept them up at night, and the good they wanted to do. Sleeping with her wasn't the wisest thing he'd done, but he'd never regretted it.

Nikki didn't speak, but her gaze followed him, as if she knew they'd elected him the spokesperson in this little charade. Yeah, it was a crock of bull. They all knew if one member of the crew was involved, they all were. They didn't turn their backs on their own. But maybe she didn't know that. And maybe she didn't know the sky was blue.

"If we do this, we want something." He hated how sleazy those words felt coming out of his mouth.

"You want to know why the FBI withheld evidence that would have prevented Michael Evers being released on bond."

Gabriel didn't know what was more surprising, that she knew what they were going to ask for or that she'd just admitted to what they'd all suspected.

The FBI had hindered their investigation.

"And who they're trying to trap." The muscles across Gabriel's shoulders tensed. She was a hell of a lot more knowledgeable than she'd admitted.

"I thought you just read the highlights." Aiden said what they were all thinking.

She turned her eyes on Aiden, relieving him of their burden.

"I did. And then I spoke to CJ."

Mutters from the others buzzed in the background. Their old handler had remained out of contact for several months following the death of his wife, a loss they were all still healing from. Gabriel, Aiden, all of them, had tried to contact him numerous times, but had been shut out. He'd been part of their crew, and yet he'd confided in Nikki? Not them? Gabriel didn't know what to make of that.

She held a file folder in front of her, one hand wrapped around her wrist. To the eye, she was relaxed, in control, and yet Gabriel was starting to see the signs of strain. It was in the corner of her mouth, on the left side. Her nails were bare. Small signs, but ones he'd grown to notice back in the day.

"How is he?" Roni asked. CJ and his wife had become part of their family, and the twins had felt their loss particularly hard.

"He's . . . dealing. I wouldn't say he's well, but he's trying to move on." For a moment Nikki didn't look at any of them. She shook her head and focused on Gabriel once more, treating him to the full scrutiny of her gaze. "I can't promise to get you answers, but I can try. Being the deputy director's daughter doesn't give me a license to do anything I want. It means a lot more people watch what I do. Especially these days."

Honesty. He'd always appreciated how Nikki told him the truth, no matter how ugly or screwed up it might be. Even now, after all this time, he still knew she was shooting them straight.

"What's the gig?" Gabriel asked.

"Bradley Wilson. He's started his own militia, supposedly to protect the US citizens from themselves. Their pitch for recruiting is that Americans are weak. We need to wake up and realize the danger we are in. The people he's gathered are all highly trained. Many of them are ex-military, former law enforcement, and straight-up whack jobs. Up until now, Wilson has been the one following orders. This group is the first time he's the one in charge."

"Do you know why?" Gabriel held out his hand and took a few steps closer. She met him halfway with the file.

"After we arrested and interviewed the people at his last 'outpost,' it sounds like narcissism and a very perverted case of Munchausen by proxy. He wants to fix America by attacking it."

"The country is sick, so he's going to cure them by shocking them awake?" Gabriel flipped through the file. There were a dozen pieces of paper, photographs, and a few maps. It wasn't a thick file.

"Something like that. His group carried out two hits on a couple gun retail warehouses, robbing them, before blowing up a sheriff's station in Tennessee. They went to ground and surfaced in Miami last week. From what I could gather, several core members are from the area, so they're starting their reeducation of America here."

"What does this reeducation entail?" Aiden peered over Gabriel's shoulder.

"So far, they haven't hurt anyone. Even the sheriff's office was completely empty. Based on their mission statement, I'd guess they're going to blow something else up, and this time they might not stick to empty buildings."

"That won't last. No one will talk about them unless they kill a few people," Roni said.

Nikki plucked the file from his hand and spread the papers out on the workbench. They each took a section and started reading.

Gabriel continued to stare at the roster of names. Most had just a single line of information on the person. This really was a startup gig. He could feel Nikki's gaze on him, peeling back the layers.

Who held her at night now? Did he want to know?

One of the smaller doors opened and their tech, Emery, stepped into the garage, followed by his girlfriend Tori. Emery tapped the headset hooked over one ear and made a beeline for the limited information spread.

"This isn't our problem." Aiden tossed the papers back onto the workbench, scowling, no doubt itching to dump everything off his station.

"Maybe not, but look at it this way." Gabriel handed the

papers to Emery, but kept his gaze on Aiden. "The Hoovers wouldn't send someone with a name like Gage down here if the gig was optional. That means that like it or not, we're going to have to do what Nikki says. Now, I can tell you from experience that she's a hell of a lot better to work with than anyone but maybe CJ. She didn't have to ask us to do this. I bet she's got a signed set of orders that will compel us to do what she wants, and instead of throwing that at us, she's coming to the table willing to bargain."

Nikki bit her lip. She always hated when people threw around her daddy's name and position.

"Is that true?" Aiden asked.

"Yes, Gabriel has hit on most of it." She tipped her chin up a bit, as if daring them to think less of her.

At least the bureau hadn't changed that part of her.

"What will they do if we don't play ball?" Aiden crossed his arms across his chest.

"I ensured Director Scott it wouldn't come to that." She wasn't dissuaded, intimidated, or shaken by any of them or this unorthodox setup. At least not on the surface. Good. If this was going to work, she would have to get her hands dirty.

"You can fight it if you want, Aiden, but what if saying no puts Madison in danger? What about you? The garage? You heard about the freelancer last month the same as I did." Gabriel had known the freelance spy. A decent enough man, but when he'd said no to a job Uncle Sam wanted him to do, they put his baby mama in jail and his kid into CPS before he could blink.

"Yeah, I heard," Aiden replied.

"I don't want to work with people who don't believe in the work we're doing," Nikki said, breaking into the staring match. "We've got a little to go on. The less time I have to spend fighting you, the more time I can spend trying to find these guys and stop them."

Gabriel continued studying Aiden, willing the man to see the bigger picture. None of them wanted to do another job right now. Their plates were full, but having Nikki possibly working for them, passing them intel, was an invaluable opportunity. She wouldn't break many rules, but she was a lot closer to the source of their problems than they were.

"We've got company," Roni announced, pocketing her phone.

More light spilled in through the windows set into the garage doors.

Who the hell was Roni talking to?

A moment later, Detective Matt Smith stepped into the garage. His gelled blond hair gleamed in the light. He still wore his badge on his hip, so this was an official visit at least.

"Do I want to know?" the golden boy cop asked. He'd had the unfortunate luck of getting involved with their crew and had become something of an honorary member.

"Depends." Nikki glanced at Gabriel, as if she were looking for his lead. It shouldn't have pushed him off balance, but it did. On some level, she still trusted him. That rapport wasn't completely destroyed.

"Probably. Matt, meet Supervisory Special Agent Nikki Gage of the FBI. We're about to take a vote on if we're going to stop some guys from blowing up Miami."

"What?" Matt glanced between them. "This is a joke, right?"

"Afraid not, Detective," Nikki said.

"Why are you even voting about something like that?" Matt's expression just got more horrified by the second.

"Who wants to let idiots with guns and bombs blow people up?" Gabriel asked, sweeping the room with a look.

No one raised their hand. Aiden pursed his lips and averted his eyes, but otherwise didn't object.

"Okay, who wants to stop some bad guys?" Gabriel raised his hand.

The others nodded, raised a hand, or in Aiden's case, flipped him off.

"All right, SSA Gage, you have our crew at your disposal. What are we doing?" Gabriel turned toward Nikki, and memories slammed into him. How many times had he asked her that? Looked to her for direction? This was how it used to work. Nikki manning the flow of information, priming the resources, while he got in the field and saved people.

For a second, there wasn't anyone else in the room besides them. It was just like old times. She'd tell him what they were doing, urge him to be careful, and seal it with a kiss. A quickie, if he was lucky.

She wasn't feeling it like he was. Her blank face told him he was the only idiot hanging on to what had been.

"I'm hoping we can decide the next steps together," she said.

"Well, consider Miami PD behind you. Can I help?" Matt kept his distance, well aware there were things he couldn't or shouldn't see, but made no move to leave.

"I'd appreciate the help. To be honest, I don't have the best relationship with the head of the local field office, so I'm not expecting a lot of support."

"I don't expect anything from them," Matt practically growled.

"Then we're on the same page." Nikki's smile was fleeting, and not aimed at Gabriel.

"What's their deal anyway?" Matt asked.

"It's—complicated." Nikki wouldn't divulge FBI gossip

to someone without the right kind of badge. Too bad, so sad for the golden boy detective.

Gabriel curled one hand into a fist and envisioned punching the cop.

Yeah, so he still had a thing for his old flame. So what? Nikki was a remarkable woman; they just hadn't been able to make it work.

Gabriel cleared his throat, and both Matt and Nikki looked back at him. "First thing, we should check the last known residences of all family ties in Miami. If someone has come home, they've probably made a visit to mom and dad. While we do that, Emery can start digging up more information, put some pictures with the rest of these names, get us some actual files going."

"That's what I was hoping you would suggest," Nikki said.

"Then that's what we'll do," Julian chimed in, giving his leadership stamp of approval.

"I can have something by the morning." Emery scratched the back of his head, lips curling into a frown.

"Fine. See you all in the morning." Aiden strode toward the offices, shutting the door behind him with more force than was necessary.

"Anything we can do?" Matt edged closer to Nikki, and Gabriel took another step toward her.

"Keep an eye on local crime. Also, missing persons. If anyone reports a man, twenty-five to fifty, former military, flag them. Wilson is recruiting heavily, and these groups often have cultlike rules that cut people off from family and friends. Chances are they won't have any idea where their loved one has gone."

"Can do." Matt grabbed a business card out of his pocket. "Where are you staying? Do you want me to send the information to you or to Emery?"

"Emery will probably be the point of contact for that. We still have details to hash out there. And I'm not sure where I'm staying yet."

The skin along Gabriel's spine prickled. Oh hell no, Dudley Do-Right wasn't going to offer to help there, too.

"Hey, Roni, is your spare bedroom still empty?" Gabriel called across the garage to the twins, who had their heads together.

"Yeah. Why?" Roni frowned.

"Nikki needs a place to crash."

"Oh. Can do." Roni stared daggers at him. He would have to tread carefully in the shop for the next week or more.

"That's not necessary," Nikki said quietly. "I can get a hotel somewhere."

"That's going to look bad on us. You stay at a Hoover hotel, you'll look like a Hoover. We have to do this whole gig in the context of our deep cover. So you have to live, work, and eat just like we do." And why did he look forward to seeing her in his element?

Nikki had always pushed for more time in the field. She'd never fully understood the danger, and he'd instinctively pushed back to protect her. Well, now she was getting what she'd always wanted, and he had a front-row seat.

Chapter Three

Nikki rapped her knuckles on Roni's bedroom door, imitating the same rhythm the woman had demonstrated to her.

"Think you got it?" Roni asked.

"Yes," Nikki replied slowly. The Chazov twins' file was an interesting read. "Why exactly am I doing this?"

"Because if you come through the front door and don't signal you're a friend, I'll blow your brains out." Roni grinned, but Nikki didn't doubt a word the girl said.

"All right then. Anything else I should know? Trip wires? Traps?"

"Nah. You should be good. Come on. You'll stay in here." Roni pushed off the wall and crossed the condo. She led Nikki to the first room on the right and nudged the door open. "The furniture used to be Tori's, but she doesn't need it now. I figured having a spare place to crash would be handy. Looks like I was right."

Nikki set her hanging bag on the bed. She was hyper-aware of her host, and already running a mental checklist on the signs of stress. People under deep cover like Roni sometimes cracked, and she'd had enough thrown at her to rattle even the strongest person.

"I'm sorry I didn't get a chance to really meet your sister," Nikki replied.

"Yeah, well, you probably won't see her much." Roni sat on the edge of the bed and wrinkled her nose looking at Nikki's bag.

"Why's that?" Did Nikki want to know? Or was this a topic riddled with land mines? She didn't want to upset Roni if at all possible.

"She's started helping Emery out. If we're as behind the game as you make it sound, he's going to want to keep her on hand to help research."

"You don't sound thrilled about that." Nikki perched at the foot of the mattress and eased her feet out of the dress boots.

"Hey, it gets the job done faster. Whatever." Roni shrugged. "Did you have any more luggage?"

"Nope. I travel as light as I can."

"Uh . . . so, did you bring anything besides your Hoover-wear?"

"Hoover? What's that mean? They said that earlier, but I didn't want to ask." Nikki stripped off the suit jacket, and instantly the sensation of sweating to death eased. It still felt as though she were breathing water, but at least she wasn't about to die of heat exhaustion.

Roni laughed and partially unzipped the bag.

"It's what we call you Feds. You're Hoovers. Like the vacuum? You suck up all the time."

"Gee, thanks."

"Look, I don't want to tell you how to do your job, but do you really think you're going to fit in with us wearing this?" Roni tugged on the lapel of another black jacket.

Nikki pressed her lips together. It had occurred to her, but the rest of her wardrobe consisted of sweatpants and hoodies. She'd become a stereotypical agent at some point in the last few years. No social life. Just work.

"I'll take that as a no." Roni studied Nikki. "Your boobs are bigger than mine, but I think I have some stuff that'll work. Come on."

Nikki stared after the redheaded woman sauntering out of the room. She'd never been in the trenches like this before. Her role was always a little more removed and a lot more official. She'd fought for this case the moment it landed on her desk, to be the person who took on this challenge. Was she going to let a five-foot-five redhead intimidate her because her fashion sense was nonexistent?

She stripped off her socks and followed in her host's wake, luxuriating in the cold tile against her feet.

The master suite was larger—and covered in piles of clothing.

"Here. Try these." Roni thrust a couple articles of clothing at her. "So your dad's someone important?"

Nikki eyed the small garments with trepidation. These were going to cover her?

"That's what people tell me." Nikki stepped into the bathroom and shed her slacks and blouse.

"You read up on us?"

Nikki could see Roni's reflection in the mirror. She flipped through a magazine. Everything about her posture was relaxed, and yet Nikki knew she had to answer the question very carefully.

"The basics, but mostly I talked to CJ. I figured he knew your team the best. I wasn't going to trust René Merlo to brief me. What gets recorded is sometimes not a first-person account. And besides, personnel files are pretty black and white. They don't tell me a lot about who the people are I'll be working with. They mostly cover what you've done and where you've been. If you've decided to work with me, that is." Nikki tugged the shorts down a bit, but there wasn't enough fabric to go around. She frowned at the mirror.

"Damn, girl, you've got a booty on you." Roni leaned against the door frame, arms crossed. Her smile was easy; whatever test she'd issued, Nikki appeared to have passed.

"These are way too short."

"They're called shorts for a reason. What's Merlo's deal anyway? Why's he such a dick?"

"Merlo wanted to head up the undercover unit, and he got passed over for the job. Someone younger, and with better connections, got it. He's never been able to let it go, even after he was promoted to chief of the Florida offices. The man has the biggest chip on his shoulder I've ever seen."

"Tell me about it. We send them shit all the time that gets ignored." Roni rolled her eyes. "Don't know why. We just bypass them and send it up the chain anyway."

"People notice. I'd be shocked if Merlo keeps his job much longer. I can't believe it's gone on this long. Do I really have to wear these? I don't want to interview witnesses with my butt cheeks hanging out, thank you very much." Nikki turned, presenting her bottom to the mirror, and once more tried to tug the hem lower.

"They are not. You've got a good two inches of clearance."

"Oh great. Two inches to save my ass."

Roni tossed her head back and laughed. "I like you."

The way Roni said it, there was no doubting the woman's mind was made up.

"Thanks. What did I do?" Nikki had no idea how she'd wrangle such an out-of-control team into some semblance of order to get the operation done. If she'd done something right, it would be nice if she could figure out how to do it again.

"I've known a lot of agents in my life, and you're just different. Most wouldn't have been so honest with us. Hell, we've had a few handlers over the years who thought they were slave drivers."

"I can understand why they'd take a tough approach. You have a reputation." Nikki turned around, presenting her rear to the mirror, and tugged on the hem again. "I can get some jeans tomorrow."

"It's summer. In Miami. Jeans are the last thing you want to wear. Trust me."

"This doesn't look professional." Nikki gestured to her pale legs. At least she'd had enough forethought to get waxed before this trip, though she didn't want to think about that choice too hard. It wasn't like it was a habit these days.

"We aren't professionals. That's why you want us. We blend in, and for you, that means booty shorts and a tank top."

"I want my suit back." Nikki indulged in the whine, feeling she was justified this once.

"Well, too bad." Roni leaned against the vanity. "What's the deal with Gabriel?"

"Gabe?" Nikki blinked, thrown off-kilter by the sudden change of topics.

"Gabe?" Roni arched a brow at her.

"We worked together."

"Seriously?" Roni cocked her head to the side.

Nikki wasn't sure if she was relieved Roni didn't know, or disappointed Gabriel hadn't mentioned her.

"Yes. It was a long time ago." Nikki turned around, surveying her appearance once more. If she wore a camisole it wouldn't be that bad. And Roni was probably right, shorts would help her blend in.

"You aren't going to tell me squat, are you?"

"Nope. Classified."

"Fuck your classified." Roni pushed off the door and walked through the bedroom into the living room.

Nikki stared at her slacks, torn between wanting more clothing and not overheating tonight.

What the hell?

It wasn't like they were going anywhere. The only person who would see her right now was Roni.

She gathered up her clothes and followed in Roni's wake. The condo was decorated in a hodgepodge of garage sale furniture that appeared rustic and a touch shabby chic. Mixed in were bright colors and an occasional plant to bring out a tropical vibe.

Roni sat perched on the kitchen counter, a pint of ice cream in one hand and a spoon in the other. She waved the spoon at Nikki, one eye squeezed shut. "Okay, so you clearly worked together, and I bet you were FBI then, too, which means I've been right all along and Gabriel really is the badass he seems like. But the way you two were staring at each other wasn't exactly work appropriate."

Nikki glanced around the room. What were the chances she could escape this conversation? She'd known her history with Gabriel was bound to come up, so the trick was controlling who knew what and how much of it. Better to go ahead and set the groundwork for the version she wanted shared instead of letting Roni come up with her own.

"We worked together for a long time and under some difficult circumstances." Nikki leaned on the bar, soaking up more coolness from the marble countertop.

"Yeah, but what I want to know—"

Roni was interrupted by a distinct knock at the door, one Nikki had just learned.

"It's me. Open up," a man yelled.

Nikki gulped and clutched her clothes to her chest.

Roni waggled her spoon at Nikki. Roni jumped off the counter and crossed the room surprisingly fast.

"Hey, me, what's the secret password?" Roni peered into the peephole and reached into what appeared to be an umbrella basket next to the front door, but Nikki doubted an umbrella was what she was reaching for.

"Roni, it's Gabriel. I need to talk to Nikki."

Roni twisted the locks and swept the door open.

Gabriel stood on the stoop, hands braced against the frame. The charcoal gray T-shirt stretched tight over his biceps and his hair was damp, as if he'd stuck his head under a faucet. He stared past Roni, like she wasn't even there, and directly at Nikki.

"Got a minute?" he asked.

This was a mistake. A big, huge miscalculation. She could not face him. Not alone at least. She wasn't even over him, as pathetic as that truth was.

"Sure. Give me a second to—"

"I'll take those. Remember the knock." Roni jerked the clothes out of Nikki's hands, leaving her nothing to cling to.

She wanted to run away, to bury herself under blankets, wrapped up in his damn shirt, but she was better than that. As much as talking to him, seeing him, and being around him hurt, if she didn't do this, she'd be stuck on him for the rest of her life. Maybe they could get past this. Perhaps she could move on.

"If you decide not to come back tonight, at least text me, okay?" Roni whispered.

"We shouldn't be long," Nikki replied.

Whatever Gabriel had to say to her, she doubted he'd

take a moment more than he needed to. He had good reason to hate her still, and that was what still stung. He hated her, and she'd never gotten over loving him.

Gabriel held the door as Nikki swept out into the night, head held high. He was not prepared for a dressed-down version of his former girlfriend. It was easier to distance himself when she was dressed like a Hoover. In a suit, he could pretend she was someone else. Someone who hadn't shared his bed and broken his heart.

Yeah, he'd had it bad for her, but he'd also moved on. What they needed was to clear the air, close that door and focus on the case. Their lives no longer intersected; they had no common ground. In a week or so, she'd be gone again and Gabriel could go back to working on his life after the FBI.

Nikki paused halfway to the car and glanced over her shoulder. The streetlight cast a halo of light around her. Her gray eyes held secrets so tight he'd never been able to really know her.

"What did you want to talk about?" she asked.

"Let's take a drive." He strode to the curb where he'd parked his 1967 Pontiac GTO. The Skyline wasn't close to being street legal, so he'd stashed it in the back lot at Classic Rides and opted to take his other car tonight.

He kept his focus above her shoulders. Damn, but she'd filled out in all the right places. He'd always had a thing for her "bubble butt," as she'd called it. Whatever shape it was, she'd fit his hands and against his body just fine.

"Is this yours?"

"Yeah." He pulled the passenger door open and held it while Nikki sat.

He took the moment to survey the quiet street. Nothing out of place, nothing suspicious. As it should be.

Gabriel circled the car, clearing his mind to the best of his ability. Where Nikki was concerned, it was messy and complicated, but perhaps they could move on from what they'd been to each other. She was an amazing woman, regardless of how she'd broken it off with him. Besides, they had to work together, and his crew had elected him their handler's watchdog.

The GTO roared to life and he smiled.

"You have some upgrades." She ran her fingers over the chrome dash he'd had built just for this car. The others could have their restored beauties. He liked the look, with all modern conveniences.

"Yeah."

Her completely neutral tone grated on his nerves. Once, she'd relaxed around him, let loose, laughed, cursed even. If they were going to talk, well, she'd have to bring down that stony front and be real with him.

Gabriel pressed his foot to the accelerator and shifted, whipping the car around the way he'd come and urging it faster. Any sound Nikki made was drowned out by the engine, but he didn't miss how she clutched at the door with one hand and clung to the seat with the other. He took perverse joy in pushing the car to perform just to hear her suck in a breath when he passed between cars, weaving his way closer to the ocean. He didn't have any real idea of where he was going. He'd lost all sense of what he was doing the moment he'd walked into the garage and seen her. She was a lighthouse and he the ship lost at sea for years now, content to drift with the tide. She reminded him of a time when he had a purpose he could believe in.

He still wanted to reach over and touch her, see if Nikki

might melt like she once had. If he went there, no. It wasn't happening.

Gabriel pulled into a beachfront hotel parking lot and shifted into park.

"Was that necessary?" Nikki sounded out of breath, as if she'd run the distance instead of ridden in a car.

"We have a reputation to keep."

She let go of the door and seat, shaking her hands out. He turned to face her, grateful for the shadows that hid some of her.

"Tell me about where you are with your assignment." She folded her hands in her lap.

She really was a great handler. It had baffled him at the time when he'd first heard her voice and realized they'd assigned a newer, female agent to him. The work he'd been doing was rough, ugly, and complicated. Back then, he couldn't hold her hand while she processed the horrors of what they were dealing with. Except Nikki hadn't needed any coddling. She'd turned the tables on him, becoming the gentleness in the storm, his safe haven where he could turn for a little respite. She'd shielded him, talked him through tough decisions and supported him when he had to refuse orders.

He was staring at her, lost in his own thoughts, and she was once more calmly waiting him out.

"What do you want to know?" he asked.

"What do I need to know?"

"This shit is complicated." He blew out a breath. Cliffs-Notes. She needed the highest level overview. "We started with a simple objective, collect enough evidence to put a kingpin in prison for life. You should know that it's personal for Aiden and Julian, but Aiden seems to have moved on. Instead of knocking it out fast, we've spent three, almost four years spinning our wheels."

"Not really. You think someone has been actively stalling your investigation."

"Yeah, we do. Otherwise, why were we never told about a hundred other connected cases? We got the boss, Michael Evers, thrown in jail, but someone was still running things for him. He got out on bail a couple months ago and has pretty much disappeared."

"He isn't checking in with his parole officer?"

"The officer says he has, but our surveillance says no. Matt's working on that for us."

"How does the assassination team factor into this?"

"Outside job, but they started working with Evers's people then against them. It was a clusterfuck."

"Sounded like it. I'm sorry about Kathy."

"It's the risk we take."

"It is."

"What else do I need to know?"

"Our crew has a pretty bad rep right now. We took out a rival street-racing gang purely by accident because of their involvement with Evers, and with his organization limping along, people think we're the new bad dogs in town."

"I see."

"What?"

"Nothing. It's just a point Roni was trying to make. I understand now." She shifted in her seat and tugged at the hem of her shorts, but there wasn't much to go around.

Now he wanted to know what Roni had said.

"What else?" Nikki prompted when he didn't speak again.

"We need to talk about Boston."

"Oh." Her eyes widened a bit. Touched a nerve, did he?

"The only people here who know about us are Julian, Aiden, and Emery." He watched her, looking for some sign that she felt something. Had any emotional attachment to him whatsoever.

"The rest will figure it out. Roni already has, so her twin probably has as well."

"Shit." He scrubbed a hand over his face.

"What is there to say?" Nikki's voice was quieter, maybe sad even?

"A hell of a lot. Damn it, Nikki, we haven't spoken since then."

"I know. A lot went wrong. What do you want me to say? I'm sorry? I'm sorry people died. I'm sorry you took the fall for what other people did. I'm sorry we didn't get a chance to clear things up before you left." She was so calm, so poised, he just wanted to muss her hair, hear a little passion in her voice. If he hadn't known her so well at one point, he might believe this was her. Instead, he knew she was holding back with him.

Could he blame her?

He'd have liked to believe that she'd dumped his personal things from her place in a box and had them sent over with a breakup note. In reality, he'd pushed her away, so it shouldn't have come as a shock when she walked out the door he'd opened.

"What do you want me to say?" Nikki asked.

Did he detect some feeling in her voice? Had he gotten through her walls?

"We both did a lot of wrong for the right reasons, *cariña*."

"It was a bad situation." She nodded. But she wasn't getting it. Not at all.

"I'm not talking about that part of Boston." He stared at her, searched her face for some sign of the woman he'd loved. "I'm talking about us. I cleared my conscience a long time ago. We can't save everyone, no matter how much we want to." He gripped the gearshift to keep from reaching for her.

"Boston. Okay." She stared at the dashboard for a moment. "You left, Gabriel. You were very clear when you said you didn't want me around and you were out. What else is there to say about that?"

When she boiled it down to those points, okay, he could see how she might think it was done with.

"When I said that, I was covered in blood and high."

"I didn't know about the addiction until later. You never said you needed help."

"It wasn't an addiction. I had to prove I wasn't a Fed, Nikki. That's the only reason I smoked the crack in the first place."

"I'm sorry, Gabe, but how is it my fault? You never told me when you needed a break. You never said you needed help. It was always *I'm fine* or *Everything's great*." She leaned toward him, her finger jabbing at her sternum. "Yes, it was my job to take care of you, and I wanted to, but I couldn't do my job when you refused to talk to me. And when you left, you finally said something, so I listened. Did I react the best way? Probably not. But people I knew died, too, and I lost you, so excuse me if I didn't behave professionally."

She was on fire now. Her cheeks flushed and there was a light in her eye that told him he'd finally touched a nerve. He wanted to be angry with her, but he also wanted to kiss her, to taste that passion she tried to bury behind a fake veneer.

This was the woman he'd fallen for.

Nikki pushed her door open and stood. In the dim parking lights he could make out the curve of her bottom just before she slammed the door shut.

"Nikki, Nikki, wait." Gabriel scrambled to follow her. He locked the GTO behind him and jogged down the wooden walk leading toward the beach.

She wasn't wearing shoes. Why hadn't he noticed that? Oh, right, because of those shorts.

She kept going, even as he caught up with her when the concrete transitioned to a wooden boardwalk that led to the sand and the beach below.

"Will you at least wait for me to take my shoes off?" he asked.

Nikki stopped so suddenly he took another step before pivoting to face her.

"Can we work together?" she asked.

"Yes." And he wanted to. Some masochistic urge goaded him on.

"Then can we agree that you should have told me how bad things were, and I should have seen the signs you were holding out on me?"

"I'm not—"

"Yes or no?"

"Fine. Yes."

"Good. Neither of us can take blame for the other agents. They knowingly stomped into our investigation with their heads up their asses. Even that cop. She knew better than to stick around once we warned her off."

"You're right." He hated it, but it was the truth.

"As for our breakup." She spread her hands. "It was going to happen. You weren't happy. I wasn't happy. We were tearing each other apart, and one way or another, we were over."

A knife to the heart would have hurt less than those three words.

I wasn't happy.

He shoved his hands into his pockets. Before he'd landed the grants to get through school and into the academy, he'd been a poor kid living in a border town with no future. He should have known better than to want someone like Nikki. She was too good for the likes of him. How could he have ever hoped to make her happy?

Chapter Four

Nikki's heart shriveled up inside her, dying all over again. God, she'd imagined this moment so many times, and she'd been right. Gabriel wouldn't fight for her, not for them or what they'd had. It wasn't worth it to him. She wasn't worth it. She didn't belong in his world. She'd never heard the message louder or with more clarity. Her rose-colored glasses were off, and she could finally see what she hadn't wanted to back then. They just didn't fit. It didn't matter how much she loved him or wanted to make it work, some things just weren't meant to be.

It was hard to breathe around the proverbial knife in her chest, but the oxygen did her good.

"Is that how you saw it?" By some miracle, her voice didn't shake. It was as though her heart and body were divided, separate.

"Yeah, that sounds about right. It's been a while, so maybe my memory is foggy." He kicked a pebble down the boardwalk.

She felt the stone's pain. Sure, four years had passed, but this was the real ending. Right here. Right now.

"Is it possible for us to work together?" she asked.

She didn't want to. Being around him, it hurt. Maybe

she'd been foolish when she fell for him. How clichéd was it, anyway?

"Sure." He shrugged. "You're cool. I'm cool."

"Good. What else do we need to figure out now? It's been a long day, and after tonight I doubt any of us will get much rest." And she had to go cry into her pillow like the sad, pathetic thing that she was. The sea breeze kicked up, blowing in the salty air. She turned to face the beach, letting the breeze dry her eyes.

Tonight, she'd make her peace. She'd cry. Get it out of her system. It was time to put the silly notion that someday Gabriel would come back to her out of her head. In the real world, they were different people now, with separate lives.

"You said you're working in a new division. What's that about?"

She didn't look at him; it hurt less that way.

"Homegrown threats. There's a lot of attention on foreign terrorists attacking, so it's incredibly unlikely we'll see another 9/11. We run more risk from people born here turning against us. The random shooters. The revenge bombers. The militia cells. They're our neighbors, friends, and sometimes our family. They're more dangerous because we don't want to see them or believe it could happen here, to us or someone we know."

"Hasn't the FBI always handled threats on our own soil?"

"Yes. Our specific focus is threats to multiple lives. We've saved people. In our first six months of operation . . . well, I can't tell you that, but we've done some good." She smiled at the memory of little arms wrapped around her neck, thanking her. That was why she'd worked so hard to follow in her father's footsteps. She'd seen firsthand the lives he'd touched, the people his decisions had saved, and she wanted to do that, too.

Her father had shown her the photo albums of clippings documenting the people he'd saved, lives protected. Growing up she'd pored over those stories, committing them to heart, and now she had her own albums of lives saved. It was small, but growing every year.

"Isn't that what this is all about? Helping people?" Gabriel asked.

"Yes."

She could recall with almost crystal clarity the third conversation she'd had with Gabriel. It was when everything changed. He'd called her in the middle of the night and warned her he'd been drinking with the people he was spying on. She'd sat on her window seat with its wonderful view of a brick wall and listened to him rant about how much he hated them, but working for them was a necessary evil to help people. To save them.

They'd bonded over that, and when he'd worked the alcohol out of his system, she'd shared what drove her. If memory served her, they hadn't hung up until close to noon, and then it was just so they could get showers and on the road to meet for food halfway between them. A face-to-face meet was dangerous, but Gabriel had been splintering and needed to see someone he could trust.

She'd been that person once.

Standing there, watching the waves beat at the shore almost empty of people, it was easy to tap into the feelings of that first time. The day when it all changed. She'd gone to see him with good intentions, but he'd checked his at the door. When he flirted with her she'd been taken aback and had no idea how to respond, but she soldiered through. Over time, he'd worn her down. If he hadn't pursued her, she'd have stayed in the nice, neat box she'd made for herself. Following the rules, coloring inside the lines. Thanks to him, she wasn't afraid to tear down a few walls if it meant getting the job done. She'd learned a lot from him, but now it was time to learn how to walk away.

"I want to go back to Roni's." The wind whipped her voice back over her shoulder, but she saw Gabriel nod out of the corner of her eye.

"Come on." He turned back toward the parking lot.

The beach called to her. If she knew how to get back on her own, she might take a stroll, walk her problems out. It might not help, but at least she wouldn't be cooped up inside with only her broken heart for company.

She turned and almost walked straight into Gabriel's chest.

"You haven't got any shoes on." He scowled down at her. Numerous broken noses and a couple thin scars had roughened up his face just enough so he wasn't someone you wanted to meet in a dark alley—or a secluded breezeway between hotels—by yourself.

"I'm fine."

"There's glass in the parking lot."

"I didn't step on any. It's fine." She hadn't seen any, either, but she'd only had one thought when she got out of the car: get away.

"Yeah, whatever." He bent his knees, and before she could process what he was doing, Gabriel hoisted her up in his arms.

"Gabe! Put me down." She could feel the cool breeze on her ass now. Damn these shorts.

"Quit your hollering." His scowl lines deepened and he kept his eyes focused straight ahead.

She opened her mouth to protest again, but what was the point? She'd learned to pick and choose her battles with Gabriel. Besides, this was her parting gift. One last chance to feel his arms around her.

He didn't speak to her all the way back to the GTO. She

was too wound up to enjoy the strength of his arms or the feel of his chest against her, which was a pity.

Gabriel set her down gently next to the passenger side.

"Thanks. You didn't have to do that," she said.

He unlocked the door and held it open for her. Once, he'd told her how manners were required in his *mama's* house, and when he was being himself, he made sure to follow her rules.

"No problem." He shut her door, and for a brief moment she was alone.

Nikki squeezed her eyes shut. She couldn't cry. Not yet. Not until she was alone. She studied the dashboard while he got in and started the car. What had he said about it?

"Did you do the upgrades yourself?" she asked to fill the silence. For a moment she'd felt a bit of their old connection back there, but it was gone now. This conversation was stilted. Awkward. As if they were strangers.

"Yeah. The other guys complain about it, but they're big into restoring cars."

"Not you?"

"Nah. Why not upgrade it?"

She asked about the details without caring about the answer. What mattered was that they were talking. It was silly to imagine him in her life again for anything but a brief moment. He'd left the FBI, and her life was the bureau.

"Thanks for the ride," she said as they pulled up in front of Roni's condo.

"Thanks for talking to me."

Thanks for breaking my heart.

"Talking was always one of the things we did best."

"I don't know about that." His lips curled up at the corners, and for a moment his brown eyes heated.

Yeah, they'd done other things well, too, which she was trying to forget.

"Good night, Gabriel." She pulled the door handle.

"Gabe. You always called me Gabe."

Nikki paused getting out of the car.

"That was then." She stared at her hand against the white leather interior.

"You called me Gabe earlier."

"I shouldn't have. You aren't that person to me anymore." She pulled up her walls, calling on every shred of professionalism she could scrounge up and surrounded herself in it.

"That's cold."

"It's the truth."

"You always were good at pushing people away."

She shouldn't look at him. But she did. His features appeared even more broken up-lit by the dash lights.

"I learned that from you."

Nikki stood before he could make some sort of reply and closed the door. Straightening her spine, she took the first step toward the condo. It was time to make a new life and stop living in the past. She felt his gaze on her all the way to the front door.

Was she running away from him?

Yes, yes she was.

She knocked on the front door, repeating the pattern Roni had shown her, and waited, listening to the sound of the GTO's engine chugging in the background. The condo door opened a crack and Nikki shoved past, into the house. She needed to get away from him before she shattered.

"Uh, wow. Going out?" Nikki didn't mean to stare, but Roni's sequined, body-hugging dress was a huge change from the shorts and crop top she'd worn earlier.

"Yeah, do you mind?" Roni clenched the doorknob in one hand and a tiny clutch in the other.

"Not at all. I'm just going to shower and crash."

"Cool. Don't wait up." Roni stepped through the door, and a moment later the locks clicked into place.

The silence of the condo was absolute.

She was alone.

Nikki buried her face in her hands and dug her toes into the rug. Pain sliced her to the bone, cutting so deep she trembled. But it was all in her head. Wasn't it? She rubbed her chest and shambled to her room. There was no one around to put on a show for. Wallowing in self-pity was completely allowed. She dumped her bag on the floor with every intention of showering, but when she pulled Gabriel's threadbare shirt out of her suitcase, she couldn't. There was no more fight left in her.

She buried her face in the fabric and inhaled the long-gone scent of his cologne. That smell she'd never been able to shake from her memory or reproduce. Slightly spicy, with hints of sandalwood, musk, and something else. Something that was uniquely Gabriel.

Tears pricked her eyes.

Fuck it.

Yes, she'd thought it.

"Fuck it," she said out loud.

Nikki stripped down to her panties, slid his shirt on, and crawled into bed. She hugged one of the pillows to her chest, buried her face in the other, and let the first sob shake her. She pulled her knees up to her chest and let the floodgates open. It was time to say good-bye to that secret wish she tried to not admit to even herself.

She still wanted Gabe in her life. She wanted to love him, to be loved by him and finally be let in. But he'd moved on. Hell, he probably had a girlfriend, too. She couldn't blame him. They'd split four years ago, and a lot had changed. She'd changed. Still, he was possibly the first man she'd truly loved, and it hurt to close the door on what they'd had. After so many years without closure, she had it now. And it didn't make it any easier to swallow.

Besides, what kind of pathetic sap held on to the idea of a man she'd loved years ago still wanting her? Working in Washington the last two years had toughened her up, but apparently not enough. When she dreamed, it was still about a man with arms strong enough to hold her, dark tanned skin, and a broken nose.

Gabriel tipped the Classic Rides coffee mug back and gulped the thick, bitter coffee. It hit the back of his throat and went straight to his veins.

"Yuck. What is Madison putting in this?" He peered into the bottom of the cup.

"She didn't make it." Aiden tossed a thick folder onto the desk in the back office of the garage and sank into the rolling chair.

"Morning." Julian stepped into the office carrying a similar mug.

"Close the door, and don't drink that." Aiden waved his co-owner into the other guest chair. They might be co-owners of the garage, but it was Aiden who did the heavy lifting around the shop.

"Do I want to know?" Julian set his mug on the desk and flopped into the too-small chair.

Gabriel remained standing. He couldn't sit, sleep, or stay put, not after the hell of last night.

"Roni made it. I took Madison to Emery's to keep her out of this." Aiden gestured to the folder he'd flipped open.

"Where's Nikki?" Gabriel asked. He'd been late to work

because he'd decided to take the GTO for a joyride and had lost track of time.

"Roni has her helping on that oil change." Aiden shifted papers around on his desk.

"'Scuse me?" Gabriel glanced between Aiden and Julian, who merely shrugged.

Roni wasn't the play nice with others type, so what was up?

"I'm not asking." Aiden held his hands up. "Emery wants Tori to help him, so that leaves me shorthanded in the garage. If she's working, I'm happy. Now, Nikki will probably poke her nose in here any second. I told her I had to wait to talk to you before we made a move this morning."

"About this morning . . ." Julian sat forward, elbows on his knees.

"Oh, what now?" Aiden scowled and dropped a pile of invoices into a tray on one corner.

"I've got that debrief in the field office with Merlo."

"Shit. Let's deal with that later." He switched his attention to Gabriel. "First thing. Find out anything?"

Both Aiden and Julian stared at him.

Despite being a former spy, he still had connections. People who didn't mind answering a few questions, so long as it wasn't a habit.

"I talked to some of my buddies. Everything Nikki is saying about herself is on target. She has a reputation for being good in the field."

Julian sniffed his coffee, made a face and put the mug back down. "Is she hot for you? Think you could—"

"No." Gabriel shook his head.

"Hey man, I had to ask. She's still easy on the eyes." Julian leaned back in his chair.

"I get you two have history, but that's why we need

you on her. She can't screw us over like the rest of them, not now," Aiden said.

"I get it." Gabriel glanced away. He doubted Nikki would intentionally. She wasn't like that, but sometimes it was just the nature of the bureau. People got shafted.

A light knock was all the warning they had before the office door swung inward. Nikki leaned a shoulder on the door frame and tilted her head to the side. Gabriel's mouth went dry. She was wearing the damn shorts again, but this time with an Invasion Car Show tank top and her hair tucked under a bandanna. She'd clearly been under a car already from the smudges of dirt and grease.

"Starting without me?" she asked.

"Come in. We were just going over our manpower." Aiden gestured to the empty chair. "We're a little under-staffed today. Madison and Tori are working with Emery, gathering intelligence. Julian has a debrief that will take him out for most of the day. That leaves you, John, Gabriel, Roni, and me to follow up on Emery's leads. Did he send them to you?"

"I was reviewing them this morning." Nikki perched on the edge of the remaining spare chair, hands in her lap. She hadn't looked at Gabriel once. "Is it possible to split up? Interview the families?"

"Unfortunately, I've still got a garage to run." Aiden spread his hands, but there was nothing apologetic in the man. "I've got two appointments in the middle of my day that I can't reschedule, and another guy flying in to look at a car. Work here has piled up. I can't afford to shut down."

"Then what do you propose?" Nikki asked.

Aiden nodded at him, and Gabriel's stomach sank. He knew Aiden wanted him glued to Nikki's ass, even if it was the last place he wanted to be.

"You and Gabriel start interviewing those families. Once Julian wraps his stuff up, I can send him and Roni out to hit what you haven't made it to yet. It's not ideal, but after today I should be able to move appointments around to keep us more flexible."

Nikki turned toward him and lifted her chin. He didn't know if he wanted her to avoid him or if it stung that she was so over him that working together didn't even faze her. Then again, she had her walls back up, so there weren't a lot of ways to really get into her head.

"Are you ready to get started?" she asked.

"We're just interviewing families, right?" he asked.

"Yeah, do a normal, looking for my buddy, approach. These guys are all military. Maybe drop their unit number, say you're looking to reconnect. Might open some of these people up more." Aiden held up his copy of the files. "You need this?"

"I've got everything on my tablet," Nikki replied.

"Then we're good. *Vamos*." Sweat broke out along his spine. He didn't know how many people they were trying to track down, but chances were, he was looking at spending the entire day with her, and that was after she'd been in his thoughts all night. It was a special kind of hell Aiden was throwing him into, one made just for Gabriel.

Chapter Five

Nikki flipped to the first list of names, keeping her eyes on the tablet screen instead of the man striding toward the car. She wished they could take something else less showy, but he'd insisted his GTO was the only option. There appeared to be some sort of macho car code going on she didn't understand. What she did get was that this car was all him. The leather even had that signature scent she hadn't been able to reproduce. Sitting in the passenger seat was like having a bit of Gabe wrapped around her.

She could see him strolling closer out of the corner of her eye.

Last night she'd dreamt about him and the things he used to do to her, how he made her feel. Waking up was a nightmare of reality checks. She hadn't even bothered to ask Roni, still wearing her sequined dress, if she'd been to sleep yet. If Nikki had to guess, the other woman had been up all night and wasn't interested in chitchat.

The driver's door opened and Gabriel folded himself into the seat. He tapped the stereo display and the radio muttered in the background.

"Where to?" he asked.

"I'm mapping the locations."

"Let's start with the ones farther away, that way when Julian and Roni hit the road they can cover more ground."

"Okay, one second. We can make a loop on the south side of Miami. Here. This address." She turned the tablet to face him.

He frowned at the address for a moment.

"Got it." He shifted and the car rolled forward.

"Ever need to use a map?" She set the tablet in her lap and watched the colorful storefronts as they passed them.

"Nope."

She smiled. Gabriel had always been the perfect navigator. He was a living, breathing GPS. His recall was only good for maps and roads, but it was a valuable skill he'd been born with.

"Where are we going?" she asked.

"Cutler Ridge?" Gabriel swung his head around to look at her from behind his sunglasses for a moment. She stopped breathing. "It's nice, gated communities, young families. Not really the kind of area I'd peg your guy Wilson to be in."

He looked back at the road and she inhaled.

"He probably isn't there, you're right. A guy like him would stick out." She made a little note on the file for the sake of doing something.

"Read some of those other addresses to me?"

She did as he asked.

"Homestead." Gabriel tapped the steering wheel as he merged onto the highway. "I bet you we find out something in Homestead."

"Why do you say that?"

"It was mostly destroyed by Hurricane Andrew in '92 and has been in recovery since then. People fight over what to do with the land. There's a lot of rural property out there.

Places to hide a group like Wilson's. What do you want to bet that's where he's at?"

"I don't know. What should I bet?"

There was a discernable shift in the atmosphere within the car. Gabriel glanced at her.

"An answer. Bet me an answer."

"Okay." She focused on breathing slow and even. What kind of question couldn't he ask her? "If nothing is in Homestead, you have to help me convince Aiden to go along with this."

"Deal. He is being a *joda*, isn't he?"

Nikki chuckled. "Is he normally like that?"

"No, usually that's Julian's job."

"I see." She glanced over the addresses. "How long will it take us to get there?"

"Thirty minutes."

She peered at the odometer. "Going the speed limit?"

"Probably closer to forty-five."

Half an hour at least, trapped in this car, with him.

Nikki stared at her tablet without seeing it.

She'd cried herself to sleep last night, promising herself today she would be over him. Too bad she was a great liar.

"What have you been up to the last couple of years?" Gabriel asked.

She blew out a breath. Where to start? She'd worked all over the country, with so many police departments and officials she couldn't keep them all straight.

"In the field, mostly. At least until I took the promotion."

"You always wanted to be in the field."

He'd done his best to keep her behind the lines. Did he realize how much of a dick he sounded like when he told her to stay away, stay safe? She hadn't felt secure enough in their relationship to ever have it out with him over that little issue. Now, well, it wasn't his business what she did or where she did it.

"And you?" she asked to get the focus off her.

"After rehab I came here. You read the file."

"Not really. I wasn't lying when I said I went for the high-level overview only."

"I didn't say you were lying. You might be many things, but a liar was never one of them. It's one of the things I always respected about you."

"What else am I?" She shouldn't ask, but he just kept prodding her.

"Stubborn." He chuckled.

"That's hardly a sin." Her determination had won her the respect of many of her fellow agents. She'd learned that from her father. "How bad was rehab?"

"After what I'd been through? Easy. If I was an actual addict it would have been harder. For me, it was more like a rough indoctrination to civilian life."

"Talk to your mom?"

"Yeah, she'd love it if she knew you were here."

"But—"

He held up his hand. "I won't tell her. She always did like you more than me."

Nikki picked at the edge of the tablet with her nail. Gabriel's mother was loud, she laughed a lot . . . and the hugs. Nikki couldn't remember anyone hugging her as tight as Gabriel's mother. Nikki wasn't supposed to have met her, but a scheduling mix-up put them face-to-face once. In the bigger picture, the meeting could have potentially put Mrs. Ortiz's life at risk. Deep down, Nikki was glad she'd met her. She was different from Nikki's mother, a by-the-book woman who'd set out to marry an influential and wealthy man. So long as she got to play house in the right neighborhood, drive the right car, and wear the right clothes, she didn't mind what else happened. Gabriel's mother was salt of the earth, family meals and manners.

"You dating anyone?" Gabriel asked.

Nikki calmly folded her hands in her lap while she imagined throwing herself from the car. She'd rather hit the asphalt at seventy plus miles an hour than talk about her lack of a dating life, but she couldn't tell Gabriel he'd been her last, stable relationship.

"Here and there," she replied.

"Yeah, it's hard, doing what we do." Gabriel draped an arm over the wheel.

He didn't even bat an eyelash at the implication she'd had other men in her life since him. But why should she expect anything? Years had gone by. By all rights, she should be happy without him. And until she'd stood in that garage and faced him down, she'd thought she was.

They drove in silence, broken only by the radio personalities talking about the news or sports or whatever it was he listened to.

There were different kinds of happiness. Nikki had known that going into the FBI meant her professional happiness was the one that mattered most. Going home at night, alone, was just how it was. But she couldn't hold on to an idea at night. Part of her wanted to hate Gabriel for shining a light on that lonely part of her soul, even if he hadn't intended to.

"We're here." He eased the car up to a guard shack and pulled out a little black box.

"What's that?"

"A transmitter and code breaker in one." He pressed something on the screen and waited. "It's not like we have a code to get in. It'll just take a second to get it . . . There."

The metal gate slowly retracted. Gabriel waited until

there was just enough room for the GTO and accelerated through the space.

"Your design?" She held out her hand and he gave her the slim, black box.

"The first one was. Emery's improved on it since then."

Gabriel hadn't been her first undercover gig, but he'd been her best. He wasn't just a good actor, he was innovative. Losing him hadn't just hurt her, it had hurt the bureau. But the agency didn't have feelings like she did.

"That one." She pointed to one of many uniform brick houses. It was easily big enough to fit five or six of her little apartment inside the one structure. "David Swiss. Thirty-seven. Army. Medical discharge after taking a bullet to the throat."

"The throat?" Gabriel turned his head, brow wrinkled.

"That's what his file said. How are we handling this?"

"Not sure yet." Gabriel killed the engine and got out.

She had to scramble after him up the walk. He flashed her a quick smile and knocked on the wooden door bracketed by two long panes of frosted glass.

"Got a plan yet?" she asked.

"Nope."

Movement on the other side of the glass indicated more than one person was home. Her pulse kicked up and she wished she'd brought her gun that was back in the car. Or pants. Pants would have been great.

The door cracked open and a woman with curly salt-and-pepper hair peered out at them.

"Hi, ma'am. I don't mean to bother you. We're just looking for David. Haven't seen him in a while and we were getting worried." Gabriel spoke with a slow drawl and an easy smile that caught Nikki by surprise. It was rather charming, if she didn't already know him.

The woman opened the door farther, glancing between

them, her penciled brows arched and her mouth formed a little *o*. Another woman stood at her back, wisps of orange-red hair framing her face and blue liner accentuating her eyes.

"Are you from the VA?" she asked.

"Not officially, we just know David from the VA. We were both seeing the same doctor. You know where he is?" Gabriel leaned an arm on the door frame and his smile widened.

The gray-haired woman pressed her hand to her mouth, and Nikki cringed.

"No. I keep asking, and no one knows where my son is." Mrs. Swiss's voice trembled.

Gabriel glanced at Nikki, the smile gone.

"I'm sorry to hear that. Any idea where he might have gone?" Gabriel asked. "We haven't seen him in a while and wanted to check on him. Worried is all. You know how it is."

Mrs. Swiss nodded, as if she knew exactly what Gabriel was talking about.

The red-haired woman took David's mother by the shoulders and steered her away from the door.

"Come in. We can talk out back," she called over her shoulder.

Nikki stared after them a moment. They were complete strangers to these women. She would never just invite someone into her house like this. Gabriel didn't appear to have any qualms about it. He stepped over the threshold and held the door for her.

The inside of the house was lush with potted plants, cheerful yellow paint, and brown tiled floors. Pictures hung on the wall. Gabriel paused at one of a young man in uniform, staring straight ahead with the American flag behind him. Gabriel glanced pointedly at her before following the two women through the heart of the house, a large eat-in-kitchen, and out through sliding glass doors to the patio where the two appeared to have been drinking coffee.

Mrs. Swiss sat staring into her cup while the other woman said something to her in hushed tones. The redheaded woman darted glances at Gabriel every few moments, with none of the same friendliness David's mother had expressed. Gabriel seemed to pick up on the unfriendly vibe and chose a seat across from the two women, while Nikki decided to take the one next to Mrs. Swiss.

"Have you made a missing persons report?" Nikki asked.

Both women stared at her and for a moment neither spoke.

"No, we haven't," the redhead replied.

"I'm sorry, I didn't catch your name?" Nikki asked.

"I'm Lucy. I live next door."

"I'm Nicole. I work the desk at the VA." She shook both women's hands. "It's how I met Gary and David." First rule of ferreting out information was to never use her real name. "Can I ask why you haven't reported him missing? It's been, gosh, how long, Gary?"

"Hard to say, I don't run into him every time I'm up there." Gabriel scrunched his face up and stared at the awning overhead.

"He's been gone for almost a month," David's mother said, her voice watery with unshed tears.

A month. That would be the right time frame for some sort of scouting mission before shifting into gear and blowing up the sheriff station. They could have picked David up by chance or on purpose.

"This isn't the first time David's gone off." The way Lucy said his name, it was pretty clear the woman wasn't mourning his absence.

"No, but he always calls." Mrs. Swiss reached for a tissue that was just a bit too far out of reach.

"Where was the last place you saw him?" Nikki grabbed the box of tissues and pulled them closer. She hated crying, but after last night she'd done more than her fair share.

"Here." She gestured at the patio. "He said he was going fishing."

"What was he wearing?"

"Jeans. A T-shirt." David's mother shrugged.

"Why are you asking all this stuff?" Lucy directed her frown at Nikki. They needed to wrap this up and get out of there before Lucy got too suspicious.

"I've seen a lot of veterans go missing, and I know what questions the cops will ask. Sorry, I don't mean to pry. I just want David to be okay. I know his mother meant a lot to him." Nikki smiled at Mrs. Swiss, hating the roll she had to play. When she could step onto a scene as Special Agent Gage, it was easier, more straightforward, but that didn't work here. Not with the undercover operation.

David's mother reached for Nikki's hand, squeezed it, and didn't let go.

"Did David talk about anyone you hadn't met? Hang around anyone new?" Nikki held on to Mrs. Swiss's hand, committing her words to memory. She hoped they could save David, and others like him, before it was too late.

"No, he hardly hung out with anyone. He was so closed off and depressed after he got out of the hospital."

Which would make him an easy target to someone like Wilson. A man with training, skills, and no anchor in life fit their profile. David was as much a victim as the people Wilson might hurt in this crusade.

"Did he have a specialty in the Army? Any specific interest?" Nikki asked.

"Why do you want to know that?" Lucy demanded.

Nikki glanced at Lucy, but kept her attention mostly on Mrs. Swiss. "Because if someone like David just got out of the Army or moved here, they might have hooked up and be hanging out together. If we know what he did, maybe we can track down who he might be with."

"He was just a telephone operator. How does someone stationed on phones get shot in the throat?" David's mother stared at her, tears in her eyes, wanting answers.

"We don't want to bother you." Gabriel leaned forward and offered the women a scrap of paper. "How about I leave my phone number, and if you hear from him, let us know?"

"That's a good idea." Nikki nodded. "If I see him, I can pull your number from his file and give you an update. How's that sound?" She dredged up a smile and squeezed Mrs. Swiss's hand in return.

"That would be lovely." She smiled and pressed her tissue to her chest.

They said their good-byes, keeping it as brief and non-committal as possible.

Lucy frowned the whole time, even when she saw them to the door. Nikki wasn't sorry to put the woman behind them.

"Phone operator?" she asked as they walked to the GTO. They really should be in a less obvious car than the purple wonder.

"My guess? He was part of a six-man long-range surveillance team, and he was their communications guy. They can get dropped behind enemy lines, spend days or weeks even like that. Dangerous shit." Gabriel opened the passenger door and held it for her.

Nikki sank into the GTO, unease churning her stomach. She chewed her lip and studied the picture-perfect house while Gabriel circled the car and got in.

"That might make him more appealing to Wilson." She didn't like admitting that. It was one thing to lump the whole group into the extremists column, but now that she'd met some of David's family, she had to wonder what they were dealing with.

"I think you're right. David would have to be made of some strong shit for a gig like that." He started the car and pulled it around.

"To Homestead?" she asked.

"Yeah."

She didn't know if she should hope to find something there or not. One way or another, she was going to pay the price.

Chapter Six

Gabriel's gaze strayed to the length of Nikki's legs. She'd crossed one over the other and now, if he didn't look too hard, the denim shorts were more like panties with the way they cut across her upper thigh. Because that was the visual he needed in his head.

"How we playing it this time?" She tapped the damn tablet screen again.

He wanted to throw it out the window, force her to pay attention to him, but what would that get him? Another carefully worded *fuck off*?

"The same." He leaned over the steering wheel and watched the street traffic in and out of the trailer park.

They'd chosen to sit back and watch before approaching the second family. A militia would be hard-pressed to hide behind a gated community where everyone was up in their neighbor's business. Lucy was proof of that. Gabriel doubted anything happened on that block without Lucy knowing about it. While there might be another version of Lucy in the trailer park, there were also a lot of transitory residents. The demographic was low-income, and not like one of the kitschy trailer parks with rows of flamingos and retirees. The trailers here were generally run down and would only last through one or two more hurricanes before being demolished. Chicken wire held siding together on several of the homes, and tires weighed down patched roofs.

He knew the types of people they'd find here. Back home, growing up, he'd played and lived in many parks just like this one. Like it or not, these were his roots. And he'd clawed his way up from the rough heritage to something hopefully better. It at least allowed him to ease his mother's life these days.

"Does Wilson have a type?" he asked, for lack of anything else to talk about.

"Mm, young and male is the only one I'm seeing. There are some older members we've identified, but they fit either the military or activist angle."

"White?"

"Nope." Nikki didn't even bother to look at him, and it rankled. "He's hit on almost every major ethnic group. The militia is mostly white and Hispanic, if that's what you mean."

"Just a guess." He leaned on the driver's side door, resolute to not look at her legs again.

"Wilson doesn't appear to have an ethnic motivation. At least not yet. I wouldn't put it past him to go that way if he thought it might help his case. He's got too many Latino and black supporters to make it about race." She dragged her finger across the tablet screen.

He could remember how that felt on his skin, the slow glide as she teased him. It took some work to bring out her playful side, but it was there. Many times, he'd woken slowly to her drawing on his arms or chest with nothing but her finger.

Damn. Now he was jealous of a stupid tablet getting more action than he was.

Gabriel shifted in his seat and focused on one trailer door in particular. A woman stepped out, carrying a disposable baking dish laden with food.

"What's their story?" He nodded at a cluster of people between the woman's trailer and the one next to it. There was a grill going and people hanging out in a redneck pool made from an old fiberglass boat covered with a tarp and filled with water.

"Hm." Nikki stroked the glass screen. "Jedidiah Williams, goes by Jed. He was military police. Was in for eight years, and—"

"Let me guess. Medically discharged?" It was the same story over and over again. Gabriel didn't like the theme he was seeing.

"Yeah. Someone lobbed a grenade over the fence. Jed didn't suffer much external trauma, but his PTSD made him unfit for service."

"The VA seems to be our link." It turned his stomach. He wasn't looking forward to pointing out this link to Julian or Aiden. Both men had served and seen some serious shit they carried with them to this day.

"Except Jed wasn't going to the VA." Nikki glanced up from the tablet and at him. Her gray eyes were so bright they seemed to shine. It hurt to look at her and not be able to touch her. "From what I can tell, he came home and has been in and out of trouble, with no job, for the last couple of years."

"Shit." Gabriel scrubbed his hand over his head. He needed to focus. To stop thinking about her. Them. Because there wasn't anything there. Just the job. "Let's do this."

He met Nikki at the front of the car. He barely resisted reaching for her hand. Some part of him had never stopped being hers. Instead, he shoved his hands in his pockets and together they crossed the street, entering the park.

A couple of kids kicked a ball in an empty lot. Some twentysomethings had their stereo systems competing with equally obnoxious music in another driveway. The neighborhood was busy, active.

At first Gabriel had wondered if Wilson's militia might be hiding out here. In an area like this, no one would think anything of half a dozen men living in a trailer together and keeping to themselves. Chances were, people would assume they were cooking meth or some other nefarious activity and give them a wide berth. He'd seen those types often enough as a teen to know them on sight. But Gabriel wasn't so certain now. From watching the Williamses' trailers, he could see a community routine. The area might not be wealthy, but he'd seen almost every other vehicle slow or pause to speak to someone at the Williamses' get-together. But could someone have seen something?

The Williams clan occupied several lots. The trailers were connected by shared yards, sheds, and the party central in the middle of it all. Kids played in the water while the men tended the grill and the women went to and fro, seeing to everyone's needs. It might not be the nicest of digs, but these were people who banded together to help each other and didn't turn their back on family. So what happened to Jed? How had he fallen through the cracks?

The trio of wingmen for the grill eyed them as they approached. Or more accurately, Gabriel. If they noticed Nikki, it was only that she was there. No one displayed the easy welcome they'd given others going by.

"Help you?" one man called out to them. He had a handlebar mustache, the sleeves were cut out of his T-shirt, and he held a can of beer in his hand.

"Lookin' for Jed. Is he around?" Gabriel put a twang in his voice, not quite mimicking the speaker's speech pattern, but enough that they might read him as familiar. Someone who belonged.

"Nope." The man shook his head and directed his attention back to the grill.

So much for getting asked to hang around. There was a distinct *go away* vibe.

"Will he be back soon?" Nikki held her hand up to shield her eyes and smiled.

Gabriel knew he was frowning, but he'd seen her smile at strangers while he got her cold professional front.

"He owe you something?" Handlebar asked Nikki, ignoring Gabriel's presence.

He got the message loud and clear. They weren't interested in answering anything he wanted to ask them. The problem there was that Nikki wasn't experienced in the field. Maybe she'd gotten her feet wet after him, but she belonged in an office—safe. Not out here doing the grunt work. That was his contribution.

"No." Nikki's brow wrinkled and she appeared genuinely confused by the question. She glanced at Gabriel, then back to Handlebar. "He said he could help . . ."

The way her voice fell at the end, it tugged at even Gabriel's instinct to protect. Damn, where had she pulled that from?

Handlebar set his beer down by the grill and strode toward them. He glanced at Gabriel, but there wasn't anything friendly about it. When he looked at Nikki, there was concern. Interesting. Just what had Jed gotten himself into before he'd disappeared? Gabriel wondered if he dug into the trouble Jed had been in, would he find a history of white knight syndrome? Not all damsels wanted to be rescued.

"He do something?" Handlebar asked Nikki.

"No, it's not that. I just . . . Jed was very nice when I met him and said if I ever needed help to give him a call, but I haven't been able to get ahold of him."

Handlebar sighed. "Jed does this sometimes. Sorry. It's best not to count on him." The man spoke like one often let down. "Chances are he went camping and will be back in a couple of weeks."

"Weeks?" Nikki's jaw dropped. Damn. She was a much better actress than Gabriel had given her credit for. That, or she'd had a lot more field experience than he realized since they worked together.

"Yeah, that's Jed. If I thought it would do him any good, I'd go haul his ass back myself, but it's best to leave him to it. Anything I can help you with?" Handlebar scuffed his boot in the dirt and offered Nikki a smile that had probably endeared him to many a woman.

Nikki glanced at Gabriel. "No, I don't think so. Thank you, though."

"Come on." Gabriel placed his hand on Nikki's back and Handlebar glared at him, as if it were he Nikki needed help with. As if.

He and Nikki might not be together, but if she ever needed help, he hoped she would call him. He'd move mountains if that was what it took.

"Thanks," she said over her shoulder as she turned with him.

Gabriel ran his fingers over the ribbed fabric hugging her waist, then dropped his hand. He could appreciate the ways she'd filled out without touching her. In fact, not knowing how she felt would probably go a long way in helping keep his sanity in check. Back when they'd been together he'd fussed at her for missing meals, eating a piece of fruit when she didn't have time to go out for anything else. She'd been so thin a hard breeze might have knocked her over.

Okay, so he was exaggerating. Even pushing paper, she'd had to measure up to tough FBI standards, and Nikki wasn't one to just scrape by.

He didn't know if it was maturity, a better schedule, or having someone in her life who prepared her lunches and took care of her, but she was even more attractive to him now. Granted, he'd always been an ass man, and hers was fantastic. Especially in those shorts.

They strode back the way they'd come, Gabriel conscious of the eyes on their six.

"Jed must have a history of rescuing women," Nikki said under her breath.

"That's what I'm thinking. You see the way he bowed up when I was trying to talk to him?"

"Yeah."

"Good move with the asking for help line."

She glanced up at him and for a moment he thought he saw surprise there.

"Thanks." She looked up and down the street as they jaywalked back to the GTO.

Gabriel refocused his thoughts on the case, and not Nikki's bubble butt. Their connection between the missing men might not be the VA, but there was a pattern developing he was willing to bet they'd hear at the half dozen different families across the greater Miami area.

"Wilson recruits these guys and cuts them off from their families. Sounds a bit like a cult," he said.

"Lots of groups use separation tactics. Wilson isn't about religion. It's a one-man show with him calling the shots. Cults operate in a different way." The act was gone and the all-business agent was back.

Gabriel unlocked the passenger door and held it for Nikki. He mulled her words over as he circled the car and got in.

Nikki turned toward him the moment he closed the door. "We should see if any of Jed's family own land out in the country. Something rural where he could go camping."

"I'll text Emery." He grabbed his phone and tapped out a quick info request. He was willing to bet they'd have an answer in minutes. "When did you get so good in the field?"

"You do know that I was trained as a field agent before I ever met you?" Nikki kept her gaze on the damn tablet, but her tone was all ice.

"Being trained and having experience are two different things." He'd worked with plenty of guys who couldn't hack it. With her, he'd never doubted her ability. The truth was he needed her safe so he could continue doing his job.

Nikki didn't respond.

Gabriel applied maybe a bit too much pressure to the accelerator as they merged with traffic. The tires squealed as he took off, but only a little. She grasped the door as he swerved around slower-moving traffic.

"What the hell?" she snapped.

"It's a muscle car."

"So you have to drive like an idiot?"

"Dang. That might be the most emotion I've seen from you yet."

Except for last night. He'd felt her frustration and anger then, but he wasn't going to bring that up.

Nikki didn't respond.

He wanted her to pay attention to him. To talk to him. It was juvenile and silly, but if the only way he could make her see him was to bug her, well fine. He'd done worse before.

Gabriel reached over and grabbed the tablet out of her hands.

"Hey!" She made a wild grab for the device.

He tossed it into the backseat. It landed with a thud and bounced onto the floorboard. If it broke, well, either Emery could fix it or the FBI could buy her a new one.

"What the hell was that about?" Her voice was raised, her brows drawn down. There was emotion behind her words.

"I'm trying to work with you and all you do is jack with that tablet." He swerved around slower-moving traffic, going nowhere fast. His destination didn't matter yet, so long as he was going somewhere.

"And I'm trying to research."

"You've read that file a dozen times over. It's not going to tell us anything new."

"What is your problem?" Nikki pressed her fingers to her temples. "I can't figure you out. You're angry with me for—what? Working? Trying to do my job?"

"I'm not angry, you just aren't seeing the case because your nose is buried in that tablet."

"Gabriel, in case you aren't aware of this, people work in different ways." She spoke slowly, as if he were a damn toddler being scolded.

He yanked the car into the lot of a fast food joint and shifted into park.

"You don't have enough experience to know that." Even as he said the words, he knew they weren't true. Nikki was an experienced, seasoned agent. She might not be used to undercover work, but she was incredibly competent. So why was he goading her? To get a reaction? He should stop, but he couldn't help himself. Not when he saw emotion simmering there just under the surface.

Nikki blinked a couple of times, her jaw working soundlessly.

"Excuse me?" she finally said.

He should apologize, acknowledge he was being an ass

and smooth things over. Yet his mouth opened and he shoved his proverbial foot farther down his throat.

"You've had what? Three or four years?" He shrugged. "That's not enough, Nik."

"You always downplay my ability." She tossed her hands up, her cool façade broken.

"I am not downplaying it, I'm just saying, there are better ways to work a case."

"You don't think I can do it. You never did. Is it because I'm a woman? Is that it? Does my lack of a penis offend you?"

"No, this isn't about gender." It was about her. About them. God, he was a wreck inside.

"Really? Because you're starting to undermine my authority all over again, and I'm not going to let you do it this time." Her voice rose as she spoke. She must be getting really riled up this time. He had to stop this.

"I never undermined your authority." He frowned, scouring his memory for a time when he'd gone against her orders.

"Yes, you always did. You're doing it now. God, why is working with you so difficult? Can't you just let me do my job and stop trying to control everything?"

"I'm not controlling anything."

"Yes, you are. You used to do it all the time."

"I didn't control you. I protected you."

"Really? Is that what you want to call it?"

"Yeah. Give me an example." He was blindsided. When had this happened? He'd only ever thought of her.

"Detroit. The warehouse?" She leaned toward him, her eyes a little bloodshot and her lips tightly compressed.

"That was—it was dangerous. You needed to be farther away from the site in case shit got bad. Which it did."

"I was supposed to be there as your backup, to pull your ass out, and I couldn't get there."

"And I got out just fine. It was safer for you."

"If I had a dick would you have cared?"

Silence.

He'd cared about his previous handlers, but not like her.

"If I'd been a man, would you have second-guessed my call to be outside that warehouse?" Nikki asked, jabbing her finger at her chest.

Shit.

"It wasn't safe—"

"If I was a man would it have been the same?"

They stared at each other for a moment. His phone vibrated, the only other noise in the car. It might be Emery or Aiden or anyone else he should answer, but not in this moment.

"Gabriel." She drew his name out as a warning.

"No. Are you happy? If you were a man or even another woman, it wouldn't have mattered. But because it was you, the woman I was sleeping with, it mattered."

"You promised me it wouldn't."

"Yeah, well, I lied. Happy?"

"Were you lying when you said we could work together now?"

"No. Yes. Maybe." He sat back in his seat, unable to look at her.

He was guilty of loving her too much back then. Of wanting to protect her at all costs, even if it meant his life and cutting him off from the one person who might have helped him through the fallout. Another woman might swoon at the idea she rated above everything else, but not Nikki. To her, what mattered first was the work they did; everything else came after that. It was another thing he respected about her. He'd made an emotional choice back then, and even now. Both times they were wrong, and selfish, but he didn't know how to stop himself. How to make it be any other way. He couldn't stop caring about Nikki, no matter what had happened and how far they'd come.

"I'll call Aiden," Nikki said.

"Don't." He reached out and grabbed her hand before he could think better of it.

They both stared at his large, dark hand wrapped around her small, pale one. Her skin was softer than his. Of course, sandpaper was softer than him, but that wasn't the point. She was everything he wasn't, and she was better. Not because of race or class, but because of who she chose to be.

He had to be honest with not only himself, but her, too. She deserved that.

Gabriel let go of her hand and sat back in his seat. He'd need a little distance to get it all out.

"I always thought I was looking out for you. I didn't realize you took it to mean I was undermining your authority." Without knowing, he'd become another hurdle for her to clear instead of building her up.

"You did. Do you have any idea how bad it looked when I would lay out an operation, only for you to change it later?" She hung her head forward and looked up at him. With her shoulders hunched that way, he could imagine the weight of everything she'd overcome pressing her down.

He should have been helping to make that burden easier.

"I never looked at it that way. I thought I was protecting you."

"I didn't—I don't need your protection. If I were a civilian, then yes, protect me. But I'm not. I am an FBI agent. The training and shit I've been through has prepared me to be out here with you. Not holding you back or letting you pull my weight. If you would just let me do my job, maybe you'd realize that."

He blew out a breath.

Of course she didn't need him. She was every bit as capable as he was. Probably more so. She could look at situations analytically, while part of him would always get wrapped up in it. He felt it in his bones. It made him great undercover, but lousy as an agent.

"I'm sorry. What can I say?" He rubbed his hand over his face. "Telling you that being together wouldn't change how we operated was my mistake. I didn't mean to lie to you, but it shifted everything. From how I called you and when, to my focus in the field. I wasn't thinking about the objective, I was worried about you, keeping you in the clear and out of it."

"Can we work together?" Her voice was quiet.

"I want to. I was out of line earlier. You just . . . It's like you shut down, and it drives me crazy."

"How am I supposed to be, Gabriel? Things have changed. We've changed. I'm behaving the only way I know how to get the job done."

"I get that. Can we find a middle ground where it's not like working with a robot? We used to have fun together."

Nikki stared at the gearshift, opening and closing her mouth.

Once, they'd laughed together. On the job, they had an uncanny synchronization because they were in tune with the other. But not anymore.

"I can try," she finally said.

"That's all I'm asking."

"Will you stop being an asshole?"

"I can't promise to go against my nature. I am a man." He smiled sheepishly.

Nikki's smile was sudden and unexpected. She rolled her eyes and relaxed into her seat.

"Did Emery get back to you?" she asked.

The heavy weight sitting between them lifted. The day was a little brighter.

Her tendency to shift focus so fast had once left him in the dust. Now he recognized it as her acceptance of the barrier they'd just blown through and a desire to get back to their objective. Which meant she was still going to work with him. A stupid, crazy part of him was happy about it.

Gabriel grabbed his phone, grateful for yet another second chance.

"I've got an address." He slid the phone into the cradle and grabbed the gearshift, the world running a little more in tune.

Chapter Seven

Nikki leaned forward, craning her neck to get a better look. The seat belt tugged at her shoulder and the air conditioner blasted her in the face.

"Cameras," she said.

Gabriel slowed the GTO to a crawl. She lowered the window and snapped a couple of pictures with the high-powered camera she'd borrowed for this trip. She'd had a vague hope this would be an evidence-gathering trip only, but the more they uncovered about Wilson's recruits, the more concerned she was getting.

The presence of white poles with the brand-new security equipment stuck out in the middle of nowhere was a prime example of what was making her worried. By all accounts this property was supposed to be undeveloped land won in a poker game. From the map, all they'd been able to tell was that it was remote, backed up onto a waterway that led to the ocean, and had no neighbors nearby. The closest occupied structure was a bait and tackle/gas station several miles closer to the highway.

"What do you want to bet there isn't just a fishing shack out here?" Gabriel asked under his breath.

The latest aerial photographs Emery had dug up showed

a ramshackle twelve-by-twelve cabin and tiny dock on the property at the end of a dirt road. It wasn't much, but for someone who wanted privacy, it was an ideal getaway—for Jed and a couple dozen of his closest friends.

"They aren't pointed at the county road." Nikki frowned and followed the angle of the nearest camera.

"Look. They're aimed there." Gabriel pointed ahead of them to a brand-new gravel drive leading away from the two-lane county road.

"That's not on the aerials." She snapped a few pictures.

"What do you think the chances are this is Wilson's new hangout?" Gabriel asked.

Nikki peered down the drive and at the cameras as they passed at a low speed.

"Why point cameras at a driveway and not the road?" she mused out loud.

"I highly doubt we're seeing all the cameras. We're probably on one now. Let's find a place to hide the car and hoof it back to their location." He accelerated a bit, putting some distance between them and the drive.

"If they have cameras on the road, then they'll get your license plate. Why didn't we take a less conspicuous car?" It was the issue she couldn't wrap her mind around. Gabriel's electric purple car stood out, even in a place as colorful as Miami.

"I changed the plates, so if they're run, they'll go back to a sedan from Tallahassee. Plus, Emery will know and we'll have something for him to sink his claws into."

"Why couldn't we just take another car? One that wouldn't draw attention."

"We need the action."

"I'm sorry, but I think I missed something." She stared at Gabriel, trying to figure it out for herself.

He turned the car off the road onto a sandy path. She wasn't so sure about this decision, but kept that to herself.

"Remember, we've got to keep up appearances. If these guys are muscling in on our territory, for whatever reason, we can spin this to help us. You can't tell me where Wilson is getting their funds from, so I bet it's something nice and illegal. Hitting them bolsters our street cred. Besides, not everyone can match cars to owners, and if they can, Emery has all of our rides masked or disguised or something."

"I don't get it, but if you say it works for you guys, I won't push it." The flashy car went against everything she'd been trained to do in covert work, but Gabriel was playing a different game here in Miami. If he was willing to let her lead in what she knew, she would defer to his judgment where the car was concerned.

"Ready to walk?" Gabriel reached under the driver's seat and pulled out a twin set of silver Desert Eagle pistols.

"That's an upgrade." Nikki eyed the high-powered semiautomatic handguns.

"Would you believe me if I said they're for looks?"

"No."

Gabriel grinned.

"You lead. I'll follow." Nikki was more at home in an urban environment. Out here, she would have to rely on Gabriel's tracking ability and knowledge of the terrain. Despite his current inner-city gig, he'd grown up tracking animals and people across the desert in West Texas and the border of Mexico. He'd proven a number of times that he was more than capable at finding his way even without streets. His sense of direction was truly uncanny.

Nikki reached into the messenger bag Roni had outfitted her with and retrieved one of her own SIG Sauer pistols.

"You're carrying?"

She glanced at him, amused by his neutral tone.

"Why else do you think I'm carrying a purse in the field? Does it look like there's anywhere on these shorts to stash a weapon? I swear, this is the most ridiculous outfit I could think of." She checked the chamber and flipped the safety off, then on again before tucking it in her waistband.

"Yeah, but you look like you belong, so the clothes do their job."

She didn't miss the way his gaze traveled slowly over her body, or the half-smile. An invisible hand squeezed her heart painfully for a second. This was about the job, not them.

"Ready?" Gabriel stood, stowing both weapons in the belt around his hips. He flipped his shirt up and over the firearms, gifting her the smallest peek at his abs. Damn, but the man had a great body.

"Ready."

Nikki pushed out of the car and looped the camera strap around her neck. It was a fairly sophisticated model that she'd been able to program to send the images directly to Emery's server so he would get the pictures almost as fast as she could take them.

"Stay ten feet behind me." Gabriel started walking into the brush. "We don't know if they're actively patrolling. I want to come at them about halfway between the water and road, where they're likely to be more lax about security."

"Okay."

She tried to tell herself this was just another intel recon. In her career, she'd done dozens of these. But never with Gabriel. Back then her role had been different and all about him. She was glad to follow him at some distance because she was pretty sure the excitement of it was going to show through. How many times had she wanted this to happen? Then there was the aesthetic joy of getting to watch him.

Sweat made the gray T-shirt cling to his shoulders. The

dappled light on his skin accentuated the strong definition of his biceps and arms. He crouched slightly as he walked, presenting her with a great opportunity to admire his firm ass. Yeah, the man was a walking, talking buffet she wanted to eat up. Too bad her time with him was over. Still, there was no harm in looking.

The ground was covered in grass and weeds that came up to her knees. Thigh-high bushes and shrubs thrived between the sparse trees that were a mix of tropical, evergreen, and what appeared to be some kind of oak. Nikki wasn't up to date on the flora enough to know more than if it came down to a shoot-out, none of the ground cover was enough to hide behind.

Without the rumble of the car, she could hear the sound of the distant ocean. She could even smell the scent of brine in the air. Insects buzzed, and pretty soon a halo of little flying things circled her head. The coarse grass cut her calves, and in a few places they had to cross open ground due to the soil being eroded down to the limestone bedrock.

There was a peaceful kind of quiet at first, but it wore thin. It was as if even the nearby wildlife knew something bad was afoot. Every so often she could hear a noise, maybe a shout or an engine that was decidedly man-made.

Ahead of her, Gabriel paused.

She hesitated, waiting for a signal from him.

He gestured for her to come closer and sank to a knee.

Nikki crouched lower and scurried up next to him. A sprawling hedge and a sagging branch provided some cover, but not enough to put her at ease.

"There's a fence line up there." Gabriel pitched his voice low and pointed.

She could make out a chain link fence between the trees, but more than anything, she could hear the chug of a diesel engine and the shout of voices.

"How many of them do you think there are?" She peered through the camera lens at the largest gap, but all she could see was the siding to some kind of structure that didn't look like a beat-up old cabin.

"No clue. I'm going to that stand of trees there." He gestured ahead of them and to their left. "I'll check it out, and if it's clear, you join me. Keep an eye open for patrols or someone wandering around out here." Gabriel drew one of his Desert Eagles and flipped the safety off.

Nikki's nerves twisted inside her for a moment. She didn't like risking the lives of good agents, but to stop the bad guys, it had to be done. For the span of a couple heartbeats, she let herself be nervous. Be human. Even though she'd faced down some truly terrible things in her life, she was still a person with fears just like everyone else. The trick was learning how to deal with them. She envisioned putting the emotion away, like she might hang a jacket in a closet and be done with it.

She blew out a breath and pulled her SIG Sauer out, disengaging the safety.

"I'll cover you. Go."

Gabriel stared at her for a moment. She couldn't begin to imagine what he was thinking. Finally he said, "Okay," pushed up into a crouch, and made his way slowly and carefully to the stand of trees.

She kept her gaze on the landscape, letting her eyes relax, opening herself up to catching the slightest movement. There were times when it was right to rely on a gut feeling, when it would give her the added edge to react faster, but nothing was screaming at her to flee. She settled in, shifting until she found a more comfortable spot, and continued to wait for Gabriel's signal.

At long last he reached the trees and dropped down to all fours.

Damn it. She should have given him the camera. If it wasn't safe, if they had to make a speedy exit, this could be their only chance to get photo evidence of what was going on. Documentation was the key to building the case. It was great and all to see it for themselves, but they needed tangible evidence. Pictures. A paper trail. Catching them in the act of a crime. Something that would stick. For several long moments nothing moved, not even Gabriel.

He flicked his fingers, curling them in a *come here* gesture.

She mimicked his traveling pose, but crossed the ground faster, eager to finally get eyes on whatever the hell it was Wilson was doing way out here.

Nikki hit the dirt next to Gabriel, going down to her belly, and pulled the camera up to peer through the viewfinder. She pointed and clicked, only waiting on the frame to focus before she shifted her target.

"*Ay, ay, ay, ay*. This is not good," Gabriel muttered.

Nikki couldn't agree more.

This wasn't a secluded fishing getaway anymore.

"I recognize some of those trucks. I bet if we run their plates they'll match up to some of Wilson's people." And here she'd hoped they wouldn't find anything.

The chain link fence enclosed maybe the whole property. A couple of acres at least. The trees and ground cover had been pushed back and even burned in places, either to make room for whatever it was they were doing or to remove places to hide. Gravel covered most of the space, cutting off anything living and any cover they might have had for a closer look. Several prefabricated sheds, trailers, and a couple campers were lined up in the far north corner, away from the water, in what appeared to be the bunk area. People moved all around with purpose, while others patrolled the perimeter.

She wiped at her eyes and sniffed. There was something rotting close by, and under that, some odor she couldn't quite place.

In the middle of it all was two barns, set as far apart as possible. One backed up all the way into the water. If Nikki had to guess, a boat could pull up inside the structure to load or unload its cargo. The other barn was maybe a dozen yards from the westernmost fence. Several vehicles were lined up along the fence out of the way, and one van idled at the gate.

Nikki frowned into the display.

Right behind the van was a conspicuous . . . car. The rear spoiler rose up above the cab. It was painted a pink and purple flames motif with a handful of advertising stickers slapped on top of the paint job.

"Anyone you know?" she asked.

"Yeah." Gabriel didn't sound too pleased.

She blinked a couple more times, but whatever was in the air was particularly strong. Where had she smelled that before?

"Is that . . . meth?" She peered at Gabriel.

"Yeah." He sounded even less pleased this time.

Nikki hadn't worked narcotics cases very often, but drugs touched almost every corner of the earth now in some fashion.

"I bet they cook it in the boathouse. If there's a fire, the water is right there. If they want to deliver it, the water is a good way to avoid detection. Man, they set this place up more than a week ago. They've been working out of here for a while. At least a month or more."

She cringed.

He was right.

How long had Wilson been working on this without anyone noticing?

"What's the other barn for?" She zoomed out and took a couple wide shots.

"I'm going to find out." Gabriel turned and put his back to the thickest tree.

"What?" She paused in her photo taking to gape at him.

"The fence doesn't go all the way to the water. The patrol isn't too tight. They aren't wearing uniforms, and there's enough people milling around I bet if I'm seen I can blend in." He checked his gun once more.

"No." She said it before she could think through her knee-jerk reply. "There is no way to get in there unseen. This isn't a good idea."

"Trust me. This is what I do best."

"No." She shook her head.

"Look, I don't want to argue with you on this or undermine—"

"This is about being smart. It's too dangerous to try to sneak in there now. It's the middle of the day—"

The pink and purple car revved its engine and sent up a cloud of smoke.

"Everyone is going to be too busy watching Hillary to notice me." Gabriel pushed to his feet and dodged toward the water, moving with the shadows.

Hillary?

Nikki tore her attention from Gabriel and looked back at the car.

A woman in painted-on jeans and a halter top hung out of the driver's window. Even from this distance Nikki could see her impressive cleavage. She snapped a few pictures, zooming in on the car and the woman.

How did Gabriel know her?

Nikki clutched the camera with both hands.

Was this someone he knew intimately? Were they some kind of car rivals?

The urge to punch the woman's lights out was completely irrational, but it felt good to visualize Hillary's head bouncing off the hood of her car.

She glanced back at Gabriel and her heart leapt into her throat.

He edged around the last fence post right next to the water. And no one saw him. At least no one she noticed. Nikki craned her neck to get a better view, but he stepped behind a truck and out of sight. She fisted the wrist strap on the camera, willing him to come back. If he came back, she wouldn't second-guess him, she'd listen to him, she'd do anything if only he was safe.

Gabriel prowled between the two box trucks. Men yelled at each other, sometimes in code. He couldn't put his finger on it, but something felt off. He reached the cabs of the vehicles and peered out.

From this angle he could see the other barn. The big sliding door was partially pushed back. A car sat in the entrance, hood up. Most people kept a little distance from the second structure. He itched to get inside that building, but the chances of him making it inside were slim.

The meth barn had a healthy amount of traffic in and out, which was plain stupid. Labs like this were highly flammable, and prolonged exposure could produce sores and other side effects just from being around the chemical process. It would make Wilson's people easy to pick out of a crowd.

He stood up straight, pushed his shoulders back, and strolled out into the open. A big part of undercover work was acting like he was supposed to be wherever he was. If he appeared as though he belonged, only people who knew better would question him.

Hillary revved her engine again. He could hear her cackling laugh over the rest of the noise as she put on the same show she'd always used. She'd been a looker once, but that was before the meth. How she hadn't died already, either by overdose or wrecking her car, he didn't know. It was only a matter of time until her poor life choices came back to bite her in the ass.

Gabriel kept his focus on the barn. One foot in front of the other.

A man exited a small door set into the wall and glanced at him, frowning.

Gabriel gave the man a sharp nod and marched forward. He did his best imitation of Aiden's walk, the way he held his shoulders, and kept going. The man made a hard right and headed in the direction of the bunks.

Nikki needed evidence of what was going on here. He'd do what he could to grab something, snap a few pics with his phone, and get out of there. Whatever was going on, he couldn't stop it right now. Not until he knew the bigger picture and what they were dealing with. One thing was for sure, this was a lot bigger than a bunch of nuts with guns wanting to teach 'Merica a lesson.

He grabbed the door and hauled it open. A wall of putrid stench hit him. It was worse than rotten eggs. His eyes began to water and his nostrils burned.

"Hey," someone called.

Gabriel glanced to his right. A man stood in the bed of a pickup loaded down with barrels of something. He was big. There was no other word for it. In dusty fatigue pants and a green T-shirt with the sleeves ripped off, he was not someone Gabriel wanted to meet. Ever. A guy didn't get that big naturally, or just for the fun of it.

"What?" He closed the barn door carefully and turned to the truck.

"We have to get this stuff inside. Grab that dolly." Big Man gestured at the side of the barn.

Gabriel strode around to where Big Man had indicated, and sure enough, two dollies sat side by side. He grabbed them both and rolled them to the truck.

"Want to get one side and . . ." Gabriel stared as Big Man hoisted one of the barrels up in his arms, took two steps to the tailgate, and hopped down, merely grunting as the liquid inside sloshed around. Big Man set it on a dolly, pausing only to swipe his forearm across his brow.

"Get that to Nico." Big Man gestured at the far barn.

A gift-wrapped opportunity to get into the barn he needed eyes on?

"Sure thing."

Gabriel tilted the dolly and pushed it through the gravel. The barrel had to weigh, what, two hundred pounds? He wouldn't say it wasn't humanly possible to lug it around like Big Man behind him had, but it was unlikely. Hell, Gabriel was having difficulty just pushing it through the deep gravel. Despite the sealed barrel, he could still catch a whiff of something he didn't like. It was different than the meth lab. Worse, actually.

Big Man trucked backward, dragging the dolly and barrel after him.

Gabriel pivoted, following suit, and found it to be marginally easier.

"What's in these, man?" he asked.

"Don't know, don't care," Big Man replied. His eyes were bloodshot, and close up, Gabriel could see the start of sores along his arms.

Wilson must be selling the meth to pay for this little party, and giving it to his men. Meth made people do things, unnatural things, like slinging around a two-hundred-pound barrel of chemicals.

"Gabriel?" a shrill, feminine voice said. "Is that you, Gabriel?"

Oh shit . . .

Chapter Eight

Nikki couldn't see Gabriel anymore. He'd disappeared from view thanks to the trees and trucks in her line of sight, and damn it, what was he doing?

She lifted up on her elbows, peering this way and that for some sign of his movements. Why did he think he had to go in there? Evidence wasn't worth putting his life at risk.

This whole situation was bad. Yes, they needed proof of what Wilson's militia was doing to figure out how to stop him and what laundry list of crimes to charge him with, but not at the cost of Gabriel. She needed to get on the phone to Aiden in case they needed backup. Emery was the only person who knew where they were, but he wouldn't know if they needed help.

She pulled her phone out of her pocket and tapped the screen.

"Damn it," she muttered as the call canceled out.

She had no signal.

Nikki surveyed the area until she found a clump of bushes bracketed by two trees about fifteen feet closer to the fence. The foot patrol wouldn't be by for another few minutes, and the people inside the perimeter were either too busy watching the woman in the car or were minding their own business. No one would notice her if she moved fast and kept low.

For a few seconds, she waited and watched, but no one looked her way.

She pushed up to her feet and crouch-ran to the clump of bushes. She hit her knees and went down to her elbows hard enough she knew she'd have scrapes.

Gabriel stepped into view, heading straight for the meth barn.

No. No. No.

She cringed. They didn't need proof of that. She could smell it. Plus, there wasn't a cleanup crew alive who could remove all traces of the meth lab fast enough.

Nikki went to her knees behind the shrubs and lifted her cell phone.

Still no signal.

Were they simply out too far? Or was this intentional? Could the militia have a cell phone jammer on-site? They weren't regulated enough to be out of the question, and it could be one method Wilson used to keep his men under control. If they didn't know about news coverage and couldn't contact their families, they remained completely reliant on Wilson and his people.

The woman, Hillary, shimmied out of the car. She grinned at someone Nikki couldn't see. A plain white trailer, like what might be used at a construction site for an office, blocked her view. Hillary stopped and spread her arms. A man with sandy blond hair approached her. It was the way he moved that gave him away. She'd watched enough footage, seen enough pictures to be able to place him. This was who they were looking for. They'd found Wilson's people, and now she had evidence.

Nikki had seen enough. She snapped a few pictures of

the passionate lip-lock between Hillary and Bradley Wilson.

The two spoke, but at this distance Nikki couldn't tell what they were saying.

Where was Gabriel?

She glanced back at the meth barn, but her gaze snagged on Gabriel and the biggest black man she'd ever seen dragging dollies across the deep gravel. Her stomach dropped. Was he fitting himself into this group? Had his plan changed? If he was able to get in with the militia, maybe he could tell her how to stop them. But it meant leaving him in an uncertain situation, not to mention her without a way to get out of there. She would manage somehow, but it was him she was worried about. They had no idea how the militia was organized, if he could simply slide in or what. It was too risky. She had to get him out of there.

The grass rustled to her right. It was shorter here than it was anywhere else, as if someone had trimmed it some time ago. There were no ambient animal sounds, no call of birds. It was quiet. It was a different sound than that of the breeze or an animal. It was a slow, controlled crunch.

Nikki went completely still. She had her camera in one hand and her phone in the other. She'd walked into a trap. There was no way for her to draw her weapon before whoever was creeping toward her could get off a shot. Her alternatives were to run, which would attract more attention; give up and be taken hostage, taking the chance she could learn something; or wait to be killed.

Something swished closer. Whoever was out there was drawing nearer.

They'd probably kill her. It was easier that way, less work. Cleanup could be left to animals and they wouldn't lose manpower.

Why had she moved?

Slowly, she looped her arm through the camera strap,

shifting it to lie across her back. If there was a cell phone jammer on the premises, it would block the camera upload as well. They needed to analyze these images, study them. But first, she had to make it out of there. Or at least the camera did.

If she made a break for it, she risked outing Gabriel. Of the two of them, his was the more precarious position.

She was in trouble. But she needed to hold her position for as long as possible.

A shadow fell on the ground in the farthest point of her peripheral vision. She tucked her phone in her bra, praying it stayed put, and grabbed handfuls of dirt in each hand.

The woman, Hillary, shrieked something Nikki couldn't make out past the thunder of blood rushing in her ears. She sensed more than heard the person stalking her move into action.

Now or die.

Nikki pushed up to her knees and pivoted, flinging the dirt up at the man. He wore green fatigues and body armor and carried a sniper rifle. There was nothing about his gear or equipment that made sense at a glance. It was as if he were supposed to be somewhere else. At war, not in backwater America.

He staggered back, swiping a hand across his face. Nikki took two strides toward him and kicked. He moved at the last second and she got him in the thigh with the heel of her boot. He swung wildly with his left hand and brought the gun up. She ducked and drew her pistol, her whole body pulsing with adrenaline.

She was going to die.

Gabriel swung his head around. His stomach sank. Why, of all the people in Miami, was it her? It wasn't so much her, as who she worked for. Who her brothers were. Between those two facts, Hillary could do whatever she wanted, which back when she used to run with the street-racing crowds meant drugs and booze. Lots of those.

"Gabriel!" Hillary strode toward him, her voice too loud. The men stared, and why wouldn't they? As far as Gabriel could tell, she was the only woman in this sausage fest and she wasn't half bad looking, though the drugs had taken their toll.

The blond man she'd hugged stared at Gabriel, gaze narrowed.

The jig was up. Sometimes Gabriel could play a situation off, figure out how to spin an angle, but from the looks of things, he didn't think there was a way to come back from this. The question was, did he bolt now or later? How could he find out the most useful information?

Hillary threw her arms around his shoulders and planted a kiss on his cheek. Her breath, or maybe it was her body odor, wafted under his nose. He was going to scrub off a layer of skin later.

"Perimeter," someone yelled.

An almost electric charge rushed through those present in the yard. All heads swung toward the guard at the fence, pointing in the direction where he'd left Nikki.

Fuck.

Was she okay? Could she fend for herself until he got there?

The blond man didn't glance away from him despite the surge in sudden, unorganized activity. People ran in all directions, yelling and giving orders that made no sense. For a military-style operation, there was no obvious chain of command.

He had to get out of there right now. There was no later. Nikki's life might depend on it. When it came down to it, she was all that mattered.

"I need a ride," he said to Hillary.

"What?" She frowned at him. Judging by the stench coming off her breath, she was high on meth right now. Which was about what he expected from her.

Gabriel grabbed her elbow with his left hand, pulling her partially in front of him. He was banking on the blond guy not wanting to hurt Hillary. The Big Man had abandoned his dolly to rush to something else. Possibly hunting Nikki down right now.

Gabriel bent his neck and spoke into Hillary's ear. The blond man never once looked away, but he did gesture for someone with a clipboard to come near. Was this Wilson? It had to be. And Hillary was his plaything. Great.

"I've got a gun," he said. "I will shoot you if you don't get in your car right now and drive me out of here."

Hillary made some sort of strangled sound in the back of her throat. She arched her back, as if he were jabbing her with the gun right now. Meth paranoia could be useful, but it also made people like Hillary unpredictable. He propelled her forward, toward the car.

"Hillary, where are you going?" the blond man asked.

"Out," she yelled back, but her voice quivered. She'd always been a bit extreme in her moods, but hyped up on meth, who knew what he was dealing with? When Gabriel still knew her, she was mostly smoking pot and doing a few feel-good drugs. Nothing as hard as meth.

Gabriel stared at the man staring at him. They both knew Gabriel wasn't supposed to be there. This man was a shark. The rest of the people on the makeshift base weren't the threat. This man was, and Gabriel was staring him down with nothing more than two Desert Eagles and a prayer.

Dios mio, espero que Nikki esté bien.

"Keys?" he asked Hillary.

"I-in the car," she stammered. Her eyes were glassy, and

this close, he could see the wear and tear drugs had taken on her formerly beautiful features. If it weren't for the drug use, she might have tempted him once. She'd aged prematurely, and while makeup and cleavage could distract from what she'd lost, there was no going back.

"Who are you?" The blond man pitched his voice over the noise, speaking directly to Gabriel.

Ten feet from the car.

"Just a friend, popping in to say *hola*."

Seven feet.

"Bradley . . ." Hillary's voice hitched at the end.

Gabriel's suspicions were right. This was Bradley Wilson, their narcissistic mastermind. He wasn't a lot to look at. Five eleven, maybe, without the combat boots. The military-style gear he wore was all store bought, probably never once dirtied. Wilson didn't have an imposing physique. His eyes were small and close set, his lips generous, yet pinched. Whatever hold he had on these people, Gabriel didn't get it. Not at all.

A gun went off in the distance.

For the span of a second, Gabriel's world stopped.

Nikki.

What if that was her? What if she'd been shot? Or what if she was backed into a corner? He wasn't there for her. He'd left her unprotected out in the open.

Gabriel shoved Hillary away from him and dove for the car. She cried out, and he saw her stumble in his peripheral vision. He jerked the driver's side door open, groped for the keys, and turned the ignition. Someone reached for him through the open window. He stomped on the accelerator and let the engine do the rest. His shirt partially ripped, but it was just clothing. Nikki was out there and she needed him. The car fishtailed in the gravel before gaining traction and shooting forward. He turned the wheel hard, barely avoiding another vehicle parked askew before straightening it out, and aimed for the fence.

Men scattered from his path. A few drew weapons. He hit the locked gate, and the car lurched. He cringed, waiting for the air bags to deploy, but the gates gave way first. He cranked the wheel, sending the drift racing car off the road and into the brush. It bounced over the uneven ground, sliding sideways until he clipped a tree with the front fender.

Gabriel threw himself out of the driver's door, which hadn't completely shut yet. He drew his two Desert Eagles and took stock of where everyone was. A handful of the militia seemed to have organized themselves and advanced out of the now-broken gate behind him in something resembling ranks.

It was past time to leave.

Nikki.

Had she shot the gun? Or was she the one getting shot?

He had to get to her. Now.

Gabriel turned, sprinting in the direction of the gunfire. He zigzagged as he ran. The blood pounded past his ears so hard it drowned out the sound of gunfire. The skin between his shoulder blades itched. The blast of a gun report broke through his single-minded determination far closer than he'd have liked it to. Shards of wood pelted him from the stray bullet, several splinters sticking into his skin.

A figure lay on the ground, the sand stained black.

Gabriel skidded to a stop, staring.

It was a man.

It wasn't Nikki who'd been shot.

"Get down," Nikki yelled.

He ducked. The flash of muzzle fire caught his eye, giving Nikki's position away. She lay low in the brush, perfectly hidden—and not at all where he'd left her.

Gabriel glanced behind him. There were easily a dozen men on his six. If he had a moment to spare, he might have paused to take in the oddity they presented. This just couldn't be right. There was no uniformity. Most militias might be patched together, but they eventually had a cohesive appearance—these were a dozen different men with varying levels of gear, munitions, everything. They didn't belong together. It was completely wrong.

One paused, gun up to shoot.

"*Vamos, vamos, vamos*." He scrambled toward her.

Nikki got to her feet. The camera banged against her side. Blood covered her right shoulder and was smeared on her face.

An invisible knife twisted deep in his chest.

She was hurt. He hadn't protected her.

His knee-jerk reaction was to stop everything. To tend to her wounds. But more importantly, they had to get out of there so they could keep breathing; then he could take care of her. If she lasted that long. It was a good thing she'd already killed the bastard. Gabriel wouldn't trust himself around someone like that.

He twisted and fired off three warning shots without aiming. Nikki sprinted ahead of him and disappeared past a line of dense brush. He charged after her, following the trail of quivering branches and beaten-down grass. Shots fired behind him and to his left, but didn't come anywhere near them.

Was that blood he spotted on a bush? Was she still bleeding?

The next time he saw a damp spot on a leaf he swiped his hand over it, and it came back red.

Nikki was hurt.

These goddamn sons of bitches were dead. All of them.

He turned and went to a knee, sweeping his gaze under the short trees and bush. A voice called out to his left. He fired. He kept firing, sweeping to his left as he went. There were a few raised commands, maybe a muted yell, but he couldn't be certain he'd hit anyone, just beat them back a little. With his anger dulled he sprinted to the north, then cut back west toward the car. The purple hood glinted between the trees.

Nikki stood in front of the car, her phone mashed to her face, blood streaked over her cheeks. The sight of her fueled his rage into overdrive. Wilson and all his gun-toting idiots were dead.

"In!" he shouted.

Something crashed through the brush behind him. He could hear voices now, distinct tones. He cursed himself. Taking those shots was the wrong call. He hadn't delayed their pursuers, just pushed them west a little.

She dove into the car and leaned across to push the driver's side door open.

He threw himself into the seat and thrust his weapons into her lap.

"Are you hurt?" he asked, digging for his keys.

"Drive!" she snapped.

He got the key in the ignition and threw it into reverse as two men carrying assault rifles breached the tree line. One went to his knee.

Nikki leaned out of the open window with his Desert Eagle in hand and pulled the trigger. The shot went wide, clipping the branch over the man poised to take a shot. He flinched and dove for the ground.

Gabriel grinned. Dust plumed up around them. His tires contacted the pavement and he whipped the car around. A distinctive pink and purple Mustang swerved into his rearview mirror.

"Fuck!" He stomped on the accelerator. If Hillary was behind the wheel, they were in trouble. Even strung out on meth, she was a first-rate drift driver and would know these roads better than him.

Street racing cobbled together a lot of different forms. It was the MMA of the car world. Drifting was all about handling a car. It was a precise, judged sport, and Hillary—God damn her—was great at it. If he were in his Skyline, all he'd need was a bit of open road and he'd outdistance her in moments. But back here, on twisting, winding roads in a heavy muscle car, it was going to take more than fancy driving and a killer engine to save their asses.

"Shoot anything that follows us." He had to push his concern to the backseat. When they were out of here, still alive, he could take care of Nikki's wounds. Until then, he had to focus on hightailing it.

Nikki twisted in the passenger seat until she was on a knee, one leg braced against the floorboard.

"Hold on," he yelled as they entered a turn.

The tires skidded and squealed as he took it too fast. He could feel it in the vibrations coming up from the floorboard and the jerk of the wheel. Nikki slammed against the door, grunted, and held on as he evened out.

Pop. Pop.

A metallic *ping* echoed through the car.

The bitch shot his car.

"Shoot! Shoot back!"

"I'm trying," she snapped.

Nikki fired twice with his Desert Eagle before thrusting it back at him and drawing her own SIG Sauer. She squeezed off several more shots. It was hard to track the nearing vehicle, and keep his eyes on the road, and watch Nikki.

He wanted to protect her. To be the one fending off Hillary and these assholes.

He hated the blood all over her, but she wasn't complaining, so he couldn't pause.

A loud boom nearly made Gabriel jerk the GTO off the road.

"Got them," Nikki shouted. "Oh shit."

"What?"

"There's a green and black car. Drive faster!"

He glanced in his mirrors in time to see Hillary's car bounce off the road, limping along with a flat tire. A bright green car with black racing stripes swerved around it, hot on his tail.

"Damn it."

"Who is it?"

"Hillary's brother. Shoot."

The road evened out into a long, flat stretch. Nikki leaned farther out of the car and fired repeatedly. He saw the following vehicle's windshield spiderweb and shatter inward. It swerved right and left, fishtailing before going into the ditch. Gabriel took the next turn in the road and they lost the visual on the second car.

"Was anyone else behind them?" he asked.

"No, not that I saw." Nikki sat back down in the passenger seat and strapped the seat belt on.

"Are you sure?" If they had Hillary and Andrew, what about their other brother Jesse? He worried Gabriel. The other two were just punks who could drive. Jesse was in a whole other league.

"Yes."

Nikki grabbed her cell phone again and immediately started chattering to someone on the other end of the line, never once addressing the blood staining her clothing. He gripped the wheel tighter as the landscape passed in a blur. She asked him a few questions about the layout of the property, and he answered on autopilot. He couldn't manage anything more than that. The one thought on repeat in his mind was: *She's hurt.*

He could have lost her today because he'd chosen to take a risk.

It was every reason he'd never allowed her this close to his work before.

She could have died.

At the edges of the Homestead city limits, he pulled the GTO into a gas station and parked in the relative shelter behind the car wash. Yeah, they were on the run, but they'd taken out the two fastest pursuing cars. They hadn't seen anyone on their tail in miles.

"What are you doing?" Nikki turned toward him, eyes wide, lips parted.

He cupped her face, brushing his fingers over the drying blood, turning her face this way and that. There were no gashes, no wounds. It wasn't hers. The blood was not hers. As best he could tell, all she had was a busted lip and some bruising.

"Oh, thank God." His hands nearly shook with relief.

"Gabriel—"

"Shh."

There was still blood spray and chunks of something sticking to her.

He grasped her arm and peeled the strap of her tank top and bra back, holding his breath as more skin was revealed. Dirt and more blood clung to her, but there was no injury. No bullet wound. Nothing. She turned her upper body to face him and didn't pull out of his grasp.

"Gabe. I'm fine. It's not mine." Her voice was steady. The calm to his storm. He'd needed that so many times. She'd been his anchor. The one point in his life he could count on.

He placed both hands on her shoulders, taking her in. Whoever that guy on the ground was, he must have been on top of her when she shot. It was the only explanation for the amount of blood on her. She'd have had to push the body off, roll in the dirt. Messy, but she was alive.

"I'm okay," she whispered.

He sucked in a breath, letting go of the fear that had gnawed on him since hearing that first gunshot.

She placed her hands on his biceps. Her gray eyes pulled him in. She was his focal point. She'd been his everything. And she was okay.

Nikki was *mi cielo*. She'd never stopped, though she'd also never known what she meant to him.

He slid his hands up to cup her face. So many mistakes. So much missed time.

She held perfectly still. Maybe she was still stunned from the attack, or maybe she felt it, too.

Gabriel placed his mouth on hers, mindful of her split lip. An electric-like current shot through him, reviving those deep recesses of himself only she'd touched. Her body jolted against his hands, but only for a second. She remained completely still. He didn't care. What mattered was that she was alive and unhurt.

Her lips parted, maybe to tell him off, but he didn't give her the chance. He suckled the sweet morsel of flesh between his lips and she groaned.

Better than I remembered.

Chapter Nine

Nikki ran her fingers through her damp hair in an effort to hide her shaking hands.

She'd only killed a man once before. Then, it had also been in self-defense. The popular theory was that it got easier, that the shock of it dulled after a time. Maybe for others, but not her. Nikki felt the loss of life more acutely than before. Whoever he was, he'd died on her watch. She'd joined the FBI to help people. To stop the threats. Of course she understood that sometimes that meant occasionally the bad guys had to die, but she didn't have to like it. Maybe that guy wasn't all bad, just brainwashed, doing his job.

"You look like shit." Roni closed the door to the garage bunk room. Nikki had retreated here after her shower in the utility room. She couldn't be around the others.

"Gee, thanks." And yet, Nikki relaxed a little with the other woman around.

"Here. Have a drink." Roni tossed a flask at Nikki.

She caught it inches from her face. The silver surface was battered and worn. Not at all the kind of flashy accessory she expected of Roni.

"What is it?" Nikki asked.

"Whiskey, I'm guessing. John said you might need it."

Roni sank onto the bottom bunk and propped her elbows on her knees. The sleeves of her coveralls were belted around her waist, holding everything up.

Nikki unscrewed the cap and tossed back a gulp. The liquid burned all the way down her throat, settling in her belly with a thud. She didn't particularly enjoy alcohol, but a single shot wasn't going to hamper her ability to function. If anything, it might blunt the edge of her guilt a bit.

Whoever he was, he was someone's son. Maybe a father. Yes, what Bradley Wilson's people were doing was wrong, but death wasn't hers to hand out. That was what justice was about.

Roni stared at her, that same laser focus she'd shown last night now aimed at Nikki. "Emery sent over an analysis of the pictures. I think Aiden is waiting on you. Gabriel is stomping around, looking for a fight. Something happen?"

Nikki glanced away.

The kiss.

She'd been trying to not think about it, but it was incredibly easy to lose herself in the memory of it. And that wasn't right. Not after what she'd done. She should feel guilt, not lust for her ex.

"Look, this gig is stressful. I don't talk about shit, but if you need to, get it out so we can keep rolling."

Much as Nikki hated to admit it, Roni was right. Nikki opened her mouth and closed it. Where did she begin? What did she say? She'd hardwired herself to avoid girl talk at all costs. Doing what she did, she had to be the complete professional. Talking about a little lip-lock wasn't in the realm of what was usually acceptable. But that was when Gabriel wasn't in the picture.

"Let's start with Gabriel," Roni prompted.

"God." Nikki buried her face in her hands. She could

still feel the whisper of his touch and the sting of rejection when he pulled away from her. They were a mess.

"That good?"

"Complicated."

"Considering you came back covered in blood and he's storming around, I get that."

Nikki couldn't bring herself to say that Gabriel had kissed her. What if she'd imagined it? What if he was going to tell her it was all an accident? A product of adrenaline? When they'd been together, the adrenaline-fueled, post-op sex had been crazy. The best. She also couldn't bring herself to talk about it when it could all be taken away from her.

"Have you ever killed someone?" She leaned against the cinder-block wall, soaking up the chill.

"Yeah." Roni shrugged, as though it were no big deal.

"Does it bother you?"

"Sometimes, but I've never killed a man I wasn't positive deserved it."

But it wasn't Nikki's place to act as judge and jury. That reasoning wouldn't work for her.

"How did you know?"

"First guy?" Roni held up a finger. "He was a Russian mobster with a *reputation*. We were . . . eighteen. Our dad was gone. This guy thought he could torture information out of us. He was going to rape Tori and make me watch. I shot him in the face."

"Shit." Nikki took a second swig of whiskey.

"Second guy was an all-around criminal of opportunity. He was wanted for the death of a couple people. Third was a hit man. My theory is, if they shoot at me, they wouldn't feel guilty if it was me that died. So I shouldn't either."

Nikki nodded. It made sense, but what if the guy she'd

shot was like Jed or David? What if he hadn't known what he was doing?

"Think you can make it?" Roni asked.

"Yeah. I'm good." Nikki screwed the cap back on the flask and handed it to Roni.

"Great. We've got plans tonight." She stood and pocketed the flask.

"What are we doing?" Nikki followed Roni out of the bunk room and into the garage. Sunlight poured in from both sides of the open bays. Music blared over the sound of tools clanking and the general busy nature of a garage.

For a moment, all eyes were on her, but the only ones she noticed were Gabriel's. He stood silhouetted by the afternoon sun, the rear yard of the garage behind him. She didn't need to see his face to fill in the sharp lines, the thinned lips. They were already committed to memory.

"Gather round, everyone," Aiden called. He grabbed a tablet from a drawer in his workstation and laid it on the top.

Nikki shuffled closer, but stayed on the outskirts of the group. By all rights, it should be her leading this powwow, but she wasn't up to it. Maybe Gabriel was right to doubt her ability. She hadn't done well today. Instead of staying low and focusing on what Gabriel was doing, she'd caused a mess that could have gotten them both killed.

"Looks like Wilson has torched his waterfront operation. Call came in to the Homestead cops about an explosion. Julian is there now with Matt Smith, who is trying to pull it into his jurisdiction." Aiden passed the tablet around.

The images were a collection of the ones Nikki had taken, with the key focal point highlighted, and what appeared to be cell phone shots from after the blast. Those had to be additions from either Julian or Matt.

"Think they set off the lab?" Gabriel asked from right behind her.

Nikki shivered and her nipples puckered. It was a completely illogical reaction to him, and yet she couldn't help the way her body responded to him.

"It looks that way," Aiden replied.

"Damn it. Our leads?" Gabriel paced three steps to Nikki's right and clasped his hands together behind his head. He was really worked up about something.

"Emery is working on tracking down the license plates in the pictures, where some of the equipment might have been purchased. Him and the girls are making a lot of progress, but he says they'll need a few hours." Aiden took the tablet back and powered it down. "Nikki, what's our next step?"

Four sets of eyes turned to her.

She cleared her throat and straightened. Think. She was a damn FBI agent. She'd logged hundreds of hours in the field. One little shake-up wasn't the end of her world.

"Can we speed up that process or is it better to leave Emery alone?" she asked.

"Honestly? He'll work faster if we leave him alone. Besides," Aiden checked his watch, "we've got to make an appearance at Stoke's in thirty minutes. Anyone hungry?"

"Hell, yes," Roni cheered.

"Stoke's?" Nikki echoed.

"Food," Roni replied.

"Shit. Aiden, I gotta bounce. I'm supposed to be on shift with the other derby refs." Gabriel thumbed over his shoulder.

"Yeah, see you there, man." Aiden waved Gabriel out of the garage.

Nikki turned away so she wouldn't have to watch him leave. Last night she'd been sure it was all over. That either

her broken heart would waste away in unrequited love, or she'd pick up the pieces and move on. The kiss had shattered her so completely. If he'd done it at another time, when she was stronger, maybe it wouldn't have touched her soul. But he had, damn him.

She was pathetic.

"Come on." Roni shimmied out of her coveralls and tossed them onto another workbench.

"I'm not—"

Roni hooked her arm around Nikki's neck and pulled her out into the back lot, grinning.

"Shut up, will you?" Roni said between gritted teeth.

Nikki held her tongue and let the other woman draw her out to her silver Dodge Viper. They didn't speak again until they were inside. Roni dropped the smiling, happy girl routine. It was rather refreshing.

"Look, we have to go tonight to support Madison, but we can split after we eat and go hang at my place until Emery calls us in. Gabriel will be busy. You won't have to worry about him because he's volunteering with the rest of the roller derby squad. League. Whatever." She turned toward Nikki, one arm draped over the steering wheel.

"I don't understand . . . I think I missed something . . ."

"Madison—Aiden's chick? She plays roller derby. We got together and decided someone needed to join the league to . . . watch out for her. Gabriel is the only one of us who can stand on roller skates, so now he referees for the league and does fund-raisers with them. Especially at the car hop, because there's biker dickbags that like to harass the girls."

"Is this something we have to do?" She hated how whiny she sounded, but didn't she get a pass after the day she'd had?

"Yes and no." Roni shifted into drive and peeled out of the Classic Rides lot. "Madison did me a solid a couple months ago, she took the fall for what was our fault, and she makes Aiden less of a prick. I like her. She should be in witness protection—"

"For the Evers case?" Nikki struggled to recall all of the details.

"Yeah. But instead she hangs with us. We show up, people know to stay clear of her, she's safe."

"It's good for appearances."

"Exactly. You're learning."

"Daddy always said I was a fast student." Nikki leaned back in her seat and rested her head against the seat.

"Don't take this the wrong way, but you're pretty frazzled." Roni didn't pull her punches. She didn't lay it out there like an accusation, but she wasn't sugarcoating it, either.

"The first time I killed someone, it was to protect a little girl. He was determined to kill the kids in the same classroom where he'd been humiliated as a child. I hated that I had to pull the trigger, but I didn't feel guilt over it. This time . . . I don't know if I did the right thing or not."

"I'm guessing you didn't punch yourself in the face?"

"No."

"And Gabriel didn't bust your lip?"

"No." But he had sucked it.

"Look, I don't know who he was, but he attacked you. Did he have a gun?"

"Yes."

"Then if you hadn't killed him, he'd have killed you. You shot him before he could pull the trigger. It's that simple."

"But—"

"No," Roni snapped. "No buts. What we do—it has to be that simple, or we'll lose our minds wondering if we're doing the right thing."

Nikki nodded. She'd heard something similar in the

academy, but Roni spoke with the kind of been there, done that conviction that resonated with Nikki.

"What happened with Gabriel?"

"Nothing."

"Big fucking lie, but if that's what you want to believe, whatever. Here." Roni dug out a small zipper pouch from the tote sitting in the floorboard.

"What . . . ?" Nikki frowned at the bag.

"Makeup."

She flipped the visor down and peered at her reflection. Her hair had a slight wave to it thanks to the humidity. The bruise on her jaw stood out under her pale skin, and her lower lip was puffy. She couldn't be sure if that was due to the elbow she'd caught with her face or the little bite Gabriel had given her during their make-out session.

Thinking about his mouth on her made her insides heat. She pressed her thighs together and plucked out a bit of concealer. It was for appearances. If she was supposed to be part of the crew from Classic Rides, she couldn't sport a fat lip and bruised jaw. It might give people the wrong impression. She smeared a bit more of the makeup here and there, keeping it light and natural.

"Find out anything today?" Nikki asked to fill the silence.

"Nah. We got word about your visit as we were heading out. Emery squeezed in some research on the other missing guys. Pretty sure they're shacking up with your man Wilson. That's crazy about Hillary."

"Who is she?"

"Drift racer. Crazy bitch. Her family on her father's side is pretty redneck. Her mother is Cuban. The brothers are pretty cool, but she's totally unhinged."

"Do you race against each other?"

"Oh, no. Drifting is done on a track and you're judged

by people who think they know shit. We just drive really fast."

"Then how do you know each other?"

"Hillary used to come out to some of the scheduled races. We do a monthly big race out in the Everglades and she'd hang around. Had a thing for Gabriel, but he wouldn't touch her with a ten-foot pole."

"How do you think she's involved?"

"Hillary is sponsored by a couple Cuban restaurants. Family connection type thing. We know the owners, not family, store drugs for the Cuban gang. It's mostly cheap or highly addictive stuff. Meth. Cheese. Whatever the latest kid craze is. The DEA hadn't been too interested in busting their people up. Betting Wilson's people make the stuff, sell it to Hillary's people, and they distribute it. The group has never been much on our radar. They're pretty satisfied to stay in their neck of the woods, but now with Evers pretty much out of the picture and us not dealing, someone has to step up and fill the supply chain."

"This was a lot less complicated when it was all about someone wanting to blow something up."

"Yeah, wasn't it?" Roni turned into a lot with a big STOKE'S BAR & GRILL marquee advertising something about Deadly Dames.

The red barnlike restaurant was flanked on three sides by a row of tin awnings. People parked under them and girls wearing less than Roni had dressed her in brought orders out on roller skates. Motorcycles clustered along the front of the establishment, and the rest of the patrons appeared to give them a wide berth.

Gabriel's car was conspicuous, both because of the color and make, but also from the group of skaters standing around the hood. He'd changed into black shorts and a striped ref shirt.

Nikki slumped down lower in her seat, jealousy gnawing on her. Roni parked the car a couple of spots to the right of his and shifted into park.

Gabriel didn't even glance their way, just kept staring at a clipboard. Maybe the kiss had been a mistake.

"He's a freakishly good skater." Roni popped her seat belt and turned to face her.

Of course Gabriel was a freakishly good skater. He was good at everything.

She knew she was being sullen, that she was allowing her less honorable emotions to get the best of her. Jealousy was the first sign of it. Gabriel wasn't hers. There was nothing to be jealous about. They'd established that last night. And yet, no matter how sad it was, he was still the man she dreamed about.

Aiden's Challenger and John's classic Ford pickup pulled into the open spaces between the Viper and GTO, making the distance less obvious.

"I like you," Roni announced.

Nikki tore her gaze away from Gabriel's bulging arms crossed over his chest and back to her driver. Had she missed something? Was like code for something else?

The confusion must have leaked onto her face because Roni tossed her head back and laughed.

"Not in a lesbian way, though you are pretty hot in shorts." Roni grinned.

"Thank you?" In the past, Nikki had gone to great lengths to cover herself up to avoid comments about her body so she could be respected for what she did, and not how she looked. It was weird hearing it now.

"I've known Gabriel almost as long as this gig has been

going on. Can I tell you something?" The way Roni sat completely still, like a snake about to strike, was slightly unnerving. Then again, there were many things about the woman Nikki found slightly scary—if they weren't on the same side.

"You're going to tell me no matter what I say."

"Pretty much." Roni shrugged.

A girl in track shorts and a bikini top with skating alligators rolled to a stop outside Roni's window. She tapped on the window and smiled.

"Aw, hell. This is Lily." Roni rolled the window down and Lily leaned through the open space, bracing her arms on the car door.

"Hey." Lily's face was framed by curling dark hair, and there was something painfully perfect about her features that made her, in a word, beautiful.

"Lily, this is my new friend, Nikki."

"Nice to meet you." To Lily's credit, she actually looked at Nikki when she said it. Judging by the way she raked her index finger over her thumb and how she bit her lip, Lily was preoccupied with something else.

"He's not coming tonight," Roni said.

"What?" Lily blinked.

Roni blew out a breath and rolled her eyes.

"Julian's out working," she repeated.

"Oh." Lily blinked a couple of times, but it was clear the wind had been just knocked from her sails.

Roni ordered for both of them after a little chitchat and the roller girl skated off.

"Do I want to know?" Nikki asked.

"God. It makes my head hurt." Roni massaged her temples. "The stuff that went down with Madison? Lily got involved for a hot second. Julian rescued her, and now she's got it bad for him."

"Okay."

"I get that you're seeing Aiden as the asshole and Julian as the more reasonable one in all of this—"

"Not really."

"I'm sorry—what?"

"I met Julian. Before. He's different now." It was a difference that made her sick to her stomach.

"He is."

"He's . . . darker."

"Yup. Which is why a pretty girl like her needs to stay the fuck away. He'd blow her mind and break her heart."

"Or she could become a target." Nikki stared across the parking lot at Lily entering their order into a terminal mounted on the side of the building. Nikki had to weigh every person who came into her life. Was she willing to put them at risk to be a friend? An acquaintance? There were costs to being who she was, and some of them were very high.

"Exactly."

"You discourage her interest?" Nikki asked.

Roni shrugged. "I didn't discourage anything. I tell her how it is. I might warn her, though. Back to you and Gabriel."

"There isn't a *me and Gabriel*."

"Yeah, right. He's hovered around you ever since you guys got back."

"He thought I got injured. He's always been the protective type."

"Not with me. Or Tori. We've got ovaries, too."

"Gabriel and I have history."

"He's not the type to let history dictate what he's doing."

Nikki didn't want to hear this. Roni was giving her the building blocks to perpetuate her fantasies. What she needed to hear was that he'd banged every one of the girls in their skimpy clothes and had a line of clingers waiting to blow him every night when he was done with work. Of course, then Nikki would want to use their heads for target practice, but that was her problem to navigate, not his.

"I didn't know about you two until you walked in the door, but now that I see you, things make sense." Roni gestured at Gabriel, who stood with one arm draped over the side of Aiden's Challenger, sipping a beer. "Look at him. He's perfectly placed himself between Aiden's car and Aiden while he does his job. He's distancing himself from the girls. I never got why a guy with a hot ride and a decent face didn't at least have someone he saw on the side. I'm not saying there haven't been girls, but they don't stick around long enough for any of us to know their names."

"What are you trying to say?" And could Roni get it out any faster?

"All I'm saying is that you two have history and maybe it's not done yet."

"It's over. It's done. There's nothing more to say."

"You don't know that."

"Yes, I do."

"Yeah, how?"

"Because look at me. Well, not me now, but me. I'm an agent. I was born into this. My choices were," she held up a finger, "become someone's trophy wife with the understanding they would protect me from my father's enemies," she held up a second finger, "or become an agent. That's it. If I didn't want to live in a glass bowl my whole life as someone's possession or direct line to my dad, the only option for me was to be an agent. I learned that about the time I figured out what boys were good for. My mother sat me down and told me there were standards, and I figured out right then that I didn't want to be her. I wanted to do something. Help people."

Nikki pushed a hand through her hair. Growing up in DC around politics and law enforcement had given her a different perspective, but also a good grasp of her worth. To the man she might marry, it wasn't about love. It was power. And connection. To the people she worked with, she was the boss's daughter. Neither situation was perfect, but she'd made her choice.

"So, what?" Roni prompted.

"Even if he'd wanted me to leave with him—which he didn't—I couldn't. I can't leave like he did. I have to stay where I'm at. And he doesn't want back in. To be honest? This gig isn't for him. He was good at it. Really good. But it was killing him. I don't want him like that. We'll never work." It wasn't true, but it was more honest than laying out her pipe dream of how to make it happen. Either way, someone would give up a chunk of themselves, and Nikki wouldn't ask that of Gabe, not now, not ever. He'd left. He'd gotten out and moved on. She wouldn't haul him back.

"Man, I wish I didn't get it—but I do." Roni propped her elbow on the open window.

"Roni, join us?" Aiden had one arm around Madison, outfitted in a skirt and pink tank top, modest in comparison to her teammates.

Nikki's gaze skipped to Gabriel—who stared straight at her. The smile was gone, he wasn't laughing or talking. Did he hate her for coming back into his life? She was starting to hate herself for walking back into it.

"In a minute," Roni yelled back and punched the button to raise the window. "I wish I didn't get it, but I do. This job sucks sometimes, ya know? The only people you can be honest with are the people who know you're living a lie. If you make friends outside of that circle or, God forbid, date, you're never honest with them. Makes it tough to . . ."

"What's going on with you?" Nikki wasn't blind. Something was going on with Roni, but she hadn't thought the other woman would talk to her about it. Oh what a difference twenty-four hours and a little blood splatter made.

"Nothing really, it's just weird not having Tori around. Don't get me wrong, I'm happy for her, it just sucks to be me right now." Roni shrugged.

"I'm not an expert on siblings, never had one, but I think it's okay to miss her."

"I do and I don't. We've been each other's shadows our whole life. In a way it's freeing to be apart, but it isn't. And I get where you're at. I really do." Roni relaxed against the seat and leaned her head back.

"What's his name?" Was that where Roni went last night in a sequin dress that fit like a second skin?

"Doesn't matter."

"Sure it does. You spend time with him."

"It's a mistake, is what it is." Roni grabbed her blinking phone and stared at the screen. Her expression was hard, unreadable. "Speak of my devil."

"A bit of bad advice?" Nikki watched Gabriel from out of the corner of her eye. She didn't dare look at him again.

"Yeah?" Roni tapped the screen with both thumbs.

"Enjoy him while you can. Even if it can't go anywhere."

"You aren't making this any easier." Roni groaned.

"Why?"

"He wants to meet up for a bit."

"Honestly? I really don't want to be here."

"Are you sure?" Roni's tone perked up a bit. Whoever it was she wanted to see, he had his hooks in her. Nikki could point them out, or she could let the woman enjoy herself for a little bit.

"Positive. I could do with some breathing room." Nikki leaned back and let her head rest against the seat. There was only one way to be with Gabriel, and she had a one-in-a-million chance of making that happen.

Chapter Ten

Gabriel stared at the cherry red door to Roni's rental. The lights were on and the girls were home. He should still be at the fund-raiser. He'd signed up to help bus the side lot so the girls wouldn't have to skate over the busted-ass concrete, but that was before he knew what would happen this week. He'd lost any ability to focus when Nikki left without saying good-bye. They hadn't spoken since those few, halted words after the ill-advised kiss.

The kiss he couldn't stop thinking about.

Ever since that moment behind the car wash, when he'd looked at her and realized she wasn't hurt, he'd lost control. His need for her had overwhelmed the good sense to keep his hands to himself. He didn't regret kissing her. He'd do it again if she'd let him, but he doubted she would. Once Nikki made up her mind, there was no going back. To her, they were over a long time ago. After their last two discussions, he could understand why it was so easy to walk out on him. All this time, he had no idea how much more difficult he'd made things for her. How he'd pushed her away with best intentions.

Which brought him back to why he was sitting in his car on a dark city street staring at the only thing keeping him away from Nikki. He shouldn't be there, yet he couldn't get away from her. For twenty-four hours his mind hadn't stopped circling her. This moment was inevitable for him. It was the truth. And it wasn't pretty.

He still wanted her. He wanted her so badly that nothing else mattered. Today he'd made a go at working with her, but the truth was that their history was going to fuck everything up. While the rest of the crew was focused on their objective, he only had eyes for her. In a pinch, he'd put her above nabbing Wilson.

The crew would meet up at their secondary, covert location later. He'd see Nikki there, but he couldn't make himself turn the car around and leave. That was the reasonable thing to do. It was what Nikki would do. Hell, if their roles were switched, Nikki wouldn't be here by choice, which made his situation suck that much worse.

He was still in love with a woman who didn't give two fucks about him.

This was the moment where he should leave.

Instead he got out, the fragrant scent of Florida flowers assaulting his nose. The palm trees rustled in a strong breeze overhead. He put one foot in front of the other and made the slow trek up the walk to the door. He might as well be dragging tires behind him for all the speed he put on.

This was going to suck, but the good thing about leaving the FBI behind was his ability to say no. To set his own boundaries, and he was sure as hell going to do that tonight. Tomorrow he might take it all back, but he owed it to himself to at least say it. To get it out there.

He pounded out the stupid rhythm Roni insisted on using and braced his hands on either side of the door.

"Who is it?" Roni asked, her voice muffled.

"Open the door, Roni." He wasn't in the mood for her shit.

The locks scraped as she freed the door and pulled it open. Roni studied him, skipping the typical banter. Something was up with her lately, but she wasn't talking to him about it, and he couldn't dredge up enough energy to ask.

"I'm headed out. Make sure to lock up when you leave." Roni grabbed a small purse and stepped over the threshold. She jabbed her finger at his chest and leaned in close, pitching her voice low. "Don't do anything stupid."

Stupid covered a lot of territory.

He didn't agree, or even nod, to her terms. What he was about to do was probably stupid, but oh well.

Gabriel stepped into the condo and shut the door, flipping the locks to at least slow Roni down if she decided to come back. He stood on the welcome mat, absorbing the feel of the place. It was different now that Nikki was here. Even her presence changed things. Look at Roni. She usually bristled whenever an FBI agent came near them, and now she was defending one. To him, of all people.

"Who was at the door?" Nikki walked out of the hall, towel-drying her still-damp hair. She stopped abruptly when she saw him, swaying on her feet, her eyes widening.

Yeah, he was just as surprised he was there as she was. What he wouldn't give to be able to move on like a normal person. Instead he was stuck on this crazy-ass merry-go-round of obsession. It'd been four years. Shouldn't he have been able to let her go by now?

"Roni went out." He thumbed over his shoulder.

"Oh." Nikki dropped her hands and the corner of the towel touched the floor.

The seconds stretched on. He knew he should say something, but he was committing this moment to memory.

Was . . . was she wearing his old training days T-shirt?

The one he'd kept at her place so he had something to change into in an emergency? Or was this a new shirt that just looked like his? It was a standard-issue FBI item. Deep down, he hoped it was his, that she sometimes thought about him when she wore it.

Was she wearing a bra? It was hard to tell with the dark navy fabric.

One of them needed to say something.

"Roni pissed about the shirt?" he asked.

"No."

"Oh. That's good."

She gathered the towel into her hands and clutched it to her chest. The fabric draped more intimately over her curves.

No bra.

Shit. The memories of the time he'd spent between those breasts. Good times.

"Did you take something for . . . ?" He gestured to his face. Her jaw was a little swollen, but the bruising wasn't any worse.

"Yeah. I did at the garage."

"Good. Good."

He shoved his hands into his back pockets and dropped his gaze to the carpet. They had literally nothing to say to each other, yet these were the best moments he'd had in months. Years, maybe.

"Gabriel—"

"Look—"

They both paused.

He gestured for her to go first.

"About earlier . . ." She hesitated. Uncertainty wasn't like her.

"Which part?" The part where he'd left her? Or the part where he'd kissed her?

She pushed her shoulders back, dropping into agent mode. "Did you come here for a reason?"

"I wanted to check on you." He shrugged. If she was clinging to that act, then they really were over. The kiss, none of it, had touched her.

"Okay."

What should he say? Was there a way to salvage this? To slap a Band-Aid on it and move on? Which was better? Professional courtesy? Or owning up to the one-sided attraction?

"I shouldn't have kissed you earlier. It's fucked everything up again, hasn't it?" he asked.

Nikki glanced away and his gut tied in knots. It was over. It was really over.

He didn't take pleasure in this response from her. He liked her angry, passionate, laughing. This uncomfortable shift, the avoidance, it grated. Once, they'd been better than this, but he'd ruined that.

"Sit, please?" Nikki gestured to the sofa.

He let her pick a spot first. She perched on the sofa, almost hugging the armrest. He settled halfway between her and the other side of the couch. Close enough, but not.

He didn't regret the kiss, even if he shouldn't have done it.

"We were in a tense situation. A lot happened." She folded the towel and draped it over the end of the sofa.

Gabriel knew what he should say, but it would be a lie. Wasn't the point of leaving the FBI shaking off the lies?

"I can't do this." He set his hands on his knees and stared at Nikki. Admitting that out loud was liberating. It didn't make the sense of dread any better, but the weight clinging to his shoulders lifted.

"Do what?" Nikki asked. Was it his imagination, or were her eyes a little bigger?

"I can't work with you," he said.

She flinched, blinking rapidly.

"I still have some kind of feelings for you. And I can't sit back and act like you being in danger is okay with me. I just can't do this. I don't want to get in the way or bail, but this isn't working for me." He knew exactly how he felt, but there was only so much he was going to share with her. No need to lay his heart out there just to get broken even more.

Nikki continued to stare at him. Problems, tangible issues, she could deal with, but he'd just lobbed a touchy-feely thing at her, and it would take her a while to figure that out. For a girl, she was really bad at the emotional stuff.

"I'll stay out of the way. You won't even know I'm here. I just . . . I can't do this with you." Of course, he'd be right around the corner, keeping an eye on her. She didn't need to know that, though.

"No," Nikki blurted.

"Babe—"

"No, you can't bail on me now." She stood up. "Gabe, I can't do this without you."

Those words elated him, but only until he considered the context. She didn't need him like he needed her. He needed her, not just now, but for all time. She only needed him for this job.

"The others are behind you. You don't need me," he said, though it killed him.

"Yes, I do. I feel things. You might not believe me, and I know I'm not good about expressing myself, but I do feel. I needed you out there today, and I'll need you tomorrow." She closed her eyes. "I can't do this op without you."

"The way I am right now, I'm going to get someone hurt. And what if it's you?"

"What are you trying to say?"

"Don't you get it? I still feel things for you."

"I need you, Gabe." Her voice was so small, so lost. She sat down again, their knees almost touching, and reached for his hand, wrapping hers around his.

She could have said anything else and he could walk out of there just fine, but not that.

He stared at the top of her bent head, muddling through the last few moments. She felt things, but what was that supposed to mean? If she needed him, he'd be there for her, but at some point this had to stop. Unless . . . unless there was more. He didn't dare hope for it.

"I screwed up my last case and—"

"And you'll be fine. The crew here will get the job done."

"Will you stop talking over me?" she snapped, bringing her head up.

His jaw clicked together, he shut it so fast.

Nikki pulled her hands from his and shoved her hair back.

"It's not about my screwup. I'm trying to . . . You know what I realized when I screwed up? That a lot of what I'm good at, I learned working with you. When we were good, it was really good, and I miss it. I miss you, Gabe." She wiped at her eyes, her voice breaking. He didn't even dare to breathe. "Even the way you talk over me and try to protect me and when you pick a fight just because."

She glared at him.

Missing him wasn't the same as still being in love with him, but right now he'd take it. There was something there. It wasn't just him. She felt it, too.

Gabriel tugged on her hand, pulling her in closer. She leaned toward him, but her glare wasn't as fierce. Maybe the whole ice queen thing was an act, a way of protecting herself, and he hadn't seen through it. Why not? She'd had years to improve on it.

He cupped the back of her head and tipped her chin up. She stared at him, her stormy gaze so intense he had to pause and soak up the moment. He could change. He could show her. She meant that much to him.

Gabriel bent his head and licked her lips. She hissed, but this time there was no startled jolt. He set his lips against hers in an open-mouthed kiss. She shook off his hand and gripped the front of his shirt so hard he heard a seam snap. Blood rushed to his head and groin.

Nikki slanted her head to the side and nipped at his lip. It was so out of character for her, and he liked it. Arousal made everything except her hazy. He pushed her back onto the armrest, reveling in the way she clung to his shoulders, dug her nails into his skin, and arched her back. Whatever dam she'd hidden behind was broken, and the woman in his arms was another creature entirely.

It was . . . better than he remembered.

Once Nikki had opened up to him and they'd become intimate, watching her grow comfortable with her sexuality was his favorite pastime. This time, she didn't appear to need the same coaxing. Which was good because he needed her now.

Nikki shoved hard at his shoulders

No, no, no.

He sat up, blinking back the haze of lust to really see her. Had he read her wrong?

"Nik?"

If she was about to take all of those words back . . .

She sat up and dove at him. There was no other word for it. He caught her and rolled onto his back while she straddled his thighs. She didn't even try to brace herself, just gripped his shoulders and pulled herself up his body. The shoulder seam of his T-shirt gave way, but neither of them paid it any mind. She could rip every thread of clothing off him for all he cared.

He remained still, more out of fascination than fear she'd lock this creature back up inside her. He had a feeling once out, this was a facet of herself that couldn't be hidden. At least not from him.

Her hair hung over one shoulder. Her cheeks and shoulders were pink from too much sun, which gave the rest of her skin a glow. She was perfect. And right now, she was his.

She dipped her head and kissed him again. He wrapped his arms around her, hungry for more. He'd spent the better part of four years seeing her around every corner, failing to replace her because no one measured up.

He shoved his hands up under her shirt and splayed them on her bare skin. Moisture and lotion still clung to her shower-fresh body. She thrust her tongue into his mouth and he nearly lost his load. He pulled her closer, mashing their bodies together. Her hips shifted, rubbing his cock through his jeans.

"Gabe." She groaned his name, notes of frustration lacing her voice.

He pushed her shirt higher and cupped her breasts. Nikki sat up and tossed the training days T-shirt on the floor. For a second, all thought stopped.

This really was an all-new Nikki.

And she really wasn't wearing a bra.

Whatever kind of support she wore on a daily basis had to be illegal. At a glance, no one would imagine her breasts were this full or lush.

He plucked her dusky-colored nipples, tugging on them ever so gently.

She moaned and he kissed her neck.

"I want to fuck you so bad right now," he said.

Instead of giving him the shocked, blinking routine that

normally happened when he said something so forward, she nodded.

"Yes."

Oh hell.

She sat up and crawled off him. Or at least enough that he could take back his legs and stand up. He grabbed her hand and pulled her to her feet. His gaze went lower, to the curve of her hip.

That ass. He hadn't touched it, but in these goddamned shorts she'd paraded around in, he hadn't been able to stop thinking about it.

Nikki wrapped her arms around his neck and kissed him. He grasped the tab on her shorts and yanked. The button pinged off the coffee table. They were seriously destroying their wardrobes, and he couldn't care less. She pulled his shirt up and over his head. He tossed it off just in time to see Nikki shimmy out of her shorts and panties.

He took a step, barreling into her, and grasped her by the ass with both hands, carrying her backward. Their mouths met, lips parted, hungry for each other. It was more passion than he'd ever painted her with in his dreams. And this was real. He squeezed her ass, lifting her onto her toes just to be sure.

Her nipples stabbed his chest and her nails raked his skin.

Hell yes. This was real.

He thrust his tongue into her mouth and walked her in the direction of the room he assumed she was staying in. She sucked and his knees threatened to buckle from the surge of lust.

She wedged her hands between them, clawing at the front of his jeans. His shin hit something and he pitched forward, driving her back into the wall. The pain didn't even register.

He slid his hands lower and lifted, hoisting her up, pinning her against the wall. She arched her back and her fingers threaded through the hairs on the back of his neck.

There was no way he was making it to the bedroom. He squeezed her ass. It felt even better than before.

This was what he wanted things to be like between them. Full of passion to the point they tore each other's clothes off.

His jeans sagged around his thighs and his erection strained at the front of his boxers. She reached between them, fumbling with the band of his underwear.

"Do it," he said against her lips. Nikki slipped her hand past the elastic. He shifted her, allowing her more space. Her hand closed around his cock and—damn. He sealed his mouth over hers, pushing her higher on the wall. Her thumb swiped over the sensitive head, but there was no room between them for more.

They weren't making it to the bed. He could feel her wetness on his stomach. Nikki might keep a tight rein on herself, but her body didn't lie. She was turned on. She wanted him, even after all this time, after all he'd put her through.

Gabriel grasped his cock and she shifted her hips. He found her entrance with his fingers, wetter than he'd expected. Had she been like this the whole time? Hot for him?

She kissed his neck, bringing his focus back to the present.

"Shit," he groaned.

"Gabe . . ."

He placed his erection against her vagina and eased his hold. She slid down onto his hardness. Her eyes widened and she gasped. He could feel her internal muscles stretching. He caught her and kissed her lips, holding her steady.

He pulled out and rocked back in. The memory of doing just this a dozen times over was nothing like this moment. He hooked his arm under her knee, opening her farther for him and easing the penetration. She clung to him, her eyes squeezed tightly shut.

"Nikki," he whispered.

She whimpered in reply.

He withdrew and thrust with too much force. The pictures hanging on the wall shook with the impact. She hissed and pulled him closer for a kiss. He rocked into her until he was fully seated inside her.

For a moment, neither moved. The only sound was their heavy breathing and rain hitting the windows. He kissed her neck, her jaw, careful to not apply any pressure to the swollen area. She was too precious to be bruised like that.

Gabriel had to move. His dick was throbbing with arousal, and before he lost it, he had to make it good for her. There was no screwing this up.

He thrust, in and out. The smooth glide of his skin against hers, the way she hugged his cock, was bliss. Again and again he pounded into her. She tossed her head back and forth, making helpless noises of pleasure. Her breasts bounced and at times rubbed his chest.

Nikki opened her eyes, without him asking, and stared at him. Her mouth worked soundlessly, but her hands dug in, holding him tight as her thighs constricted around him, her heels driving into his ass and thigh.

She was beautiful. She was his *mi cielo*.

Her spine arched and she nearly screamed, a primal, soul-deep sound he'd never heard from her. He continued to thrust, keeping an even, steady rhythm. Something fell off the wall with a heavy clatter and crunch of glass, but he didn't stop. She tightened her grip around him, pulling herself up his body. This time, she nipped his lower lip, driving him even crazier.

He planted a hand against the wall for better leverage. The remaining pictures thumped with each pass of his skin against hers. Nikki groaned, arching her back even more.

His balls drew up and before he could shift, he came. The sensation rolled up from his toes. He thrust into her in a few short, jerky motions, burying his face in the crook of her neck, and leaned against the wall, pinning her there.

Her fingers stroked over his face and hair while she kept her limbs entwined around him.

That was the best damn thing. Better than a memory.

They could do this. They could be together again. Couldn't they?

He leaned back, all the warm, fuzzy feelings dying at the look of abject horror on Nikki's face.

"What? What is it?" he asked. If she said it was a mistake . . .

"You didn't use a condom," she whispered.

"No." They never had before.

She closed her eyes and sucked in a deep breath. Her hands still clenched his shoulders, so at least she wasn't punching him in the face.

"I'm not on the pill anymore," she said calmly.

Shit. Oh, shit.

"I—I'm sorry. I didn't even . . ." Think. He hadn't thought about how things might be different. He'd just gone for what he knew.

He eased one foot, then the other to the ground. Nikki covered her face with her hands, rubbing her eyes.

"Nikki, I—"

"You didn't know. It's not your fault. I just . . . I just need to clean up."

She side-stepped him and made the right turn down the hall, leaving him with his pants and boxers around his ankles.

What had he donc?

Chapter Eleven

Nikki shut the bathroom door and wrapped her arms around herself. She'd left her clothes and the towel outside and stood on the cold, tile floor completely naked.

How could she be so stupid? But Gabriel did that to her. He drove her crazy, until she lost all reason and ability to think. She'd wanted him so badly she'd ached inside. They were both at fault here, though what they were guilty of besides a moment of irresponsible lust was lost on her. How could something that felt so right be wrong?

If she got pregnant . . . The thought didn't fill her with terror. Having his baby wouldn't be such a bad thing. Once, they'd discussed it. Children just weren't what she'd planned on yet.

"Oh, God."

She wiped away the moisture leaking from her eyes. Was she crying? After sex?

That was unlike her. Except . . . The kicker was that— he was it for her. And being with him again, it was showing her just now much no man would ever measure up to him.

She'd dated a handful of men since him, and no one could inspire this kind of all-consuming desire. Only

Gabriel. After that display there was no going back. She couldn't pretend like this was some booty call, a little revisiting the past. The way she'd acted, he had to know. Hell, he'd seen her wearing his shirt. If there was a more pathetic banner advertising her everlasting devotion, she didn't know what it was.

"Nikki?" Gabriel tapped on the door.

"I'll be out in a minute." Her voice managed to stay somewhat steady.

There was no way she could hide in the bathroom forever.

She turned on the tap and splashed some water on her face to get her thinking. As her mind switched into gear, she grabbed a washcloth and proceeded to clean herself up.

The most responsible thing to do was to find the closest drugstore. There were morning-after pills. A few days of being uncomfortable while the drugs did their thing was prudent. And yet . . . she didn't want to.

What if she was pregnant? It wouldn't exactly fit into her life plan, but she could make it work. The biggest concern was how much of a target a baby of theirs could be. Gabriel would never consent to not be part of a child's life, so then there would be trips to visit his family. He would always be there, and if they couldn't make things work it would be a slow, painful kind of death to have him around and not be able to love him.

But what if they could make it work?

There was a slight chance her pet project could get the green light. It was unlikely. But Gabriel would be perfect for it. That was a pipe dream, though. She wasn't one to depend on fantasies. Which was why she needed to be reasonable. Which normally she excelled at, unless Gabriel was around.

Her phone sat on the vanity where she'd left it after smearing ointment on her bruises. She pulled up the app store and downloaded one of the highest-rated ovulation calendars. A few clicks later, a little personal information and it generated a graph that showed her squarely in the least fertile part of her cycle.

Good to know.

It wasn't scientific proof, but she drew an easier breath.

Intellectually she knew it was unlikely she could be knocked up, and yet there were hundreds, if not thousands, of one-night stand babies born every year.

If she was pregnant, if they decided not to go the route of a contraceptive pill, she'd love the child. If not, well, maybe it was time to start thinking about her future—with or without Gabriel. She might only be able to love him as the leading man in her life, but there were other ways of having children these days. And she wanted them. Now wasn't the right time, but—what ever happened according to schedule these days?

She glanced around the bathroom, but there were no towels. It wasn't like Gabriel hadn't seen her naked before. The difference was her. He was the only man she'd ever been with so intimately, which was one more clear sign. Pushing her shoulders back, she opened the bathroom door.

A small stack of clothing sat on the tile floor.

Damn him for being so thoughtful.

She smiled and scooped them up. Gabriel was a really great guy. And he was probably freaking out right now just as much as she was. At least she'd picked a good one to fall madly in love with.

Dressed and ready to have a calmer discussion, she poked her head into the bedroom Roni had lent her. Gabriel sat on the bed, elbows on his knees and hands clasped in front of him. He was shirtless, clothed in just his jeans and boots. He was paler than usual, but she didn't take that personally. In their line of work, they couldn't make accidents.

He glanced up at her, lips parted as if he wanted to say something.

What did you say in a moment like this?

She sat on the bed next to him and reached for his hand.

"I'm sorry. I didn't even think," he said in a rush.

"Neither of us did. It's not like we ever had to use condoms before." She squeezed his hand. "It's unlikely that I'm pregnant."

Gabriel's expression didn't change. If anything, she felt the slice of sadness to her bones. Gabriel would make beautiful babies.

"I haven't been with anyone since my last physical," he volunteered.

"Me, too." It was two physicals ago for her, but she'd keep that tidbit to herself.

"I would never knowingly put you at risk like that."

"I know. That was my fault."

"I should have stopped and asked. I've never done that before." He wrapped both his hands around hers. "But . . . what if you are pregnant? Should we do something? How early can you tell?"

"No clue. I've never run that risk before. I'd imagine it'll be a few days, maybe a couple of weeks." She took a deep breath. Just because she'd accepted the consequences of what they'd done didn't mean the choice was entirely up to her. "I could take a morning-after pill."

Gabriel's face twisted up. He didn't tell her no, but his old-fashioned inclinations showed through despite his good intentions.

"I thought that's what you'd say." She smiled weakly.

"If that's what you want to do, I mean . . ."

"I don't."

"Then—"

"If you're going to start with the overprotective bullshit—stop."

Gabriel grinned. She rarely cursed, and it seemed half the time it was because of him. He brought her hand to his lips and buzzed her knuckle with a kiss.

"I was going to say that we needed to do that together," he said.

"Oh."

Both of their phones began to vibrate. Hers in the bathroom and his in his pocket. Before either could move, Gabriel's phone chimed with an incoming call.

"It's Julian." He frowned and answered it.

Nikki snagged her phone from the bathroom to get ahead of whatever was going on. The text was gibberish to her, but she had Gabriel to translate it for her.

She scurried back into the bedroom and pulled out another pair of shorts from the pile of castoffs Roni had given her. They weren't ideal for the field, but she couldn't argue that the majority of people she'd seen wore stuff even more revealing than this.

Gabriel stood and wiggled the phone at her. "Julian. Says they identified a lot of people from the pictures. Detective Smith put together a whole file for us to go over. You need a few more minutes?" His gaze traveled down her body.

"Just need socks, boots, and my bag." She grabbed the first two from the bedroom and led the way out of the house, snagging her bag from the table next to the entry.

"If Roni asks about the picture, tell her I did it."

Nikki glanced at the now-conspicuous hole on the wall of beach pictures. Several were askew.

That was going to be fun to explain.

Later.

Now, they had a job to do.

Gabriel pulled the door shut and took the new set of keys Roni had gifted her with earlier.

She was glad they had work to focus on. If not, who knew what they might end up discussing? It was too soon to admit how she felt about him. Besides, having feelings for her didn't mean he was in love with her. It was a hard reality to remember.

Gabriel stood at Nikki's back. His hands itched to reach for her. Hold her hand. But he kept his distance. Now wasn't the time to get their emotions mixed up in the job.

The crew was gathered in the bunk room at the Shop, all attention focused on the digital whiteboard Emery was commanding at the far end of the room. He'd zoomed in and cropped each face in Nikki's pictures from earlier in the day, highlighting those he'd been able to name. What that man could do in a couple of hours was scary—and amazing, since he was on their side.

"They're almost all veterans." Aiden scowled at the screen.

"Correct." Emery gestured at the screen where an American flag was displayed predominantly on both barns. "Wilson's rhetoric is very pro-America, protect America, et cetera. It resonates with a lot of the veteran crowd. He doesn't take in everyone, which was one of your questions, Agent Gage. I found a forum where Wilson did some recruiting. The account is disabled, but not deleted. I've also officially requested documentation on all his activity there. It appears he was banned for a blowup with some people he turned down to join his militia. Seems they didn't take too kindly to being told they weren't the right kind of patriot."

"What's the right kind?" Tori asked, her gaze still on Emery.

"I'm guessing the blow-myself-up kind." Roni glanced toward Nikki and rolled her eyes. Yup. The two least likely people to get along were somehow buddies now. But that was Nikki. Always turning expectations on their head.

"What's our next move?" Aiden pivoted toward Nikki.

Gabriel fought the urge to step in front of her. Aiden's aggressive stance and frustration telegraphed plainly to the rest of the room. And why wouldn't it? Aiden was a veteran and took Wilson's actions personally.

Nikki didn't miss a beat. "They have to have a target picked out. Where's the list Detective Smith made up? We narrow that down, we get ahead of them."

Emery's gaze flicked to Gabriel so fast, if he hadn't been watching he might not have noticed it. Since Gabriel and Roni had arrived at the same time, no one had appeared to notice that Nikki had been in his car, not Roni's. Julian had told Gabriel about that list, and Gabriel was willing to bet Julian had learned about it from Emery, which meant Nikki had just subtly outed them to the perceptive members of the crew.

"Yes." Emery brought a calendar up on the screen with at least a dozen different events filled in. "Here are the public and private events for the next two weeks for the greater Miami area, including a fifty-mile radius around us."

"Shit. That's a lot of ground to cover." Aiden crossed his arms.

It was a big list, but that didn't mean everything on it fit their parameters.

"The fashion events are out. It wouldn't even occur to Wilson to hit those." Nikki paced forward and crossed her arms.

This was where she would shine. For all his field experience, there was still something to be said for a profile. And that was what Nikki was doing while the rest of them ran down clues. Her profile of Wilson and his group would be the tool to get them ahead of the game. It was the measuring stick by which they could evaluate a situation, an event, possible avenues of action, and deconstruct Wilson's plan.

"The beach concert thing, is that a big deal? Are there sponsors? Any media coverage?" she asked.

"To the twentysomethings, yeah," Roni replied.

"No idea on the media coverage. Probably some radio stations, but I can check into that." Emery grabbed his tablet and got to work.

"Okay, so that's a possibility given the age range of the militia. Wilson is young so he is going to have a different approach than what we're used to when it comes to these freedom fighters. He's got a grasp of how to use the media and public opinion, but he is still narcissistic, and his urge to be seen as the fixer for our problems will drive him to create a scene." Nikki paced toward the map. She tapped a range of three squares highlighted in yellow. "What about this one? Homestead?"

"Ah, yeah, the Homestead 100." Roni pushed to her feet and gestured at the screen. They'd all heard about the event, but who hadn't? "It's something like a hundred different races and competitions over three days. They've got a lot of different kinds of racing going on. It's kind of a weird new event, but the pre-sales are something like fifteen hundred, plus the drivers, crew and vendors, it's probably a five- to ten-thousand-person event. The stadium seats around sixty-five thousand, so in comparison to the venue it's still small."

"Big space. What are the chances your friend Hillary was supposed to drive there?" Nikki pivoted, glancing at Gabriel.

"I wouldn't call her a friend," he replied.

"What's this?" Nikki tapped another yellow square back in central Miami.

"Political college rally, liberal audience." Emery tapped his tablet and the screen shifted to display an event flier.

"Crap." Nikki took a step back. "That's got Wilson written all over it."

"There's literally six to eight events a day over the next two weeks that have some kind of potential for Wilson's group." Emery brought the calendar back up. "I've done my best to sort and highlight them into categories, but it's still a lot of public events to wade through."

"This . . . is not good." Nikki rubbed her face. The trouble with profiling was that it was a taught skill. Even if Gabriel wanted to help her, he'd never pursued that line of education at the academy.

"How do we want to tackle this?" Aiden asked.

Nikki blew out a breath and opened her eyes. There was a plan brewing, Gabriel could feel it. God, she was amazing.

A siren blared inside the warehouse. For one short second no one moved. Eyes widened, jaws dropped. Gabriel reached for the handle of the Desert Eagle pressing into his back.

The crew moved as one. Almost in unison, they drew weapons and keys jangled.

"It's Wilson," Emery called out over the noise.

"He shouldn't . . . no." Nikki shook her head. Maybe something in her research and profiling of Wilson was off. It didn't matter right now. What did was protecting their asses.

"Come on." Gabriel grabbed Nikki by the hand and pulled her out of the bunk room. He glanced around the warehouse as he hauled her into the next room behind Aiden.

Madison stood beside a metal locker, strapping on a Kevlar vest. Her hands visibly shook, but she got through the practiced routine of it on her own.

Gabriel grabbed one of the smaller vests and thrust it at Nikki. He wouldn't presume to put it on her.

"What is going on?" she demanded, but didn't pause in slipping it on like a pro.

"Wilson's group has breached the perimeter." He strapped on his vest as the first gunfire pinged off the building exterior. It didn't appear as though the actual building was breached, but they were going to be ready regardless.

For years the Shop was their go-to place for all their covert needs. It housed their cache, surveillance equipment, and extra vehicles, and no one had ever tracked them here. Of course they employed a number of means to keep the Shop safe, but this moment was inevitable. Wilson's militia was made up of highly trained soldiers. It wasn't surprising they'd finally done it; it was the speed with which they'd accomplished it that shocked Gabriel.

They exited what amounted to their armory, hand in hand. Bullets hit the reinforced walls and bounced off from all sides.

They were surrounded. He didn't need Emery's equipment to tell him that.

He turned to Nikki and fear settled in his stomach. She could be carrying his baby. She was the most important thing to him, and she was in danger if he couldn't protect her.

"Stay close to me," he said.

She opened her mouth to speak, but never got a sound out.

One of the side doors exploded in a flash of light and heat. The initial blast knocked Gabriel off his feet. Nikki's hand was torn from his. It all went dark after that.

Chapter Twelve

Nikki crouched behind one of the steel support columns and fired into the dusty clouds billowing up around the partially ripped-open section of the warehouse. Smoke and the crackle of flames rose up in the background, while inside, it appeared as though a giant toddler had upended almost everything in the Shop. Beyond this slice of hell, she could see the evening sky spread out above them, calm now that the rain had passed.

Everything in her said to go to Gabriel, but she'd lost sight of him in the scramble for cover. She didn't know where to even begin to look for him.

"One o' clock," Roni shouted.

Nikki adjusted her aim and nailed the target. He stumbled, but the bullet didn't take him down.

"They're armored," Nikki yelled back.

She adjusted her aim again and squeezed the trigger on an exhale.

The man went down to his knees.

She couldn't watch. This operation was supposed to be about gathering intelligence, and somewhere along the line it had changed. She should be collecting paper, not toe tags.

"Behind you," a man, John, yelled. He was somewhere

above them. Nikki didn't dare take her gaze off the breached door for fear that another handful of Wilson's militia would trickle in.

"Got it." Roni turned, putting her back to the blown-out door, and aimed.

There were too many of them. She counted at least a dozen, probably more like twenty, trying to get past the metal door, which had become its own land mine. The fire made it treacherous to cross, trapping their crew inside and Wilson's people outside. These weren't good odds. Eventually Wilson's people would get in, or the smoke would force them out.

"Fall back," Aiden bellowed from somewhere to her right, back toward the armory. She couldn't see too far in that direction, thanks to the haze. It was starting to sting the back of her throat and her eyes had long since begun to water.

She put her back to the column and nearly swallowed her tongue. Aiden and Julian were in a vicious hand-to-hand combat with three men. Where had they come from? Gabriel was nowhere to be seen and Tori was partially dragging Madison into a car. John was on top of a truck with a sniper setup, but it wouldn't be enough. They were outmanned and overpowered.

"Grenade," John yelled from the truck.

Nikki dove away from his position and rolled, covering her head.

The blast shook the foundation. A sickening creak of metal made her skin crawl. The lights flickered out and— *BAM!* Part of the roof collapsed in a shower of sparks and flame.

Hands grasped at her shoulders.

The militiamen.

They'd found her.

Nikki rolled and punched upward at her attacker.

"Oof! It's me." Gabriel grunted.

Stunned, she let him haul her to her feet.

"Come on." He threw an arm around her. She wasn't about to argue. Aiden had given the fall-back order and they wouldn't win anything by sticking it out here. Together, she and Gabriel half crouched and half ran through the still-settling debris. An electrical wire sprayed sparks overhead, and men called out to each other in the smoke.

"The others." She tried to stop, but Gabriel picked her up and carried her to the GTO.

"They're leaving, too."

He shoved her in through the driver's side and twisted the key in the ignition. The car lurched forward before she'd even made it to her seat or the door was closed. He revved the car and steered it out through a narrow opening, just tall enough to squeeze under. Ahead of them another set of taillights turned out onto the street.

The others?

Had they really made such a fast exit?

Something thumped against the side of the car, but they made it out through the opening without mishap. The car bounced over the curb before hitting the pavement.

"Did everyone get out?" she asked. They couldn't leave anyone behind. She twisted in her seat.

They'd gone through what now appeared to be the side of the building. It was partially pulled up in what would otherwise be an invisible door. A secret exit for quick getaways?

"I don't know."

Gabriel grabbed a Bluetooth earpiece and hooked it on his ear, jabbing the side.

"Where the hell is everyone?" he said.

Nikki stared at the quickly shrinking warehouse.

"Good. Everyone out?" He turned the car hard right, gunned the engine, and jerked the car into an empty parking lot in front of another nondescript building.

Three other cars idled, looking worse for wear.

Roni, Tori, Madison, Aiden, Emery . . . Where were Julian and John?

She straightened, looked at Gabriel, and noticed the blood running down his forehead. Her breathing stopped for a second and her hands squeezed the pistol still in her grasp.

"Gabe, you're bleeding."

"Later." He pulled out both his guns and reloaded.

"What's happening?" Why were they just sitting there?

Gabriel pressed a few buttons on the display and several voices started jabbering over the loudspeaker.

"Equipment is fried." That voice was Emery.

"Goddamned motherfuckers. Where are you?" a man's voice said. She couldn't make out who it was.

"Julian, is John with you?" Aiden. That had to be him. Which would make the other voice Julian.

"Yeah, he's out cold. Took a bullet in his arm. He'll be fine."

"Get to cover, now. Detonating the charges."

"Wait—what?" Nikki blinked at Gabriel.

He punched the display and the microphone icon began to flash red.

"If this location was ever compromised, we were instructed to blow it up. Cover your ears." His features were grim, his gaze resigned.

"Fire in the hole," Aiden said over the line.

A second later a blast came, so strong it shook the car, set off alarms, and broke glass in shop fronts up and down the street. A secondary explosion boomed just as loud, followed by small pops, pings, and lesser detonations as whatever stores of weapons remained in the armory were set off by the heat.

The building crumpled in on itself. Tongues of fire licked the night sky. Nikki could only watch with her jaw hanging open.

They'd been attacked.

They could have all died.

What else would Wilson's people do if this was their logical next step?

She'd profiled Wilson. Clearly things had changed since her initial research. The Bradley Wilson she'd encountered before was bluster. Big talk, little game. Something had happened, some trigger she didn't see to make him capable of issuing an order like this.

A black car pulled into the lot behind them. It looked like Julian and John inside from the silhouettes.

"Movement, north side," Emery announced over the speakers.

"Get out of here, guys. Go to ground." Aiden's car peeled out, heading not away from the blast, but toward it.

"What is he doing?" Nikki stared at the swiftly shrinking tail lights.

"Fuck, he's going to be a distraction to give us time to scatter." Gabriel grabbed his handgun.

"You can't let him do that."

"You're right. We can't. You good on ammo?"

Nikki reloaded as swiftly as she could. Gabriel let the other cars head toward the highway before he followed in the wake of their stupid, fearless friend. This whole situation was so beyond anything she'd ever dealt with before. To Gabriel's team's credit, they weren't batting an eye at what had to be done, unlike her, who was struggling to keep up.

Gabriel whipped the car around the first turn. The heat

from the blaze was so intense it made Nikki's eyes water. Ahead, Aiden's white and blue Challenger skidded on gravel inside the fenced-off yard. The Challenger fishtailed slightly as he turned, avoiding shots fired from men behind a truck. Little pops of light here and there weren't part of the warehouse fire . . . they were muzzle fire. The sound of the guns was barely audible over the roar of the engines and inferno. The setup in the yard was more elaborate. Out here, it was clear to see the organization it had taken to breach their facility. Several large vehicles had the exits blocked, but also served as cover for the men on foot inside the yard.

"They've got him penned in. Fuck. Hold on." Gabriel steered the car over the curb. It bounced and slammed into the chain link fence. The car lurched. Metal groaned. The fence gave way under the sheer brute force of the muscle car.

Nikki didn't wait for Gabriel's order. She leaned out of her window, squeezing off rounds, aiming for tires, people, anything that might move. Her tactical training kicked in and she operated on need alone.

The need to survive.

Her heart pounded and all she could do was shove all her fear, doubts, and adrenaline to the back of her mind. She focused on the next shot.

"Watch out!" Gabriel grabbed the back of her shirt and yanked her in the car.

She felt the displaced air of a bullet whiz past her head. The rear window shattered, spraying the back of the car with glass.

"The green car. Shoot out its radiator."

The same green and black car from earlier was headed straight for them, tracking their movements through the large, fenced-in lot.

It wasn't time to point out she didn't know what a radiator was or did. She leveled the barrel at the front of the car and emptied the rest of her clip. A plume of smoke and steam went straight up into the air. The car lost its momentum and crashed into a box truck that looked like it hadn't moved in years.

Aiden's car charged through the hole they'd made, a Jeep and an SUV on his tail. Gabriel turned the car and it skidded on the gravel. He gunned it, but a large truck cut him off.

"Fuck, fuck, fuck." He cut the wheel, barely avoiding a collision with the truck.

The yard was a mess. It was littered with three smoking vehicles. There weren't any bodies to be seen, just six cars slowly trying to herd Gabriel into a corner with the warehouse at their back.

"Another gun." She held her hand out and took Gabriel's heavier Desert Eagles. They felt wrong in her hands, but screw it. They needed an out.

The car bumped over debris and potholes as he accelerated suddenly, aiming for a hole.

A heavier car aimed straight for them, coming up fast on Nikki's side. She could see the outline of the driver. She blew out a breath and pelted the windshield with one bullet after another in quick succession. The car swerved wildly. Gabriel pushed the car harder, swinging to try to get out of the careening vehicle's way. The other car clipped the back of the GTO, sending them into a spin.

Nikki almost cartwheeled across the car, but her belt snapped tight. Her head whipped around and just when she thought they had to tip over, the car straightened out and they blew past the fence. Something scraped along her side, but they were out of the death trap.

"Aiden, do you copy?" Gabriel bellowed at the dash.

"Yes. Where the hell are you?"

"Getting my ass out of Dodge."

"Good. I lost my tail. Get out of there, now. That's an order."

"Yes, sir!" Gabriel punched the dash, then handed Nikki a box of ammo from under his seat. "Reload."

She didn't ask questions. Wilson's group was a much bigger threat if they were going to launch that kind of attack in the heart of Miami. Things were much worse than she'd realized.

Nikki watched the clock on the dash roll past midnight before Gabriel turned into a quiet, unassuming neighborhood. The house he stopped in front of had a seven-foot wrought iron fence surrounding it and a gate with a hefty lock in place. A few lights on up and down the streets attested to some of their neighbors still being awake, but not many. Their movements would hopefully go unnoticed.

"Where are we?" she asked.

"Little Havana. Wilson's people will stick out here. Stay in the car."

Gabriel got out, unlocked the gate, and parked in a detached garage behind the house.

She wasn't going to argue with him. Not after this night.

The garage was a big cinder-block double-car structure. The walls were barren save a few gardening tools. She could only glimpse the exterior of the house, and if she wasn't mistaken, it was pink. Considering Gabriel's preferred mode of transportation was a purple car, she was willing to bet he'd been in on the color choices. The man didn't shrink from bold statements.

He got the gate locked back up and closed the garage door, flipping on an overhead light. There was a grimness to the set of his lips she didn't like.

Nikki got out of the car and surveyed the damage. The

paint was chipped, the back window gone, the bumper on her side was crunched in, and a handful of bullet holes peppered the sides.

"Is the car reinforced or something?" She eyed a few holes way too close to where she'd been sitting.

"These older models were tough." Gabriel drew his gun and placed his hand on the trunk.

Why did he need a gun to open the trunk?

She pulled her pistol out of her waistband and waited for what he would do next. He inhaled, the sound loud in the quiet space, and yanked the lid up, pointing his gun at whatever was inside.

Nikki stepped up beside him, offering additional cover.

A man lay in the fetal position, a gunshot wound on his arm. Blood leaked sluggishly from the injury, soaked up by the upholstery. He wore the mismatched fatigues of one of Wilson's men and dog tags that had seen better days. His eyes snapped open and he lunged out of the GTO.

Gabriel stepped back and the man tumbled out of the car onto the concrete floor.

"What the hell?" she blurted, keeping her eyes trained on their prisoner.

The man swayed on all fours and spat blood.

"Get up." Gabriel grabbed the man by his shoulder and hauled him to his feet. "Stand against that wall."

The man dragged his feet, not even motivated by the press of Gabriel's gun to the back of his neck. In a few seconds Gabriel had him positioned against the far wall.

"I am David Swiss." He rattled off a string of numbers.

She didn't dare take her gaze off the former soldier.

David Swiss? As in the very man whose family they'd visited that morning?

"Saw him come in the side door of the shop, figured I'd do his family a favor," Gabriel said.

David continued to stare impassively at the floor. He clenched his jaw. Holding back pain? Or he didn't like them talking about his mother?

"There's some handcuffs in the glove box. Grab them for me?" Gabriel asked.

"Sure thing." Nikki walked backward to the car, sat down in the driver's seat, and glanced away just long enough to pop the glove box and snag two sets of cuffs.

Gabriel took the handcuffs from her. She didn't begrudge him this task. He had at least a good twenty pounds of muscle on the smaller man. Judging by the gauntness of his cheeks, time with the militia hadn't treated David too well.

He approached slowly. David was a puzzle. Something wasn't right, and not just his wounds or fashion choices. There was something *off*.

Gabriel hesitated less than two feet away. David took the opportunity and swung with his uninjured right arm. Gabriel dropped the cuffs, but kept his gun in hand. He caught David's arm, kicked his leg out from under him, and shoved David to the ground, face first, bending his arm behind his back.

"I will not hesitate to shoot you." Gabriel spoke with deadly calm, gun pressed to the back of David's skull. "Cuff him."

Nikki moved in, grabbed the cuffs, and slapped them around David's wrists.

"If you don't cooperate I'll hogtie you with the cuffs, understand?" Gabriel said.

Nikki backed up, but didn't allow herself to relax. David Swiss was still a very real threat without his hands and injured, if he was what they thought he was.

Gabriel hoisted David up to sit with his back against the wall.

"There. Now, care to tell me why you're working with a terrorist like Bradley Wilson?" Gabriel asked.

David did not deign to reply.

"Come on, man, you're facing a long time in prison if you can't give me one hell of a reason why you're doing this." Gabriel put his weapon away and held his hands out.

Nikki had conducted all manner of official FBI interviews, but nothing like this. In the field, messy interrogations were out of her league. Why the hell had he thought this was a good idea?

"Your mother know where you are?" Gabriel asked.

"Don't talk about her," David snarled. He drew his legs up and Gabriel pulled his Desert Eagle just as fast.

"Take it easy. Your mother's worried about you, David. If I were you—"

"Fuck you! What kind of American turns traitor?" David's face flushed red, his brow furrowed.

"Traitor? Me? You're the one attacking civilians." This time Gabriel didn't put his weapon away.

"Yeah, civilians helping ISIS." David's lip curled in disgust.

For a moment both Nikki and Gabriel stared at the man. The accusation didn't make a single ounce of sense.

"What do you think we're doing?" Nikki asked. She wanted to crawl inside his head and understand him. What made him throw his allegiance in with Wilson? How did this whole thing seem to work?

"You're working with the enemy. When the people back home find out," he shook his head, "you're going to wish you'd never been born."

"Where do you think you are?" Gabriel asked.

"Where'd you take me?" David glanced between them. His color was sickly, and the scars across his neck were enough to make her wince at how much they'd hurt.

"What city were we in when you attacked us?" Nikki asked.

"Kobani. We're taking it back from you."

Gabriel turned slightly toward her.

Kobani was in Syria. Half a world away from Miami, Florida. What the hell was going on?

David shoved to his feet and rushed Gabriel, hitting him shoulder first in the stomach. The momentum carried both men back against the GTO. Nikki closed the distance, but David threw himself sideways, into her. They went crashing to the ground, him on top of her. His weight drove the air out of her lungs and her head hit the concrete hard enough to jar her teeth.

Gabriel roared something and pulled David off her. He threw the man up against the wall, gun shoved up under David's jaw.

"Nikki?" Gabriel said with clenched teeth.

"I'm okay." She winced as she got to her feet and recovered her gun.

"Give me those other handcuffs. You, down on your knees." Gabriel backed up, but didn't decrease the pressure he applied with the gun.

David never once flinched. He slowly lowered to his knees and waited.

She snagged the second set of cuffs, larger than the ones around David's wrists, and fastened them one around each ankle with the chain looped between his hands, effectively hogtying the man.

"You aren't going anywhere," Gabriel said to David. He pressed his hand to Nikki's back, urging her toward the small side door. They stepped out into the evening air. It was deceptively calm, maybe even pleasant.

"What was that?" she asked in a whisper.

"Are you okay?" Gabriel's hand gently cupped her

cheek. He peered at her head, but it was too dark to see anything.

"I'm going to have the worst headache known to man soon. What happened back there?"

He ignored her question and pulled her in close, tucking her head under his chin, and gently hugged her. She leaned against him, inhaling the scent of smoke and everything awful they'd survived tonight. She'd never again wear the training days shirt and have good memories. Not after tonight.

"Something's knocked loose in that man's head. He's going to hurt himself or us."

Gabriel's voice rumbled against her ear. Holding on to him was such a guilty pleasure. She'd forgotten what it was like after an op, how the reality that she could have easily lost him always slapped her in the face.

She stepped back and tried to clear her head. The situation was even more complicated than a bunch of gun-toting militiamen with an agenda.

"We can't continue to question him. He's not right. If he thinks we're actually in Syria . . ." She shook her head, unwilling to believe such an absurd lie.

"You're right. We can't trust anything he says. Here. Inside the house in the fridge is a stash of medicine. We need a tranq." Gabriel handed her his keys.

"What are you going to do?" she asked.

"Watch him. Whatever he did before now, it was some bad shit. I don't want him getting loose here, especially if he thinks he's in unfriendly territory."

"Okay."

Nikki let herself into the pink house while Gabriel returned to the garage. The furniture was sparse, livable but not comfortable. There was no decoration that spoke of personality. At least until she looked in the fridge. It was stocked with medical supplies. Lots of them.

Nikki read through the handful of bottles and picked one she recognized as a weak sedative. She ripped open the packaging on a new syringe and needle before drawing a small dose. This was a risk. They had no way of knowing what else was in his system, if anything. Adding to that potential cocktail could risk his life, but David had already proven he was willing to attack and kill others. When it came down to it, Nikki was going to protect civilians from him first.

She returned to the garage. David sat where they'd left him, and Gabriel crouched at his feet. The two men were having some sort of stare-off.

"The bullet went straight through him," Gabriel announced.

"Hold him." Nikki examined the syringe to make sure there were no air bubbles.

Gabriel grabbed David and pinned him to the wall with his knee. Nikki used Gabriel's belt knife without asking and sliced away David's sleeve. His veins were protruding, probably due to the adrenaline keeping him going. She inserted the needle and injected the clear liquid.

They stepped back and watched David, who glared at them.

"What's next?" she asked Gabriel. Process was out of the window.

"He needs a hospital. I know someone who can help us get him there."

David spat empty threats and profanity, sometimes in languages other than English, but eventually the drugs won out and he slumped over sideways.

Gabriel pulled out his cell phone and hit a single button.

"Hey, Matt, it's Gabriel. Got a favor to ask of you. Two actually."

Nikki relaxed. She didn't like the idea of holding a veteran who was already confused and out of it like a prisoner. Whatever David Swiss's sins were, they didn't merit that.

Her head throbbed. With David out cold and Gabriel arranging everything else, she headed back inside the house to study the contents of the fridge and pick her own solution.

"This should help." Gabriel reached over her shoulder and plucked a bottle from the top row.

She didn't say it, but not having to make the choice herself was a relief. Her head was really starting to protest all the abuse today. She was tough, but there were limits to what her body could take.

"Thanks."

Gabriel popped the top, doled out three white pills for her, and snagged a plastic cup from on top of the fridge. She leaned against the counter, content to let him do this. He poured her a glass of water from the tap and held it and the pills out for her. Some girls wanted roses, she swooned for a healthy dose of painkillers.

She downed all three in one swallow, then drank the whole glass of water. Gabriel remained almost toe to toe with her until she set the cup down. The moment it was out of her hand, he yanked at the straps keeping her bulletproof vest on. He stripped her out of it, tossing the heavy, constricting garment on the floor. His followed suit. A moment later he squeezed her to him, burying his face in her still-damp hair. She gripped him tight and wished he didn't smell of smoke and death.

Chapter Thirteen

Gabriel ran his hand over the Skyline's hood. It wasn't every day he let someone else drive his creation, but the GTO was in some serious need of repair. Plus, he was going to need speed.

"The only thing legal about that car is that you switched the driver's seat." Matt crossed his arms and eyed the car.

"Yeah, never could get used to driving it on the other side." Gabriel pocketed the keys.

"Do I want to know?" Nikki stood in the side entrance, arms wrapped around herself. The meds from earlier had hit her pretty hard, but she insisted the pain was gone.

"The Skyline." He thumbed over his shoulder. "They never sold them in America, so the driver's side was on the right when I got it."

She shook her head.

"There's a bag of clothes and stuff in the passenger seat." Matt glanced over his shoulder at the EMTs. He'd done them a solid and led a disguised med van to their safe house to pick up David Swiss and bring Gabriel a new ride. The EMTs were busy getting their new charge strapped down and his vitals recorded. "I also pulled more info on Swiss. Let me know if I can help."

"Keep an eye on Classic Rides?" Nikki pushed off the door frame and strolled closer. She was a little worse for wear, but Gabriel was there for her to lean on if she needed it.

He eyed her, surprised by the request. Was she getting the bigger picture? Or did she understand that if Aiden lost the garage, he was likely to jump even farther off the rails than Julian?

"I already do that." Matt shrugged. "Perps think we're just looking for a chance to bust these guys, but it's cover enough to watch over things."

"Watch it closer. Wilson could try to make it a symbol or something to his people. Classic Rides would be more valuable than the Shop, and losing that could hurt the ongoing investigation here." She looked to Gabriel, who nodded, appreciating her breadth of thought.

What he wouldn't give for her to be their handler. An agent like her could make a lot more happen, not that CJ and Kathy hadn't done their best. But their last name wasn't Gage. Nikki might not like it, but other agents gave her preferential treatment on the off chance that doing otherwise might draw the stink eye of her father. And Deputy Director Gage was a man better left uncrossed.

"Right. Looks like my ride is ready to leave. You guys need anything else, just call." Matt glanced between the two of them, but neither Gabriel nor Nikki extended an offer to stay.

"Later, Matt." Gabriel offered his hand and slapped palms with the pretty-boy detective.

"See you." Matt waved at Nikki, strode to the passenger side of the van, and climbed in.

Gabriel could only hope that their neighbors were fast asleep and unaware of their late-night activity.

The large vehicle rolled forward and onto the quiet street. Gabriel followed on foot and locked the gate after them before retrieving his bag and the folder of information on Swiss from the Skyline's trunk. Nikki was nowhere to be seen, which hopefully meant she was inside, taking it easy.

He hated that their job put her in danger, but he couldn't deny that both this morning and tonight, she'd handled herself as well as any of his crew. The only difference was that she didn't love him.

Not like he loved her.

And she could be carrying his child.

He stuffed that thought back into the mental closet it came out of. Thinking like that was only going to distract him. They had a lot on their plates.

Nikki sat curled up on the sofa, one of the spare tablets perched on her thigh. He couldn't remember if she'd left hers in the GTO or if it had wound up left at the Shop. Doubtless, there would be dozens of things that cropped up as casualties of losing the warehouse. The loss hurt. In the beginning, the warehouse was where he'd gone to acclimate, to figure himself out, at least until the Classic Rides garage became home. The two facilities represented two of his primary identities.

The spy and the man.

Tonight, Wilson's people had taken out their covert headquarters, effectively scattering them to the wind. But they'd come back. Their crew was made of stronger stuff.

Nikki frowned at the tablet screen and scrolled through pages of what appeared to be photocopies of handwritten notes.

"Here's what Matt gave us." Gabriel pulled the report folder out of his bag and joined her on the sofa.

"Why didn't we see this when Emery pulled his information?" Her frown lines deepened.

"Because this isn't in his police record." He flipped to the first page. Nikki gasped and reached for the folder, but he pulled it from her fingers.

"How did he get David's VA file? Emery hasn't been granted access yet."

"I don't want to know." He spread the file open on the coffee table. They bent over the pages, scanning and turning them. There was more jargon and acronyms than he could wade through, but the big picture was plain. "Okay, so what we know. David Swiss was discharged after a gunshot wound to the neck. He suffers extreme PTSD. Look, he's been admitted eight times. This doesn't look good."

Gabriel flipped to the handwritten notes some doctor had made regarding David's time in the hospital. He tracked each line with his finger, the sense of dread increasing with every word.

"What if . . . what if the others are like this?" Nikki asked.

It was the question he hadn't voiced out loud. Not since the moment in the garage when it clicked and he realized they were dealing with a person who wasn't rooted in reality. At least not this one. If Wilson had a group of veterans who thought they were still in the Middle East in an active war zone, there was no telling what they would do. They would see every person on the street as a possible enemy—not as Americans. How deep did the delusions go? And what if there were some who were completely aware of what they were doing and actively encouraged the fabled reality?

There was nothing good about what they were discovering. The more answers they uncovered, the messier and more disgusting the situation became. These men, who had given so much, were being manipulated and used to further one sick bastard's plan for self-gratification.

"This is making my head hurt," Nikki announced after half an hour of going through the doctor's chicken scratch.

"Then let's be done." He flipped the folder shut. There was only so much they could do tonight, and he wasn't about to let Nikki burn herself out.

"Hold on. I need to recap everything." She cradled her head in her hands. "Wilson presents his movement as pro-American, motivating the civilians to awareness by using random acts of violence. Because that's a great idea."

Gabriel took her hand. He liked even the touch of sarcasm in her tone. It sure wasn't professional. Just one more crack in her ice-queen act. The real woman under all those layers of protection was just as vibrant as he remembered.

"We believe he's going to target some public event," he said.

"Or private. We can't even track some of those. God damn it, I hate this."

He smiled at her use of profanity. Little more than twenty-four hours around him and he was already eroding her perfect little agent front. Success.

"We have to stop him, and for your 'street cred' it needs to be something public. Something where you can make a lesson out of him." She rubbed the heel of her hand over her eyes.

"Let's not worry about that right now. Stopping him needs to be our first priority."

"But if we don't, you lose all the ground you've made on your undercover op." She dropped her hand to her lap and curled her fingers around his.

"True." He liked the feel of her holding on to him.

"Where are you with the Evers thing?" She turned to face him, crossing her legs and dismissing the Swiss file.

"Nowhere, really. He's vanished."

"That's so hard to believe that someone with that much visibility would vanish. Someone's covering for him. It really ticks me off how solid that case was. You had a slam dunk." She frowned and he wanted to kiss the little creases around her mouth away, but held back.

"All we can figure out is that there has to be another motive for why someone would want him out of prison." Gabriel shrugged and packed up the tablet and file.

"What are you doing?" Her frown deepened once more.

"Nikki, it's past three in the morning. I don't know about you, but I hardly slept last night. Tonight was exhausting. If Wilson's people were going to track us all down, we'd have heard about it, but it's quiet. Last check-in, everyone else was bedded down for the night except us. Come on. We're going to crash." He held out his hand and waited for her to put hers in his.

He wished he could offer her more. That he could lead her to his bed for hours of lovemaking, or lay her down in the lap of luxury. Too bad neither were options tonight.

Instead, Gabriel led Nikki to the only bedroom with a bed in it. The safe houses weren't outfitted with more than the bare essentials. They'd begun to set up more than the four they had before in the last three months, since the hit team. Already he was making a mental list of what they needed to add to the safe houses to make them more useful.

Nikki stared at the bed. He could hear her brain working.

"We can either both sleep in here or I can take the couch," he offered. He wouldn't impose on her if she wanted space. They were making huge leaps from barely speaking to . . . whatever they were to each other now.

"You wouldn't even fit on that couch. It's tiny." She unfastened her shorts and they hit the ground.

He watched her crawl into the bed and scoot over next to the wall.

She hadn't told him to take a hike.

Did he dare lie beside her?

If he took the couch, he'd stare at the door all night.

He removed his jeans, taking his time to allow her to get comfortable. Her bra sailed over the side of the bed, catching him off guard. He snagged the garment before he could think better of it. It was plain white material, sort of satiny and soft. She'd never been one for flashy clothes or panties, but that was because Nikki was constantly trying to camouflage what was inside.

Gabriel set the bra on top of her shorts and put it out of his mind. He slid into the bed next to her and lay on his back, arms crossed under his head, not daring to move a muscle.

He was exhausted.

Too exhausted to sleep.

The house settled into complete stillness, the only sound that from outside. The occasional car passing by. A plane overhead. The rustle of the palm trees and shrubbery as the evening breeze kicked up. It was quiet.

And yet his brain buzzed with thoughts. The case. Nikki. What the hell was up with Roni. The changes in Aiden. His worry for where Julian was headed. John's injury. If it wasn't one topic, it was another his brain ricocheted between.

Nikki rolled over onto her back. The clock on the nightstand told him all of ten minutes had passed.

"I can't sleep," she whispered.

"Me either." Between their op and having her back in his life, it was hard to quiet his mind.

"Do you like living in Miami?"

"It's all right."

"What's your plan for when this job is done?"

"Don't know. Haven't really thought about it. I came here for something to do, and I never ran out of stuff to do."

"Are you happy?"

He paused, rolling that word around.

"Some days," he finally replied. "The rest I miss you."

Silence.

Her hand groped for his under the sheets. He held it out and she curled her fingers around his.

"I miss you, too," she said, her voice small and quiet in the darkness.

Was there hope? Could there be something for them together if they were just willing to work for it?

"What do you want to do about it?" He was wide open to suggestions, but experience had taught him not to get his hopes up.

"I don't know. What can we do? You know I can't leave the FBI, and you can't come back." She was talking in concrete facts, which was what Nikki understood best. There was no denying he wouldn't go back to the FBI, but that wasn't the only gig out there.

"There's other work I could do." He rolled to his side, studying the lay of shadows across her face, the pale glint of light on her eyes.

"You wouldn't be happy. I moved into DC. It would kill

you there." Her lashes lowered, casting long shadows on her cheeks.

She was right on that front. If he was going to wear her down and find a way to make it work, he had to be patient.

"Ya know, I think we have enough problems right now. What if . . . what if we just take each day as it comes? This thing with Wilson could be a while sorting out. We can figure out what to do later when we cross that bridge."

Even in the darkness he could feel her frown. Of course she wouldn't like a vague answer like that, but it was his best solution right now. If they agreed there was no option for him in her life, she'd close that door again, maybe to protect herself or him. He didn't know. What he did know was that he wasn't ready to lose her yet.

"Come here." He looped his arm around her waist and pulled her to him, tucking her body alongside his. "There."

She covered his hand at her waist, pressing it closer.

What if she was pregnant? He wouldn't say it, but he could imagine her carrying his child. He'd always intended to leave undercover work behind, take up a boring job somewhere in the bureau that would be more conducive to family life. Or at least in his dreams that was what he wanted.

Nikki turned in his arms until they were face-to-face. She lifted a hand to his jaw and traced it with her fingers.

"There's more scars," she said.

"They add character."

She pressed a kiss to the scar from a knife fight, then one from when he'd taken a swan dive off a building and busted his chin. Blood rushed to his groin. She'd kissed him earlier like she couldn't get enough of him. He wanted that again. Now. But it wasn't the right time.

"You have to stop," he said, though it killed him.

"Did I do something wrong?" She was so earnest, and yet did he detect a slight tremble in her voice?

"No, sweetheart. You knocked your head pretty hard twice today and I loaded you up on those pain pills. I don't think you're thinking clearly right now."

"On the contrary, I'm probably as lucid and coherent as I was earlier." There was no question about which *earlier* she was referring to.

"Earlier was pretty damn nice."

Nikki ducked her head, hiding her face against his chest and the mattress. He'd enjoyed the hell out of coaxing her into embracing her sexuality the first time. If she'd let him do it again, fuck. It was even worth putting a little of himself on the line.

"It might be better than I remember it. Except that one time at Padre Island." He whistled. "That was . . . well, you were there."

She said something into the mattress he didn't understand.

"What was that?" He chuckled.

"Shut up," she said clearer.

"What? I can't talk about the sex we had?"

"No. Not right now." She pushed at his shoulder and turned her back on him.

"Why not?" He leaned over her, peering at her face, fully enjoying himself.

"Because."

"Because why?" He wrapped an arm around her and she squirmed in his hold.

"Because . . . if we aren't going to do *it*, I want to stop thinking about *it*, or I'll never go to sleep."

"I'm sorry, but what is *it*?" She thought about it, too?

That was the best news he'd heard all day. Well, except for her saying yes earlier.

"Sex." She smacked his shoulder. "You're teasing me. Stop."

"It's fun to tease you." He caught her hand and kissed it.

Gabriel bent his head and pressed his lips to her cheek. She turned toward him and their mouths met. He kept it brief so he could uphold his promise to himself. She really did need to rest.

"If I agree to this *go with the flow* plan of yours, what does that mean?" Even in the darkness he could feel her shrewd gaze.

"What do you want it to mean?"

"I don't know. That's what I'm asking." The frustrated notes were there, telling him she needed more.

"If you feel like kissing me, kiss me. If you want sex, tell me."

She was quiet a moment. Did she want less? More?

"So it's just a sex thing?" The shadows were too dark to read her expression, and her tone was carefully under control again.

"No, we'll spend time together, too."

"Are you seeing someone?"

"What? No." He trailed his fingers over her face and gently stroked the tendrils of hair clinging to her cheek. "I haven't been with anyone else in a long time. I just haven't been interested. This is just between us. And if you need something else, let me know."

"Why do you still want me? After I turned my back on you?"

"It took two of us to be in a relationship, and it took both of us to destroy it. Neither of us were blameless. I can't forget the good times we had. For me, they outweigh any bad there was. I'd like to think that now it might be even better if we give ourselves half a shot. What do you say?"

For several long, agonizing seconds she didn't say anything.

"Okay . . . But—we need protection."

"Already on it." He kissed her once more, a quick peck on the lips, and settled his head on the pillow. "What else do you want?"

"You're terrible." She pushed at his shoulder and turned her back on him, but he spooned her close and was rewarded with a kiss on his arm.

He might be terrible, but she wanted him.

Tonight, he'd hold her. Tomorrow, well, he hoped they had a little downtime, because he had a list of things he wanted to do to her all over again.

Chapter Fourteen

Nikki sat on the cool tile floor with the sofa to her back, but she couldn't read a word on the tablet in front of her. The bed squeaked in the other room and Gabriel groaned. It wasn't one of his nighttime sounds. It was that *I just woke up and don't want to be awake* groan. At one point she'd catalogued things like that. She'd made a study of him, the way he moved, how he ate. They were all her treasures. Their private moments captured in memory for her to savor when he wasn't around.

Except he was here now, and she was getting reacquainted with everything to do with him again.

Last night she'd slept the sleep of the dead, wrapped in his arms. Of course, it had only lasted a few hours before her mental alarm kicked her out of bed and back onto the job. She was glad for the short period of quiet she'd gotten to herself, because Gabriel was nothing but a distraction.

As if thinking of him summoned the man, Gabriel stepped out of the bedroom and leaned against the wall. His eyes were barely open and he'd only bothered to step into his jeans and pull them up. Fastening them seemed beyond him still. The front gaped open and his belt jangled as they hung precariously off his hips. Her mouth went dry remembering all the time she'd spent on that part of his anatomy. The groans from those episodes were particularly entertaining.

"You're up," he mumbled.

"Hope I didn't wake you."

"No." He shuffled toward the couch and, instead of sitting on the furniture, sank down to lounge next to her. His shoulder bumped hers and he buzzed her cheek with a quick kiss that froze her for a moment. "What have you gotten done?"

She cleared her throat and flipped to the beginning of what Emery and Matt had sent her that morning.

"I've got VA files on everyone we know about. Almost seventy-five percent have some sort of PTSD or psychological disorder. Wilson has a type." She handed the tablet to Gabriel.

"Matt send you these?"

"Yes. He's very resourceful."

"I wish he wouldn't be." Gabriel scrubbed the side of his face.

"Why?"

"Because his mentor got busted for an Evers investigation that didn't stick and Matt's going to have a target on him for helping us. I wish we didn't need him so bad."

"He wants to help and he knows the score." Besides, Nikki had seen the way Roni *didn't* look at Matt. Nikki was pretty sure she had pointedly avoided Gabriel just as much as the other woman shunned the detective.

Nikki also hadn't mentioned that the bag of clothes Matt provided them with included the rest of the clothes Roni had set aside for her, which meant Matt had more access to their team than Gabriel realized. Perhaps she needed to have a girl-to-girl chat with Roni about the dangers of dating on the job. If nothing else, someone who wasn't emotionally invested needed to be keeping an eye on the detective for his own safety.

"Talked to Emery or Aiden yet?" Gabriel asked, pulling her back to the moment.

"We had a quick conference call earlier after Matt sent the stuff. John's okay. Everyone was able to get somewhere. Worst injuries were some burns and scratches. John's wasn't that bad. Just some stitches. Matt was able to be on-site and says everything was destroyed, so there's nothing to link it back to you guys. He's going to keep an eye on it."

"We owe him." Gabriel shook his head.

"Yeah, well, I think he likes being one of the good guys doing something." And being close to Roni.

He pushed the tablet onto the coffee table and turned his head to look over his shoulder at her. For a moment he didn't say anything, just looked at her. She often wondered what he saw, how she measured up in his eyes.

"Sleep okay?" he asked.

"Yeah."

"How's your head?"

"Good. Doesn't hurt. I'll have a bit of a bruise, but I took some general painkillers earlier. None of that stuff from last night. You tricked me with that."

"Hey, you said it hurt bad, I gave you something to make that go away." He grinned, completely unapologetic. "What's our next move?"

"Breakfast?" She was starving. The burgers hadn't been enough to last.

"Mmm." His lids dropped to what she called his *come hither* look. At least when she got the chance to read a novel for fun and the men gave the heroines lustful stares, she imagined they were a lot like how Gabriel was studying her now.

She swallowed and dug her nails into the tile, even as her body responded to him. All it took was a look from him and she was a goner. Her heartbeat increased, her skin felt tight, her breasts grew heavy, heat pooled low in her belly, and she didn't care about being hungry.

Gabriel leaned in and she held her breath. His lips closed around her bottom lip, his tongue caressing that bit of flesh. Heat waves swept her body. She turned toward him. After last night's candid discussion, what reason did she have to hold back? There was little to no chance of this going anywhere, so she would enjoy him while she could.

He cupped her face, forcing her head to tilt to the left, and deepened the kiss, licking into her mouth. She slid her palm down his chest, reveling in the feel of him, all that lean strength. For now, he was hers.

His hand slid up under her T-shirt and cupped her breast. She arched her back into his palm, her nipples constricting and her sex throbbing with arousal.

Hungry to horny in five seconds.

That had to be a record.

Gabriel lifted his head and squeezed his eyes shut.

"What is it?" She battered down the stray thought that she'd done something wrong.

"Condoms. I didn't get any condoms." He dropped his head to her shoulder.

Nikki screamed inside.

"Oh . . . well . . . there's always later." Unprotected sex again was out of the question. Once in the height of passion was forgivable, but right now she was in control.

"I've got a better plan." Gabriel pushed up to his knees.

The way he said it, she wasn't sure she was going to like this plan . . . or maybe the problem was that she'd like it too much . . .

He grabbed her around the waist and tossed her up

onto the couch. She gasped, unaccustomed to the way he manhandled her. There was something appealing about it, the way he was strong enough to throw her around and never hurt her.

Gabriel leaned over her, pushing her down into the cushions with his weight. He cupped her face, holding her prisoner to his kisses. Not that she gave much protest. He stripped her of her shirt and held her gaze as he released the catch of her bra.

The way he looked at her, she felt beautiful. It wasn't a word she claimed often, but in these moments with Gabriel, she embraced how he saw her.

He slid her bra off her arms and let it fall to the floor. She held her breath, waiting for what he would do next. He kissed her lips, her chin, and the dip of flesh above her collarbone. His fingers plucked her nipples, gently squeezing and lifting. She arched her back, moaning.

"*Eres hermosa.*" He spoke against her skin, dragging his mouth down her sternum.

She curled her toes into the upholstery.

He called her beautiful.

Had she told him she'd studied Spanish in the intervening years? It didn't seem like an important point of conversation in the moment or something she could just work in casually.

"Do you know what I'm going to do to you?" He stared up at her, a hand on either breast, his lips lightly grazing the valley of flesh between them.

"No." It was hard to speak, but she got the word out.

"Good."

He lifted his face to her left breast and sucked the tip into his mouth, swirling his tongue around the tightly furled nipple.

"Oh." Nikki groaned and closed her eyes. She couldn't

grasp his short, black hair, so she cupped his head instead, but found herself urging him on, pressing him closer. He gently bit her breast, not hard, just enough for her to suck in a breath and squeeze her thighs shut.

Gabriel shook off her grasp, lifting his head.

"*Quiero estar dentro de ti*."

"Yes," she hissed. It was almost a crime he couldn't be inside her again. She was glad he was just as impatient about it as she was.

Gabriel switched breasts, attacking the other with the same amount of passion as the first. His free hand slid down her stomach and unfastened her shorts. She gripped his shoulder, bracing herself for his touch. Instead, he bit her breast. She dug her nails into him and didn't relax until he released her.

He chuckled against her skin and shifted, sliding his hand into her panties. She sucked in a breath. He pushed her knees farther apart, making room for his hand.

"Look at me."

She pried her eyes open. The morning light fell on his face, casting him in a golden glow. He slid his fingers through her slit. Her legs and his hand were both trapped by the unforgiving denim. Why were they still wearing clothes again?

Gabriel lowered his head and kissed her, sweetly. His lips to hers. She curled her arms around his shoulders, melting into this moment. He pressed two fingers inside her. It wasn't the same as his cock, but it was still him.

He lifted his head and rocked his hips into her, pushing his fingers deeper.

"I'm going to do this later." His voice was low, rough.

"Promise?"

"Oh yeah."

He kissed her lips and worked his fingers in and out,

stroking her inner walls and curling them just right. In a matter of moments she was a boneless, whimpering wreck.

Gabriel sat up and slid his hand out from her shorts. She almost protested, but he grasped her twisted shorts and panties and pulled them down her legs.

She could work with that.

Her shorts joined the rest of her clothes somewhere on the floor.

He sat back on one leg that was curled under him, the other braced on the ground. He stared at her for a moment and her stomach did flip-flops. Did they need a condom?

Yes.

The answer was yes.

But she wished they didn't.

Gabriel's lids drooped and her heart fluttered in her chest. She gripped the cushion under her head with both hands. The seconds ticked by. Finally, he leaned forward and planted his hands on the cushion between her legs. He'd done this to her before. In fact, he'd taken great pleasure in tormenting her like this. Something about how she lost control.

He pushed her legs apart, spreading her completely and sinking down to his forearms. There was nothing rushed about the way he moved, but her heart raced.

Gabriel dipped his fingers into her channel. Unprepared for the intrusion, she gasped. His calloused hands were a completely different sensation from his velvety smooth cock.

He bent his head and kissed her mound. Thank God she'd splurged on getting her legs and bikini line waxed. Every caress, even the feel of his breath on her skin, was more acute. He spread her folds with his thumbs and kissed her again, more intimately. His tongue traced her seam and her back arched off the couch. All the blood rushed to her extremities, her sex and nipples throbbed.

She wanted him, so badly. He cupped her bottom, kneading her ass, and thrust his tongue inside her.

Nikki cried out and shifted her hips. He stroked in and out of her, rubbing the flat of his tongue along the walls of her channel. She rocked into him, riding his face, and he moved with her. There was nothing like the feel of Gabriel inside her.

She wanted more.

Gabriel had always urged her to pursue her pleasure in whatever form it took. There was no reason to be shy or afraid with him.

She let go of the cushion and stretched her hand down to her mound. Her clit throbbed with her pulse, completely untouched save when he had his hand down her pants. She rubbed the hard nub with her thumb in bold, sure strokes.

Gabriel pushed her hand away and shifted his mouth to her clit. Her eyes snapped open and she stared at the ceiling as he thrust at least two fingers inside her vagina while gently sucking on the bundle of nerves.

"Oh, my—my—Gabe!"

Nikki planted one foot on the tile and draped the other over his shoulders. She lifted up and undulated against him, moving in tandem with his fingers. His head bobbed with her, never breaking contact with her clit. She babbled, chanting his name, losing all sense of control.

The tightness in her abdomen released the very moment she thought she couldn't take any more. She groaned, her body caught in a cascade of pleasure that went all the way to her toes.

Gabriel kissed her mound and eased his fingers from her body. She held out her hand and he took it, touching his lips briefly to her palm.

She loved this man. This amazing, selfless man.

"I'll get us some breakfast." He squeezed her hand and let her go, but she held on.

As if.

They might have been apart for four years, but his habits were committed to memory.

She pulled him toward her and he sat down hard on the cushions. He must still have been partly asleep, because she managed to get him sitting and straddled his lap before he could voice a protest.

Nikki curled her arms around his neck and kissed him. He tried to talk, to probably point out something sweet. For a man who could kill with one hand, he was surprisingly gentle. Too bad for him he awakened something in her that would not be shut down.

He grasped her ass with both hands and hauled her closer. Despite coming, she wasn't done. Okay, she might be done in the orgasm department, but there was a whole other pleasure she got from just being with him. His hands in her hair, their bodies touching.

She slithered to the floor, dropping out of his grasp. He braced his hands on the cushions, blinking down at her. She smiled and grasped the jeans that were already sliding south.

"Nikki—"

"Don't pretend you don't want . . ." She fumbled for what to call it.

"I'm not pretending anything." He braced his hands on his knees and leaned toward her. "My dick is hard. There isn't an immediate solution. I'm dealing."

"There are other ways."

He grasped her chin between his thumb and forefinger. "You know the only kind of sex I'm interested in."

Gabriel was maybe the only man she'd ever met who

had zero interest in receiving oral sex. Not that it was high on Nikki's list of things to do, but for him it would be number one.

"Then what are you going to do?" she asked.

"Ignore it. Hope it goes away."

She laughed.

"What? Is my dick funny?" He gestured at the erection tenting his boxers.

"No, but I know you. That isn't going anywhere."

"What do you suggest, then?"

"I don't know. Help you out?" Was she being ridiculous? It was hard to think about the bigger picture instead of the single-minded desire to get him off.

For a moment they stared at each other. This was crazy, why was she pushing it? Heat crawled up her neck, and she knew he could see her blush. She was too pale for it to not be painfully obvious.

Gabriel stood, hooked his thumbs in his boxers, and shoved his clothes off. She reached greedily for them, stripping the jeans off his legs. He sat back down, crossing his hands behind himself, and nodded at his erection.

"Go ahead," he said.

Go ahead—what?

She froze.

Okay, so her vague plan didn't exactly cover this, but it was all about what felt good, wasn't it? Gabriel wanted passion, to feel her, so she'd give him that. She inhaled a breath and slid her palms up and down his legs. The wiry hairs tickled her and grounded her all at once. She leaned forward, letting her breasts brush up against his knees.

She grasped his cock with both hands. The muscle twitched in her palm. A reassuring sign. She stroked his erection, hand over hand, running her fingers along the bulging vein and under the mushroom cap. At first Gabriel sat impassively watching her, but slowly little tells seeped through. A tensing of his jaw, a slow blink, until he outright groaned.

There wasn't enough slide in her grip and she definitely hadn't come prepared with lube. So she'd use the next best thing.

Nikki bent her head and licked his stiff flesh, root to tip. It wasn't a bad taste. Salty, masculine, and distinctly him. She sucked the crown and stroked him, thrilled when he lifted his hips just a tiny bit. He might not like oral, but he liked her.

She let him go and glanced up. His cheeks were sunk in and his eyes seemed darker, almost black. She leaned toward him and kissed his chest. His erection notched between her breasts.

There was an idea.

She pushed her breasts together, capturing his cock between them, and sank down.

"Fuck," he muttered.

She grinned, enjoying the bewildered look on his face. She swiped her thumbs over her nipples as she rose and fell, stroking him with her breasts. He scooted forward, giving her more room to work with and better access. As her skin began to drag unpleasantly across his, she bent her head and took him once more in her mouth, as much of him as she could.

"Come here," Gabriel growled.

He hauled her up onto his lap. She straddled his thighs, his cock jutting up between them. He dug one hand into her hair, twisting it around his palm, and kissed her. She fumbled between them, seeking his hard length. She wrapped her hands around it and stroked. He cupped her ass with his free hand while he devoured her mouth. She ground her hips against his, moving in time with her hands, rising and falling as much as his tight hold on her would allow. He lifted his hips, thrusting into her hold.

He let go of her hair and cupped her mound, thrusting his fingers inside her. It was so unexpected she gasped. She was a one-hit wonder when it came to orgasms, but it felt so damn good to have him in her, she didn't care.

"Oh, yeah," he muttered.

The hand on her ass squeezed, changing the angle of his penetration. She groaned as warmth spread through her lower body. He continued to thrust, lifting his hips, their sexes grinding together with his fingers doing amazing things inside her.

Nikki's vision hazed and her breath caught.

"Gabe . . ."

"Yeah."

"Oh!"

The second orgasm caught her completely by surprise. She pitched forward, curling around him as her body went limp.

He wrapped his hand around hers and guided her, the thrusts growing jerky and uneven.

"*Te amo,*" he whispered against her shoulder, so low she doubted he meant for her to hear it. "*Te amo muchisimo.*"

He—what?

Te amo wasn't exactly hard to understand.

Stunned, she was hardly aware of the guttural shout, signaling his orgasm.

He's just said he loved her.

He so did not know she spoke Spanish.

Chapter Fifteen

Gabriel admired the silhouette of the woman sitting in his passenger seat through the tinted glass. He strode across the gas station lot without fear of getting run over. This early, they were the only patrons, though in an hour or two this place would be bustling with people grabbing a drink or snacks for the beach.

God, she was something else. Utterly and completely amazing. He pressed the key fob to unlock his door, opened it, and dropped into the driver's seat. Nikki'd left her dark hair down, and dressed in a bright blue tank top and shorts, she almost looked Miami enough to belong.

"Everything okay?" she asked.

"Yup." He tossed the plastic bag into her lap, just for the sheer joy of seeing her turn red when she realized what he'd bought.

He watched her peer at his purchase out of the corner of his eye while he shifted into gear and eased onto the street that would take them straight to the beach.

"Only three?" she asked.

Her demure tone surprised a laugh out of him. Well hell, he liked this confident and sexy side of her.

"I figured that could get us through the morning." He winked at her.

Nikki's eyelids slid shut. She held them closed for a second before opening them again. Was that her version of a count-to-five technique for dealing with him?

"Where are we going again?"

Ah, ignoring his teasing. That was okay, they had time to get around to the fun stuff.

"Miami Beach," he answered.

"Why?"

"Because I think best there. And breakfast."

"Well, all right then." She placed the bag on the floorboard. "Emery hasn't been able to track down where Wilson's people are. All of the images of their vehicles can't read the license plates, either."

"That could be due to anything. Hell, clear gaffer tape works in a pinch to obscure license plates."

They pulled into one of the many parking lots along Miami Beach. A food truck was doing brisk business. He parked across the road in the free lot to avoid any kind of bank or paper trail and walked over to the vendor. The cooks offered a variety of breakfast tacos, fruit, and bottled drinks. People in suits waited next to the morning swimmers, a testament to just how good this particular truck's food really was. They left the tablets and files in the car and, armed with only breakfast and coffee, took to the beach. It was still early enough there weren't many people out. Good, because he wanted to be able to do a bit of brainstorming while they sat and ate.

They settled in the sand, far enough away from anyone else that he wouldn't have to be concerned about eavesdroppers.

"What does finding out where they're holed up do for us?" he asked between bites.

"Tells us where their new base of operations is, it could give us leads to their connections, and it might reveal something about how Wilson has established himself." She sighed. "There's some trigger, something that's happened to Wilson recently that's the inciting action for all of this. After last night, though, if we can find where they are, we can call in—everyone—and get them stopped."

"I'm thinking he already has a secondary place ready. They torched that waterfront property way too quick."

"What are you thinking?"

"The water access made it ideal for moving meth to fund this thing. At this point, he doesn't care about the money—okay, he probably does, but it's secondary. He might ditch the meth business altogether and focus on his main objective."

"Which is hitting an event. That's my guess based on the profile."

"Exactly. I'm willing to bet that whatever he was really working on wasn't there. It was too open. That's what's been bugging me."

"I can see that. So, he's got two places. One where he keeps his expendable people, makes the meth, and deals with people like Hillary and her brother."

"Brothers. I don't know where the others are. One was in that green car at the Shop, which tells me Hillary is more involved than I thought." And that had dangerous complications he didn't want to deal with.

"Great. So then what would he have at this second location?"

"No idea." He pushed to his feet. "Let's walk."

Gabriel offered Nikki his hand and helped her to her feet. They strolled along the beach for a few minutes, like any normal couple. Of course the majority of people weren't packing a 9mm on their morning date. Still, this was about as typical as it got for them.

"It's pretty here," she said.

"I guess."

"Is this where you thought you'd end up?"

"No."

"Where did you think you would go?"

Gabriel hesitated. Should he speak the truth? Or give her a pleasant answer?

What the hell did he have to lose? He was going to put it all on the line with her, like it or not.

"I didn't think things would change. I didn't expect to go anywhere." He didn't look at her, but he could feel her gaze.

Back then, he'd thought he would be a lifetime FBI agent. They'd end up in different departments, but hopefully in roles that were as nine-to-five as possible so they could have a life together. It was crazy, especially for a guy like him, raised poor on the wrong side of the tracks, but he'd dared to hope for more. And he'd almost had it. Second chances didn't come very often for people like him. This time, he had to make it count. She had to know just what she meant to him. What he was willing to do for them to last.

"What should I have done differently?" she asked.

That was Nikki. Assessing the situation and evaluating to improve her performance. She never shrank from blame, but this wasn't on her.

"I don't know that you should have done anything different. Me? There's a lot I would have changed looking back." He glanced at her. "I'd have listened better, for one. You wouldn't have kicked me out if I hadn't stacked the deck."

"Gabe—"

"It's the truth, *mi querida*. I knew I'd screwed up, but I

had no idea how badly until you told me the other day. If I'd been honest with you instead of trying to shield you, maybe we'd be in a different place. I still think I'd have left, but who knows what would have happened to us? Maybe we could have salvaged our relationship? Maybe it wouldn't have been an end?" Maybe he could have moved in, started that life together. Found a different job. Just like what he was thinking they could do now.

"But then you wouldn't be here. This team obviously needs you."

"They'd get by."

"I'm glad we have this time together."

She smiled, and though he heard the period in her tone, he didn't think there was an end for them. Not unless she meant to cut him out of her life. He'd let her go once, and that was his mistake. He wouldn't do it again. He'd lived four years without a piece of himself, and now he was whole again. He had a lot of time to make up for. There were hurts deep down that couldn't be healed in a few days, but if she gave it a chance, he knew they could get there.

His phone rang, breaking the moment.

Gabriel pulled it out and glanced at the screen.

Julian.

He answered and turned to look back the way they'd come. "Yeah?"

"Where you at?" Julian asked.

"Miami Beach."

"John and I will be there in ten."

Julian hung up, leaving Gabriel stuck. He wanted more time alone with Nikki before the shit started hitting the fan, but the job called.

"What's up?" Nikki asked.

"Julian and John must be in the area. Emery probably

told them where to find us. Come on. We'll meet them back at the car."

"What do they want?"

"Probably to talk about what we should do."

It wasn't a secret Gabriel haunted this beach when he wanted some air. He'd spent many mornings here, on his own, before the garage opened, thinking over his mistakes. What he'd do differently. Today, though, he had opportunity by his side.

They turned and headed back to the car, hand in hand. He savored this moment. If he could convince her, this wouldn't be a one-time thing. They could be together again. But that would have to wait until after the case, when he could devote his full attention to winning her back.

Julian would be out for blood, but that was nothing new. He'd chilled a bit after losing one of their own, but probably because he'd realized he was a liability. Gabriel didn't count on that change of mind to last. Anything could happen today, but he doubted it would be of the good variety. Losing the Shop was a hit to their morale. How many cars and equipment had they lost? Tori's Bel Air sprang to mind. The engine wouldn't even turn over, but she'd had plans and parts to start work on the car that fall. One of the structural charges was all of ten feet away from the Bel Air. The car would have become shrapnel.

"Have we heard anything about David?" Nikki asked.

"No. You're the one that's talked to the others, remember?"

"I didn't know if you called them while I was in the shower or something."

"Babe, the last people I want to talk to after coming like that would be these guys. The only reason I wasn't in that shower with you is because we actually have stuff to do today. If I had my way, we wouldn't have left the house at all." He wouldn't mention that he wanted to keep her at the house so she would be safe. He liked breathing after all.

"There's always later." Her prim-and-proper attitude so did not mix with what she was telling him. Damn, but he liked when she talked dirty.

He kept his reply to himself. Two figures strode through the sand toward them and he didn't want Julian or John privy to their private life. At least not yet, and never in that much detail.

"Figured you'd be out here," Julian said as they neared.

"You look like shit." Gabriel inclined his head toward John, who merely nodded.

"Did you get something to eat? Those tacos sure burn your throat." Nikki stuck her hands in her back pockets. Gabriel kept his eyes away from the interesting way the pose thrust her breasts forward.

"You let Gabriel pick for you, didn't you?" John shook his head. "He only likes stuff that burns when they go down. No taste buds."

Nikki chuckled.

Their little group descended on a picnic table near a parking lot. By the looks of it, Julian had a pretty bad leg injury with the way he was limping.

"Well, where are we?" Gabriel asked after they'd settled two on each side.

"When are the Feds getting here to take over? There has to be plenty of evidence by now." Julian leaned on the table, somehow managing to make menacing an art form.

To Nikki's credit, she returned his stare with an equally calm one.

"The local field office has begun an investigation. Merlo said that since your operation is out of their control, they need to do their own legwork. And because they're a bunch of assholes, they won't accept our research either.

I'm going through channels at the bureau and pulling in Director Scott, but it'll take some time. Maybe a day or two to get it sorted out."

"Fuck, Wilson's bunch of crazies are going to pull something off before then. They've got to know that," Julian said.

"It's process." Gabriel detested the red tape, the proper procedure of it all. People were dying. They might be the bad guys right now, but they weren't all that bad. At least not before Wilson poisoned them.

"Chill out, man," John drawled. "Don't act like you expected anything less. What do you want to bet that was the suits' intention all along? I bet this is exactly what they wanted. So what? We keep working the case. Show them the list and let's get on with it."

Gabriel wanted to high-five John, but didn't think Julian would appreciate the gesture. The list of people who could give Julian straight talk was down to two: Aiden and John. Gabriel was pretty sure the moment he and Nikki got on good terms was the last time Julian would take him seriously. Add to it Julian and Aiden were butting heads more often than not these days and it was shaky ground.

"List?" Nikki perked up. They were speaking her language.

"Got a list. Six events going on today that might be of interest to Wilson." Julian spread a receipt out, facedown. Several lines were scrawled on the back.

"We could divide and conquer. What're Aiden and the twins doing?" Gabriel asked.

"Aiden has Madison somewhere he won't even tell us." Julian glanced away. Aiden was his best friend. Or had been. "Last I heard from him, he was going by the garage to shut it down, then swing by and pick up Roni, maybe Tori depending on if Emery needs help or not."

"Then we each check out two of these, see what's going on?" Nikki picked up the list and studied it for a moment.

"Sounds like a plan." Julian tapped his knuckles on the metal surface.

"We'll take these two. This one and this one are sort of close together, and so are these. Should cut down on our time spent driving." Gabriel tapped the corresponding events, seeing them as points on his mental map.

"Got it. Let Aiden know. We're out." Julian pushed to his feet, followed by John, who cast Gabriel a knowing look. The two men ambled to Julian's new ride and were gone in a plume of exhaust and burnt rubber.

"Do I want to know?" Nikki asked.

"Probably not." He sighed.

Gabriel understood Aiden's choice. The job was just that—a job. Julian couldn't see past it. It was all that mattered to him. Once, Aiden had been like Julian, but Madison had rescued him. Maybe more than he'd rescued her from her scumbag of an ex-husband. There was more to life than work. Family. Love. Happiness. Those were the reasons why Gabriel had signed up for the FBI in the first place, to protect those things. At the end of a day, he couldn't hold a job at night. It wouldn't care for him when he was gone.

He hoped the others would understand. Someday, probably sooner than he intended, he'd leave the crew. He wouldn't look back. Because as much as they'd become his family, this was still a job. And he wouldn't put a possible new life on hold just to check off a couple tasks.

It was beyond difficult to focus. Nikki's gaze kept blurring as they walked the lines of booths along the street fair. She needed to be on the lookout for Wilson's people in case they were canvassing the location, setting up for a hit, but her mind kept going back to that morning.

Gabriel had said he'd loved her.

It didn't matter that it was in Spanish, he'd still said it. And she wasn't all that convinced that it was a momentary slip of the tongue during a passionate moment. He'd never said it to her before, and they'd been damn near moving in with each other.

"This doesn't look like Wilson's scene." Gabriel paused at the intersection of booths and turned a slow circle.

"No. It really doesn't."

The arts fair was billed as a ten thousand plus event with booths featuring all sorts of new age art, alternative medicines, and meditation events. It appeared to be the kind of thing that would offend Wilson's hard-core stance. A bomb here would make the news, but not create the kind of splash he wanted. Plus, there was no way ten thousand people would fit on the grounds set aside for the fair.

"Let's bail." Gabriel placed his hand on her back and gently propelled her toward the parking lot. "Any word from Julian or Aiden?"

She pulled out her phone and scrolled through the new messages while they waited at the crosswalk. Gabriel started walking and she fell into step beside him.

"Julian says—"

Tires squealed and an engine revved in the distance. Gabriel shoved her forward roughly. Nikki stumbled, righted herself, and sprinted. He wouldn't shove her for no good reason.

"Go! Go! Go!" Gabriel yelled at her back.

She glanced up the street at a pink car that had seen better days barreling down at them, far closer than she'd realized. The car jumped the curb, heading straight for them.

Gabriel picked her up and tossed her over the four-foot fence that separated the parking lot from the street. She hit the hood of a car, back first, her head tucked, arms lifted to protect her already abused skull. Metal crunched and glass sprayed her.

"Gabe!" She pushed herself up and leaned over the fence, searching the street for some sign of him as the pink car made a hard right turn.

"Here." He grunted.

She turned and gaped as he pulled his leg out from the busted windshield of a late-model sedan.

The glass and metal crunching wasn't Hillary hitting him, it was Gabriel getting away from her. Mostly unhurt.

He shook glass from his jeans and leapt to the pavement. More tires squealed not too far away.

"Come on, she's doubling back." He helped her down and they ran for the Skyline, parked a little away from the others.

The sound of Hillary's car grew closer. A metal crash wasn't that far away.

"Shit, hide." Gabriel pushed her between cars. "Are you carrying?"

"Where am I supposed to hide a gun in these shorts?" Nikki crouched behind a pickup truck, peering under the vehicle. She'd debated carrying the messenger bag, but opted not to since it didn't seem likely they would run into any of Wilson's ilk here. How wrong she'd been, the one time she decided to not carry.

"Here," he whispered.

Tires hugged by a pink body rolled into view.

Gabriel slid his spare Desert Eagle across the asphalt to her.

"No, no, no." She cringed.

The car stopped perpendicular to the truck she was hiding behind. Nikki glanced at the gun, just sitting there. Hillary, or whoever was driving the car, had to see it.

"Go," Gabriel mouthed, waving her away.

Nikki shook her head. He was pinned down in the corner of the lot if she bailed on him. Unless she drew Hillary away.

It wasn't a bad plan.

"Nikki. Nikki," he continued to whisper.

"Get the car," she mouthed back.

She crept to the left side of the truck. Sirens wailed in the distance. The cops wouldn't get there fast enough to save them, so they were on their own.

Nikki crawled past the break between the truck and nearest car. She glimpsed at the pink stalkermobile but couldn't make out anyone in the interior. Now, a little behind the car, she rose into a crouch and crept the length of the vehicle. She wanted Hillary's attention, but she didn't want to die in the process.

Before Gabriel could do something even more stupid than what she was planning, Nikki straightened. She pushed off the car and sprinted with all her might, arms pumping, away from Hillary.

Tires screamed and the car's engine whined.

She didn't dare look behind her.

Nikki dodged across the aisle and between two cars. She glanced behind her as the pink car whipped to a stop, the windows down. The driver leaned out, gun in hand.

"Shit!" Nikki cried.

She ducked, hitting the ground behind another car. Glass shattered, spraying down on her. The car revved again and she crawled in all haste away from her shield.

A moment later the vehicle she'd hidden behind lurched into another car.

"Nikki," Gabriel bellowed. He leaned out of the Skyline and squeezed off a couple rounds, hitting the pink drifting car.

She scrambled toward him as Hillary reversed. Gabriel accelerated, overshooting her position, but also blocking her from Hillary as she ran behind the Skyline and dove into the passenger seat.

The pink car rounded the line of parking spaces, and the two sat facing each other with almost forty yards between them.

Nikki twisted in her seat. Where was the exit?

Behind Hillary.

Nikki grabbed her bag and pulled out her two SIG Sauer pistols. Gabriel threw the car into reverse. Someone leaned out of the passenger seat of Hillary's car and started firing.

"God damn it," Gabriel yelled.

Nikki held on as he whipped the car around a ninety degree angle, then another one. She punched the automatic window button, lowering it, and pushed her upper body through the widening space.

"What are you doing?" he demanded.

"What does it look like I'm doing?" She aimed and squeezed. They couldn't risk stray bullets here. She hit the side of the car, ahead of where she'd aimed.

She fired again, then ducked as the passenger returned fire. Gabriel pushed the Skyline faster. Hillary was closing the distance, even as they neared the end of the row. Gabriel slowed and jerked the car at a clean, right angle, then shot backward, sailing out of the parking lot and onto the street, just ahead of the cops.

Hillary didn't make the turn so neat. She clipped the cars at the end of the row before straightening out.

"They aren't going to make it." Gabriel shifted into drive

and they shot forward, making a clean getaway. The car hadn't even been hit once.

"Are you sure?" Nikki twisted to watch the back window.

The first cop car swung wide and barely missed being hit by the pink car.

"Shit. Go!" Nikki shouted.

"She'll never catch us."

Gabriel shifted lanes, passing other cars as if they were standing still. He blew through lights, cut across intersections, and all the while the pink speck behind them grew smaller and smaller. Nikki's head spun and she clutched at the door, not sure if she should be more in shock about what had just happened or their speed.

"Oh my God." She tucked the pistols under her things and pushed her hair back. That was close. Way closer than she liked.

"What were you thinking?" Gabriel snapped.

"What?" She knew perfectly well why he was pissed off.

"You should have stayed hidden."

"And let you do what? Get trapped in that corner? She'd have shot you."

Gabriel opened his mouth, but she held up her hand.

"Would you have this same argument with Aiden or Julian?"

His teeth made an audible clicking sound. She could feel the heat of his wrath.

"Look, I know I'm not as strong as you. My reflexes aren't as sharp. I'm not accustomed to this kind of deep cover. But I'm well aware of my abilities. If I say I can do something, I can. I gave you the opening to get the car and get us out of there, didn't I?"

"Yes."

"I appreciate that you want to protect me, but that's not possible in our line of work."

"I'm never going to like this." She could almost hear his teeth grinding over the sound of the engine.

"That's fine. You don't have to like it, but this is how it is."

They drove in silence, headed God only knew where.

"It's hard to be okay with you putting yourself in danger. I'm never going to be comfortable with that. If that's wrong or it pisses you off, well, too bad. I can try to react better."

"I would appreciate that. Yelling at me for saving your ass isn't very gracious."

Gabriel barked a laugh. "Did you just say *ass*?"

"I did. You are a horrible influence on me." She peered up at the roof of the car and smiled, unable to contain her joy at that little victory. She'd never fault him for wanting to protect her. It was nice, actually, because unlike many of her coworkers, Gabriel wasn't condescending about it. His motives for wanting to keep her from harm were completely different.

Because he loved her.

A thrill shot through her. She still wasn't sure how to handle that information, but she needed to make a plan. Figure things out. What she needed was to talk to her daddy. Not the deputy director, but her father. Boy, that was going to be a fun conversation.

Chapter Sixteen

"Where now?" Gabriel asked Nikki. They were just cruising, keeping an eye on their tail while Emery pulled cameras, Matt worked the cop angle, and they collected what intel they could.

"How do you think they found us?" She glanced through the rear window. Again. Hillary's attack must have shaken her more than she was letting on.

Gabriel tightened his grip on the gearshift. Fucking Hillary.

"Who knows? Maybe Hillary was scouting the site? We could have put the brakes on one of their hits." He was spitballing. Truth was, they had nothing.

"But that wasn't their speed." She tipped her head back and stared up at the ceiling of the car.

"No, it wasn't. Hey, call Matt. See what he knows."

Nikki pulled out her phone and dialed. She'd put her hair up once more, revealing the long line of her neck. He wasn't about to tell her to take it down and cover the slight hickey he'd left there this morning. Of course, with the road rash on her knees and new bruises, the others might just assume it was another battle scar instead of a mark of passion. All the better. This was still just for them. Not for long. The others weren't stupid, but right now they didn't need anyone messing with what they had.

"Hi, Detective Smith, this is Nikki—we're breathing. How are you?" She pulled the phone away from her face and put it on speaker.

"I'm at the scene of a . . . hit-and-run? Shoot-out? What exactly happened here?" Matt asked.

Gabriel filled in the holes for Matt, using a few choice words but keeping it brief. The less Matt knew, the more deniability he had when it came to looking for the people involved.

"Did you find a green and black car at the warehouse scene last night?" Nikki asked.

"Yeah. It's being processed," Matt replied.

"Think you could try to ID any bodies inside that car?" Nikki asked.

"What are you thinking?" Gabriel asked.

"If Hillary isn't after us for Wilson, what if it has to do with whoever was in that car? Didn't you say she had brothers?"

"Shit. Yes." Gabriel squeezed his eyes shut as they waited at a light.

"I'll work on that, but things move slow," Matt warned.

"How's our patient? Any word there?" Nikki asked.

"He's lucid and talking, last I heard. Things have been busy, so I didn't get a chance to swing by and hear what he's saying yet."

"Think we should pay him a visit?" Gabriel glanced at her.

"It's better than anything else we've got going on."

Matt rattled off the address for them and hung up.

Gabriel turned the car, heading deeper into the heart of Miami. The hospital they'd taken David Swiss to was a smaller establishment with less traffic. Probably to better monitor who came and went in an attempt to identify any friends of his. They parked and sat in the lot for a moment, watching the other visitors come and go.

"Think they know he's here?" Gabriel asked.

"Hopefully not. If they did, I imagine Wilson would try to eliminate him. I'd like first crack at him. Something has happened to Wilson to trigger all of this."

"You'll figure it out. Come on." He got out and gave the Skyline a quick once-over. By some miracle, they'd escaped without a scratch on the car. Good thing, because with the GTO already in need of some TLC, he couldn't lose this ride, too.

They strode into the hospital and Nikki went straight to the admissions desk. She glanced around before pulling a slim wallet out of her bag. Inwardly he groaned, but couldn't fault her for using the tools to get what they wanted in the fastest manner possible.

Gabriel turned and kept an eye on the other people, ensuring none got too close while she flashed her credentials at the hospital staff. He couldn't make out their hushed voices, which was for the best. If he couldn't hear them, none of the others milling around could either.

"Gabe, let's go."

Nikki led the way to a bank of elevators. In the relative privacy of the nook, he edged closer. He didn't speak until they were safely inside the compartment, being whisked up a couple of floors.

"What did they say?" he asked, pitching his voice low.

"They weren't surprised to see me at all. I'm guessing Matt warned them we'd be by."

Gabriel reached over and took her hand, soaking in the simple pleasure of the feel of her skin against his for a few brief moments.

The lift dinged and the doors slid open, dumping them out into a small, empty waiting room. The medical posters were sunny and cheerful and touted healing proverbs. The chairs were newer, the floor free from scuffs. This wasn't one of the county facilities. What strings had Matt pulled to get David Swiss into a private ward?

Nikki approached the desk, this one enclosed by a thick glass window. She spoke to a woman on the other side through a speaker.

After a few exchanged words, the person on shift buzzed them past a locked door.

This wasn't just any hospital level.

"Psych ward?" He glanced around, taking in the fresh flowers and colorful décor. It wasn't exactly white padded rooms and fishbowls.

"Makes sense to me." Nikki gestured at a secure, metal door as they passed. "It's got security, has cameras and a single point of entry." Nikki stopped abruptly at an intersection of halls.

"What are we waiting for?" he asked.

A young nurse with a perky smile stepped out of a nearby door.

"This way," she said, clutching a folder to her chest.

"How is Mr. Swiss this morning?" Nikki asked the young woman.

"He's doing well. I can't tell you more than that." She even said her apologies with a smile.

"Understandable. Have you notified his family of his whereabouts?" Nikki had slipped back into her agent mode, and despite the clothing, she screamed Fed.

"No, because of the safety concerns." The nurse was quiet for a few strides. "Also, he has moments where he's completely lucid and he sounds like he knows what he's talking about, but it's not always the case."

"Meaning whatever he tells us is unreliable evidence."

"I'm sorry." The nurse paused at another intersection.

"His room is the third on the left. I'll let you go in. He doesn't like me very much right now. He might be calmer if I stay out here. I'll wait here if you need anything."

"Thank you."

Nikki strode toward the room and Gabriel lengthened his stride to keep up with her head start.

"Because he's going to be happy to see us?" he said under his breath.

"We need him to talk to us."

Gabriel couldn't disagree. They were running out of leads, fast. Both of the events they'd checked that day were all wrong.

Nikki pushed the room door open and hesitated in the entrance.

David Swiss sat in a hospital bed, his arms loosely bound to the rails. The furniture seemed too small for a man of his stature, but Gabriel was willing to bet they'd held scarier patients. David's wounds were bandaged and he looked younger without soot, blood, and dirt on his face.

He stared at them, his eyes widening slightly and lips parting. It was better than screaming profanities or trying to attack them.

"You're real," he said.

"Yes, I am. Hello, David." Nikki took a few steps toward the bed, but stopped well out of reach. "I'm Supervisory Special Agent Nikki Gage of the FBI."

"You got a badge?" David's gaze was resigned. He glanced at Gabriel, and there was defeat there.

"Of course." Nikki produced the same badge she'd shown the hospital staff and in turn offered it to David.

"Who's he?"

"You don't want to know who I am." Gabriel crossed his arms. "We want to ask you some questions."

David handed the badge back to Nikki and rested his fingers against the rails of his bed.

"What do you want to know?" he asked.

"How are you?" Nikki set her messenger bag down in one of the guest chairs and took another step closer.

A tactical maneuver. She appeared unarmed, the lesser of the two threats. Going for the personal approach would hopefully turn David sympathetic. But what did they really know?

"They have me on suicide watch." He lifted his arms and rattled the restraints. "How would you feel if you found out you were trying to kill people you knew?"

"Your mother is very worried about you. She wants you to come home."

"I'm the last thing she needs." David scrubbed his hand over his face. He darted a quick, tortured glance at Nikki. "Did I—I hurt you, didn't I?"

Remorse. David Swiss regretted what he'd done so much he'd considered suicide.

"No." Nikki shook her head. "You did try, though."

"You screwed up," Gabriel said.

Both sets of eyes shot to him, Nikki's telling him to shut the hell up. David nodded, agreeing to what he said. Good.

"You can help fix it." Gabriel stared hard at the man. It wasn't David's fault he'd been taken advantage of by a sicko like Wilson, but he'd carry the weight of this sin the rest of his life. If they didn't give David the chance to redeem himself, he might actually hurt himself.

"I'm guessing you don't actually mean I'm going to get out of this hospital bed and go fix this myself?" David asked.

"No, man." Gabriel shook his head. He wasn't without forgiveness, but if David thought he was getting out of that bed, Gabriel would slam his ass back into it. The man needed medical attention first and foremost. "You need to stay here. What would help is if you can tell us what you remember."

"It's . . . it's not all right in my head." David stared at the wall, but he wasn't seeing anything on this continent, that was for sure. "There's whole chunks that don't make sense. Other times, I was positive we were all back in the Middle East."

"That's okay. We're aware that anything you tell us may not be what really happened. But maybe something you saw or heard will help us." Nikki's statement seemed to put David at ease. The man had a long road to recovery ahead of him, if he stuck to it. This was just the first step.

"When did you meet Wilson?" Gabriel asked.

"General Wilson. He's not a general, is he?" David's face said he knew the answer.

Nikki glanced at Gabriel before replying. "No, he's not. He's never been in any branch of the military or law enforcement."

"I met another guy, Keith, at the VA. We hung out, and he later introduced me to Wilson."

"Who was Keith?" Nikki asked.

David spoke staring at the blanket draped over his lap. Every so often he moved his hand, but not often. "He was the real deal. Infantry. We hung out and he started talking about going back over there. Making a difference. Skipping the red tape. I was angry. It sounded like a good idea."

"What's the deal with Keith and Wilson?" Gabriel asked, anxious to get to the point already.

"Keith is one of Wilson's top guys. Keith would get me and some others together, we'd hang out and he'd start talking shit. About how things are fucked up and we can do something about it."

"Keith recruited you," Nikki interjected.

"Yeah, I guess so."

"Tell me more about Keith, please? What can you remember about him?"

"He's an all right guy. Stuck to Wilson's side, though."

"So he told Wilson everything you guys said or did?" Nikki took a small step forward. She was being cautious. They both knew that just because David's wrists were tied down didn't mean he was safely restrained. He was a trained, seasoned soldier.

"Yeah." David nodded.

"Did something happen to Bradley? General Wilson? Something he'd talk about? Or maybe something he's touchy about?"

"No, no." David shook his head, each side-to-side motion losing speed.

"David? What is it?" Nikki asked.

"There was . . . I think . . ."

"Close your eyes for me."

David did as she asked.

"Take a deep breath."

His chest rose and fell.

"Okay, think about what you were doing when you heard about what happened. What are you doing?" Nikki edged to the foot of the bed and grasped the railing.

"I'm cleaning my weapon," David replied.

"Good. Where are you?"

"In my trailer behind HQ."

"Is Wilson there?"

David tilted his head to the side and his brow furrowed. "Yes. He's on the other side of the trailer. He just came back. He was away for a while . . . someone died. Someone close to him."

Nikki turned to Gabriel, eyes wide. He wasn't sure what that meant, but apparently it was something.

"That's good, David, really good," she said.

"Do you know what Wilson is trying to do? We know he's planning something, but not what or when," Gabriel said.

David opened his eyes and shook his head. "Plans changed all the time. Only person who will know what they're going to blow up is Nico. He makes the bombs."

"Nico?" Gabriel frowned. He'd heard that name from Big Guy. "Who is that?"

"Keith always kept us away from Nico. Said he was bad blood. Something about kids. Not a team player. I got the feeling he wasn't there willingly."

"I guess it's Nico we really want to talk to." Gabriel glanced at Nikki. Nico wasn't exactly a common name. What were the chances they could track him down?

"How does Hillary fit into this?" Nikki asked.

"Hillary?" David frowned.

"Drives a pink car?"

"Doesn't ring a bell." David shook his head.

"This chick." Gabriel thrust his phone in David's face with Hillary's racing head shot.

"Wilson's hooker?"

"Hooker?" Nikki echoed.

"Who is she?" David asked.

"That's what we're trying to find out," Gabriel replied. A romantic relationship made sense. Hillary would be attracted to power and money. She might hop in and out of beds, but she was still relationship driven.

The questions continued, but David's answers became wilder and it soon became obvious that whatever lucid window they'd lucked into was shut now. They excused themselves and met back up with his nurse waiting for them in the hall. Nikki gave the woman a quick rundown of his behavior and they saw themselves out.

"How much of that do you think we can use?" he asked Nikki as they stepped back out into the sunshine.

"No way to tell what's real and what was in his head. The names, I'd bet those were real."

"What was that about the dead relative?" Gabriel asked.

"Wilson's mother. She died a couple months ago. The pieces fit."

"Talk to me like I'm five."

"Okay, up until now Wilson has been someone in the background. He hasn't called the shots. I'm willing to bet his mother kept him in check to some degree, and his sense of Munchausen by proxy would drive him to keep her alive. So until her death, they were codependents."

"How do you know this?"

"Mrs. Wilson was a colorful character. She spoke at a hearing for Wilson once, and I watched the tape. Without her there, he's searching for something else to fix. He's angry because he no longer has her to keep him in check, and the person aiming him is now this Keith person. It makes Wilson completely unstable."

"That doesn't sound good."

"No, it's not." She pulled out her phone. "I've got a text from Matt. He wants to meet us at the morgue."

"That's not going to be good either."

"Do I need to ask if you know where it is?"

"No." He unlocked the Skyline and held the passenger door for Nikki, taking the moment to admire her legs. She was right. There wasn't anywhere to keep a SIG Sauer in those shorts.

He jogged around the car and got in the driver's seat.

"I feel like we're spinning our wheels." Nikki stared out the passenger window as he guided them back to the main drag.

"We took a big hit last night. We're making progress. We've got a name. Send that over to Emery."

Nikki tapped the screen of her phone, then dropped the device into her lap.

"I hate Wilson," she announced.

"Right there with you," he replied. It was a special kind of scum who could use a person's own mind against them. Who knew how many people he'd trapped inside their own heads and manipulated to work for him?

"This isn't a clear-cut case anymore. We can't turn this over to the FBI."

"Why's that?" He was curious at her reasoning. Chances were, he'd already arrived at the same conclusion.

"It's more like a hostage rescue situation. We've got Wilson and his team holding people hostage and making them perform his acts of violence. But the FBI won't see it that way. I'm not saying these men don't need to answer for what they've done, but not in the way the FBI will make them pay. You know?"

"Yeah, you read my mind."

"What do we do?"

"We take care of it. Stop Wilson. The FBI is still going to take them all when it comes to arresting because you'll be the agent on the scene, but your reports will change how they're processed."

"It's a lot of weight to carry."

"You're up to it."

"Thanks."

He reached across and took her hand.

They arrived at the morgue in short order. Matt's SUV sat by itself, with the man in question standing out front, phone pressed to his ear.

"He hasn't slept," Nikki muttered.

"What?"

"Look at his clothes. They're the same ones he was wearing last night."

"I see." And he had other theories now.

They got out and met the detective between the vehicles.

"What do you want us to see?" Gabriel asked.

"Glad you two are alive. That was some stunt this morning. I didn't want to be there, by the way." Matt placed his hands on his hips.

"You don't want to know about this morning," Gabriel said.

"You're right. I don't. Come on." Matt led the way into the morgue and flashed his badge, bypassing any questions the staff might have asked.

He led them past rooms, down to the lockers where the bodies were stored.

"This is going to be cold," he warned, and opened a walk-in freezer lined with bodies on gurneys.

"All of these from last night?" Nikki asked. She pulled a pair of rubber gloves from a box by the door and put them on.

"No. We've had a bunch of bodies wash up. First ones were already released to the families, but they had similar markings on them." Matt pulled on gloves and led them to the first body, nearest the door. He gestured to little sores all up and down the man's arms.

"Meth," Gabriel said.

"Yes, but . . ." Matt picked up the corpse's hand and showed them the fingers.

"There's no fingerprints." She reached out and swiped her finger over the dead man's digit.

"Nope. Burned off postmortem. The bodies from last night have the same cocktail of meth in their systems and their fingerprints have been removed." Matt walked to the back of the freezer and gestured to a badly mangled body. "I was able to ID this one. You aren't going to like it."

"Lay it on me." Gabriel held his breath.

"Andrew Rivas."

"Fuck me." Gabriel squeezed his eyes shut.

"Why is that bad?" Nikki asked.

"It's Hillary's brother."

"Hillary? I'm guessing that was the other car from this morning?" Matt asked.

"Yeah." Gabriel's lungs burned from lack of oxygen, so he breathed through his mouth. "We think they were running the drugs for the Cubans. They've been beefing up their distribution since Evers has gone MIA."

"That would make sense, actually." Matt gestured at the door, and Gabriel couldn't get out of there fast enough.

"What else do we know? What does this mean for us?" Nikki seemed distracted, which wasn't like her.

"That's about it," Matt replied.

"Was anything recovered off the bodies?" Gabriel asked.

"Not a lot."

"Can I look it over?"

"Sure." Matt shrugged.

"Do you need me? Or can I make a phone call real quick?" Nikki asked.

"Honestly, there isn't much to see," Matt said.

"I'll meet you at the car?" Before Gabriel had finished speaking, Nikki was headed for the doors.

Chapter Seventeen

Nikki retreated from the building, out into the bright sunshine. She pressed her second speed-dial number and pressed the phone to her ear. What did it say about her that her boss was her first speed dial and her father second?

"Hello, Nikki, your father's finishing something up." The cheerful voice of her father's secretary wasn't unexpected. It was rare that he answered his own cell phone even at the office.

She listened to the sounds of papers shuffling and muted voices for a few moments. She glanced back at the doors to the building, but Gabriel hadn't followed her.

"How's Florida?" Her father had a pleasant, easygoing disposition that disarmed most people. Which was their mistake.

"It's hot."

"That bad?"

"Yeah, but I think we've got some leads to work with."

"Anyone get hurt in that explosion?"

"You heard about that?"

"You landed yourself in a hot mess down there. I didn't want to step in after the decisions were made, but I wouldn't have put you with that team."

She smiled. "Is it because of Gabe, Dad?"

"Not entirely. Their operation is . . . complicated."

She held her tongue. Now wasn't the time to press for answers. Her father knew more than he was letting on.

"Do you have time to talk?" She crossed one arm across her chest and drew in a deep, calming breath.

"About ten minutes."

"Gabe told me he loves me. In Spanish. He doesn't know I understood him." She began to pace the length of the Skyline. This was a conversation most girls would have with their mothers, but hers wasn't a great source on the subject. Not that her father was, either, but he had more feeling.

"You never got over him." Not a question, a simple truth. "Wrap up the case. Then worry about the rest of it. I'd imagine any man you would fall in love with would also understand your sense of duty. Everything I've heard about Gabriel tells me he's a man who will land on his feet wherever he ends up."

"Yes, sir."

"Good. Maybe I'll meet him this time?"

"I'd like that."

"Get back to work. Worry about the rest of it when the bad guys are in prison."

She hung up, feeling a little less desperate.

Gabriel loved her.

That fact still made her insides go warm and mushy. Of course she'd felt strongly for him before. They'd made plans together, but they hadn't said those words. At least not yet. She'd been waiting for them, unsure how she would say them back—and it never happened.

How would she tell him she loved him in return?

Could she say it?

Words had never been intimidating, but those three little

ones stacked together were so profound. They symbolized her vulnerability, her hopes, everything she'd wanted for them to be, packed in a tight little sentence.

Part of her wanted to wait until this operation was wrapped up and they could maybe take a little time off. But the hard truth was that they didn't know if they'd survive. They'd had three close calls in less than twenty-four hours. It was a lot to handle.

But should she tell him? Their lives were separate. One of them would have to give up everything for the other. She didn't want to ask him to leave Miami, and yet she knew deep down she couldn't leave the FBI. Not yet. Not until there was something better to go to. Someplace where she could do more good. Gabriel would understand that. It was their dream. The vision they'd shared and bonded over.

Maybe she shouldn't tell him. Not yet, at least.

A message from Emery waited for her.

No leads from A/R or J/J. Got a couple #s for Nico Silva. Medical discharge, lost a leg. Explosives badass. Baby mama/daughter missing.

There were three numbers, with no other information. What was the best course of action? How should they approach this lead?

She glanced toward the morgue doors and bit her lip. This was her case, but from the moment she got here she'd shared the responsibility with Gabriel. She swiped the text off the screen and tapped her phone, dialing Gabriel's number from memory.

The line barely rang.

"I'm coming to you."

"I've got three possible numbers for Nico. Emery just

sent them over. Also, it looks like his kid and her mother are missing."

"Did you call the numbers?"

"No, I thought we should consider how we want to approach this. There's no telling if these numbers are even good. We can't just call him and say we're the FBI, we want you to cooperate."

The double doors to the morgue opened and Gabriel strode toward her. Nikki's heart did a somersault in her chest. His body language, the way he walked and carried himself, inspired confidence when hers was lagging. He hung up the line and slowed to a stop.

"Think the kid factors in?" she asked.

"Yeah. Give me a number," he said.

She read the first number to him.

"What are you going to say?" she asked.

"Depends on if he answers the phone." They stood there in silence for a few moments. Gabriel shook his head. "Invalid number. Next."

"Seriously, what are you going to say?" She tamped down on the anxious excitement and read off the second number. It was probably a long shot to hope they'd get the man on the phone, but they could give it a whirl.

"It'll come to me."

"Gabe."

"I don't know yet. It depends on how he answers the phone—if he answers." He pressed the phone to his ear. "That one's not working either. Next."

The moments dragged on as she waited. One side of Gabriel's mouth hiked up.

Was it ringing?

"Not picking up," he muttered. "Voice mail . . . Hi, Nico, this is Bobby. I'm a friend of David Swiss. He gave me your number and said we should chat. Hit me up."

"Was that him?" Nikki asked.

"Not sure. It was one of those automated voice mails. Come on. Let's go." Gabriel opened the passenger door for her.

She wanted more answers, but what else was there to say? The man hadn't answered the phone. They were exactly where they'd been before the calls were made.

He strode around the front of the car, pausing near the driver's side. She peered through the window at him as he stared at his phone. He tapped the screen and held it to his ear while he sank into the driver's seat.

"Hello?" Gabriel started the car, jabbing at the Aux buttons.

"Bluetooth enabled," the car computer announced.

"I don't know a David Swiss." The man's voice was suspicious, and rightly so. By now all of Wilson's people probably thought David was dead.

"David knew about you."

"Who are you? What do you want?"

"Is your name Nico Silva?" Gabriel asked.

"Who wants to know?"

Gabriel glanced at her. "I'm a federal agent."

"This conversation never happened," Nico said.

"I guess you don't want help finding your daughter, then?"

Silence.

"You can't help me." Nico's voice was just as cold and hard as when he answered. But he'd hesitated.

"Maybe we can. Meet with us. Let me show you that you can trust us."

"No."

Nico hung up.

"Shit." Gabriel dropped the phone into the cradle mounted on the dash. "Text Emery. Find out what happened to that kid. He thought about it. That means something is up."

Manipulated veterans. Strung-out fanatics. And now a missing kid. Could the case get any more convoluted?

"What next?" She typed out the request to Emery and sent it off, bobbing her knee.

"Hillary. She might be our way to find these guys."

"Where are we going?"

"Back to Little Havana. Several of Hillary's sponsors are local businesses. I bet she runs drugs for them. Her brother Jesse owns a garage over there. Does a lot of lowrider cars."

"You sure that's a good idea?"

"Jesse is the smart one. He won't want to start something with us."

"Okay."

The stereo muted and the phone rang.

"*Bueno?*" Gabriel said as the call activated.

"I have to make a pickup in Coral Gables. Can you be there in twenty minutes?"

It was Nico.

"I can be there sooner than that," Gabriel replied.

"Don't be. They drop me off at the entrance to the storage unit there off 976 and Twenty-ninth. Circle around to the Quick Mart while I pick up what I need. They usually leave me for maybe ten minutes. Don't be early."

The line cut off.

Gabriel executed a U-turn and accelerated, heading south instead of west.

"What changed his mind?" Nikki asked.

"There's something going on with the kid."

"Or . . . it could be a trap."

Gabriel barely blinked. The silent tension in the car was thicker than the Miami humidity. From their position across the street from the storage facility, they could see the two main points of entry. The gas station was down the street and around a corner.

Now they just had to wait and see if this was a trap.

"How much time?" he asked. They'd arrived with eight minutes to spare.

"Any second now. How will we be able to tell it's him?"

"Wait for a car to pull in, then leave?" He shrugged. "You know, this probably means that wherever Nico was, it's close. Ten minutes this time of day won't get you far."

"What if they were in the area?"

"If that's what you want to believe."

"I'm just pointing things out. It does give us a grid to search."

A large pickup truck pulled into the storage facility. He heard Nikki draw in a breath.

They waited.

Gabriel turned around, checking down the alley behind them, but it was clear.

The Bluetooth rang through the speakers.

Gabriel clicked the answer button on the steering wheel.

"You there?" he asked.

"Yeah."

"What unit?"

"4315. Don't be seen."

"This isn't our first rodeo."

Nico hung up on them.

As much as Gabriel wanted to run in there, he waited. The pickup truck emerged and turned toward the gas station. He held his position until the vehicle ambled around the corner, out of sight.

He gassed it, shooting across four lanes of traffic and into the storage facility. They bypassed the first three rows and turned down the fourth. Partway down, a rolling door was raised about a foot. The number painted above it was 4315.

Gabriel shifted the car into park.

"Stay here for a second." He released the seat belt.

"Gabe—"

"If you were a dude, I'd still say we shouldn't both walk in there, so please. He's spoken to me. He's expecting me. If it's not a trap, you come, too. Leave the car running."

"Fine."

"Is that a woman fine, or a *fine* fine?"

"Gabriel, go. Stop wasting time." Nikki rolled her eyes.

"Then it was a fine." He got out of the car and drew his handgun. There was nothing to trust about this Nico. He approached the partially open door from the side. "Nico?"

"Open the door, slowly."

Gabriel used his toe and nudged the rolling gate upward, holding his breath. He grabbed it with his left hand and lifted it the rest of the way, gun trained on the man with a shotgun in hand.

"Is that any way to say hello to your new friend?" Gabriel asked.

"You aren't a Fed. Who are you?" Nico had a white-knuckle grip on the gun.

"Easy." Gabriel held up his firearm. Nico was scared. A glance told Gabriel Nico was no joke. His hard exterior was genuine, forged in trials of blood. And he was scared.

"Who. Are. You?"

"I'm the Fed." Nikki stepped around Gabriel, unarmed saved for her credentials. "Special Agent Nikki Gage."

"Gage?" Nico's brows drew down and he gestured for the badge.

Nikki tossed the slim wallet at him and backed up.

Nico stared at the document long enough for sweat to begin beading on Gabriel's brow.

"Why does Gage sound familiar?" Nico asked.

"My father is Deputy Director Gage."

"Shit." Nico slapped the wallet down on a set of low shelves and turned, pointing the shotgun at the ground.

Gabriel drew an easier breath and stepped in front of Nikki.

"So we talking or you done?" he asked.

"You're the real deal?" Nico turned abruptly, but didn't lift his gun.

"Yes, we're the real deal," Nikki replied.

"What about him?" Nico nodded toward Gabriel. "He's a street racer. His crew deals drugs."

"Don't worry about that," Gabriel replied.

"I have to worry about all of this, don't you get it?" The tendons on either side of Nico's neck stood out. The man was operating with a hair trigger.

"Ever heard of a thing called undercover work?" Gabriel asked.

"Fine. Okay. So, what did you want to talk about?" Nico set the shotgun down on one of the long metal shelves that filled the storage unit. Boxes, bottles, and large barrels filled of God only knew what.

"Why'd you agree to meet with us?" Nikki asked.

Nico shrugged.

"Anything to do with Wilson having your daughter?" Gabriel asked.

Nico flinched and glared at Gabriel. "How do you know that?"

"I didn't," Gabriel replied.

"He has her? And her mother?" Nikki asked.

"Yeah." Nico stared off in the distance, as if he were somewhere else.

"Why?" Nikki asked.

"Because I said no when he offered me a job. So he made sure I couldn't refuse the offer again." Nico's smile didn't reach his eyes.

"We want to stop Wilson. We could use someone like you to help us," Nikki said.

Nico shook his head. "I help you, they kill her. No."

"What if we could get your daughter?" Gabriel asked.

Nico paused. His gaze sliced toward Gabriel. "Her name is Becky. Her mother is Sarah. She's only eight."

"Can you tell us anything about where they're holding Becky and her mom?" Nikki asked.

"Yeah. There's a few others with them. Wilson has about six of us he's blackmailed into this shit storm he's created. They've all got someone there. He calls whoever is holding them once a day, and one of us gets to talk to our family. There's two women that answer. Hillary and Isabella."

"Shit," Gabriel muttered. Hillary. Again.

"What can you tell us about the people Wilson has working for him? What his plans are?"

Nico held up his hand. "You get Becky, I'll answer all your fucking questions. Time's up. You gotta go. They're going to come back soon."

Gabriel nodded. It wasn't the time to press their luck.

"Come on," he said to Nikki. "We'll be in touch, Nico."

Nico waved and started grabbing things off the shelves at a furious pace. Gabriel hated climbing back into the Skyline, leaving Nico to collect the materials to create some monstrosity. Wilson was willing to blackmail Nico to get use of his abilities. There were any number of guys these days who could Google and become self-taught bomb makers. But that wasn't what Wilson wanted. Whatever the plan was, they needed someone with skills far beyond that of a common explosives junkie. Leaving Nico there went against Gabriel's gut instinct. What other option did they have?

They got out of the storage facility via a back entry, dialing Emery as they made their exit.

"What?" Emery snapped.

"Trouble?" Gabriel asked.

"Everyone wants something. I can't do it all."

"Well, whatever anyone else wants you to do gets put on hold. We've got a squealer."

"I'm listening."

"Nico's being blackmailed into helping Wilson. Wilson has his kid and the kid's mom. Says Hillary and a woman named Isabella are holding them. We need to find this Isabella and where they are. Once we have the kid, Nico will help us. He could be our ticket to shutting this thing down."

"There isn't an Isabella in Hillary's family."

"Is there an Isabella with a rap sheet?"

"At least a couple dozen."

"Okay, so how about one with ties to the Cubans? Hillary runs drugs for them, so maybe it's an organizational tie."

"This will take time."

"Go."

The line went dead.

"What do we do now?" Nikki asked.

"It's getting late. We need to eat something. We're going on empty. I say we get some gas, go back to the house, and let Emery do his job. That way when we have a lead, we're ready to move. It might not be until the morning, though."

"Sounds good to me."

"Okay, let's go hit the hay."

The hay wasn't all he was hoping to hit.

Chapter Eighteen

Nikki opened the garage door a few inches, just enough to see Gabriel's bent shoulders as he went through a regular cleaning exercise with his Desert Eagles. There was something calming about the actions. Everything fitting where it went. Knowing that when your life depended on the trigger, it wouldn't misfire.

Watching Gabriel was a joy by itself. He was different from other men. His movements weren't always the most efficient, but they were . . . fluid. Graceful in the way of a stalking predator. She'd failed to respect that years ago. He would never be typical. Aiden might go back to civilian life when his time was up, but Gabriel would always need to help people. It was part of who he was.

"Coming in?" Gabe asked without looking at her.

"How long did you know I was there?" She entered the garage and pulled the door shut behind her.

"The back door scrapes as it opens, so three minutes?" He turned his upper body, but never took his eyes off what he was doing. "What did you find out?"

"Wilson's mother really is dead. I had the ME pull her autopsy. Looks like someone killed her brutally."

"Think it was Wilson?"

"Maybe? He hadn't shown this kind of brutality yet, but maybe this is who we're dealing with now?" And that was a terrifying thought.

"Anything else?"

"Yeah. We were able to pull the card number from the gas station Nico's buddies went to. Emery hacked the account and is tracking the last two weeks' worth of purchases. We have a better map of their activity now that we know more names. Want to see it?"

"Sure." He drew the one word out for several seconds, never once looking at her.

Nikki watched his hands fly, fitting the gun back together and laying it on the waist-high table built against the side of the garage. He wiped his hands and turned toward her. No matter how many times she saw him, the first hit of his eyes on her made her tingle in all the right places. But that was for later. Right now was work.

She held her tablet out and showed him a map of Miami, with digital pins overlaying it.

"Black pins are the family members of people he's recruited." She tapped the one they already knew represented David Swiss.

"That's a lot of people. He must have been recruiting heavily here. Why?"

"My guess? The drugs." She tapped a blue pin. "These are drug related. Busts. Known dealers. He's producing a lot more than we realized, and thanks to their particular blend of ingredients, we can reasonably link all of this to him. Now, we know the waterfront location was where he made it, but the cops busted another location a few weeks ago Matt thinks was also theirs. These guys set the place on fire and bailed, so there wasn't much evidence, but he thinks that was their distribution center."

"Damn. For once, I want a case with no drugs. How does his Kentucky base fit in?"

"Remember David talking about Keith? Matt was able to pull more information about him." She flipped to the encrypted PDFs. "Keith White is from Miami. Judging from his arrest records, he must have been in the same militant cell with Wilson. My theory is that they struck up some sort of twisted friendship and moved on to start their own thing before that cell got raided. Keith does have a violent record, but nothing as brutal as what happened to Wilson's mother. The Kentucky property? That belonged to the family of another militia member who died, which is probably why they pulled up stakes and left for Miami."

"So what are we thinking? They pull back to Kentucky, organize there, but have the secondary operation running down in Florida?"

"I bet they indoctrinated people in Kentucky. Made them think they were getting ready to go to war, then dumped them here and the switches flipped. It's a stretch, but I think we're starting to get the bigger picture."

"Isn't it ironic that he wants to wake people up, and at the same time he's making a drug to just fuck them up?"

"You're right, but there's often gaps in logic with these groups. They want to achieve their end goal so badly that they're willing to overlook the means to getting there."

"What are the rest of the pins on the map?"

"Oh. Yellow are any incident that the cops recorded in the last six months with one of Wilson's group. If we follow with the theory that the most accidents or crimes happen in a five-mile radius from where they're located, we can draw a circle around each grouping of crimes to one, determine where they might have a base, and two, to figure out which crime or accident doesn't fit the pattern of our profile."

"And they're either looking to get something at these places—or scope out a location."

"Exactly what I'm thinking."

"It's progress."

"We're stretching things."

"Maybe, but it's a good theory. Any word yet on Isabella or Hillary?"

"Not yet, but I had another thought there. Not a good one, but . . ." Nikki bit her lip.

"What?"

"Use me as bait."

Gabriel stared at her. His lips thinned and his gaze had a hard quality that would have intimidated her if she wasn't positive of her actions.

"She's angry because I killed her brother, but she doesn't know who I am. She knows it was someone in your car. So use me as bait to draw her out."

"How would I do that?" His tone was cold, but she refused to fidget under his scrutiny.

"I don't know. The car-racing network?"

"Not happening."

She opened her mouth to protest.

"No one in this crew will back a plan like that. We've been down that road. Madison was kidnapped and it led to an ugly standoff. A lot of people got killed. Kathy was killed when the hit team tried to take Tori. We just have a bad history with our people being bait."

"But those were accidents. Unintentional. If we controlled how she found out and where she came to 'find' me, it wouldn't turn out like that."

"And what if she brings Wilson's people with her? Or her brother, Jesse? Andrew was a hothead and stupid. Hillary is high half the time. Jesse? You don't want him involved. He's street smart, and even the Cuban gangs here in Little Havana leave him alone. That tells me all I need to know about him."

"Okay, okay. It was an idea. I just wanted to suggest it."

"We discussed it. And it has nothing to do with it being you. I would be opposed to hanging any one of our own out as bait. We aren't like that."

She held up her hands. "I'm not arguing with you. If that's the call you want to make, I'm good with it."

He stared at her a moment longer before nodding. His hands unclenched and the lines around his mouth softened.

"Heard from anyone else? I've only spoken to Emery and Matt." She leaned against the workbench and relaxed.

"Aiden is still incommunicado, but Emery said he got a confirmation of receipt on some texts, so he's at least seeing them. We're trusting that he's just taking Madison's security very seriously. This would be a great time for someone to try to snatch her."

"I hadn't thought of that. We could arrange a protective detail . . . ?"

Gabriel shook his head. "She'd shake them and go right back to Aiden."

"Okay, so we leave them be. What about Julian, John, and the twins?"

"The twins are helping Emery. I get the feeling Roni is ready to split. Julian and John spent the day checking locations, scouting a couple sites for events that are coming up, and drove down to the Homestead track. We're the only ones seeing any action."

"Because we made ourselves targets."

"True."

"Well, we're the best equipped to deal with this, so that's probably a good thing."

Gabriel laughed and slapped his thigh.

"What?" she asked.

"You."

"What about me?"

"Just—" He straightened and wiped the smile off his face. "If they're going to shoot at someone, it should be us."

"Am I wrong?" She couldn't help chuckling at his impression. To anyone else that statement would be crazy.

"No, I just . . . nothing." He shook his head, smiling a bit.

"What?" She pushed his shoulder. It felt good to not have to be so restrained with him. It was liberating. Sure, it could come back to bite her in the ass, but when things worked between them, it was great.

"I just like working with you again."

She gulped as the warmth inside her rose a couple of degrees.

"I was just thinking the same thing." She fought back a tremble at the admission. Around other agents she couldn't admit something like that, but Gabriel was part of her.

"Where do you think we'd be now if I hadn't left?" His question extinguished any rising desire. Oh the bitter memories.

"I . . . don't know."

Together still. Married. A kid on the way. Or shattered, husks of the people they once were because they couldn't let go and they couldn't change when they were too busy propping each other up.

"I don't think we would have both fit in your apartment." One side of his mouth hitched up in a devastating smile.

She had to pause to remember that apartment. She'd moved out of it years before.

"Maybe not, but it would have been cozy." She didn't point out that him moving in with her wouldn't mean more than a few weeks here and there spent with her. His undercover work was often long-haul stints.

"Cozy. That's a cute word for cramped." His smile spread and her knees seemed to lose all ability to hold her upright.

"It wouldn't have been for long." She leaned her elbow on the workbench to keep herself standing.

"You moved. You told me that."

"I did."

"Remind me, where are you now?"

"I moved into DC not quite a year ago."

"DC? Man."

"Yeah. I guess I glossed over that detail. When we started this division it was decided we would be in the DC metro area. It's different."

"I must have missed that detail. I wasn't exactly ready for you to just step back into my life."

"Should I apologize?" Did he not want her here? He could *not* want to love her, just like she'd tried a million times to stop.

Gabriel took a step toward her and closed the distance. He cupped the left side of her face, pushing his fingers into her hair, and bent his head.

"No."

His nearness drove whatever thoughts she should be having out of her head. All the neat mental piles of information went up in a puff of smoke when all she could see was him.

"Sometimes I think about what life might have been like if we'd stuck together. If I'd pulled my head out of my ass, got some help. I wonder if we'd still be together. I like to think that we would."

She lifted her hand and splayed it on his chest, because when he was this close, why not indulge in the feel of him?

His heart beat under her palm. She heard the whisper of his confession in the back of her mind.

Oh, God. He had no idea she'd understood him earlier. It was always Gabriel taking that first step, leading her down the path. She hated her paralysis when it came to things of a romantic nature. Maybe it was something bred into her by her mother's cold, callous approach to matrimony, or maybe it was just her. How she was wired. But she could choose to change.

"I speak Spanish," she blurted.

Gabriel frowned a little and blinked.

"*Hablo español con fluidez. Aprendí cuando te fuiste.*" She gulped and forced herself to look at him.

His brows drew down, making him look more confused. She saw the moment the realization hit him. It was a completely unshuttered sucker punch she saw play out in his eyes, the slack-jawed surprise. All of it.

"When?" he asked.

"I started learning about six months after you left. I'm fluent, or mostly fluent. I understand everything you say." Okay, so learning had been useful. She'd interacted with a lot more Latino assets, and not needing an interpreter was invaluable. But she'd also learned because of him. Because she was a sap and making that effort had somehow, in her twisted inability to let go, made him closer to her.

"Everything?"

"*Me dijiste que me amabas mucho.*"

"You heard that." His Adam's apple bobbed.

"I did. I just . . . it didn't occur to me that I hadn't told you already."

"Okay, then." He glanced away and she felt the atmosphere change. It was cold. As if he'd already decided what she was going to say and didn't want to hear it.

"I didn't know what to say . . ." She clasped her hands

together and wiggled her toes. Her insides squirmed. This was not a conversation she wanted to have, but it had to happen. "It didn't seem like the time to have a discussion about *it* and . . . I didn't know what to say. You know how I am. I have to think about things. I need to wrap my head around how to respond. I'm not good in the heat of the moment like you are."

"It's okay, we can just—"

"It's not okay, Gabe. Stop cutting me off. I'm trying here." She pressed her fingertips to her temples. The door wasn't shut between them. There was a small chance that something good could still happen. "I hate that it's taken four years for us to get back together. I wish I'd have come seen you sooner, but I think we needed time apart. You've changed. I've changed. But we're still the same people we were. Leaving was the best thing you could have done for yourself, and I hated you for leaving me because . . . because I loved you and I was scared shitless without you. When you left, a piece of me was gone, and I feel like some days, the only thing that keeps me going is the job. That's no way to live. You showed me more than that, and I still miss you."

What was she saying? She was circling the drain on this one, pouring out all the words, and none of them were what she needed him to know. Nikki took a deep breath and stood a little straighter. He'd told her he loved her, she could put a little of herself out there for him.

"I've slept in your shirt at least once a week since we broke up. I've never really gotten over you. I don't think I stopped loving you. Ever. So when you said that . . . I couldn't think. I didn't know how to get it out. I can't express emotion like you do. I'm just not wired that way and I know it annoys you, but I can't help it."

"What do you feel now?" he asked.

"Right now? Fear. I'm scared. What if telling you how I feel means . . . I don't know. Something bad will happen? I don't like being afraid, but if you've taught me anything, it's that fear shows us what we really want."

"What is it you want?" He was so quiet, his exterior stony and unreadable, but the undercurrent had changed.

She stared him in the eye.

Now or never, right?

"You," Nikki replied.

Chapter Nineteen

Gabriel took a small step toward her and grasped her hand.

"I'm right here," he said, squeezing her fingers.

She smiled weakly and clung to him. It was that or fall on her face. Her legs were jelly and her head was spinning. For five years she'd held on to that secret, never uttering those words out loud.

"I know." She reached for his other hand, needing that contact and his reassurance. He was still there. "And . . . I love you. It doesn't make sense or fit any of the boxes in my life, but I love you, very much. You should probably remember this because I'm actually talking about feelings."

He laid a finger across her lips and she stopped talking.

"Remember our deal? You tell me what you want and I make it happen."

She nodded. Their candid conversation last night was a little hazy, but the important parts had stuck in her mind.

"I've always loved you, too. I just never thought I'd hear you say it in quite so many words."

Nikki blew out a breath that turned into a nervous chuckle. Her palms were damp with sweat and her knees nearly knocked together. He was worth it, but she didn't know if either of them could pay the price. Right now all that mattered was hearing him say those little words to her face.

He bent his head. She held her breath, waiting. His lips brushed across hers, his skin blazing hot. She kissed him back, clinging to his arms, pressing closer. A heady rush of adrenaline pumped into her system.

She'd told him she loved him, and he'd said it back.

How many times had she dreamed this moment? It wasn't perfect, but this was them.

"Speak Spanish to me," he whispered against her lips.

"What?"

"I've never heard you speak Spanish. I want to hear you say something."

"*Te he extrañado.*"

"You already told me you miss me." He looped one arm around her waist and pulled her against him.

"*Te amo muchísimo.*"

His gaze darkened and a tremor of awareness shook her. She'd both forgotten and remembered the hunger that always seemed to be there. Gabriel had a voracious appetite.

She licked her lips. Between them, he was the initiator, but she'd changed. She'd never be as bold as he was, but she had a voice now.

"Would now be a bad time to say I want you?" Her head was buzzing too much to even attempt another language right now. English would have to do.

Her nipples brushed his chest; she felt his jeans against her thighs. He lifted his hands to her face, fingers stroking the little hairs at her temple that never behaved.

"It's never a bad time," he said.

He swooped down, pressing her back against the workbench, and kissed her. Devoured her was more like it. His tongue thrust into her mouth, rubbing against hers. He

shoved his knee between her thighs, rubbing her already
sensitized sex. She gripped his shirt with both hands and
wished she could just rip it off him already so they could
be skin to skin.

She loved him. And he loved her. She'd suspected it
before they broke up, but having the freedom to say those
words intensified the emotion swelling within her breast.

He loved her.

Gabriel leaned into her, bending her almost backward
over the table. He trailed kisses down her neck, across her
collarbone. His calloused finger traced the neckline of
her tank top, and suddenly her clothes were too confining.
She needed them off.

He covered her breast with his palm and she stopped
breathing. She even stopped thinking. He gently squeezed
and lifted the full mound.

"Oh, God," she muttered under her breath.

"Close enough." Gabriel's voice had gone deep, until it
had more in common with a growl.

"Not funny."

Nikki scrambled to get a hold on him, but he was so
toned all she got were handfuls of his damn shirt. It was
just getting in the way. She yanked the garment up to his
armpits. For a second Gabriel just looked at her, and she
wondered if he was going to let her have her way or not.

He took a half step back, grasped the hem of his shirt,
and whisked it over his head. Her mouth went dry. Sure,
she'd gotten up close and personal with him a few times,
but she still found pleasure in looking at him. He was a
hard man, but life had made him that way. She loved everything about him. The tan lines where he went from light
to dark, the scars, the body honed by a tough life, and
the smile lines that would only grow more pronounced
with age.

"Nikki." He closed the distance and pinned her to the bench with his hips. "Don't look at me that way."

"What way?" She flattened her palms against his chest and slid them down, over his ribs and abs, luxuriating in the feel of him.

"I need you out of this shirt. Now."

She lifted her arms and he pulled her tank top off. There was no awkwardness or shyness about her partial nudity. Not when he'd seen so much of her before. Not when she'd already revealed the most private part of her heart to him.

Gabriel sealed his lips over hers and splayed his hand over her back, covering the catch of her bra. She held on to his shoulders and barely registered the moment when he unfastened the plain white garment. She shrugged the straps off and the bra fell between them. Her nipples puckered despite the warm temperature. Sweat trickled down her spine and she could already feel tendrils of hair sticking to her neck and face.

"We aren't going to make it inside," he warned, his lips never once leaving hers.

She grinned against his mouth. Were they supposed to? Beds were overrated.

He backed up, pulling her after him. There was mischief in his gaze and the twist to his lips.

What was he up to?

She grasped his biceps and slowed her pace. The scratched-up GTO was right behind him.

"Gabe—"

He pivoted with her. She yelped and a thrill of adrenaline mixed with arousal shot through her body. She braced her hands against the hood of the muscle car behind her, halfway resting against it. Her heart pounded in her throat. A dozen different scenarios played out in her head. He stared at her and she licked her lips.

What next?

Gabriel took one step closer, his knee between her thighs. His chest brushed her breasts and she shivered. Nikki lifted her chin, eager for a kiss that never came. Instead, he grasped the waistband of her shorts and yanked them down over her hips, dragging her panties with them.

She perched on the hood of the car while Gabriel stripped her of everything but her boots. The rational part of her brain said she shouldn't do this, but she was done listening to that part of herself, at least for the next half hour.

Gabriel grasped her knees and pushed them open. He kissed her knee and inner thigh.

Butterflies swarmed in her stomach. Okay, so maybe she would never be as bold as him, but she was coming around.

He cupped her mound and slid his fingers into her, curling them to rub against the walls of her vagina. Sparks of color blossomed behind her eyelids and she gasped.

It felt so good.

But not as good as he did.

Gabriel withdrew his hand and stood, taking a step back. She pried her eyes open and watched him swipe the back of his hand across his mouth. The hardness was back. And not just in his jeans.

"Turn around," he said.

She'd been wondering when he'd demand that. All her life, her bubble butt drew the wrong kind of attention. She'd hated that part of her anatomy. But Gabriel changed how she thought about herself.

She turned and braced her hands on the car, swallowing down the same old nerves that clamored in the back of her mind. Nothing could ruin this moment. It didn't matter what anyone had said a hundred years ago about her ass. What mattered was this compassionate, funny man found her attractive, and he had a thing for her butt.

Gabriel smoothed his hands over her hips, down over the globes of her ass, and squeezed them. She drew in a deep breath and closed her eyes. She was a Plain Jane, and yet she turned him on. That was something, right?

Heat and pressure.

Gabriel bit the curve of her bottom.

Nikki yelped and would have jumped had he not had her captured between him and the car. He let go almost immediately and chuckled. Okay, it wasn't the first time he'd bitten her, either, but it had been a while. There was something primal in the way it appealed to her. As if he were marking her as his woman. Sure, the rational, feminist part of her was appalled by the idea, but being his meant he was also hers.

Gabriel smoothed his hand over the mark, the sensation already fading.

"I missed this."

"Me, too." It was hard to speak. Hard to draw breath. The humidity was drowning her, but she wasn't about to stop their forward momentum.

He gripped her ass in both hands and she rocked up on her toes. His thighs pressed to the back of her legs, holding her here. She hated the rough denim. Why couldn't he have gotten rid of his clothes already?

There wasn't a man alive who could do this to her. Desire thrummed in her veins until she thought she might explode.

"Gabe . . ."

"What?"

"I want you now."

Silence.

He let go of her and stepped back. She rocked back to her heels, but didn't look for him. He wasn't about to leave her. She knew he was there.

The gentle rustle of denim was the loudest sound in the garage. She tilted her head to the side, but only saw the wall of his chest as he pressed himself against her. The heat of him seared her backside, all the way to her core. He planted his hands over hers, covering her body, and nuzzled her neck. She could feel his erection against her bottom.

"Here? Like this?" The wicked tones in his voice undid whatever reservations she might have had. When he spoke like that, he blew her world.

"Yes." She rested her head against his shoulder and lifted her hips.

"Shit." He placed one hand against her stomach, arching her back, fitting their bodies together. He buried his face deeper against her neck.

She pushed back against him, wanting more.

"Gabe."

"You know how many times I've thought about you like this? Bent over my hot rod?"

"Is that a euphemism?"

He chuckled.

"It could be." He kissed her cheek and straightened. "Stay right there."

She peeked over her shoulder. Her mouth dried up. Damn, but he was fine. Tanned skin as far as the eye could see. His abs—people airbrushed to get that kind of definition. And he was all hers.

He slid his wallet out of his back pocket and removed a condom. One of the precious three they'd bought that morning. She missed the days when they didn't have to pause for that, but there was too much on the line to indulge in that kind of thing. She couldn't trust the cycle calendar that she wasn't pregnant already. Until they knew for sure, until this case was wrapped up and they could figure out what the next step for them was—if there was anywhere to go—this was their new normal.

He turned toward her, one side of his mouth twisted up, and winked at her as he rolled the condom on. Heat crawled up her neck. She would probably never get over all of her shyness, but she sure as hell enjoyed looking at him.

Gabriel leaned over her again, one hand on her hip. Their noses bumped and her heart clenched.

"God, you're beautiful," he whispered.

It wasn't the most dignified position, and yet, the way he looked at her, the reverence in his voice, she felt it. To the tips of her toes, she was beautiful. For him.

She spread her fingers wider, bracing herself on the car. There was no need to tell him what she needed. Not now. Not when their bodies were so in tune. Gabriel squeezed her hip with one hand and guided himself to her entrance with the other. He gently pressed into her, sinking a few inches into her channel.

"Oh . . ." She scooted her legs open wider and pushed back, closing her eyes as the intrusion stretched her. It had been so long since she'd been with anyone. Their hurried coupling had left her a bit sore, but in the best way possible.

"Easy," he muttered.

He pulled almost all the way out of her and pushed back in. It was good, but not entirely right. She eased down to her elbows, bracing herself fully against the car. Gabriel grabbed a handful of her hair and kept the other hand on her hip. This time, he slid deeper, the penetration effortless and right.

"Oh, damn," he muttered.

Nikki moaned. Words were too much effort right now. She laid her cheek against the car and surrendered herself to the feel of his cock moving in and out of her. His balls gently tapped her mound with each thrust. His weight shifted not only her, but the GTO as well. She curled her fingers, but there was nothing to grab hold of against the hood.

The hand at her hip slid around her pelvis. Her breathing hitched and she rocked up onto the balls of her feet.

Oh . . .

His fingers brushed her mound and down over her clit. Electric tendrils of awareness snaked through her body. A pleasant warmth wrapped around her, reducing her muscles to goo and her bones to jelly. He stroked the bundle of nerves again and the sensation grew sharper. She wiggled her toes and clenched her muscles as he thrust.

"Oh, baby," Gabriel said against her ear.

She lifted her hips and this time he stroked and thrust at the same time.

"Oh, oh—Gabe!"

"That's it."

She arched her back and stared at the side of the garage without seeing it. A cascade of pleasure began deep inside her, growing and spiraling up and out of her. His movements became harder, but they never lost the regular rhythm.

He captured her clit between his fingers and rolled it gently.

Nikki tossed her head back and let out a startled shout.

The orgasm was sudden and all consuming, riding up from her toes, rolling up through her body, and robbing her of her senses while Gabriel continued to move in and out of her.

He grasped her ass in both hands while she lay mostly spent across the hood of the GTO. Her breath fogged up the paint, but she doubted he cared about that. The thrusts grew harder, pushing deeper. She pushed up on the balls of her toes, reveling in the feel of him moving inside her. Even now, after she'd come, it felt so damn good.

The sounds of their labored breathing and the slap of flesh mixed together with the creaking of the car. It was an erotic soundtrack, one that would be burned into her mind.

Suddenly, Gabriel pulled out of her.

"Gabe—?" Foggy-headed, Nikki lifted her head.

He grasped her hand and pulled her upright.

"What's wrong?" she asked. Was it her?

"I want to see you." His voice was savage and deep.

He picked her up and sat her on the edge of the hood. The metal bent a little under her weight, but he didn't seem to care. He pushed between her legs and thrust deep all in one motion. They both gasped, and she lost herself in the dark depths of his eyes.

She eased down onto her elbows while he leaned over her, braced on the car. He withdrew and thrust. Her breasts rubbed against his chest and her sex throbbed.

"Gabe," she whispered.

He didn't reply, but he did move, slow at first, then building in power until the car shuddered under each thrust. This was what life with him would be like. He would be there to catch her, to love her, to make her laugh. He was it. All of it. In one hot, hunky package.

Tears pricked her eyes, but she blinked them away.

Gabriel's eyes grew unfocused and the tendons on the side of his neck stood out. She grasped his hips, driving her nails into his skin, urging him on.

All at once the movements stopped and he groaned, burying his head in the crook of her neck. She wrapped her arms around him and kissed the crown of his head.

She could live the rest of her life with him and be happy.

His body relaxed over hers, pressing her down against the hood while they caught their breath. She stroked his shoulders, his arms, feeling the scars she remembered and the new additions. She slowly became aware of other sounds. The neighbors, a lawn mower, children playing somewhere on the street. Had they heard their lovemaking?

Nikki squeezed her eyes shut. Good thing this wasn't actually Gabriel's home. She'd hate to have to see these people regularly after this.

Gabriel moved first. He propped himself up on his elbows and kissed her briefly. She adored the sleepy, sated expression on his face. He eased out of her and shuffled over to a trash can that still had the price tag dangling off one side. She was too boneless to move. She tilted her head to one side and swallowed down the laughter threatening to bubble out of her. Gabriel's jeans and boxers pooled around his ankles. He hadn't even bothered to remove them.

He glanced her way, a lazy grin on his face, and winked again before pulling his clothes back up and on. She sighed. It was probably time to do something else. Something responsible.

"Stay right there," he said.

She froze in her halfhearted attempt to get up and remained sprawled across the car. He crossed to her and gently helped her off the car. They turned and eyed the sweaty outline of her body against the purple paint.

"It's a shame that'll wash off," he said.

"Is not."

She rested her head against his shoulder and reveled in the simplicity of being happy.

"Here," Gabriel snagged his T-shirt and pulled it on over her head. The garment hit her mid-thigh, and honestly, after their little workout, she needed a shower before she put on any more clothes.

"I want a nap. Think there's time for that?" She stretched, looping her arms around his neck.

"One sec, babe, and I'll make that happen." He turned away and grabbed the Desert Eagles on the workbench.

He wouldn't be the man she loved if he absently left guns lying around. Any other woman might be offended that he paused to pack up the tools of his trade, but not her. Their jobs were dangerous, but there were some risks they didn't have to take.

"Anything else?" She hugged the soft fabric to herself. She'd tried to recreate his scent, to capture some essence of it for herself, but she'd never been able to do it. This was all him, and it was wrapped around her now.

"Nope. Just you."

He scooped her up in his arms and carried her into the house. It was a needless show of strength, and yet she adored him for moments like these. When he treated her like she was precious. He might try to protect her too much, but she understood why. Love made all the difference. It didn't make them perfect, but she could forgive him when he went too far.

He laid her down in the bed and set his firearms on the nightstand. She lay on her side and watched him strip down to nothing and join her. She shed his shirt, wanting to feel him. He pulled her to him, wrapping her in his arms.

She loved him. And now he knew. Whatever came next, they'd figure it out.

Chapter Twenty

Gabriel's eyes popped open before he'd actually achieved consciousness. Unlike the numerous times he was awoken, alone, by his memories, this time, there was someone with him. A soft, warm weight held him in place, but it wasn't Nikki who woke him. The low hum of his cell phone sliced through it all, triggering him to action. He uncurled one arm from around Nikki's shoulders and blindly reached for the source of the buzzing on the nightstand.

"Mmm?" Nikki shifted, but didn't move from where she'd sprawled across him earlier. She peered up at him, her lips curled into a sated smile, reminding him that not all that long ago they'd been doing other things.

"Emery. What?" he said into the phone, now fully alert. It was—what? Four in the morning?

"I found her. Isabella. It's really Isabella Lopez." There was tapping in the background. Most likely Emery was still on the hunt for some bit of information that eluded him.

"Where?" Gabriel jabbed the speaker button. Nikki needed to hear this.

Both of them sat up, staring at the phone.

"You won't believe it," Emery said. "Three blocks from your current location."

"Here? In Little Havana?"

"Yeah. Bad news? Guess who Isabella's brother is."

Gabriel's stomach twisted up so tight he could taste bile in the back of his throat. This was worse than bad.

"Shit." He squeezed his eyes shut. "Don't say Miguel Vargas."

"Yup." From the grim sound of Emery's voice, they both knew what this potential tie might mean for them. This operation, and their own, was about to get a lot more complicated if all of the pawns were connected to the same major players in the crime scene of Miami.

"Where are Julian and John? What kind of place is Isabella holding the kid at?"

Nikki stared at him, her brows drawn down and a frown pulling at her lips. She didn't understand the implications yet, but she would. And then they were going to need every FBI gun they could get in the field.

"Tori is calling Julian and John now, then she'll wake Roni up. I'm still digging into the house she's holed up at." Emery would have that information in no time. Gabriel wasn't concerned about that.

"Damn it." He sighed. "I was hoping Hillary and Andrew were the only Cuban connections. If Wilson is working with Miguel, this is going to go to hell fast."

"You're telling me," Emery said. "We'll want to leverage what Matt knows about them. I've noted the increased activity since Evers left town, but nothing specific. They are actively growing their reach since there's no one to compete with them directly at the moment. Not since the Eleventh went away."

"I know. Shit. Send me the address. We're going to drive by. Have the others meet us at . . ." Gabriel rubbed the side of his head, dredging up the address for a twenty-four-hour diner outside the Cuban neighborhood. He rattled it off and hung up on Emery.

"I'm guessing this is bad?" Nikki pulled the sheet up under her arms and leaned against the wall, her legs crossed.

"Yes." Gabriel tossed his phone down onto the bed. "See, when Evers moved into Miami, he eliminated a lot of the competition. Quietly, but once you knew what to look for, it all pointed back to him. Little Havana used to have a lot of gangs, and he effectively cleaned them up. A couple years ago Miguel was just a drug dealer, but he's become more. Especially with Evers out of the way and no competition. Miguel pretty much owns this area. Stores and families pay him a security deposit to ensure their property is safe. His foot soldiers deal drugs to the kids, who in turn get hired or recruited into his organization. He's building. Fast. And no one has been able to curb that yet. Not even the cops."

"If he owns this area, so to speak, why are we staying here?"

"We aren't anymore. Come on. I want to be leaving in five. We will not be coming back here." This safe house was officially off their list. At least until someone did something about Miguel. Which, if he was involved with Wilson, might mean their crew would be the ones to take care of it.

Gabriel got out of bed, making way for Nikki to crawl out after him. As much as he wanted to spend a few moments admiring her, they were in a dangerous situation. God willing, there would be more time together. Later. For now, they got dressed in a matter of moments, shoved clothes and supplies into bags, and were packed up in less time than it usually took him to brush his teeth.

"Ready," Nikki announced.

His phone vibrated. He glanced at the screen and the address.

"Let's split. I've got the location."

He flashed his phone at her as they strode to the door.

They locked up the house and stepped out into a balmy early morning. It was peaceful, the houses dark at this hour and no traffic on the street. They entered the garage without a word, each snagging the few things they'd left there during their interrogation and other activities.

"What are we going to do with the GTO?" Nikki grabbed the clothing he'd torn off her earlier.

"Leave her here for now. I'll tow her back to the garage later." After the memories they'd made on that hood, he was never getting rid of that car.

He opened the passenger door of the Skyline and held it for Nikki.

"Isn't this vehicle too recognizable?" She frowned when he closed the door instead of answering.

He quickly opened the garage door and unlocked the gate before getting into the car.

"Yes, the Skyline is a flashy car. Yeah, someone like Jesse will recognize me in it. But it might save our asses. Miguel has a couple of guys that race, and those are some mean sons of bitches. I'm faster than they are. I've beaten them before. Plus, Hillary is still out there. I'd rather be behind the wheel of something I can trust to outrun them than something that might blend in."

"Okay."

"That's it? Okay?"

"You've got reasons. They make sense, especially after yesterday. I don't want to be in a heavy, slow-moving SUV around these people. I'll trust your judgment. Where are we going?"

He locked the garage and gate behind them before easing out onto the deserted street. Four a.m. was always quiet, but now the silence had an eerie feel. What if Miguel knew where they were? What if he was involved and they were being watched? Gabriel hated that Nikki might have been in danger when he'd told her she was safe.

"What's our objective?" Nikki fired up her tablet, no doubt familiarizing herself with Emery's latest finds.

"Just scoping the place out. Seeing what's around it. If there's any activity." He draped one arm over the steering wheel and reached across to grasp Nikki's hand for a moment.

"Do we know what kind of relationship Isabella and Miguel have?" She glanced at him, and he wished there was more light so he could see her eyes. Her ice-queen routine was gone. Now when she looked at him, he saw volumes she wasn't saying. That he'd never before been able to understand.

"I didn't know about Isabella until now, so I'm guessing they aren't tight." He lifted her palm to his lips and kissed her knuckles, then released her back to her studies.

"You know Miguel?" She pulled her hand back and curled her fingers against her palm, but didn't go back to the tablet just yet.

"He likes cars, so our paths have crossed a few times." Gabriel shrugged.

"Does he race, too?"

"No, he's not the type."

"What type races?" He saw her tilt her head to the side and could imagine her expression, one side of her mouth screwed up into an amused half-smile, her eyes dancing with what amounted to mischief.

"Adrenaline junkies," he replied.

"That makes sense." Nikki chuckled. "What type is Miguel?"

Just the mention of Miguel's name squelched any stray happy thoughts. Miguel had gathered enough power right now to be a threat, and they'd let him because they were too focused on other things. "The corporate criminal type. He's smart. He's young. And he's made a lot of money. He'll want to protect that. The car he drives is for show. Sure, it's kind of fast, but for him it's a statement of his wealth, power, and ability to protect those in Little Havana from gangs who want to move up and take Evers's place."

"But if they want to take Evers's place, doesn't that mean they'd have to knock your crew off the top?"

"Yes."

"Gabe, this is . . . this is a mess. What if stopping Wilson starts a gang war?"

"Then we deal with it. Fast. The Feds would have to step in and stop it. I'm pretty sure the only reason they haven't is because the people getting killed are the bad guys and us."

"I'm going to do some digging later. Nothing about what's going on with your crew is proper procedure."

"It never has been."

"What's Isabella's address?"

"It should be up here on the right." Gabriel slowed down and leaned forward, arms draped over the steering wheel.

"That doesn't look very secure." He could hear the frown in her voice without looking at her.

The white house in question was by far the worst-kept house on the block. The paint was peeling, part of the brick wall surrounding the property was crumbling, and the landscaping was worn down to dirt.

Gabriel breathed a small sigh of relief. "I'm guessing from the looks of things Miguel and Isabella are on the outs. If they weren't, he'd have his guys clean this up. He wouldn't let family live like this. Not when it would reflect badly on him."

"That's good, right?" Nikki glanced at him, but he kept his gaze on the house. There had to be something going on here.

"Yeah, it is."

Gabriel took a right at the next intersection, then a left, and parked the Skyline behind another car lining the street of houses.

"What are you doing?" Nikki asked.

"I'm going to have a look around." He pulled his Desert Eagles out from under his seat and checked the chambers.

"Not without me." She popped her seat belt and groped on the floorboard, probably for her bag.

"Nik—"

"Gabe."

He didn't need the light to see her glare. He could hear it.

"Fine." He sighed. There was no fighting her on this. "We do it together, but let me take the lead. Sound good?" He hated this. For all they knew, Isabella wasn't living in the house and a handful of Miguel's gangsters were. Having Nikki at his back meant making her a target as much as himself, but he knew better than to expect her to stay behind. It was a constant battle he wasn't sure how to navigate.

"Good." Nikki popped her seat belt and got out of the car before he did.

She was the love of his life and she could be pregnant with his child. He wanted to shove her in the trunk and lock her up, but then she'd probably make too much noise and ruin his stealth approach. Besides, she was probably the best person to have covering him if shit went sideways. He still didn't have to like it.

He locked up the Skyline and joined Nikki on the sidewalk. She'd left the tablet in the car for once, but he could make out the bulge of her SIG Sauer pistols under her shirt at the small of her back. He did appreciate a woman who showed up prepared.

Hand in hand, they strolled down the palm tree–lined walk. An occasional car rolled down the street or one of the crossroads, but otherwise it was quiet. In another hour or two people would be getting up, the sky would lighten, and they couldn't do this.

"I'm thinking we approach from the back. The rear neighbor's fence looked low enough to vault over, and I didn't see any floodlights. Thoughts?" He pitched his voice low, for her ears only.

"They had a Beware of Dog sign. Might not be the best in case the dog is out."

"I totally missed that."

"I saw it in the mirror when we turned. My suggestion?"

"Shoot."

"Go through the backyard on the two houses next to it."

"I like the way you think." He grinned at Nikki and was rewarded with a smile. "One condition?"

"What?" The smile vanished.

"I go first. Let me look through a few windows, make sure we aren't walking into a trap or anything. If it's clear, I'll whistle. Before you argue, I'd make the same deal with anyone else. It's—"

"I wasn't going to argue," she said over him.

"Seriously?"

"Yes."

"You've got to be kidding. Arguing with me is your favorite activity." He squinted at her and pulled her closer.

"Is not." She stared straight ahead, but tipped her chin up a bit.

"You sure?" He leaned down until he could smell the hint of whatever fragrance she'd worn yesterday.

"Yes."

"Then what is your favorite activity with me involved?"

She shrugged his arm off, or tried to. He wrapped an arm around her back, keeping her close to his side.

"Let's focus on work." She chuckled and pushed at his chest.

"I am focused." He grabbed her hand again. "Let's see, what do I think you like best?"

"Gabe, be serious." She squeezed his hand.

"I am being serious." He tugged her closer again and pitched his voice lower. "I'm also making us look—and sound—less suspicious."

"By talking about activities?"

"Yes."

"You're crazy." She shook her head.

"And you love me."

Nikki sputtered, and damn if his heart didn't do a little flip. She wasn't denying it, though she wasn't yet comfortable with the declaration. There was always the chance she was professing love as some sort of a ploy to use him, but that wasn't the Nikki he'd come to know. She'd changed, but not that much. Deep down, she was the woman he'd fallen for years before. The deck was still stacked against them, but he'd figure out how to make it work. There had to be a way.

"Everything looks quiet. I'll wait there for you." Nikki gestured to the darker shadows cast by several tall palm trees up against the corner lot's fence.

They slowed as they reached the agreed-upon spot.

Getting over the fence would be a quick leap, then a fast dart across the yard.

"I don't see any motion detectors or lights," Nikki said.

"Me either. See you on the other side." He turned and captured her face with both hands. He kissed her, hard, fast, and quick. The sound of her gasp spurred him on as he vaulted the wrought iron and landed in thick grass.

This was the best night ever.

Nikki followed Gabriel's movements through the shadows, but her mind was mush. He couldn't kiss her like that anymore. At least not when they were in the field. Now all she could think about was the way her body tingled, remembering every place those lips had been lately. Her head really needed to be here, now.

She glanced up and down the street, but all was clear.

It was too easy. And she didn't like that. She couldn't shake the sense of unease, that something wasn't right about it all.

For one, she and Gabriel had been just down the street. She didn't like coincidences. In her line of work, coincidences meant someone had screwed up and the bad guys were closing in.

Gabriel leapt into Isabella's backyard and hunched, hands on the ground. She held her breath.

Nothing happened.

Her lungs began to burn, but she didn't draw breath yet.

Gabriel rose and crossed to the side of the house, peering into a window. He reached for his gun and she wanted to grab hers, too. She tore her eyes from him and turned, taking in the still-quiet street. A few houses had lights on now, rising with the sun as it cast the horizon a dark gray.

A bird call startled her. She turned and Gabriel gestured, waving at her.

That was her signal.

She stepped up onto the brick retaining wall and vaulted over the wrought iron sticking out of the masonry into the first yard. The grass cushioned her steps, muting them while she made her way to the next fence. A light switched on deep inside the house, casting the outer rooms with a bit of illumination.

Crap.

Nikki hustled over the fence, crouched low, and ran across to the second. She used a flower box to boost herself up over the mostly brick wall into Isabella's backyard.

Gabriel had his face pressed up to the sliding glass doors, hands on either side of his eyes.

"What is it?" she asked.

"Looks empty."

She glanced into the windows as she crossed to him, and sure enough, the rooms weren't furnished much, if at all. In fact, dust and cobwebs covered most of the glass, and what she could see inside was mostly overturned.

"I'm going to try to get a window open. Think you can get in there and let me in?" Gabriel asked.

"Easy." Granted, they didn't have a warrant or any sort of legal reason for being there, but she was fast learning how Gabriel's crew operated.

"Cool."

He went to the next window that looked into what should have been an eat-in kitchen. Even the refrigerator was gone. It was clear no one had lived here in some time. He grabbed the bottom of the window and hoisted it up. The window groaned in the casing, but rose slowly. He got the window up most of the way before it refused to budge anymore. It was plenty of room for her to squeeze through.

Nikki bent double and leaned through the opening with her phone out and the flashlight activated, searching for traps, a trip wire, anything, but there was nothing. At least in this room.

"How's it look?" he asked.

"Good. Hold this." She gave him her phone and maneuvered her leg through the window. She rolled her weight onto her right foot and stood up, only partially in the house.

Still nothing.

She held out her hand for the phone and pulled her other leg through the window.

"I'm going to look around. Stay there," she said.

To Gabriel's credit, he didn't protest the order, despite it being contrary to what he'd said before. There was something off, and before they both entered the premises, she wanted to be sure that there wasn't a trap waiting for them.

She drew one of her pistols, and armed with her light, she edged through the open archway into the rest of the house. Each room was more of the same. Dusty. Haphazard furniture arrangements, mostly on their side or turned over. No personal touches. And most importantly, no traps waiting for them.

Nikki holstered her gun in her waistband and let Gabriel in through the sliding glass door.

"It's clear." She nodded over her shoulder. "I'd like to do a room-by-room check, look in the closets, see if there's anything I missed. This doesn't feel right."

"I know. Let's do it fast."

He strode to a hall closet and opened it.

More nothing.

"Emery said the phone was routed here," Gabriel said.

"It's a landline, but that still doesn't mean they're here. Besides, if I were Wilson and if I wanted to blackmail highly trained solders into doing my shit, I'd be careful, too. I get the feeling Nico wouldn't mind killing Wilson."

While Gabriel checked the hall bathroom, Nikki stepped into the master bedroom and took a slow stroll around, examining the walls for places where they'd been patched and the fixtures for bugs and hidden cameras. She touched a cream-colored phone cord running out of a phone jack, stapled to the wall, and going into the master closet. She opened the door and stared. "Gabriel. Call Emery."

"What is it?" He stepped up behind her, crowding her into the walk-in closet.

A nest of wires and boxes with flashing lights was mounted to the wall.

"That. That's our landline." He pointed at a phone wire. He aimed his light at it.

He squeezed past her and followed the cords with his fingers, tugging on one, caressing another. She followed the path of his hands, familiar enough with the tech to know what they were looking at.

"They're bouncing the line somewhere else. This is pretty sloppy." He grimaced and she resisted the urge to smile. Gabriel might not be a field tech per se, but the man could make some seriously handy devices in a pinch.

"I'll send some pictures to Emery. Hopefully he can figure out where it's going." She snapped a dozen from different angles, catching make, model, and serial number where she could, and sent them off.

"Well, this makes me feel better," he said.

"Why?"

"If it was this easy, I'd be worried we were missing

something big, but this tells me we're on the right path. Also, the Cubans might not be involved, which is a relief."

Nikki's phone vibrated with an incoming call. She answered it and switched it to speaker.

"That was fast," she said.

"It's old school." Emery tapped away in the background.

"Well, what can you tell us?" Gabriel asked.

"I called the number," Emery said.

"You what?" Nikki's heart jumped to her throat.

"It went to a standard voice mail recording. With a phone number registered to Isabella. It's her cell phone. She's routed the landline directly to her mobile," Emery explained.

"See? Sloppy work." Gabriel shook his head.

"Okay, where is she?" Nikki asked.

"No clue. At least not until the phone is turned on. Isabella's online presence is . . . it makes my head hurt. When Tori gets up I'll have her look at it. She might understand it better than me."

"No location data?" Gabriel asked.

"None." Emery grumbled something under his breath. "I have to give her credit for that. Most people these days make it easy to tell where they've been or where they are. She at least has that under control."

"Okay. Let's get out of here. You have an eye on this phone?" Gabriel ushered her out of the closet.

"I do. I'm making it official and putting in a request for the phone records of both lines, but I should have everything in a few hours. Just need to crack the database."

"I'm going to pretend I didn't hear that." Nikki shook her head. These guys would be the death of her if she stuck around too long, but she was willing to bet it would be a hell of a time.

"Call us if you get anything," Gabriel said.

She hung up and they finished an unexciting check of the house. Everything else was dusty and unconnected to the case.

"What now?" she asked Gabriel.

"Lock up and leave. I say we grab some food and get ready. Emery's going to find her, and I want to be prepped to move on it as soon as we can." He patted her ass then stepped through to the patio.

Heat crawled up her neck that had nothing to do with the Miami climate.

Chapter Twenty-One

Gabriel handed the hot breakfast burrito through the passenger window. Nikki reached for it without looking, her eyes locked on the bright tablet screen.

"What could you possibly be doing now?" He draped an arm on the top of the Skyline and bent to look over her shoulder.

"My e-mail. I haven't read much of anything since I got here." She unwrapped the food and took a bite before he could warn her it was fresh off the grill.

"Hot?" he asked. It wasn't as drool worthy as yesterday's fare, but it was fresh. With a little hot sauce it would be perfect for his taste.

She glared.

"Anything good?" He tried to keep his tone neutral, but he was dreading the talk of work. He'd leave Miami and the crew for her if they could work things out. She'd said she loved him. There was hope. But he was also skeptical. Her life would have to change, too. He couldn't be the only one giving something up.

"Maybe." She blew out a breath.

"Do I need to know something?"

"No. It's a distraction." She powered off the screen and turned her attention on the food. Without the tablet, her face was layer upon layer of shadows.

"Why not tell me now?" He should drop it, but damn it, there weren't any certainties between them.

"Because I'm trying to not get my hopes up."

Was she trying to get him reinstated? The food suddenly tasted rotten in his mouth.

"I'm not going back to the FBI."

"I wouldn't want you to." Her reply was quick, honest. But she wasn't going to share this secret with him.

Did he trust her? Yes. But he didn't like secrets.

She opened the door and he swung it open, offering her his hand as she rose to her feet. Together they strolled to the concrete wall that separated the sand from the parking lot. It was one of many beach areas in Miami. In a few hours, joggers, shoppers, and tourists would overtake the sidewalk. For now, it was the two of them and the sound of the waves.

"How do we make this work?" He studied her profile, needing some answer. A solution.

"I'm assuming you aren't talking about Isabella, Nico, or Wilson?" She unwrapped the rest of her food and leaned on the hip-high retaining wall.

"You know what I mean."

"I don't know anything for certain, but I want to try." There was a wistful note of hope in her voice he wanted to nurture. She'd given them some thought, and she saw a way.

"You've got a plan."

"Maybe." Now she looked away at the ocean. "It's all up in the air. I don't want to get your hopes up."

But she was working on a permanent solution for them.

The tension knotting his shoulders released, turning into warmth and curiosity.

"Did you mean for this to happen when you came here?"

"No." She answered far too fast. He watched her for a moment longer. "Rationally, no. There was nothing to make me think you would forgive me, or that anything would be different. My best hope was for an amicable understanding. Maybe we could be friends." She turned her head and studied him. "But like I said, I never stopped loving you. My heart, it hoped for this."

"We'll figure something out."

"You think?"

"Do you want to stop now?"

"No."

"Then we'll have to work out a solution. I don't want to give you up again. I've learned from my mistakes. We'll be better this time."

"I'd like that."

"I get that we will never have a normal life, but we could have something."

"You wouldn't like normal. You left the FBI for normal, and look where it got you." She gestured at the beach, but he knew what she meant.

He laid his hand on his chest and winced in jest. It was a truth. Civilian life was something he wasn't cut out for, try as he might. He had the job, the hobbies, and even a few people he might call friends outside of the crew, but it was still part of his identity. Something he would shed in a heartbeat if it meant a life with her.

"What would normal look like for us?" She sat on the wall and took a bite of her burrito.

"I imagine a lot like this. Messy fieldwork, coming home at all hours. I'm going to insist on traveling with you."

"You aren't—"

"Talk to your dad about it. I'm sure he won't be that opposed to his only daughter having a personal bodyguard his people trained."

Nikki glared daggers at him.

"I'm just saying, I want to be near you. Even if that means my new job is you." He was serious at least. She might not like it, but it was a viable option.

"I don't need a bodyguard."

"No, but imagine how useful I could be. Outside the system. I don't have to play by your rules. Think about that." He even liked this solution.

Nikki shook her head. "That would never fly."

"Then what do you have in mind? I know you have a plan."

She chewed her lip. A bit of streetlight glinted off her eyes, making them shine.

"I do, but like I said, nothing is certain right now. I don't want to get your—our—hopes up. But if there is a way, yes, I want to see if this will work. But we are different. We aren't picking up from where we were at back then. Things have changed. I've changed. You've changed."

"You're right."

She was more assertive. Before, she'd have caved to his insistence rather than butt heads with him. He liked it.

"When this is done, we'll figure it out." She took a bite and turned to watch the ocean.

He was satisfied with her answers. At least for now. They couldn't plan things until this op was done and Wilson was behind bars. After that, well, he was keeping her.

"Would it be a bad thing if you were pregnant?" His voice lilted up at the end, try as he may to keep his tone even. God, what would it be like with her as the mother of his kids? They'd have a better life than he had, for sure. He tore bits of the burrito wrapper, taking his nerves out on the paper while he waited for her reply.

"No," she said at last. "Timing isn't ideal, but it wouldn't be the end of the world. That doesn't mean no condoms."

"Hey, I never suggested that." He held his hands up, placated for the moment.

Nikki Gage, mother of his babies. He'd spend the whole pregnancy telling her to take it easy. Then . . . maybe this was the answer. If she was pregnant, they couldn't leave their child with just anyone. He'd be a full-time dad while she stayed on with the FBI. It was a gender swap for sure, but in the long run, if only one of them could be there for 24/7 protection, he was better suited for the job.

"Stop smiling." She pushed his shoulder. "We don't know if I'm pregnant. It's unlikely, you know?"

"Says who?"

"The Internet." She glanced away from him.

"The Internet also says a cat pooped the earth."

"What?" That got her attention. She stared at him like he'd lost his mind.

"I'm just saying, not everything out there is fact."

"All right, what I mean is medical journals, people who study women's cycles, say it's the wrong time for me to get pregnant."

"When is the optimal time?" He took a small step toward her and laid his hand on her stomach.

"We are not ready for a child." Her tone was so no-nonsense. He dug it.

"I'm just saying, it might be a good idea to know these things."

"I have to track my cycle for more than a minute to figure that out." She pushed his hand away.

"Are you open to it?"

"What?"

"Having kids?"

"Yes."

It was his turn to stare at her. He'd always wanted children, but Nikki had never struck him as the nurturing kind. Honestly, he'd never asked, assuming the answer was no.

"What?" she asked again.

"Nothing, just surprised. I thought, with the way you were raised in an FBI family, it . . ."

"It might not be something I wanted?" she finished his thought.

"Something like that." He leaned on the wall instead of touching her as he wanted.

"I want children. More than one. I want their lives to be different than mine, which is why I think now is a bad time. I'm going to be stuck on the road, doing a lot of time away from DC. It would be better if I waited, but if it happens now, I—we—make it work."

"I like the sound of that."

His phone rang, interrupting an otherwise tender moment. He pulled it out of his pocket and his pulse jumped.

Emery.

"Yeah?" he said into the phone.

"I got something. Sending you an address. Isabella has ordered pizza to this house a dozen or more times."

"We'll check it out."

He nodded toward the Skyline. Nikki dropped to her feet and strode for the car. He held back a few paces, appreciating the view. Man, he'd missed that. He opened her door before circling the car and getting into the driver's seat.

"Well?" Nikki asked.

"We have a location. Checking it out now." He pulled up the address on his phone to show it to her and placed it in the cradle.

"Is backup coming?" She reached under her seat and pulled out her pistols, checking that each was loaded.

"Not yet. If we find anything, Emery will send them our way."

"Okay. Is he getting a warrant?"

"Probably not."

"Gabe . . ."

"What? It's not like we work within the law most of the time."

"Yes, but we need one for anything to stick in this case."

"If there's something there, we can get one." He'd grown used to doing things as they pleased that going by the letter of the law chafed.

"I'm calling Matt. Maybe he can get us something?"

"No. Think about how that'll look. Us. The cops. We're already raising too many questions as it is. We can't go that route. Trust me."

"I do trust you, but I want to put Wilson behind bars. There are kids involved, Gabe."

"Fine. Call Matt. Have him meet us there."

They drove the entire way in silence. Nearly half an hour later Gabriel pulled onto the street, melding with early-morning commuters, and passed by the quiet bungalow. It was neat, well maintained, even had a statue of Mary out front surrounded by rosebushes.

"That's where she is?" Nikki leaned forward, peering at the house.

"Possibly." Gabriel pulled around the row of houses until he found the back alley that led to the unending privacy fences and garage entrances.

He parked the Skyline in the empty drive of the house with a For Sale sign out front and checked his firearms.

"What's the plan?" Nikki asked.

"Just looking around. I'll get close, you keep a lookout, okay?" He got out of the car, tucked his gun back in his waistband, and strode for the alley.

"Gabe, what about Matt?" Nikki pitched her voice low, but he still heard her.

"He'll get here when he gets here."

They couldn't afford to drag their heels anymore. He tracked the small sounds of Nikki getting out of the car and following him to the edge of the property without looking over his shoulder.

The alley was quiet in dawn's early light. Most people were still asleep or just waking for the day, so he still had the cover of shadows for this stroll.

The back of Isabella's bungalow was updated with a brand-new fence. He couldn't peek through the boards at all. Which left going over it or through the gate.

"Gabe, no," Nikki whispered right behind him.

"I thought you were staying in the car." He frowned at her.

"I thought you were waiting for backup."

"That was never the plan."

He picked up a wire hanger from the street, bent it, and inserted it through the wooden boards of the gate. Closing his eyes, he moved the hanger by feel until the weight of the lever settled into the crook of the wire. He pulled, adjusting his grip until the one-way door released and swung open.

Gabriel drew his gun and peered around the yard. It was dark, and the shadows could conceal any number of things, but nothing advanced on them. The house was dark, completely still.

"Christ, Gabe, this is a bad idea." Nikki peered around the gate, back the way they'd come.

"Stay here. I'm going to look around." He'd prefer that anyway.

"You are not going in there alone."

Too bad he didn't expect to get his way.

"Fine. Stay close." He stepped into the yard, keeping his eyes on the house.

Three wide steps led up to a deck that let into the house through a set of sliding glass doors that were a primary feature in most Miami homes. He spied a bar on the interior door, wedging it closed. The windows were all dark, the blinds drawn. He kept to the shadows and made his way around to the side of the house.

All of the windows had blinds on them, save one. It was boarded up from the outside. A new tree was planted right in front of it, blocking it from view. Anyone who looked over the fence wouldn't be able to spy the boarded-up window through the leaves.

"Gabe," Nikki whispered.

He held up his hand, gesturing for silence, and crept toward the window. He pressed his ear up against the wood.

Silence.

There was no indication that Isabella was there, and yet his gut said that behind this window were the missing children and their mothers.

He tapped on the wood with his knuckles, keeping it quiet.

The seconds ticked by. He thought he heard a bump from inside the house, but it could easily have been his imagination.

Nikki stood at the corner of the house, glancing at him every few moments. Her nerves ate at him.

A soft, almost inaudible knock echoed his.

Someone was inside.

Someone was answering him.

He placed his palm against the plywood. They were going to get these kids out of there. He walked the rest of the yard, all the way to the fence in front, but the windows were shuttered. There was no outward sign this was where Isabella was, except a feeling. The rest of the houses were all typical suburban homes, except this one. It was the Virgin Mary statue that gave it away.

"Come on, we need to go," Nikki said.

"No, we're going in."

"Gabe—"

"I have a hunch."

She stared at him, and he could feel the inner war. There was something to be said for an agent's hunches. They were what kept him alive in the thick of it and gave him that added edge. This time it said the kids were here.

"What do you want to do?" she asked.

"Go in." He pulled a set of slim rods from his pocket. He'd grabbed them earlier just in case they needed to actually break into the first house.

"Shit. We don't know they're in there."

Headlights turned into the drive, slicing through the spaces between the boards. Nikki must have shut the gate, which was good for them.

He grabbed her arm and pulled her around the corner of the house, listening to the idling of a car. From the whine of the engine, he was willing to bet it wasn't the best-maintained set of wheels on the block. The headlights were too low for an SUV or truck, so it had to be a car. Probably something common, with four doors and a large trunk.

The engine died and he held his breath. The car door clicked and creaked open. Older model, then, probably easier to transport people in the trunk. Some of the older land-shark cars could fit up to four bodies in them. He'd seen a few do just that in his time. The car door closed and a single set of footsteps scuffed the concrete up to the garage. The hum of the automatic opener broke the stillness.

"Stay here." He crossed the yard to the gate and pressed his back to the boards, peering between the slats.

The garage door stopped halfway up and a woman ducked under it. He had the impression of dark hair, a glittery top, and long legs before she was gone.

Gabriel opened the wooden gate, drew his gun, and ducked, going to a knee and sliding under the garage door as it closed. The dim garage held stacks of something.

A cardboard box crashed into him. It was light, but the sudden impact tipped him back. He swept out with his foot, knocking the woman off her feet. He lunged, putting a knee in her chest as she landed on the concrete and setting the gun against her cheek.

"Don't you fucking move," he said. "Isabella?"

"*Vete al carajo.*"

"*También hablo español*, Isabella." The words flowed from him, faster than English. He grabbed her wrist and pulled her arm behind her back, then rose, hauling her up by force. Isabella cried out, no doubt experiencing a little discomfort. He didn't have a lot of pity for a woman who helped kidnap and hold children.

"I won't say anything." She turned her head a bit, glaring at him.

"That's fine. I'm guessing the people you helped kidnap and hold here will be willing to do all the talking." They'd probably bury Isabella, and he'd give them a shovel to do it, too.

The interior door to the house banged open. Gabriel tensed—except it was Nikki, gun up. He ground his teeth. He'd tell her to stay put if he thought she'd listen.

"What the hell?" She relaxed a bit and switched her focus to Isabella. "That her?"

"Think so. Lights?"

Nikki patted the wall. A switch clicked and halogen lights flickered on, buzzing as they filled the packed space with harsh light.

"Oh my God." Nikki lurched down the three steps to the garage floor, her attention on something behind the boxes.

"What?" he barked, not liking to be left out. He pushed Isabella forward. "Move."

She shuffled to the back of the garage where he could see Nikki kneeling next to a woman handcuffed to the wall of the garage. The boxes around her were broken and beaten in. Dry blood flaked off the side of her face, and her clothes had seen better days.

"She alive?" he asked.

"Yes. We need paramedics. Something." Nikki held her fingers on the woman's pulse for several moments.

"Give me your handcuffs."

Nikki pulled her handcuffs out of the messenger bag that had become part of her. They should think about a better method to carry her gear. He was getting the point of how impractical the shorts were, but he was biased. There'd never been a better view than Nikki in those shorts

He relaxed a tiny bit once Isabella sported the new hardware around her wrists,

"We know where Matt is? What's the house look like?" he asked.

"My guess is she's dealing meth out of here. Lots of paraphernalia. Want me to call Matt?" Nikki rocked back on her heels and looked up at him.

"Yes. Isabella and I are going to have a look around the house."

"I'm coming with you." She wedged the phone between

her head and shoulder while getting to her feet. "Hey, Matt. Any chance you're here? . . . You are? We're three houses down. There's a Buick in the driveway. Knock on the garage."

"Please tell me he didn't bring anyone with him." He could see it now, the whole op thrown off the rails by the cops horning in on their action.

"No, just him, unmarked vehicle."

Bang. Bang. Bang.

"It's me." Matt's voice was muffled by the garage, but clearly distinguishable.

Nikki crossed to the switches and toggled the garage door open.

Matt ducked under the door, gun in hand. He glanced around the space, taking in the disheveled boxes and the handcuffed woman glaring at them all.

"Shit. What did you do?" He eyed Isabella.

"Grabbed the competition. Hold her, will you? We need to sweep the house." Gabriel gave Isabella a little shove, propelling her toward the detective. "There's one down over against the wall. She's out cold. I'm guessing someone did a number on the woman."

He glared at Isabella, who stared at the wall, nose up. She might have been an attractive woman, but all he saw was a disgusting, vile person who had no qualms about terrifying innocent children.

"You got this?" he asked Matt.

"Yeah. Go on." Matt took out a second set of cuffs and hauled Isabella over to the wall.

"Come on, Nikki."

"Already ahead of you."

"What the hell? How did you get in so fast?" Last he knew, lock picking wasn't a skill of hers.

"She had one of those plastic stones. You know the ones

you hide keys in? I just let myself in. She didn't wedge that bar in place well enough." Nikki lifted her pistol and walked slowly ahead of him, down the hall back into a sitting area, dining room, and kitchen combination.

The table was covered in plastic with little bits of something here and there. The scent of acetone hung thick in the air.

"Shit. Their meth must not be good quality. That shit reeks." He swiped the back of his hand across his face.

"Something tells me they don't care." Nikki aimed her gun through the open archway into the rest of the house.

"She doesn't have backup here. If she did, they'd have jumped us by now." He flipped on the lights, but kept his gun out and ready.

"The room is back that way." She gestured to a hall they could now see across the living room.

"Let me go first." He stepped in front of her and advanced toward the hall. The hair on the back of his neck rose, and that same sense of foreboding weighed in his gut.

He wasn't going to like what they found on the other side of that door.

"Lights," Nikki said softly.

He nodded.

The overhead fan spun to life, shedding illumination from a single bulb. The house must have been as pretty as the outside once, but the inside was squalor. Trash parked on top of trash. Old pizza boxes. It was, in a word, disgusting.

He walked slowly down the hall, eyes drawn to the door with multiple locks and a chain securing it shut.

Isabella deserved the worst kind of retribution.

"Don't suppose there's a plastic stone for these keys." He opened the last two rooms to ensure there weren't any surprises and almost retched. The second room smelled of old sweat and sex, while something must have been left to rot in the third.

"God, that's disgusting." Nikki coughed.

He closed both doors and returned to the first, holstering his gun and drawing the lock picks back out of his pocket.

"Keep a watch out. We don't know if she has friends nearby," he said. It wasn't unreasonable that another house on the block might house security for this one.

Nikki kept her back to the wall, standing so that she could see the living room and him at the same time. Everything about her posture said she was in control. Damn, it was sexy.

"What happened to just having a look around?" Nikki frowned, but kept her eyes peeled.

"I saw an opportunity to grab her and I went for it."

He fit the picks in the locks and let his awareness shift to the feel of the tumblers against his fingers, the way all the little mechanisms fit together. The first padlock opened and he moved on to the next. Three locks and a chain secured the door. It wasn't even an interior door. Someone had custom-fit an exterior door into the frame. They'd probably thought it was enough.

"Ready?" he said low.

"Yup." Nikki pivoted, directing her gun toward the door.

He knocked on the metal surface.

"FBI, back away from the door." Nikki pitched her voice so it carried.

Muffled sounds inside the room had his gut clenching. What kind of conditions were these kids living in?

He pushed the door into the room and held back, ready to throw himself in front of Nikki if the prisoners were violent. Who knew what living like this had done to them?

A lamp cast light on two women huddled against the wall, next to the window. Four children clustered around and behind them. They were dirty, and from the stench, he was willing to bet they hadn't had facilities or a shower in a while.

"Becky? Becky Silva?" Nikki still had her weapon up.

A little girl with dark eyes and blond hair peeked out from around the women. She was the smallest child by far, and her hair had the same wild curling quality as the woman's in the garage.

"Becky, you're safe." Nikki lowered her gun. She tilted her head slightly toward him. "We need to call this in."

"Come out, guys. We're going to get you help." He stepped into the room and the children shied away from him. What the hell had Isabella done to them?

"How do we know you're really FBI?" a Hispanic woman asked. The oldest child could have been her doppelganger.

"Would you like to see my badge? We're not going to hurt you." Nikki reached into her bag and pulled out the slim wallet that contained her credentials. "I'm Supervisory Special Agent Nikki Gage. What's your name?"

"Where's my mom?" Becky asked. She thrust her chin forward, and damn, but he could see Nico in her already.

"She's with a friend. He's helping her," Nikki replied.

"I want to see her," Becky demanded.

"I'll take you to her." Nikki held out the badge for the woman to look at.

"Do you have an ID card?" The woman barely glanced at the paper.

"I do. That's smart to ask for the badge and ID." Nikki slid the card out from behind the badge and held them up. "We can call the local office, too. We came to investigate a tip thanks to Nico."

"He's working for them," the woman snapped.

"He's also working with us." Nikki's entire focus was on the room of hostages. She exuded security, calmness, and comfort. He couldn't handle the situation with the same kind of grace, so he stepped back and let her lead.

"I want to see Sarah," the woman demanded, yet there were notes of fear in her voice.

"Okay, follow us."

Nikki turned and walked slowly back the way they'd come from the garage. Gabriel followed, though he didn't like having anyone at his back. These people had lived for God only knew how long in this environment. Who knew what they'd do? Hostages weren't his strong point. More often than not, the people he hoped to save were already dead by the time he arrived, so he'd have to trust Nikki. He was just glad they were all alive.

Chapter Twenty-Two

Nikki finished wiping down the kitchen counters, or at least enough to satisfy her need for order for now. The whole house needed bleaching after what had happened here.

The three women and four kids sat around the dining table that had held Isabella's current inventory of meth all of an hour ago. They ate cereal and drank juice, their gazes darting around, as if they suspected someone to shove them back into the prisonlike room.

They'd kept Isabella out in the garage, away from her former prisoners, to help keep them calm. Isabella still wasn't talking, and Nikki didn't expect her to. There wasn't any reason to offer her a deal unless she couldn't help it, and after what she'd seen of the room, Nikki didn't want to offer her a deal.

Gabriel stepped into the doorway, and for half a second all movement ceased. He'd passed some test and everyone continued on with what they were doing with barely a beat missed.

"We need to talk," he said, looking at her.

Nikki crossed the floor to him. Mari, a Hispanic woman, pushed to her feet, glaring at them. Her husband, also former military, was a city engineer. Gabriel merely turned and walked into the living room. Nikki let Mari go first, unsure including her was the right idea, but she'd made it impossible to leave her out.

"What is it?" Mari asked, keeping her voice low.

"You aren't going to like it." Gabriel placed his hands on his hips and glanced at the floor.

"Me, or Mari?" Nikki asked.

"Neither of you are going to like it. Hell, I don't like it."

"Tell me," Mari said.

Gabriel screwed his lips up in a grimace. "My boss is headed here. He thinks our best bet to lure the man who had you kidnapped back here will be to keep you and your kids here." Gabriel grimaced.

Mari's eyes widened and she jabbed a finger in Gabriel's chest. "What? Stay in this place?"

"I know, I know. I want you out of here, too, but let me explain?" He pushed her hand aside.

Nikki tamped down on the urge to push the woman back, off her man. It was a completely irrational thought, but it was stuck in her head. Another thing to figure out how to handle if they were going to continue to work together.

"Wilson rewards your husband for doing what he's been asked to do by calling here and getting Isabella to let you out long enough to talk on the phone for a few minutes. If Wilson can't get a hold of Isabella or you, then he'll know we've been here. Aiden wants to clean this place up and set up here with you, then man the phones to keep Wilson in the dark while we catch him unawares. I realize it's a scary plan, but it's the best we have right now."

"You've been through so much. We realize this is a lot to ask of you, but at most, we're talking about a day or two." Okay, so Nikki didn't know that for sure, but that was what she was hoping for.

"What if they come here?" Mari asked.

"Have they before?" Gabriel asked.

"No. Just the junkies." Mari glanced away, clearly not on board with the plan.

"It would help us put an end to this," Nikki said.

"Fine. I will talk the others into it. But—I get a gun. I have a license. My husband made sure I knew how to shoot. I don't want to be unprotected again."

"I'll see what we can do." Nikki didn't like it, but it would be many sleepless nights before these people were able to rest in peace without waking at the threat of shadows, much less real danger. Besides, Mari had only asked for a gun. Not the bullets.

Gabriel grimaced but didn't protest her decision.

"Let's talk to the others, then?" Nikki gestured at the dining table. Already a little soap and water had improved the morale. The kids chattered and women talked.

Matt stepped into view from the garage. He'd stayed with Isabella on the off chance she'd start to talk.

"Anything?" Gabriel asked.

"Nothing." Matt shook his head.

"Come on, we're going to have a chat." Nikki ushered them all into the dining nook and took a seat.

Matt and Gabriel remained standing, but leaned against the cabinets, doing their best to appear nonthreatening.

"I've agreed to stay here, to help trick Isabella's people into believing we are still captured." Mari laid her hands against the table top.

"What?" Sarah stared at her.

"We will have an FBI agent in the house," Nikki added.

"And there will be an increased police presence," Matt chimed in, jumping onto the plan with zero information.

"You can't be serious," Sarah said.

"I am. And you should be, too. If we don't do this, if they find out we escaped, you think they'll just let us go? We help them. We end this. Then we move on." Mari spoke with authority. She might have never been enlisted like her husband, but the woman had the knack for command.

"That's easy for you to say. It's your husband out there." Sarah leaned forward.

"Watch what you say," Mari warned and glanced at Becky.

Nikki leaned forward, drawing both women's gazes. "Sarah, this is a hard situation and it's tough to understand, but I get where you're at." Nikki clasped her hands in front of her, steeling herself for the sharing of personal details. Sharing wasn't her strong point, but she'd learned from watching Gabriel and the truly great agents that sometimes the personal connection made all the difference. "It's not fair that because of Nico, you're put in danger. I get that. I really do."

"How could you?" Sarah rolled her eyes, on the verge of tears.

"My dad made enemies. He makes them simply by doing his job. I grew up in a fishbowl, always watched, always protected in case someone who wanted to get back at him came for me. It's not an easy way to live, am I right?" She paused until the women had nodded. "You can walk out of here now and try to put this behind you. Wilson may decide tracking you down is too much trouble. Or he may come after you." She glanced at Becky, sitting at her mother's side, back straight and a spoon clenched in her hand. This experience would change her forever, but Becky was a tough kid.

Sarah wrapped an arm around her daughter.

"I could stay with my family," Sarah said.

"And put them in danger?" Gabriel shook his head.

"We're going to keep you safe," Matt chimed in.

"This is how we can help." Mari glanced around the table, meeting the gaze of each of her former cellmates.

"Fine." Mari scrubbed a hand across her eyes. "I want out of here as soon as possible—and I do not want to see *him*."

Nikki couldn't argue with the woman's demand, even if she didn't entirely agree. She didn't know how their family fell apart, what had happened for them, but when she'd met Nico, she knew the most important thing to him was ensuring his daughter's safety. He was willing to do whatever was necessary—for her. As wrong as his actions were, Nikki could appreciate what he thought he needed to do.

"Right. We're going to organize security, get you some more food." She stood and nodded toward the front of the house. They couldn't risk the backyard, and Isabella would hear anything they said in the garage, so their options were limited until the house could be cleaned up.

Gabriel and Matt followed her into the living room.

"This the best plan?" Matt asked.

"Yes." Nikki braced her hands on her hips, wishing she was in a suit for these conversations. It was easier to be taken seriously. "Keeping them here is not ideal, but we've already put Wilson's people on the run. We want to control this, let them think their specialists are all still under their thumb."

"Aiden and Madison are coming here to watch them," Gabriel said.

"You sure about that?" Matt arched a brow. "He won't like putting Madison in danger."

"He didn't, but we're short on people," Gabriel replied.

"We need to let Nico know we have them. That happens first." She nodded at Gabriel's phone that hadn't left his hand since they started pulling strings to get balls moving. They needed to loop Nico in quick so they could get ahead of whatever plan Wilson had in the works. Besides, the man had seemed anxious for word of his daughter.

"I'll do that now, then we can get a start on today's events." Gabriel tapped the screen of his phone, then held it to his face.

"Events?" Matt asked Nikki, voice low.

"Yeah, we're checking out all the events we think Wilson might hit," she replied on autopilot.

Nikki held her breath. They were banking on Nico jumping ship. If he didn't, at least they'd rescued the hostages, but it might lose them more lives if it triggered Wilson's plan. There was just no way to tell if they'd made the right decision yet. If they could trust Nico. She prayed he answered, that he was as invested in getting his daughter back as he seemed, and that they hadn't just played into a trap.

"No answer." Gabriel grimaced. He adopted a drawling, good-ol'-boy tone. "Nico, it's Bobby. I got that boat we were talking about the other day. It's real nice. You should come by and see it sometime."

He dropped his arm, the screen dark.

Shit.

That wasn't good.

Gabriel made a left turn and a gust of sea breeze caught him in the face rushing in through the open windows. The sounds of the current Top 40 pop hits, the beach, and street traffic were their backdrop. It could be any Miami morning, except today they were on the lookout for bombs.

"It's up here, isn't it?" Nikki leaned forward. She'd put her hair up into a messy ponytail. He couldn't stop thinking about taking the elastic out and running his fingers through her hair. "Gabe?"

"What? Oh, yeah." He checked the street sign as they passed. "Ever thought about growing your hair out longer?"

"My hair?" She blinked at him. "Well . . . not really. It's long enough I can put it up or leave it down. Any shorter and it would be annoying. Any longer, it would be everywhere."

"Oh."

They rolled on in silence for a few seconds.

"Do you . . . like my hair?" Nikki asked without looking at him. She flicked a speck of dust from the screen of her tablet.

"Yes. I was just curious is all."

"Oh."

"Here." Gabriel pulled the Skyline to the curb.

The park was full of activity. People, mostly in their early to late twenties, were erecting a stage in the middle of a paved area. Signs promoting the University of Miami were stuck in the grass. It was an event in the first stages of setting up. And everyone appeared as though they belonged.

"I think the liberal talk would attract Wilson, but I don't know. Kids, though, it makes the news if you hurt someone's kids." Nikki shook her head.

"Yeah, but—"

His phone rang, cutting him off. Emery's name flashed across the dash display.

Gabriel jabbed the window buttons with one hand and activated the call with the other.

"Do you ever sleep?" Gabriel asked.

"Nico is at Classic Rides right now." There was strain in Emery's voice, the kind Gabriel hadn't heard since the hit team was in town. Their tech had to be burning the candle at both ends.

"What?" Gabriel glanced in his rearview mirror and shifted into drive, whipping the car around back the way they'd come. A few pedestrians scampered out of his way, one of whom flipped him off.

"He's at Classic Rides. You're the closest. Julian and John are out in Homestead, Tori, Roni, Aiden, and Madison are at the meth house with the hostages. It's you guys."

"On our way," Gabriel said.

"Did you call him again?" Nikki asked.

"Yes, he didn't answer," Emery replied. "The phone has to be off. I'm not getting any GPS data for it."

"What if he got our message, gave Wilson the slip, and is trying to get back to his daughter?" Nikki grasped the door handle and held on as he wove through traffic, cutting it close.

"Shit. I hope he has something to tell us." Gabriel pressed the accelerator out of a turn and the tires squealed.

"Keep me updated. Later." Emery hung up and the stereo went back to the radio.

"How far away are we?" Nikki asked.

"Thirty minutes, maybe? Call him." Gabriel nodded at the dash.

Nikki tapped the display and brought up Nico's contact, then hit dial. The line rang. And rang. The automated voice mail answered.

"Fuck." He hit the End Call button on his steering wheel. "He must not have the phone on him if we can't get him to answer."

"Why can't things go according to plan for once?" Nikki groaned and threw her head back against the seat.

"We had a plan?"

"Not really, but this wasn't it."

"Honey, best-laid plans."

"Shut up and drive."

He laughed and she glared at him. Man, he dug it when she was angry. It was better when she smiled or laughed, and best of all when she moaned in pleasure, but he'd take this moment. What a difference a few days made. She'd gone from cold and professional to hot and passionate. Okay, passionate was maybe a stretch, but she was trying, for him. For what they might have. It was more than he'd ever thought might happen.

"What are you smiling about?" she asked.

"You."

"Me?"

She just didn't get it.

"Yup." He grinned and lowered the window a bit, exhilarated by the rush of the wind and her presence.

"You don't make any sense."

"I don't have to."

"I'm done with you."

"Babe, you just started."

She shook her head and stared out of the window.

He cut through a few alleys and drove as fast as he dared all the way to Classic Rides, shaving off a good five minutes on the drive. Since the shop was technically closed, he pulled around behind the garage and parked on the street. On the off chance this was a setup, he didn't want to trap himself in the garage yard.

"I'm going around the front. You go through the garage. Remember the codes?" He pulled his gun from under the seat and checked the ammo.

Nikki rattled off the codes like a pro.

"Great."

He reached across, cupping the back of her head, and planted a kiss on her lips. She squeaked, probably in outrage.

They were in deep on this case, but they couldn't forget to live, to savor these moments together, because they weren't promised more. What they had was now, in the moment, and he wouldn't give that up.

Gabriel leaned back, cherishing the pink tinge on her cheeks, how her lips parted and she blinked at him. Nikki had no clue how much she meant to him. He didn't just love her, she was his whole world, and he'd been without her so long it hurt. Nothing could fill that place inside him.

"Get inside." He got out of the Skyline while she stared after him. It wasn't every day he could rob her of words. When he finished wringing Nico's neck, he'd have to put this on his calendar as a day to remember.

He kept close to the fence that lined the back lot of Classic Rides. Several hopeless cases of restoration sat covered in tarps next to a few others that were up for sale. That was the nice thing about being here. There was never a lack of projects to be done. If they weren't tracking down the bad guys, they were fixing cars. It had kept him happily occupied for nearly four years, but he wouldn't miss it. When this was over, he was leaving Miami with Nikki. The others would have to understand.

The low metal fence was barely bumper high. He stepped over it and quickstepped to the side of the garage. The parking lot that he could see was empty, but that didn't mean anything. He spared one glance behind him, making sure Nikki was inside. If it came down to it, Emery would engage the panic security system and she would be locked in, safe and sound until help arrived. It was a dirty move, and she'd probably chew him out for it if things went sideways, but she would be alive.

He pressed his back against the metal siding and drew his gun, keeping it behind his thigh in case some passerby got an eyeful they didn't want.

This corner of the shop was partially glass, so those in the front part of the office could see the streets on all sides. He could also look through the windows and get a better view of the front of the shop.

A man in flannel and jeans stood with his back to the shop, staring out at the street.

Why hadn't Nico answered his phone?

Gabriel walked slowly to the corner of the building.

"Nico, stay right there," he said.

To Nico's credit, the only indication he'd been startled was a slight hunching of his shoulders.

"I thought you'd be here faster," Nico said.

"What do you have on you?" Gabriel didn't care what Nico thought or if they'd failed his stupid test.

"Nothing." Nico slowly lifted the tail of his shirt and turned. He patted his pockets, swiping his hands back and forth to show he was completely empty-handed.

"Why didn't you answer your phone?"

"They were watching me. I trashed the phone and headed here."

A bit of movement inside the shop caught his eye. Nikki emerged from the dark hall and into the shop front.

"Shit," Gabriel muttered under his breath. To Nico he said, "Inside."

Nikki glanced between them before approaching the front door and unlocking it. Gabriel brought up the rear, aiming his gun at Nico's backside, right between his shoulder blades. Gabriel could drop him in a single shot if he had to. And if the man made a move against Nikki, he'd do it even faster.

"I can appreciate the caution." Nico held up his hands and glanced behind him.

Gabriel locked the front door, amused that Nikki also had their guest at gunpoint. "Sorry, we aren't all that trusting. That's why we're going to get along so well, Nico. Down the hall."

He spared a glance at the street, searching for any watchers, any indication they were being fooled, but it was quiet. Besides, Emery no doubt had all eyes and ears on at the shop, so he would know the moment there was trouble.

Chapter Twenty-Three

Gabriel pulled Nikki behind him and followed Nico closely.

"Turn right," Gabriel said as they reached the last door on the hall. It was the main office, Aiden's domain, but it also had an emergency exit and two cameras since the safe was also hidden here. Most of the time both doors were locked, but since Nikki had entered through here, they were open.

Nico stopped in the middle of the office, hands held out at his sides.

"Is Becky okay?" His voice was stone hard. This was a man who would come unglued if a hair on his daughter's head was hurt.

"She's okay. Have a seat?" Nikki gestured to one of the two guest chairs in the office.

Gabriel pushed her around to Aiden's chair and dragged the other guest chair a little distance from Nico and turned it to face him.

"What do you want me to do?" Nico practically collapsed into the chair, all the air leaving him. How much stress had he been operating under, knowing the lives of his daughter and ex-wife were resting on his not screwing up? On his doing exactly what a madman wanted?

Nikki pulled her phone from her pocket, tapped the screen, and set it on the desk in front of Nico.

"You are aware you're being recorded?" she asked.

"Yeah," Nico replied.

"Can you state your name for the record?"

"Yeah. My name is Nico Silva. I used to build bombs for the army before one took my leg." He rattled off his numbers and stared at Nikki so hard Gabriel wondered what the man was going to do.

"We need to know what Wilson had planned." She leaned forward, one arm braced on the desk. She was a federal agent again. But she was still different. She didn't just want to close the case; somewhere along the line she'd become invested in helping Nico Silva.

"All I know is that Wilson had me make fifteen barrel bombs and a dozen smaller ones. I'd make them and he'd take them somewhere else. I don't know what he wants to blow up. I tried. I tried telling him the kind of explosion he wanted needed to be tailored, but all he said was make it big."

"So you have no idea what or who he wants to blow up?"

"No. I have no idea."

"Shit." Gabriel sat forward, resting his elbows on his knees.

"That wasn't the agreement, Nico. We said we would rescue Becky in exchange for information about what Wilson wants to target." Nikki's voice changed, going icy cold and hard.

"I don't know. Wilson doesn't trust anyone with that kind of information." Nico spread his hands.

"Then you need to go back and make him tell you." Nikki leaned forward, resting her forearms on the desk.

"Your plea deal hinges on that information. Without it, you're going down with Wilson for all of this. It'll be you and him taking the hardest fall because these were your bombs. You've already admitted that."

Gabriel watched the woman across the desk. She was going to withhold the help she'd promised Nico? That wasn't like her. He no longer knew her. At least, not like this. She was a creature of the FBI, spouting the black-and-white lines he'd always hated.

"Yes, but—"

"There are no buts, Nico." She didn't raise her voice, but the cool quality of it sliced through Nico's protest.

Nico's gaze narrowed. Whatever rapport they'd built with him was gone. "He'll kill me, and what will that solve?"

"He's going to kill other people if we don't find out what he's targeting," she countered.

"If we find the bombs before they go off, I can disarm them."

"That's a big 'if' I'm not willing to bet lives on. Go back, or no deal." She shook her head.

"You can't do that." Nico scrubbed a hand across his mouth. He bounced his foot and picked at the fraying edges of a hole in his jeans.

"Yes, I can. You've only admitted your own role in all of this. You have to give me more if I'm going to be able to get you out of this mess, Nico. Do something so I can. Becky is an awful lot like her father."

"Don't. Don't bring her into this." Nico thrust his finger at her. Gabriel tensed. If Nico made another move . . .

"You did that, Nico. Maybe not intentionally, but you did that." Nikki stared right back at Nico, not the least bit cowed by such a hard, dangerous man.

"It's not like that." He leaned forward, hands clenched.

"Easy, man." Gabriel held up his arm. They needed to calm down. To take it down a few notches. "Look, the FBI doesn't just cut a deal because you were in the wrong place at the wrong time. There are rules we have to follow. You and I, we have to trade something. Information. If we do that, Nikki and I will do everything we can to haul your ass out of the fire, okay?"

"What about the others?" Nico swung his head around to look at Gabriel.

"What others?"

"The others like me? The ones whose families were kidnapped?"

Gabriel glanced at Nikki. They didn't want these men talking too much, but if they worked together they might uncover more. Besides, if they didn't stop Wilson soon, it would be too late to help them at all.

"We can make a group deal, but that's if you get us something we can use," Nikki said.

"Fine. I gotta get out of here." Nico pushed to his feet and pivoted toward the door.

"Be safe, Nico," Nikki said.

"I was safe. Now I've got to be stupid." He stalked out of the office and down the hall.

"Hey, wait up, man." Gabriel spared a glance at Nikki, tucked his gun in his waistband, and followed Nico out.

Nico paused in the front of the shop, surrounded by shirts and floor mats. He turned, his lip curled in a sneer.

"Hey." Gabriel held up his empty hands. "I know she's being hard on you, but it's the rules we have to play by. They aren't fair."

"They never are." Bitter words.

"Tell me about it." He shook his head. "You going to be okay going back there? It sounds like Wilson had a lot of people working for him that need help."

"That's an understatement. Someone needs to stop him."

"That someone can be us." Gabriel held out his hand.

Nico glanced from Gabriel's face to his hand and back again. The moment dragged on as the other man weighed whether or not to accept the gesture. Finally, Nico placed his hand in Gabriel's.

"You've got my number. Things go sideways and you guys need help—call me. Nikki has to follow all the rules. That's why she busts your chops like that. I don't." At least he hoped that was why she did it.

"I'll pretend I didn't hear that," Nikki said.

She stood at the entrance to the hall, arms crossed. She didn't look at Gabriel, but her expression was softer.

He was in deep shit.

Hadn't they just talked about him sticking his foot in it?

"Need anything, man?" Gabriel turned his attention back on Nico. One problem at a time.

"Get away from you guys." Nico turned and let himself out through the front of the shop the way he'd come in.

Gabriel had a bad feeling about this. Sending Nico back, when he might already be under suspicion, was asking for more trouble. But on the other hand, he knew the FBI couldn't guarantee him safety without more to go on. They had plenty of evidence to slap on Wilson and get it to stick, so Nico's testimony would be another brick in the prison, but not enough to get him off the hook.

"He might die," Gabriel said.

"I know, and I don't like it." If possible, Nikki's voice was even frostier than before.

He watched Nico stroll down the sidewalk, hands in his pockets, until he disappeared from sight, shielded by the neighboring buildings.

"You totally undermined my authority," Nikki blurted

out. Part of Gabriel liked the anger, but not when it was directed at him. Not like this.

"We were going to lose him. You were too hard on him." He squeezed his eyes shut. This was not a conversation he wanted to have.

"Too hard on him?" Her footsteps were near silent, but her voice grew louder as she approached him. "Gabriel, the man is involved in a bomb plot. He made no effort to stop things until we became the blockade in this plan."

"I know that, but look at him." He threw his arm out to where Nico had been and turned to face her. "That man has had one too many shit storms in his life. He needs a hand. Can't you see it?"

"And we need to stop Wilson. I can't believe you would blatantly go behind my back like that again. After we just agreed this wouldn't happen." She turned and stalked down the hall.

"Nikki, Nikki, wait." He followed her, closing the distance fast.

She wheeled around and he almost barreled over her.

"I believed you when you said you never went against my orders intentionally. Now I'm not so sure. You sure as hell meant to do that." She jabbed his chest with her finger.

"I did. Because we were losing him. Didn't you see it?"

Nico was breaking. The man was close to shattering, and putting pressure on him would only make it worse.

"Did you read Nico's file?" Her voice was eerily calm.

"No." Shit. He should have, but everything was happening so fast.

"Nico was taken prisoner once while he was serving. The account by his commanding officer was . . . enlightening. Nico traded false information for his release. He was in a situation out of his control, and he did exactly what he had to do to save his ass. He sent the terrorists after their own people and escaped in the process. It was brilliant. Until you look at the situation we are in now. Even if Wilson kidnapped Nico's kid and her mother before approaching him, he had choices. What's to say he isn't taking us for a ride and buying time for Wilson and his militia?"

Gabriel felt the blow of her words in his gut.

"Shit." He scrubbed his face. "I didn't know."

"No, you didn't, so instead of trusting me, you undermined my authority. I just can't win with you." She wheeled around and strode back into the office.

He'd just broken one of the cardinal rules of undercover work.

Assume no one is your friend.

Gabriel had looked at Nico and, in some ways, seen himself as he could have been. A highly skilled man with no place in society, caught in an impossible situation. So Gabriel had offered Nico what Julian had offered him. A way out. The problem was, Nico wasn't him. They didn't know that Nico hadn't been corrupted. That he was telling them the whole truth. Adverse conditions made men do strange things. What if Wilson had turned Nico? What if he was buying the militia time and throwing them off the trail? Nico wasn't all that concerned about his ex-wife. Maybe he planned to run off with Becky after this was all done?

Worst of all, he'd done exactly what he said he wouldn't.

Gabriel followed Nikki into the office at a slower pace. She sat in Aiden's chair, her phone to her ear, and didn't once look at him.

"That's right. Can you start on that for me? I'd appreciate it . . . No, that's not necessary. I'll handle it . . . Okay . . . When you're done, send it down here and I'll have it signed . . . You and me both . . . Okay, bye." She hung up the phone and laid it on the desk.

"I screwed up," he said. He couldn't fix what he'd done.

If Nico called on him, he'd have to figure out how to make it all right, by both Nico and Nikki.

"You did." She lined her phone up to the edge of the desk calendar taking up most of the surface.

"I'm sorry."

"Thank you."

"Will you look at me?" He stood with the desk between them, not daring enough to get closer. In her current mood Nikki would probably cut him with a look.

She lifted her gaze to stare at him, but not with agent-cold eyes. There was anger in their depths, and it was well deserved. He might have just offered a killer a way out.

"I should have made myself as familiar with the files as you were instead of assuming you would tell me what I needed to know. Here—that's the way it works. It's not bureau perfect, but it's the system we've been using. I do trust you. I need to be better at showing that to you, *mi amor*."

"No, you do not get to play the relationship card." Nikki held up her hand.

"Relationship card?" He frowned. "I'm telling you I fucked up and I'm apologizing for it. That's it. If you want me to be perfect, you picked the wrong man to love, *mi cielo*."

Nikki blew out a breath and pulled her feet up into the chair. She looked younger, softer than she ever had before. He liked to think these were positive changes thanks to him. Around her family and the bureau, she'd revert to her tight-laced, ever-perfect persona. But not around him.

"I don't expect you to be perfect, Gabe, but you consistently undermine my authority. It's a constant reminder that you don't trust me."

"I do trust you. I told you this time it was a judgment call. I made the wrong one."

"That's just it. You don't trust me enough to let me go out on a limb even if it's the wrong one."

"I shouldn't have done that, you're right. I'm trying here. What do you want me to say?"

Nikki closed her eyes. "I want to know you trust me as much as I trust you."

"I do, Nik." He circled the desk and went to a knee, turning the office chair until he could drape his arms over either side.

She looked down at him, her lips twisted up into something kind of like a frown.

"I won't make an excuse or reason away what I did. I made the wrong call and I'm admitting that, *mi cielo*."

"My sky?"

He chuckled. She was changing the subject, which meant she wasn't ready to let the argument die, but it was mostly over. She'd forgive him and grumble about it.

"You're being too literal," he said.

"Then what does it mean when you say that?"

"When I call you *mi cielo*?"

"Yeah."

"It means *my everything*. You are my world."

"Oh." She blinked a few times, but she didn't shift or brush him off. She was growing, and hopefully becoming more comfortable in their relationship.

"What do you think about that?" he asked after a moment.

"I think I don't know what to say."

"Can we at least agree I fucked up and move on?"

"You did fuck up." She unfolded her legs, sliding them between him and the chair.

"And I did apologize."

"You did. And thank you. I'm still . . . frustrated about it."

"I'll make it up to you."

"I'm not keeping a tally or anything."

"You sure? You spend a lot of time looking at that tablet."

"Because unlike you, I'm studying." She smacked his shoulder, but it was in fun.

"Well, you are the brains of this operation."

"Someone has to be."

He leaned in and kissed her lips, once, twice, light, barely there kisses. She didn't pull away or turn her head. He even felt her smile a bit.

"Come on, before I bend you over the desk." He pushed to his feet and held his hand out to her.

"Gabe!" She glanced pointedly at the cameras.

"Fine."

"Where are we going?" She put the chairs back into position while he locked the interior office door.

"First, we pick up some bulletproof vests. Then we follow Nico. Emery has cameras all up and down this street. We can track him as far as we can trace him. He knows where he's going, which means he probably knows where Wilson is at least." He wanted the soldier to be on their side, but Nikki was right, there was no guarantee he wasn't fleecing them. Too bad he hadn't listened to her in the first place, but he didn't mind making up with her, either.

You are my everything.

Nikki took a swig of her water and stared out of the windshield.

How could he drop that on her without warning? They'd gone from one extreme to the other in four days, not to mention fighting to full-on raging hormones. It was a big adjustment. Sure, deep down she'd had a fantasy of coming to Miami and picking up with Gabriel once more, but she hadn't actually thought it would happen. Not after the way things had ended. But here they were.

There was always the chance that their intense situation was a perfect breeding ground for rekindling their relationship. Once Wilson was gone, the way they thought and felt about each other could change. She hoped not. Her poor heart might not be able to take a second breaking.

"You're quiet," Gabriel said.

"I'm keeping an eye out for Nico. Emery hasn't been able to get a read on the plates." She checked her phone again for a new message from the tech and adjusted the lay of her Kevlar vest. A few days without wearing one, and now it felt foreign. "He said earlier he thinks Nico must have one of those plate protectors over it."

"Does Nico have a truck?"

"Not one registered to his name, but there's no telling. He could have bought one and never transferred the title."

"Or he could be in one of Wilson's trucks." His tone deepened into dangerous notes.

Gabriel hadn't stopped beating himself up over the missed details on Nico's file. She appreciated how seriously he was taking the incident, especially his apologies. He'd never apologized for that before. It was progress.

"What was the last you heard from Aiden about the hostages?" she asked.

"Nothing. They're getting the place cleaned up and food delivered. That's it."

"Matt send the EMT team to check them out?"

"Earlier."

"Good. He really is resourceful."

"Tell me about it. I just hope he doesn't get his ass handed to him for helping us."

"It does seem like he's making himself part of your team."

"You could say that. If we didn't need him so bad, I'd run him off for his own good."

"No, you wouldn't." She smiled.

"Why not?"

"Because you're like him."

"Like the golden boy cop? Ha. No way."

"Of course you are. He wants to do the right thing. He wants to help people. Sounds a lot like you."

"Great. Next you're going to tell me I'm like a Care Bear."

"You have the stare down."

"Shut up."

She chuckled, soaking up the lighthearted moment. There were too few of them now.

"You realize we're within ten blocks of the storage unit?"

"No, I hadn't." She sat up a little straighter.

"Our theory that their secondary location had to be close to this seems right on the money."

"Should we drive it, street by street?"

"Text Emery. Get him to do a search of the properties. We need to know anything that was sold in the last year. Large space, like a warehouse or something. Shop fronts would be too conspicuous."

Nikki grabbed her phone, jotting down the list of parameters, and sent it off to Emery. If she had to guess, they would get a reply in under fifteen minutes. Still, it wasn't quick enough. They needed Nico's insider information.

"Hey," Gabriel tilted his head toward her, "let's pull the others in closer. I know we need to check out all the events happening today, but if we know this is where Wilson's people are, we have more chance of cutting it off here."

"Agreed."

She made quick calls to Julian and John, then Roni and Tori. Until they were in the clear, Aiden would have to remain camped down with the hostages. It was a small team to work with. A little slimmer than she'd have liked, but the local office still hadn't responded to her request for the paperwork to process Nico's potential plea deal, and they couldn't tip off the cops more than they already had without risking interference. They were playing too fast and loose to involve local law enforcement without some sort of warrant or evidence. Nikki and Gabriel's eye-witness accounts just weren't going to cut it.

Gabriel's phone rang through the speakers.

She didn't recognize the incoming number.

"*Bueno*." Gabriel threw on a heavier accent, disguising his voice a bit.

"Half the goods are gone." Nico's voice was pitched low.

"What? Where?" Nikki sat forward in her seat, clutching her phone.

"No clue, but they're loading up the rest of us in a dozen different vehicles." The noise bleeding through the line was all yelling and the rev of engines.

"Where are you going?" Gabriel asked.

"My guess? Homestead Track. Look, the guys and I, we're in two vehicles. We'll do what we can to stop them, but it's already started. They were gone before I got back, man."

"I know, you did what you could," Gabriel said.

"Where are you now, Nico?" Nikki tapped the text icon and hovered her thumbs over the keys.

Nico rattled off the address without hesitation. She fleshed out the text and sent it to Detective Smith. Chances were the location would be empty, but they couldn't risk not covering every option. Which meant their hand was being forced. It was time to involve cops. Bomb squads. SWAT. Everything they could, but she couldn't coordinate that. She'd have to leave it up to Emery and Matt.

"We'll meet you at the track. Try to hold off doing anything until then," she said.

"I'll try. Hurry. I don't know what they're planning. None of us do." Nico hung up, leaving them in silence.

Gabriel took a hard left turn. The squeal of the tires broke the tense moment.

"I'll redirect everyone," she said. A couple of quick texts and their crew was covered.

"Good. Also, warn the track. We need uniforms there. And—get a vest from the backseat."

She dialed, chanting *Please pick up* over and over again.

"Homestead Police Department. How may I direct your call?" a chipper woman said on the other end of the line.

"Hello, my name is Supervisory Special Agent Nikki Gage. I'm with the FBI currently in an undercover operation. I need to speak to whoever is handling the security at Homestead Track."

"Uh, one moment, please."

The line went quiet.

"What's going on?" Gabriel demanded.

"I'm on hold."

"What?"

The speakers rang with an incoming call on Gabriel's phone.

"What?" He swerved and a car horn blared at them.

"There was an explosion at that art fair you checked out yesterday." No emotion colored Emery's voice.

"What?" Nikki gasped.

"Shit." Gabriel pounded the steering wheel.

"Ma'am?" Another woman answered Nikki's line.

"Yes?" Nikki refocused on the emergency call.

"Anyone hurt?" Gabriel asked Emery.

"I'm trying to verify you with the local office, but they say you aren't working with them." The woman's tone was all doubt.

Emery's voice broke in. "No one was hurt. It opens late today, so it was poor timing on their part, lucky for us."

"Hold on, Emery," Gabriel barked. He pulled the hand brake and sent them around a turn with squealing tires.

"What?" the woman on Nikki's phone asked.

"Let the cops and Feds answer that one. Wilson's people will be long gone," Gabriel said. It was a good, rational call. Whoever placed the bomb would have left as soon as they could. If it went off without hurting anyone, it might have even been on a timer. They just couldn't tell without examining the fragments.

"Shit. I'm not working *with* the local office. I'm out of DC working with an undercover unit. Let me give you a different number. Look, there's a bomb threat for the track. You know the explosion that just happened in Miami? It's the same people."

"Bomb?" Now the woman sounded even more skeptical.

"Look, call Deputy Director Gage, or Detective Matt Smith with Miami-Dade. They will both back me up on this. This is not a prank call." If she could reach through the phone and wring the woman's neck, she would.

"Hang up," Gabriel said.

"You want me to call the deputy director of the FBI?" the woman asked.

"Yes. I'm Nikki Gage. The deputy director is my father."

"That's rich. Hold on." Judging by the woman's tone, she was in no hurry.

"What is with people? It's a bomb threat." Nikki held the phone away from her face.

Gabriel grabbed the phone and thumbed the End Call button.

"She likely doesn't know about the first bomb. And sad to say, there are too many bomb threats these days to take them all seriously. That's on her, not us. Still, she has to report it, it'll get passed along, and hopefully someone is ready when we get there."

"Damn it. I don't like it, but you're right." Nikki gripped the door and stared straight ahead.

She'd always known there were more bad things in the world than what the average civilian was aware of. Now she knew exactly what was out there. The good guys saved the day more often than they didn't. She just hoped that today was one of those days. That they didn't lose anyone. That they could stop the bad guys. All of them. Even the ones that might not know what they were doing.

Gabriel took turns at a breakneck speed and wove through traffic so fast her stomach was ready to revolt, yet it still wasn't getting them there soon enough.

"Can I talk now?" Emery asked.

"Yes," Gabriel and Nikki said at the same time.

"Matt is handling the art fair. He's going to keep us up to date on what they find. John, Julian, Roni, and Tori are behind you. Aiden is just leaving, so he'll be there last. Uniforms are staying with the hostages and Madison. You're going in first. Be careful."

"We will. Anything else?" Gabriel asked.

"No."

"Have you considered hacking the cameras at the track?" Nikki suggested. It wasn't ethical, but in the face of how many lives they might lose, she was willing to turn a blind eye on some things.

"Already in. I'm focusing on points of entry."

Nikki didn't mention how relieved that bit of news made her feel.

"Okay, we're twenty out. Check in when we arrive," Gabriel said.

"Drive faster," Emery said before the line went dead.

Nikki closed her eyes to shut out the death-defying driving, but that only made her stomach begin to do sickening flip flops. God, she hoped they got there soon. She'd had no idea how close they were cutting this investigation when she got here. It was so much more dire than what she'd thought, and she'd dragged Gabriel into this. Still, there was no other man she wanted at her side for this kind of thing. They'd faced bad things together, but never like this, side by side.

"Gabriel?" She opened her eyes and looked at him.

"What?" He didn't spare her a glance, not that she wanted him to.

"I love you."

He glanced at her, brows drawn down.

"What's wrong?" he asked.

"Nothing. I just thought I should say it."

"We're going to stop them, *mi cielo*."

She hoped he was right. She hoped that they stopped the bad guys and got to drive off together, putting this whole crazy operation behind them. If not, she didn't know how she'd live without him.

Chapter Twenty-Four

Gabriel hit Dial without looking at his phone. Ahead, several lines of cars slowly edged toward the stadium.

"Do you have any idea how many rednecks are at this thing?" Emery grumbled something and jabbed at keys in the background.

"A lot," Gabriel replied.

"It could be any of them. I know our profile isn't necessarily redneck, but there's so much camo out there I can't tell the civilians from the militia. I've got facial recognition software running, but these cameras are shit. All I've got are grainy pictures and blobs."

"I know it's difficult, but we really need your eyes," Nikki said.

"Do what you can, man. Any word from Nico?"

"Nothing. Wait . . . I just got approval from the NSA to use their satellite."

The call cut off abruptly.

"What the . . . ?" Nikki reached for the dash display.

"Leave him. We need him focused on that satellite, especially if it can get us a better view of what's going on." Gabriel peered in his windows. "There's got to be another way in."

They didn't have time to go through the front gates like everyone else.

"There. What are they doing?" Nikki leaned forward and pointed to a truck pulling off the main road into the stadium. It was pulling a flatbed with a sleek car strapped down.

"Exhibitors. Hang on."

Gabriel turned on his blinker and cut the wheel, forcing his way through the two lanes on his right. The shoulder opened up, empty all the way to the turnoff. He pushed the accelerator to the floor, and the car surged forward.

"Shit! Overkill much?" Nikki scrambled to grasp the edge of her seat.

"Nah, I just like hearing you cuss."

"You bring out the worst in me."

"Or the best." He flashed her a grin.

He used the hand brake to maneuver the car in a neat ninety-degree turn. Nikki yelped and clung to the door.

"Get your credentials out."

The signs for the exhibitor entrance continued to point them ahead, down a long stretch of empty road. His gut tightened. Somewhere in there, Wilson's people were already set up, probably in a few locations. He seriously doubted they were outside somewhere. He hated how far behind their crew was. This whole op, they were nothing but ten steps behind everyone.

A set of security staff manned a gate leading into an area that butted up against the stadium. From the RVs and trailers, it was safe to assume this was where the exhibitors parked and kept their rigs, while the show cars went out to the infield to be displayed before taking to the track to really shine.

Nikki leaned across Gabriel, flashing both her credentials and ID out the driver's side window at the older gentleman with a clipboard.

"FBI. We need to speak to the head of security. Now."
She spoke with authority, but the man didn't seem moved
at all by her rank.

"Well, I'll get on the phone to him." He grabbed a radio
off his belt.

"There's no time for that." Gabriel gripped the gearshift.
"If you haven't already heard about the bomb threat, it's
too late."

"Bomb threat?" The man's brows drew down into a line.

"Shit." Nikki groaned.

Gabriel punched the gas, shooting past security. Pedestrians turned to look, but no one moved to stop them.
Probably because someone was always skirting security at
these events.

"There. There. There." Nikki pointed at the archway
leading through the stadium.

A set of flashing lights and a siren blossomed behind
them.

"Well hell." Gabriel glanced in their rearview at the cop
car spraying gravel as it made the turn behind them.

"Stop. Gabriel, stop."

"We don't have time to stop."

He turned down a makeshift street between vehicles.

"Fuck," he spat.

Two cars sat across most of the available space.

"There!" Nikki pointed at the far side. There was just
enough distance from the second car and under a goose-
neck trailer for the Skyline to squeeze past.

Gabriel kept his speed low, cautious on the gravel, and
slid through, surprising at least one pit worker who turned to
yell at them. Rocks flew up in their wake.

"Where is the damn entrance?" He leaned forward, peering past trailers and trucks.

Behind them, the cop car made it past the road block.

"Turn right up there," Nikki said.

He cut the wheel hard right, going between two double-decker trailers, yards before Nikki's proposed turnoff.

"Gabe, God damn it!" She pressed back into the seat.

"Chill out."

The cop car hesitated before passing up the alley between trailers.

Gabriel eased out from between the two movers and into a larger thoroughfare between the parked vehicles. The two-way traffic was steady, but he didn't have time to wait for a break. He pulled out in front of a drifting car and slid ahead of another headed toward the track.

He pushed past two cars before the cop car showed up behind him, too many lengths behind to make a difference as they neared the tunnel. They descended into darkness, the sound of engines and the siren mixing together in an ear-shattering cacophony. Red lights flickered down the line, closer and closer, until all the brake lights were on.

"Come on." He slammed his hand against the steering wheel.

"Calm down," Nikki said. She peered into the rearview mirror, the reflected light casting a rectangle across her face. "Cops are headed to us on foot."

"We don't need this shit right now." It was enough to make him wish he had a badge and a uniform right now to cut through the crap.

"Cool it."

He shifted into park.

"Get to the infield on foot. I'll handle these guys."

Nikki twisted in her seat.

The cops were out of their car and progressing toward them, guns drawn. It wasn't a good setup. He hadn't expected that kind of a response. That was on him. Not Nikki.

"You sure?" she asked.

"Yes. Find Nico. Stop whatever it is they're planning."

Nikki opened the passenger door and slithered out, keeping low and to the shadows that clung to the side of the tunnel. He didn't spare a second to watch her or think about the danger he was sending her toward.

Gabriel pushed his door open and stood, lifting his arms. He squinted into the light, focusing on the silhouetted officers behind his car.

"Gabriel Ortiz," the closest officer yelled.

This was not his day, but they couldn't afford to be divided between running from the cops and chasing the militia today.

"I'm not resisting," Gabriel said, pitching his voice over the sound of engines.

"Are you Gabriel Ortiz?" The officer was close enough that Gabriel could see the crinkle of skin at the man's eyes and the deep lines around his mouth.

"Yeah, I'm Gabriel." He frowned. Why the hell would they know that already?

"Just got a call from a Detective Smith, said you needed an escort." The man holstered his gun and waved at his partner, who turned around and jogged back toward the cruiser.

"What?" Gabriel squinted. Had he heard the officer right? The engines were loud.

As if on cue, several cars revved their engines at once.

The officer leaned closer and practically yelled, "I said, we're going to get you through."

Gabriel turned, looking back the way he was headed, searching for some sign of Nikki, but she was out of sight.

"Get me through," he said.

The officer waved at someone down the line and walked ahead of Gabriel's car. What were the chances Matt had saved their ass on this one? The detective was really proving his worth.

Cars inched forward, pulling to the side as the cop slapped hoods and gestured with his flashlight. A couple drivers threw rude gestures, but were ignored. Gabriel didn't know what Matt had told the older officer, but in the span of a couple moments he had the Skyline through the tunnel and onto the track. He still didn't see a sign of Nikki.

Gabriel rolled down his window as the officer approached on foot.

"Thanks, my man." He reached out and shook the cop's hand. "Detective Smith tell you what's going on?"

"Said there was some kind of threat and you're some kind of Fed." He gripped his belt and looked down his nose at Gabriel.

"It's serious. You see anyone suspicious, anything strange, call it in. Also, I've got people headed here."

"I know. Smith told me. Do me a favor and tell them to wait for an escort? If I hadn't gotten that call when I did, we'd still be chasing your ass."

"I'll give you a call." Gabriel grinned. The cops could chase him all they wanted, but in this car, there was no catching him.

Homestead Track was a huge, asphalt oval that hosted hundreds of races from NASCAR to hobbyists. The stadium could seat a whole city, and the infield could practically qualify as a township on the big race days, yet it still boasted a pond in the middle of the infield.

From the maps of the multi-race event, the best he could tell was that the track was being utilized in a handful of different ways. This early, most of the course was devoted to agility sports on bike, car, or truck. He rolled across the width of the track toward the infield, where all the consumer action was taking place, and likely, where Wilson's people were going to be.

"God damn." He scanned the hundreds—thousands—of people. They'd not only driven in, but walked and camped.

If a bomb went off there, it would be chaos as civilians stampeded for safety.

He jabbed the dash display, scrolling back to Nikki's phone number. In crowds like this, he'd never be able to find her on his own. Her number was still so new, he hadn't even had an opportunity to use it. They'd been together since she had arrived, except for that first night. The drive to find her was strong, but the case had to come first. Didn't mean he wouldn't check up on her.

A phone rang on the floorboard. It was Nikki's.

Nikki strode down the track, heat radiating up, baking her. If she ever got out of this, there was no way she was coming back to Florida of her own free will. The heat she could handle, but the humidity suffocated her.

Ahead, several rows of shiny trucks sat with their hoods up. They were showy, pretty vehicles, not like anything the militia had driven. But between the sleek sports cars and these, this fit Wilson's profile better than the other events. Except he'd hit the arts fair when they hadn't expected him to. Had she missed something?

Men stood in lines around the trucks, kicking tires and talking. The clusters of groups didn't fit the militia either. Those men would be dirty, probably in camo or other appropriate work attire. Their combined mission and mental state wouldn't allow them to socialize with others, so they would be aloof, holding themselves apart a little. The people here were the targets.

Part of her wanted to stand on top of the barricades and scream at them to all run. To get away as fast as they could. But that wouldn't stop Wilson's militia. She'd seen well-intentioned people do exactly what she wanted to do, and the body counts were high.

When a crowd panicked, there was a greater chance of unintentional harm. People getting trampled, hurt in the rush to get to safety. And then there was the reaction of the bad guys to the wrench in their plans. In almost every situation she'd seen or read about, the target panicked along with the crowds and attacked without rhyme or reason.

If Wilson thought they were going to stop him, he might opt to go down in a blaze of glory, killing not only himself, but his people and hundreds more attendees.

She walked the line of trucks, forcing herself to slow to an almost casual stroll. Sweat trickled down her spine and around the handgun at the small of her back. A well-trained eye would spot her firearm under her tank top, but she'd at least thought to grab her credentials and shove them in her pocket before fleeing the Skyline.

The crowd thinned out the farther she went until an open stretch of asphalt separated the drifting trucks from a course set up around the first turn at the end of the track. She held her hand up and shielded her eyes. It was an awfully long way to walk, and she didn't want to be that up close and personal with the cars as they went through their paces, sliding sideways and around cones.

She turned and surveyed the infield, with the press of wall-to-wall people and cars. If she were Wilson and she wanted to cause the most chaos, she'd be there. Right in the thick of it.

Where the hell was Gabriel?

Had he gotten arrested?

Nikki reached into her pocket, brushing her credentials, but no phone. She peered down, patting her pockets without luck.

Her phone was gone. Or she'd left it in the car. Regardless, she was on her own.

"Fuck," she muttered.

There wasn't time to go in search of Gabriel. Her focus had to be on the case and stopping Wilson. She circled the lines of trucks and headed back the direction she'd come from. The traffic from the tunnel was gone, so either Gabriel's stunt had caused more of a disruption than she'd expected, or whatever event the cars were headed to was under way. It left the track open to pedestrians strolling back and forth, admiring the lines of cars.

Gabriel's Skyline was still nowhere to be seen. She didn't know a lot about cars, but she would expect his to draw attention. So where was it?

He was a trained agent, so if he'd made it onto the track, Gabriel would go to the infield. And so would she.

Nikki angled her path to the strip of concrete leading to the heart of activity, weaving through people. The scent of fried foods and exhaust mixed together in a totally unique fragrance. It wasn't as disgusting as she'd expected, though after they wrapped this case up she'd want a shower for sure.

A woman's laughter cut through the din. Nikki glanced around, frowning. Why was that sound familiar? She swung her head left, then right, searching for the source.

There.

A woman had her arms wrapped around a man's neck. She leaned in as if to kiss him. Her brown and blond locks hung down her back in heavy, beachy curls. Hell, her hair covered more of her back than the halter top did, and Nikki's shorts were conservative in comparison. She could see at least three inches of ass cheek.

The woman stepped back, her face in profile.

Hillary.

Nikki ducked behind a cluster of people and changed direction, cutting between two trucks while keeping her eyes on Hillary.

This was the perfect setting for the woman. Why hadn't she thought about the risk of running into her here?

The men she was flirting with didn't appear to be Wilson's people, but that might not mean anything. She'd gathered from Gabriel that Hillary ran with a different circle, so it made sense.

Nikki crept closer, using the trucks as shields, keeping her head down. Hillary waved at the man she'd almost kissed, then sauntered away, glancing once over her shoulder to ensure her male audience was watching the sway of her hips. Nikki itched to grab her pistol, but it was too soon. Hillary could lead her straight to a bomb. Or the bombs. Maybe even Wilson.

Nikki fell in behind a trio of men striding with purpose. She had to almost jog to keep up, but not once did any of the men Hillary had entertained glance her way. It was difficult to keep Hillary in sight. Clearly Nikki had missed the memo about bleached hair and skin.

There.

Hillary bypassed the entrance to the infield and instead headed toward three lines of cars packed in nice and tight. They appeared to be in queue, waiting for their turn at the agility track. Which made sense. Gabriel had told her about Hillary's drift racing.

Nikki's focus narrowed to keeping her gaze on Hillary. In this press of people, she couldn't risk losing the other woman. Nikki's shoulders burned from the intensity of the sun, and her heart pounded against her ribs. What if Hillary wasn't involved in the bomb plot? Nikki could be chasing a dead end, but it was the only lead she had right now.

She broke from the main crowd heading toward the infield, and the creeping sensation between her shoulder blades intensified. Luck had been on their side lately, but what if someone saw her and recognized her?

Hillary meandered from one group to another, never pausing long. There were fewer people clustered around the cars, but enough Nikki hoped she could blend in. Hillary was her best lead to finding the militia.

The cars here were in four lines. There was an occasional pop-up tent that seemed to be a staging ground for groups of drivers. Logos were plastered on some, others wore similar shirts. She was probably looking at teams, or people who competed for the same sponsor. For all she knew, Wilson had his own tent and the cars were the bombs. She eyed the closest car. The midnight blue paint gleamed. Why hadn't she considered the cars might be the transportation? It wasn't like there was a lot of security.

Nikki needed to find Gabriel. They had to have more boots on the ground here, or they were going to end up casualties.

She searched the milling crowd for Hillary, but she was gone.

The hair on the back of Nikki's neck rose.

She casually turned her head, but there was no one behind her. Nothing to be alarmed about. Yet she couldn't shake the sick sensation that something bad was going to happen before they could stop it.

Hillary was still their best ticket. Arrest her, dangle a deal, and get answers. It wasn't a great plan, but Nikki was desperate. She strolled toward a line of three red tents where she'd last seen the other woman. Clusters of men and a few women drank beer, poured cold water over their heads, and chatted, none of them paying her any mind. But still there was no sign of Hillary. How had she disappeared so fast?

She walked the line of tents, eyeing the solid backing that provided more shade for the patrons.

Nikki walked between the tent and the next car, peering

around the plastic banner serving as the back wall to the tents advertising . . . something. The space was completely empty giving way to the infield and a short distance of nothing.

A small, soft hand grabbed her left shoulder, and the hard barrel of a gun pressed against her ribs.

"Fucking Fed."

The smell of Hillary's breath was enough to make Nikki's eyes water. Meth did foul things to the body, one of which was the worst breath imaginable. Nikki had smelled decaying corpses with a better aroma.

She didn't dare make a move against Hillary. Not with so many bystanders. If she shot the gun wildly, someone would die.

"Hillary," Nikki said, clinging to her inner calm.

"I'm going to gut you, you piece of trash." Hillary clawed at her back, grasping Nikki's piece and pulling it out.

She glanced around, hoping someone was watching, but they were conveniently covered by the banner and far enough away from the infield activity that no one would be able to see what was going on.

Shit. This was really not good.

"Would Wilson like that?" Nikki could still get some information out of her.

"Shut up. Walk that way." Hillary jerked Nikki around until they were side by side. Hillary had one hand up under Nikki's shirt, holding on to the gun, and the other at her side, under the Kevlar vest. The six-shooter was out in the open. If only someone would just look their way.

"Where are we going?" Talking, Nikki had to keep her talking, engaged. A meth head like Hillary was a paranoid, delusional individual.

"Walk."

"Wilson know you're here?"

"Bradley can't keep you alive."

"Does Wilson want me alive?"

"You killed my baby brother," Hillary snarled, leaning in close. "Get in the damn car."

Hillary shoved Nikki at the door of a silver Mustang. It sat perpendicular to the neat rows of cars on the very edge. Hillary pulled Nikki's gun out from under her shirt. There was no other option for the moment. Nikki opened the door and sank onto the seat. The interior smelled of paint and rubber. Hillary slammed the door shut, glaring at Nikki.

Did she make a run for it when Hillary stepped away? There wasn't anywhere for Nikki to go, and she didn't see security anywhere. If she ran and Hillary followed, she would have two guns to fire. Unless she used the car to run her down. Both ways, more people got hurt.

She stayed right where she was, gaze locked with Hillary until she climbed into the driver's seat.

"Where is Gabriel? What do you have on him?" Hillary shoved her gun at Nikki, pressing the muzzle against her shoulder.

"I don't know where he is." A truth.

"You killed my brother." Hillary pulled back the hammer, her face twisted into a mask of rage.

This wasn't how Nikki saw her life ending. Especially not now, not when she'd found Gabriel again. This couldn't be her end.

Chapter Twenty-Five

"Gabriel!"

He turned, scanning the crowd for Nikki. Instead, Roni and Tori parted the flow of people, headed straight for him at a fast pace.

"Where are the others?" Roni glanced around.

"On their way," Gabriel replied.

All around them, people milled here and there, enjoying the day with no idea what was going to happen if his crew didn't find Wilson's people. The trouble was, they could be anyone. And Gabriel could barely focus on any of it.

Nikki was still missing. It didn't mean anything, but they'd had enough close calls that he was anxious with her out of his sight and incommunicado.

Tori pulled her phone out of her back pocket. "Julian and John just got here. They're coming through the tunnel."

"Have you seen *them*?" Roni pitched her voice low. There was no mistaking which *them* she wanted to know about.

"Nothing. You?" He turned in a circle, scanning the crowds, letting his eyes follow whatever caught his attention.

The infield was mostly retail and show space. On the grass, between the vendor areas and the track, people had coolers, chairs, and umbrellas set up to watch the drift cars go through their paces. Hillary's pink and purple car was noticeably absent. An event like this was her bread and butter. She should be here, except she was in bed with Wilson and her brother was dead.

"Where's Nikki?" Roni asked.

"She's canvassing the area, but left her phone in the car. Keep an eye out for her?" Gabriel managed to keep his worry to himself. Nikki was a seasoned agent. This should be routine for her. Or as routine as tracking down rogue bombers could be.

"Hey, John and Julian want to know where we are." Tori wiggled her phone at him.

What was it with everyone suddenly looking to him? Four years of being a yes-man, and now he was calling the shots. He kind of missed it.

"Tell them to come straight through to the infield, take a left, and go to the end. My Skyline is down there. We can meet up, figure out how to divide the area, and search on foot."

"Okay." Tori nodded.

He turned, heading back the way he'd come. Roni fell in line beside him and Tori followed, no doubt relaying his message to the others.

"What are you thinking?" Roni asked.

That I want Nikki beside me.

But she was working the case. Just like he should be doing, instead of obsessing about her safety. He pushed aside the urge to find her and focused on process. What the hell were they doing next?

Gabriel glanced around. "Matt got through to security. I imagine we'll see an increased uniform presence shortly.

We need to try to find these guys before that. They feel the heat, they're going to react. We want to be on them by then."

"Any word from that Nico guy?"

"Nothing." And that worried him, too. What if they'd gotten Nico caught? Or what if Nico pulled one over on them? There were too many uncertainties.

Julian's black Nissan 300ZX and John's classic red Ford truck rumbled past, earning several admiring looks and a couple whistles. The classics were seriously underrepresented here. He could already hear Aiden's voice in his head calling it a crime. Gabriel could hear the whole argument, that without the innovation of the American muscle car, none of the current models on the track would have been made.

Streaming the tirade didn't distract him for one second. Nikki was still absent and he had no way to get a hold of her.

Julian and John met him and the girls in front of the Skyline where they circled up for a situation report.

"What's the plan?" Julian's expression was grim. Usually Julian or Aiden took the lead in these circumstances, but that was because their crew specialized in covert, quiet actions. This was a whole other kind of operation, one Gabriel had been part of more than a few times during his FBI days.

"We know Nico made a series of barrel bombs and pipe bombs. Nikki believes Wilson has had some sort of psychotic break that has triggered this. He's got an endgame in mind, and we want to stop that." Gabriel turned in a circle. "Let's split up. Check the vendor areas, the trash cans, we're looking for sealed barrels. The ones I saw were blue, but there's no telling how they disguised them. Check in every five minutes via text, and if you see Nikki, keep her with you, okay?"

"Why? Where'd Nikki go?" Julian frowned.

"She doesn't have her cell on her," Roni said before Gabriel could.

"And to think, when you started this kind of work, no one had cell phones." Julian gave Gabriel's shoulder a push.

"Let's go." Gabriel turned and stalked away. Nothing would placate him until he got to put his hands back on Nikki.

He approached his first garbage can near their cars. It was a big, plastic contraption with a lid. He pushed the swinging flap open and stuck his hand into the open space, but there was nothing there. Just emptiness. He kept his gaze roving over the displays and ducked in to stroll through a Nissan booth with their latest models. They needed to check inside trailers, the cabs of trucks, but that would take time, finesse, or maybe a warrant. What they needed was for Nico to make good on his end of the deal, but the man was gone.

He glanced across the way at John, digging down into a barrel, his face screwed up. Yeah, this was not a glamorous job. If they were a fully run FBI operation they could have bomb sniffing dogs on site already, but they had to work with what was on hand. Themselves.

John glanced up, catching his eye, and shook his head.

"Shit," Gabriel muttered. He lifted the lid off another garbage can and bits of paper and trash spilled out.

Nikki would know a better way to do this.

Nikki tried to pull her wrists apart, but the bandanna Hillary had used to handcuff her was too old and worn. The fibers caught against each other, working better than a pair of handcuffs right now.

"What do you think they're doing?" Hillary laughed and sneered.

Nikki tilted her head to the side, as if she too were curious why Gabriel was dumping out yet another garbage can. Smart. No one would suspect the trash bins to be dangerous.

"They aren't going to find anything there." Hillary leaned in close and poked Nikki's cheek, scraping her broken nail down the side of Nikki's face.

"Did you have a funeral yet?" Nikki stared straight ahead.

Hillary sat up, but even without looking directly at her, Nikki could still see her face twist in rage. Hillary growled, sounding more animal than human, and swung her fist at Nikki. Hillary's knuckles dug into the side of Nikki's face with enough force to shove Nikki against the door.

She grunted in pain, squeezing her eyes shut.

God damn, that hurt.

"Fuck." Hillary cradled her hand. "You killed him!"

"He shot at us first." Nikki sat up, despite the pain radiating down her spine and bouncing around in her skull. Angering Hillary was her best bet at getting the woman to leak information.

"Because you're a Fed."

"I never said I was." And how had they figured that out?

"Bradley knows you. He knows all about you. You're supposed to be someone important, right?" Hillary leaned back against the driver's side door and extended her leg toward Nikki until she could jab her in the thigh with a toe.

"Depends who you're talking to." Nikki shifted away, but not much. If she didn't act like Hillary's taunting bothered her, the other woman would grow more agitated, and maybe the meth head paranoia would kick in.

"I don't give a shit what Bradley says about you." Hillary picked up the six-shooter from the driver's side door and aimed it at her. "I'm going to kill you. He can have the pieces."

"Is that so? Why would he care about me?" Nikki stared at Hillary, not the gun. When had she become Wilson's target? "Shouldn't he care more about you? His girlfriend?"

"Girlfriend?" Hillary laughed. "He wishes."

"Oh, I just assumed you were the woman he was talking about . . ."

"What?" Hillary's gaze narrowed.

"Nothing."

"Tell me." She leaned forward, the gun still a very real threat.

"Why should I? You're going to kill me."

Hillary seemed to reconsider for a moment.

"I'll let you say good-bye." She nodded toward Gabriel, who was having a yelling match with one of the vendors. Probably about the trash he was spreading around.

An opportunity to talk to Gabriel would be invaluable. There was a very real chance Nikki could escape this situation alive. If Hillary was really dead set on killing her, she'd have done it already. Dragging it out meant she had other things on her mind.

"I am an FBI agent." There was nothing wrong with admitting the truth now. One way or another, Hillary would be going away when this all went down.

"See!"

"There was an NSA report, and one of the things that tipped us off that Wilson was in Miami was that he was making arrangements for a lady friend here. I just assumed that was you." The lie felt cold on Nikki's tongue.

"What kind of arrangements?" Hillary's gaze narrowed.

"A condo. A car. The necessities." Nikki shrugged. If she supplied just enough details, Hillary could fill in the blanks.

There was no such report, but Hillary wouldn't know that. It wasn't the most ethical thing Nikki had ever done to keep a suspect talking, but her life was on the line.

"That bastard," Hillary spat. She turned and chewed on a nail. "I knew he was seeing someone else, but putting her up somewhere? That's rich. And here all I've been doing is helping him with this stupid plan. This stupid, stupid plan." She slapped the steering wheel with the heel of her hand.

Nikki eyed the six-shooter. How was the trigger weighted? What were the chances it would go off in the car?

"What plan?" Nikki asked.

"Like I'll tell you."

"You're going to kill me. Might as well tell me, right?"

Hillary studied her for a moment. There was something not quite right about the way her eyes looked. As if they were slightly unfocused.

"You could be wired," she said.

"Wired?" Nikki held out her hands and looked down at herself. "Where the hell would that go?"

"It could be small. In your hair, in your clothes, something tiny. I'm not telling you shit."

"Fine. Fine. Okay." The situation was far too calm. "I guess this other woman is the one with all the info. You were just a mistake, then. God, I can't believe I didn't see it." Nikki sighed and rubbed her forehead.

"Who is she?" Hillary demanded.

"Beats me."

"You know where this condo is, right?" Hillary twisted

the key in the ignition and the Mustang rumbled, chugging to life, spitting up smoke behind them.

Shit.

"I've never been there." Nikki scrambled to remember the crew's addresses.

"But you know it?"

"Yeah."

"You won't find the shit there," Hillary screamed at Gabriel, leaning forward and gripping the wheel.

Where should we look?

Hillary flopped back, slashing her gaze toward Nikki.

"They aren't in the trash." Hillary smirked. "You want to know where they are?"

Yes. Yes, I do.

"Not here." She pressed the accelerator and the car lurched forward. A few pedestrians scattered. "I think I'll kill you in this bitch's bed and make Gabriel come to me. That should be fun."

Nikki closed her eyes.

Please, let the crazy lady crash.

Or security stop them. Or one of the crew find them. Nikki wasn't all that picky right now, she just wanted out of Hillary's death trap of a car.

"Where are we going?" Hillary asked.

There was only one condo she knew the address for.

Roni's.

Nikki hoped the other woman would forgive her for what they were about to do.

"Anyone see Nikki?" Gabriel searched the crowd.

"No," Aiden replied. He'd finally made it and joined their search.

"Damn it," Gabriel muttered. Was he being paranoid, or was that not good?

"I don't like it," Roni said, voicing his sentiment.

"Neither do I." Gabriel placed his hands on his hips and stared out over her head, willing Nikki to pop out from behind a car or come strolling toward them with the whole situation in hand. "I'm calling Emery."

He hit the tech's speed dial, hoping against hope he wasn't so buried he couldn't find Nikki for him.

"What?" Emery said.

"We can't locate Nikki. You heard from her?"

"No, I've been on with the bomb unit."

"Well, can you find her?"

"Maybe."

The line cut off, probably intentionally. Gabriel wasn't going to push his luck calling Emery back. The tech did his job amazingly well, even better when people like Gabriel weren't underfoot.

"What if Nico set us up?" Aiden asked.

"It's a possibility. Lure us here while he and everyone else hit another location." Gabriel didn't like admitting they'd screwed up, but it was possible. "What events are on the docket for today? Maybe they're waiting for something?"

"Then what?" John asked.

"Hold on." Roni whipped out her cell phone and tapped at the screen. "Drift racing. More racing. A demo. Nothing more than what's going on now. I mean, there'll be a concert in the parking lot, but that's it. This is about as much action as this place is going to see."

"Okay, then what races are later in the day? They'll be the most popular, right?" John shrugged.

"Then, what? We hang around all day and wait to see if they set up?" Roni asked.

Gabriel's phone began to vibrate in his hand. He glanced down, but didn't recognize the number. Nikki could have borrowed someone's phone to call him. He clicked the answer button and turned, putting his back to the bickering group.

"Yeah?" he said.

"Gabriel, I've got your girl."

"Hillary." Her pouting voice made him grind his teeth. "Where are you?" He turned, surveying the people, looking past them to the cars, but none of them were her signature pink and purple.

"Gabe—" Nikki's voice cut off in a grunt.

"Shut up," Hillary said, her voice slightly muffled.

"What is it?" Roni stood very still, her voice low, watching him, but Gabriel couldn't reply. Not when psycho Hillary had Nikki.

The one time he backed off, and Nikki was kidnapped. What were the odds? Why had he listened to her? Sure, she was a capable agent, but even agents had partners. Backup. For exactly this reason.

"Hillary, where are you? It's me you want, not Nikki."

The crew stood close, no one speaking. They watched the crowds, searching even as he turned a slow circle. Hillary had to be in sight. The same sounds he heard echoed on her end of the line. Hillary was still here, but maybe not for long.

"She pulled the trigger that killed my brother. I've got everything I want right here."

The line died.

A silver Mustang peeled out, making a hard right into the tunnel.

"Hillary's got Nikki. Get Emery to track that car." He thrust his finger, pointing at the Mustang.

He was willing to bet his Skyline was faster.

Gabriel pushed past Julian and reached for the driver's side door.

A boom, louder than the backfiring cars or roar of an engine, cut through the noise. For a split second, there was almost silence.

A bomb.

One of Wilson's explosives.

Gabriel pivoted, searching out the location of the blast. It wasn't a big one, not nearly strong enough to be a barrel bomb, but even a small explosive could do a world of damage.

The screaming began.

People turned, running, others yelled from where they'd been tossed prone onto the ground.

"There!" Tori pointed at a truck listing dangerously to one side, sitting alongside the entrance to the infield. It was a food vendor in a midnight blue truck that hadn't set up for the day, except now the back door hung partially ajar.

A big blue barrel sat inside the door.

People lay on the pavement around the truck and popups that served as a general dining area. The explosive couldn't have been very big. The damage done to the displays and vendor areas was minimal. At a glance, there weren't many injured either.

Tori and the others sprinted toward the truck and the source of the blast

Nikki. He needed to save Nikki.

But these people were in need of help right now.

It was an impossible choice.

"Fuck."

Gabriel jogged after them, keeping his gaze on the injured, the people still on their feet, searching for people watching the carnage. Chances were Wilson would have his men there to ensure there was damage done.

Tori and John climbed into the truck with Roni standing at the stairs, hand on her barely concealed gun. Gabriel circled the truck to where the worst of the damage was. Julian and Aiden were already tending to the worst of the wounded.

A badly mangled man lay next to the broken pieces of a cooler, propped up against the van's now-flat tires.

"Nico."

Gabriel drew his gun and crossed to the downed man.

Nico's prosthetic leg lay a few feet away. Blood smeared his face, and most of his clothing was reduced to shreds. Had he gotten caught by his own bombs? He reached for Gabriel, blackened, bloodied fingers clawing at the air.

Gabriel aimed his gun at the other man and knelt.

"Coolers. They're in coolers." Nico's voice was a rough whisper, barely audible over the noise of people. "Eight. We got six. Bryan was disarming the other. I didn't get to this one in time. Find Bryan."

"What do you mean? The bombs are in coolers?" Gabriel eyed the busted-up and melted bits of a blue cooler.

"Yes, damn it. Find Bryan. His wife—she was in there with Becky. Find him."

"Is there a barrel bomb in this truck?" Gabriel tapped the truck.

"No." Nico shook his head, his breathing labored, as if even that action were too much.

Another boom shook the stadium, but it was farther away. Gabriel leaned over Nico, shielding him with his body. Nico hadn't betrayed them—he'd saved God only knew how many people. Eight bombs? In coolers? If their goal was more chaos than destruction, that would be one way to achieve it.

John strode around the truck, covered in . . . flour? Some sort of breading?

"That one was up in the stands." John knelt next to Gabriel.

"John, we need to get Nico some help." Gabriel stripped off his shirt. There were many deep lacerations to Nico's chest, steadily oozing blood. "Roni!"

Roni jogged over, more of the white powder on her.

"Where is the rest of the militia?" John knelt and pushed Gabriel's hands aside. "Find Nikki. I've got him."

"They're gone. Just . . . just Bryan and me. We deserted 'em. Four other locations." Nico patted his pocket.

Gabriel dug in the man's pocket, but the fabric and whatever was inside it was shredded.

"Nothing's in there. Can you remember? Do you remember where Wilson's going to attack?" Everything in Gabriel screamed to go after Nikki, but he couldn't. Not with so many lives hanging in the balance.

Nico tried to speak, but all that came out was a pained groan.

"He can't tell us," Roni said.

"Roni, I need you to find out where that blast came from." Gabriel ripped Nico's shirt down the middle and helped John lay him flat. "There's a man named Bryan. I think he's black, his wife's name is Mari. We rescued his wife and kids. Find him."

"Gabriel. Gabe." John grasped his wrist. "I've got this. Go. Get Nikki. We'll tell you where to go next."

"But . . ." Gabriel looked around. There were maybe a dozen downed people. The EMTs on-site were arriving, a few security vehicles had shown up as well.

"Go," John said again.

"Call me when Roni finds Bryan. I want an update on Nico." Gabriel pushed to his feet and shoved his gun into his waistband. No shirt. No credentials. He could only hope the security guard from earlier would vouch for him if some poor soul tried to stop him.

He strode through the gathering crowd of onlookers straight to the Skyline. Blood stained his hands and arms, but he didn't bother to wipe it off before dropping into the driver's seat and starting the car. His phone rang almost as soon as he shifted into drive.

"Where is she?" Gabriel reversed onto the grass, cut through the infield straight to the track, and drifted to the outside line. No one stopped him.

Emery said, "Headed back to Miami. I'm trying to hack Hillary's phone, but there's no way to tell where they're going. I'll send you turn-by-turn directions. We'll get her back."

"Thanks, man."

The words tasted bitter in his mouth.

Emery didn't know if they'd get Nikki back. None of them did. The best they could do was hope he got there before Hillary did something he'd have to kill her for.

Chapter Twenty-Six

Nikki gripped the door and gritted her teeth. Hillary had none of Gabriel's finesse sliding through traffic.

Another car honked as Hillary cut them off.

"Fuck you." She flipped the driver off, swerving between the lines.

Nikki didn't know if she should hope a cop would pull them over or that they would make it to Roni's condo. A cop might only get caught in the crossfire. At least at the condo there was a chance Nikki could contain the situation.

"Another explosion just rocked South Beach."

"Turn that up." Nikki reached for the volume, but Hillary swatted her bound hands away.

"My car. My controls." She cranked the volume up.

"Authorities are split between three locations across Miami today as someone is setting off small explosives."

"What the hell, Bradley?" Hillary smacked her palm against the steering wheel.

"Was this what he had planned all along?" Nikki feared this was just the beginning. Incite fear, stir up the city, then hit them with a message. Something big. The barrel bombs. She'd seen the cooler explode. Watching those people knocked down as if they were paper dolls was horrifying, but most had gotten up after the blast.

"I don't know." Hillary's voice swung up in pitch.

"You realize your name is attached to this. Whether or not I live, you're connected to him."

"I didn't know he was going to do this! I thought . . . I thought . . ." Hillary shoved her hand through her hair. Sweat beaded her brow. In the close confines of the car, the lingering odor of meth use was nauseating.

"What did you think he was going to do? Did you realize he was building bombs?"

"No. Not really. Maybe? I don't know."

"Yes or no, Hillary, there is no maybe."

"I knew he was doing something, but not this."

What the hell had Hillary thought Wilson was doing? Nikki schooled her expression into one of calm.

"Get out of my damn way." Hillary jerked on the wheel, fitting the car in front of a box truck with inches to spare, and stomped on the accelerator.

"Hillary, you can walk away from this. Go in with me."

"And what? Let you get off for killing my brother?" Hillary slapped at Nikki, batting at her arms and shoulders.

Nikki held her hands up, shielding her face. When all was said and done, Nikki would have to answer for that death, but not at Hillary's hands.

"You'll be on the run for the rest of your life. The FBI will want you in connection with Wilson and with my death. The cops will want you for the meth. It's not a good situation for you. If you cooperate, tell me what you know, maybe we can work a deal."

"Shut up. Shut up. Shut up!"

Hillary reached for the gun in the driver's side door, but yanked her hand back. Her gaze locked on the rearview mirror for a moment.

"Fuck."

Nikki twisted to look out of the back window.

A familiar car zipped between the lanes behind them.

Gabe.

"He will not get you. He will not get you!" Hillary drifted onto the shoulder and ran up on the bumper of another car. Effectively blocked in by slower-moving traffic, there was nowhere else to go.

Nikki twisted her fingers around, clawing at the bandanna. She'd made a little headway on the knotted and ripped fabric, but not much. There were only so many ways this situation could play out. If they ever got off the highway, she could possibly throw herself out of the car and pray she didn't get hit or run over. Nikki didn't see a way for this to unfold without someone getting hurt, or worse.

"Move, damn it!" Hillary swung left into the shoulder and gassed it. The Mustang chugged, the whole frame vibrating with the power behind the engine, and rolled on, putting several cars behind them before Hillary cut back into the far left lane.

"Your exit is coming up." If Nikki could get her off the highway, Gabriel would have a better chance of stopping them.

"Shut up," Hillary snapped. She kept peering into the rearview mirror, watching Gabriel close the distance between them.

Hillary drew the six-shooter from the driver's side door and gripped it with the steering wheel in her right hand.

Of course she wanted to kill them both, but Nikki couldn't let that happen.

Suddenly, Hillary jerked the car right, slicing through three lanes of traffic, and took an early exit for Roni's condo.

There was hardly any traffic around them as Hillary turned right, striking off away from 95.

Did Nikki risk letting Hillary get to Roni's house? Did she wait for a street confrontation? Or did she act now?

Hillary's focus jumped from the road ahead of them to the street behind them.

The closest car to them was forty feet away, on a canal bridge. Heavy concrete and steel beams.

Nikki lunged, grasping the steering wheel and yanking it to the right, sending the car into a turn, except the tall concrete pillar at the end of the bridge impacted the front of the car. Hillary screamed. The seat belt snapped taut, jerking Nikki back. Hillary struck out, pistol-whipping Nikki in the shoulder.

Her stomach lurched.

The car tipped and the scream of more metal on metal rent the air. All Nikki could see was a flash of clear blue sky, then palm trees. Her stomach jumped into her throat as the car dipped, much like a roller coaster.

Water filled her vision.

Stunned, she watched it rush toward her while Hillary's screams drowned everything else out. The nose of the Mustang hit the water and everything went black.

Gabriel threw the Skyline into park and jumped out of the car. His stomach was in his throat and his heart pounded in his belly.

The bumper of the black Mustang dropped from view. The impact was both a crunch and a splash.

He sprinted to the bridge, gripping the railing with one hand. Below, the Mustang bobbed in the water, the nose already sinking into the blue depths. The current there wasn't all that strong, but the car would sink in minutes, aided by the seven-hundred-or-so-pound engine weighing it down. If Nikki hadn't passed out on impact, she'd have scant moments to draw and hold her breath until the car sank enough for the pressure to equalize. But if she was passed out, she could die before that, if the impact alone hadn't killed her. He was betting on the air bags being disabled, but if they weren't, she could be pinned in and unable to free herself.

He couldn't think of that, or anything else.

Gabriel sprinted another ten feet. He paused to kick off his boots, jerking at the laces, then vaulted over the side of the bridge. He tucked his arms in close and held his breath. Hitting the warm water jolted him for a half second. Little bubbles rushed around him and the weight of his jeans pulled him farther under the surface.

He kicked, propelling himself toward the sinking vehicle. Here in the canal, the water wasn't crystal clear. The slightly murky quality made it difficult to identify more than two darker shapes inside the vehicle. But at least that told him the air bags hadn't deployed.

He swam over to the car and grasped the door handle to pull himself lower. The passenger side remained closed, but he could finally take stock of the passengers. Namely Nikki.

A few bubbles skittered across the glass, but otherwise the car was completely submerged. Nikki's body bobbed in the dark water. Her hands tapped the glass.

Was she gone already? Was that blood?

He punched the window. The thud was dull and the impact useless.

Nikki's body jolted. Her head tipped up and her eyes opened. She stared straight at him.

She was alive.

Gabriel pulled out his gun. There wasn't time to wait on

the car to depressurize so he could simply open the door. He had to get her out of there now.

She pushed against the glass, retreating across the cab.

He aimed the Desert Eagle still on him at the glass and pulled the trigger. The blast sent up air bubbles. Spiderweb cracks spread out over the window. He hauled back and punched the window. It gave way slightly, but most of it was still held inside the frame, not near broken enough to come away.

His lungs burned.

Time was not on their side.

He said a silent prayer his gun was good for another shot. Gabriel aimed a second time, pulled the trigger.

Nothing.

He checked the chamber, ensuring a bullet was there, and fired a third time.

The blast was duller, but the bullet broke through the window and hit the windshield.

He pried the glass out and reached for Nikki. Behind her, Hillary didn't move. Her limbs hung in the water like the broken pieces of a marionette.

Gabriel wrapped his arm around Nikki and kicked off the car, propelling them toward the surface. He hugged her tight, refusing to give up hope. She was stronger than this. She would make it.

They broke the surface of the water. Above them people stared down, and in the distance sirens blared. He gasped for breath, spitting salt water out of his mouth.

"There's another body in the car," he yelled.

Nikki coughed, but it was weak.

He reached out, pulling at the water, and kicked, heading toward a dock attached to a private residence. It was the easiest way out of the water since he couldn't go up the way they'd come. He latched onto the wooden dock with one arm and hauled Nikki to the ladder. She grasped the rungs and he tossed his waterlogged firearm onto the dock. It wouldn't do him any good right now.

"Get Hillary." She gulped down big breaths, but held steady to the ladder.

None of the onlookers had leapt to their rescue.

Not good for Hillary.

Gabriel sucked down oxygen and pushed off the dock, swimming back to where the car had gone into the water. The current pulled at his jeans, weighing him down.

One more deep breath and he dove back under. Plumes of silt rose around the car, where it had settled on the bottom of the canal, but no oxygen bubbles. Dread settled low in his gut.

He grabbed the busted-out passenger window and ducked his head into the car.

Hillary floated against the top of the vehicle, lifeless, little trickles of blood oozing out from a dozen different injuries.

Gabriel hooked his arm in hers and pulled her from the car.

Hillary hadn't been the best person, but she didn't deserve to die like this.

He hauled her corpse to the surface and backstroked to the dock. Nikki was already out of the water and helped haul Hillary up. By the time Gabriel climbed the ladder, Nikki had begun chest compressions.

"Nikki."

"Breathe."

"Nikki."

"God damn it."

"Nikki." He grasped her shoulders and pushed her back onto her heels. "She's gone."

Nikki covered her face with her hands. Red lines circled her wrists.

"She was alive a minute ago." Nikki's voice broke.

"I know. Did she crash the car?"

"No, I was trying to run it into the concrete. I didn't know it would go over the rail." Nikki's dark eyes were desperate. "I didn't mean . . ."

"*Mi cielo*, she chose her path." He grasped her hands and kissed her fingertips. Hillary had chosen this life. She'd had opportunities and the means to do better, and she'd still chosen drugs and crime.

"What—what do we do? What about the bombs?" Nikki sat down hard on the dock. Tendrils of hair stuck to her forehead.

"Nico disabled all but two at the track, but got caught in the first blast. Another man who was blackmailed into this was able to get the second up into the stands, away from people."

"Hillary didn't know about the bombs. She freaked when that happened. I think she knew something was going to happen, that's why we were waiting, but I don't think she realized he was making bombs."

"Where was she going?"

"I told her Wilson had another woman he was keeping in a condo. I didn't know what else to do. We were going to Roni's."

"Good call. Come on." He pushed to his feet. Someone would have called 9-1-1 by now. The authorities would have to deal with Hillary's body and the wreckage.

"Where are we going?" She held up her hands and he hoisted her to her feet. There wasn't time to be gentle.

"There are more bombs. I'm hoping the others found the

other deserters like Nico. They might know what his next target will be. I can drop you at a hospital—"

"No." Her spine straightened.

"All right then. Let's hoof it back up to the car." He didn't relish the idea of walking on the sunbaked asphalt, but his boots were up on the canal bridge.

They walked up the dock to the waterfront property. Despite all the commotion, no one had emerged from the residence to see what was going on. If they were lucky it was just a couple of snowbirds, already gone.

"What do we do about Hillary? Policy dictates I should stay here." Nikki glanced over her shoulder.

"If you're able to keep going, I need you with me." They were shorthanded as it was. Besides, she was the only one with credentials. The cops were just as likely to arrest him as they were Wilson's people.

"They blew something up on South Beach."

"I heard."

"Any fatalities?"

"Maybe Nico. He was hurt pretty bad."

"Oh no."

They skirted the house and made it all the way to the side street that connected with the main drag Nikki had sailed the Mustang from. Gabriel steeled himself and set one foot on the sidewalk. The heat of a thousand suns radiated up through the sole of his foot, into his leg, and straight to his head. He hissed and back stepped onto the grass. The water dripping down his jeans almost outlined where his foot had been.

"You aren't wearing any shoes," Nikki said.

"Yeah."

"I'll get the car. Wait here."

"Nikki—"

"You want to argue this?"

"Be easy on the accelerator."

"I'll coast."

She let go of his hand and strode up the sidewalk. Her soaked shorts and shirt stuck to her body. She was beautiful to behold. He'd just pulled her from a sinking car and it hadn't even made her pause. Oh, there'd be fallout later, but she'd be alive. And he'd be there by her side, because that was where he belonged. With her. Forever.

The moments ticked by. It was completely ridiculous that the lack of shoes, of all things, meant he was stuck. At least one cop car had passed the street entrance already, and he was willing to bet there were more on the scene. He was eyeing a couple elephant ear fronds, wondering if he could fashion shoes out of them, when an all-too-familiar engine revved.

His blood pressure probably spiked in that moment.

He trained his eyes on the entrance to the street and waited, gripping the edges of his pockets with both hands.

The Skyline whipped around the turn, fishtailing slightly, windows down. It stopped in a skid of burned rubber a few feet away.

"Nikki . . ."

She popped out of the driver's side door and tossed his boots at him.

"Hurry. Wilson's next target is that student rally. The one we were at. It's supposed to kick off in twenty minutes."

"What? The rally?"

"Higher concentration of people. Kids. Not as spread out. Come on!"

Gabriel caught the boots and shoved his feet into them. He jumped into the driver's seat and was shifting into drive before Nikki even got in.

"Gabriel, you there?" Emery's voice spoke through the car speakers.

"Yeah." He concentrated on his mental map, drawing up the fastest route to the rally. It might start in twenty minutes, but Wilson's people would want to set it off ten or twenty minutes after it started. Students weren't punctual, and if they wanted the biggest bang for their barrels, they'd wait.

"This is the target. The big one. Nico's buddy, Bryan, is en route with the others, but I'm not sure they'll make it in time."

"Who is Bryan? What do you want us to do?" Nikki asked.

"Bryan is Mari's husband. I don't know what you should do." Emery's voice was grim.

"Have the authorities been warned? Are they evacuating?" Nikki strapped in and clung to the door as he pushed the car to really perform.

"The Florida field office has stepped in. Finally. Merlo doesn't want the rally called off in case Wilson's people decide to target something else or detonate early. There's something like a couple thousand kids there."

"They're setting a lot of people up to die." Gabriel could feel Nikki's gaze on him. This was almost as bad as it could get.

"Oh, God. Okay." Nikki rubbed the heel of her hand across her eyes. "We need to get there. If I'm there, I can pull rank. This is my case, they have to listen to me."

"Do we know who or where the other guys are? We've got their families. They're going to want them back." Gabriel didn't like using people, especially children, as leverage, but in the bigger picture it was all they had.

"Bryan said the other two were in different groups. He's hoping they got his message and will be able to help, but for now, don't count on them. What route are you taking? I'm going to give you green lights the whole way if I can.

The bomb squad is on their way, but they won't get there any time soon." Emery typed furiously in the background.

Gabriel listed off the intersections he anticipated turning at. A grand total of six. It was a long distance to cover, but the traffic was lighter today. Maybe people were aware of crazy shits blowing stuff up and decided to stay home instead. Whatever the reason, it was shaving precious seconds off his drive time.

Two 18-wheelers lumbered side by side, taking up the width of the road.

"Watch out. Watch out. Watch out!" Nikki braced a foot against the floorboard and an arm against the hood of the car.

Gabriel swerved into the street parking and gassed it, shooting past the Mack trucks. He came abreast of the cabs as they crossed into an intersection. Ahead, the sides of the street were lined with cars. He pressed the pedal harder and flipped the NOS switch. The car shuddered the moment the nitrous oxide hit the system, propelling him forward, far ahead of the trucks. At the last second, right before he would have slammed the Skyline into a parked car, he cut over in front of the truck.

"Another thought, Emery. We need to bury as many details about Hillary and Andrew's deaths as we can. The last thing we need is to start something with Jesse or the Cubans."

"I'm on it. ETA?"

"Five. Nikki, under your seat there are two backup Glocks. Load them." He still had his second Desert Eagle and Nikki's SIG Sauers.

She bent and dug the additional firearms out from under her seat. In an ideal setting, they would be wearing body armor, going in with the full crew and additional backup, but they were working with what they had.

"What's the plan?" Nikki asked.

"What makes you think I have a plan?"

"You haven't asked me if I have one."

Emery made a strangled, chuckling sound in the background.

"You won't like it," Gabriel admitted.

"Just tell me." She moved on to their backup primary weapons, ensuring those were fully loaded. They just might need every bullet they had.

"We need to get the students out of there. I'm going to drive straight into the rally, scatter people and see who sticks around."

"That's . . . not a plan."

"You have a better one?"

Nikki didn't look at him. "No."

Chapter Twenty-Seven

"Emery, do we know where Smith is?" Gabriel asked.

"Matt's at the South Beach site."

Gabriel turned the car down the same street they'd traveled earlier, before anyone was there. Now the sidewalks were full of people, most of whom strolled toward the park up ahead. Part of the street was barricaded and students milled around. Loudspeakers blared pop music.

"They haven't started yet," Nikki said.

"There."

A man in a bulky flannel shirt pushed a dolly with two kegs stacked on top of each other.

"It could be a vendor."

"Yeah, but why would a vendor wear that much clothing in Miami?"

"Look over there." Nikki pointed at a rolling gate sliding slowly up. From their angle, they could see pallets and stacks of blue barrels inside.

"There's no way to tell what is what." He hit the steering wheel with his palm.

"Drive into the crowd."

"Then what?"

"Then I'm going to do something stupid."

He couldn't argue with that. They needed to clear the area. He hadn't anticipated this many people attending the student rally. Just by the concentration of bodies, even the cooler bomb would do ten times the damage here.

Gabriel pressed the accelerator and focused on the space between two barricades. The foot patrol officers would try to stop him. There were probably FBI agents stationed among the crowds who would move in and try to put an end to it.

Nikki leaned out of the passenger window. In the mirror he could see part of her arm pointing straight down.

One, then two gunshots rang out. He heard the bullets hit the pavement and at least one bounce off the car.

The crowd seemed to flinch. Crime was high in Miami these days. Everyone knew the difference between a gunshot and a car backfiring.

The cops at the barricades reacted first, but the car flowed past them, crashing into the barricades. People were already scattering, running, taking cover.

He slammed on the brakes and turned the wheel. At such a low speed, the momentum didn't carry them far. He accelerated, sending the car up and over the curb, into the cobblestone area where the crowd had been thickest.

Cops rushed up behind them, guns drawn.

"Shit," he muttered. This was going to get hairy, and fast.

A gunshot from the rear took down one officer, sending him sprawling onto the pavement.

"Shots fired." Gabriel tore the seat belt off and pushed his door open.

"I think that came from the rooftop," Nikki said.

The remaining three officers couldn't seem to decide if they should aim at him or wherever the shooter was.

He kept his gun drawn, but the shooter was out of sight. Movement to his right drew his attention. He pivoted just as a man wearing a hunting vest and a trucker hat stepped out from behind a palm tree, a shotgun in his hands.

Gabriel fired first.

Trucker hat went down clutching his chest.

They weren't all wearing body armor. Maybe none of them were. He couldn't be certain.

Gabriel ran to the fallen officer. The man was curled up on his side, clutching his thigh. Blood oozed from the wound far too fast for Gabriel's liking.

Another gunshot, again from the vicinity of the roof across the street, broke through the screaming turmoil. Gabriel ducked and threw himself over the body of the fallen officer.

"I've got you," Nikki yelled between returning fire.

"Where are the FBI?" Gabriel yelled at the officer. He grabbed the man's dropped weapon and shoved it into his hands.

"Stage right," Nikki cried out a moment before firing.

"FBI? They aren't here yet." The older officer was pale, his skin ashen.

"Shit." Gabriel flinched as a bullet bounced off the pavement not two feet away.

He pushed up, grabbing the officer under the arms, and dragged him back to the Skyline.

"Shoot anyone in plainclothes with a gun," Gabriel said.

"Who are you?" the officer asked.

"The other FBI. The ones Matt Smith works with."

That explanation would have to be enough. He turned, focusing on where the last shot had come from. Where were the three officers? Had they scattered as well? Or had the militia already taken them out?

Their position was terrible. No defensive potential, out in the open. If he'd expected a gunfight, he certainly wouldn't have driven in here.

"Over here," Nikki yelled.

Gabriel glanced at the fallen officer.

"Go." He waved Gabriel off.

Gabriel jogged toward Nikki's voice left of the stage. He peered around the stage and his stomach dropped. Nikki had the top to a metal barrel partially pried off.

"What are you doing?" He rushed to her side and snatched her back, away from potential danger.

"It's one of the bombs." She backpedaled with him.

The hair on the back of Gabriel's neck rose. He threw them sideways a second before bullets ripped through the air right where they'd been. They landed on the stones, Nikki under him.

"We need to get out of here," she said.

"We can't leave them here with the bombs." He pushed to his feet, dragging her with him. They skirted a side tent and some temporary bathrooms.

"Where is the FBI?" Nikki walked backward, gun trained on the ground.

"The cops said they haven't made it here yet."

"What the hell are we doing?"

"Keeping them occupied. Let the cops surround us, sort it all out later."

The speakers crackled to life.

"Supervisory Special Agent Nikki Gage," a man said through the PA system.

"Oh, shit," Nikki muttered.

Gabriel peered around the stinking porta-potties at the back of the stage. There was a small collection of heavily armed men clustered together, most in casual clothing, a few with hunting gear strapped to them. Was that where the voice was coming from?

"Agent Gage, you are becoming a nuisance. Do you know what I do with nuisances? I put them down."

"Wilson?" Gabriel asked Nikki.

"Yeah."

"Agent Gage, I'm going to start killing people unless you come out here, understand? The first to go will be—what's your name?" Muted voices muttered over the speaker. "The cop goes first. Where are you, Agent Gage?"

"Oh, God." Nikki put her back to the plastic restroom and stared up at the sky.

Gabriel stepped in front of her and leaned in close until she had to look at him.

"We end this, okay? Now," he said.

Nikki nodded, but there was fear in her eyes, fear and dread and more. But he couldn't think about that. Not right now.

"They can't operate without Wilson. I shoot him, this whole thing goes to shit. Step out there, get his attention, I shoot. That's it. Take cover immediately, okay?"

"Five," Wilson intoned over the speakers.

"Oh, God, Gabriel." Nikki breathed through a sob.

"Don't. Don't think it. We do this. We get out. Understand?" He cupped her cheek and kissed her lips. He wouldn't allow this to be the end for them. It just wouldn't.

"Four."

"Go." He turned her, and though it went against every fiber of his being, he propelled her toward the open courtyard. But neither one of them was the kind of person to let others take the fall for them. He might be willing to let a hundred people die if it meant he could hold her one more night, but she would hate him for that. This was what she wanted him to figure out.

"Three."

Love meant standing beside her in the hard decisions. Like right now.

He darted to the right, hiding behind another vendor booth, his body going cold. Now he could see Wilson, standing over the body of the cop in the middle of the courtyard. Not behind the stage. Out in the open. He'd dragged the officer a bit away from the Skyline and stood with three armed men to his back.

"Two."

Nikki paused at the end of the line of restrooms. He very nearly snatched her back. They could sprint through the park, get away. But then the cop would die. There were things he'd done that he had to live with, but the death of another cop wasn't something he wanted sitting on his shoulders for eternity.

Nikki held her hands up, her gun dangling from her thumb, and stepped into the open.

"There you are, Agent Gage."

Gabriel straightened, aimed, and fired.

Once, twice.

Wilson's body jerked. His jaw went slack and eyes bulged. He fell backward, almost on top of the men standing guard.

The guards didn't hesitate, not like what Gabriel had anticipated. They raised their firearms, pointing them at Nikki, not him.

No.

Not her.

Gabriel sprinted, throwing himself in front of her.

He heard the shots, then he felt them ripping through his back. Fire and pain like he'd never experienced before. He hit the ground, trying to draw breath, to move. Nikki needed him. But his legs didn't seem to move and things were dark.

He couldn't lose consciousness. That wasn't how this was supposed to happen. He couldn't leave her, not like this.

* * *

Nikki crouched next to Gabriel, transfixed by the blood filling the little lines between the stones. It was so much darker red than the masonry.

Yelling. Someone was yelling at her.

She lifted her gaze, bringing her arm up automatically. One man knelt over Wilson's fallen body while the other two were pointing and yelling at her.

Gabriel's breath rattled. He was still alive. There was a chance he wasn't dead, but he would be if these men got hold of him.

She snatched Gabriel's dropped weapon with her left hand and fired with her right. She clipped one of the men in the leg and the other dodged, swerving. Gabriel's gun was heavier in her hand, so her aim was off.

The second armed man pivoted toward his fallen comrade, lifted his gun, and fired, hitting him in the skull. Nikki gaped as he then shot the remaining militiaman assisting Wilson.

One of Nico's fellow defectors?

Voices. Yelling from behind the stage.

The rest of Wilson's people.

Nikki grabbed Gabriel under the arms and tried to drag him, but he was too heavy, and with his wounds, she was afraid what moving him might do.

He couldn't die on her.

Not now. Not when they'd finally found each other again.

She couldn't move him, but neither would she leave him.

Nikki straightened and blew out a breath. The tears she couldn't help, but right now, she had to focus on protecting her heart. Gabriel. Without him, she couldn't feel, couldn't love. He was her heart, and he was possibly bleeding out right now.

The shooter put his back to the stage and gestured at her to stay where she was. The rest, she didn't understand.

Her brain wasn't working as fast. She watched him, trusting this man with not only her life, but Gabriel's, and prayed it was the right thing to do.

Her friendly shooter nodded and stepped back, raising his assault rifle.

Nikki leaned around the restroom, using it for cover. Easily a dozen men advanced toward them in military style.

Two against twelve.

Hadn't there been more?

The first fired at her unexpected backup.

She fired back, wounding the person in the lead. Their attention swiveled toward her.

Nikki fired again. And again. She went to a knee, blinking rapidly to keep the tears out of her vision.

She was going to die.

There was no way the crew or backup would get there in time.

A shot pinged off something metal.

The barrel.

She closed one eye and fired through the group. Again she squeezed the trigger.

Fire erupted, and the blast threw men off their feet. Nikki dove, covering Gabriel with her body. Shrapnel hit her side and legs. Metal creaked.

Pain erupted on the side of her head, and her vision swam, fading. If this was how it ended, at least she'd be with him. It was all she'd ever wanted.

Chapter Twenty-Eight

Beeping. The sound grated on Gabriel's nerves, and even those already hurt.

Either he'd been taken prisoner and beaten within an inch of his life, or he was in the hospital. The last memories were a little fuzzy.

He pried one eye open.

The room was dim, lit mostly by the screens flashing numbers and squiggly lines.

Aw hell. The hospital. His least favorite place.

He opened his other eye. What had he gotten himself into?

All he remembered was driving the Skyline into a crowd and . . . Nikki.

He inhaled, and pain did laps around his chest.

"Shh, don't do that." Hands grasped his arm, soft fingers twined around his.

Cold dread sat heavy in his stomach. He turned his head and stopped breathing.

Nikki had a line of stitches going up her cheek and temple, which appeared more severe because of the tight pull of her ponytail. She wore sweatpants and a T-shirt he was pretty sure he'd seen on Roni a few times, and her arm was in a sling.

"What happened?" His tongue didn't seem to want to work. "How long have I been out?"

"Take it easy, for me, please?" Nikki sat on the edge of the bed and grabbed a cup of water.

He took it from her and sucked down as much as he could.

"You should be in bed. What happened to you?" The last time he could remember seeing her, she'd been sopping wet but otherwise okay.

"Uh, well, how about I start at the beginning?" She took the cup back and clasped his hand once more in hers.

"Where is everyone?"

"Can I answer one question before you ask me another?"

"Yes." But he wanted answers now, damn it.

"You've been out maybe twelve hours. It's a little past one in the morning. Everyone was here until a couple hours ago when they kicked out all the visitors. I might have lied and told the nurses you're my husband so they'd let me stay. They don't seem to care about the whole FBI bit."

"Okay." Hell, he had zero issue with that lie.

"You got shot. Twice in the chest. The bullets did some damage to your right lung and there was some internal bleeding, but they think you'll be okay. They wanted you on the ventilator, but you were fighting it so hard they decided to take their chances."

"I hate being in hospitals. What happened to you?" He reached up and ran his finger along her hairline, not wanting to hurt her.

"Let me finish, okay?"

"What about Wilson? The bombs?"

"Seriously, I'm going to ask them to knock you out again if you don't shut up."

"All right, fine."

"You shot Wilson. He coded in the ambulance after the

blast, but they revived him. I think there's a good chance he'll live and go to trial. One of Nico's defectors turned on Wilson's guards, shot them, then we got into a gunfight with the rest of their people. The barrel bomb I found detonated, probably from a stray bullet. It blew up the stage, did a lot of damage. Killed three of the men. Shrapnel did this." She pointed to the stitches. "Help got there not long after and pulled us out."

"What about the bombs? The rest of them?"

"Between Nico, Wilson, and the other two, they were able to locate all of them. The only fatalities were on the militia's side."

"Seriously?"

"Yeah. Getting people out of there was the best crazy plan."

"What about Nico?"

"He pulled through. I talked to him earlier. He's going to be a star witness in the trial. We're going to put Wilson and his buddies away for a long time. Then a lot of other people are going to get help. Help they need."

"The others?"

"Everyone's fine. It's just us that got a little banged up."

"Come here." He blew out a breath and tugged on her good arm.

"They sliced you open."

"I need to hold you. Don't make me get out of this bed, I might pull something." Okay, he doubted it, but he wasn't above guilting her into doing what he wanted.

He gritted his teeth and scooted over, making enough room for Nikki to stretch out on her side next to him. She unfastened her sling and let her injured arm lie across his chest. He felt the weight pull against the stitches holding him together and was glad for it. Each ache and pain was just another indicator that he was alive. And so was she.

They could have died. He could have lost her. But they'd lived.

"I tried treating you like the others and almost got you killed. You should know that from now on, I'm going to be completely unfair about protecting you."

"It'll be a long time until anyone lets me in the field again. I've been put on leave until internal affairs investigates the whole case, and I've got to answer for the people I killed."

"They'll clear you." He kissed her brow. It was routine. He'd gone through it a number of times, and though the questioning was intense, it was to ensure no life was lost that didn't have to be. "You're a good agent. Talked to your father yet?"

"Yes."

"What aren't you telling me? I'm tired of the secrets, *mi cielo*."

"It's not that I'm not telling you, I'd just like to have this conversation somewhere more private. I love you, Gabe. I don't want to keep things from you. I want . . ."

"What?"

"Nothing. Later."

"Tell me."

"I want to share my life with you."

"What? Like marriage and babies and stuff?" He smiled and stared at the ceiling. Yeah, that was what he wanted, too. It was worth everything to him.

"Yes." Nikki's voice was very quiet, as if sometime in the last twelve hours she'd forgotten they'd already crossed this bridge.

"You realize this means I have to meet your dad?" His mother would do him worse than Wilson if he didn't ask Nikki's father's permission before the real proposal. And next to Nikki, the one person he didn't want to anger was his mother.

"He'll be here tomorrow."

"Guess I better get the guys to bring me a change of clothes. I don't want to meet the man wearing a gown. Did we screw up so badly he has to come fix it?"

"It's not a work trip. He's coming to see me. Us. He has to be back in DC tomorrow night."

"That's awfully nice of him."

"Mmm-hmm."

Why did he get the feeling it wasn't a family visit? What was Nikki keeping from him still?

Nikki fiddled with the hem of her sleeve. After a few days of shorts and tank tops, her suit felt foreign. She perched on the chair, watching the entrance to the hospital.

It didn't make sense that Dad would come all the way to Florida for a wellness visit. Something was up. She could feel it, and Gabriel had picked up on it. She wanted to tell him, but hadn't figured out how to put her concerns into words. So they'd eventually stopped talking. He'd sent her away so he could get dressed, against the nurses' wishes, but he wasn't one to care about that. At the rate he was progressing, they might be persuaded to release him today. And then what? Did they stay in Florida? She would need to report soon for evaluation.

A sleek black town car pulled up to the entrance. The passenger door opened and a man wearing a suit and earpiece got out, sweeping the area once with his eyes before opening the rear door. Her father emerged, standing straight and buttoning the top button of his jacket. He had a way with always appearing perfectly pressed that she'd never quite managed.

She got to her feet, feeling the ache and pull of every protesting muscle. In theory sleeping with Gabriel was nice, but not in a hospital bed wearing a sling.

Her father entered the hospital alone and made a straight line for her.

"Dad." She opened and closed her mouth. What did she say? She'd screwed up, even though she'd gotten the bad guys shut down.

He folded his arms around her, gently pulling her closer.

"Don't scare your old man like that ever again, okay?" he said for her ears alone.

"Would you believe me if I said I didn't mean to do any of it?"

"Yes. But we can talk about that later. Right now I'm here as your father." He stood back and gave her a once-over. "How's the arm?"

She wasn't buying the *I'm here as your father* line at all. They might be close, and she didn't doubt her dad loved her, but this trip was completely out of character. It wasn't the first time she'd been injured in the field, just the worst. But she wasn't about to call him out on that in a public hospital.

"Good. They said I should be able to go without the sling soon. It's not broken, just wrenched out of the socket." Didn't mean it hadn't hurt. She'd screamed when they set it.

"Ortiz still here? Or did he break out already?" He smiled, and there was a bit of mischief in it. She had the sneaking suspicion Gabriel and her dad were going to get along just fine.

"Yes, he's still here. Probably not for much longer."

"Good. Let's go see how he's doing." He rested his hand against her back and urged her toward the bank of elevators.

Nikki led the way even though her better judgment was

screaming at her. There was something up. Something she wasn't sure she was going to like.

They rode all the way up in silence, which only proved again that he wasn't there just to ensure his only progeny was well.

The nurses eyed them as they passed. Probably hoping she was there to take Gabriel away. He wasn't a cantankerous patient, but he wasn't good at lying there and doing what he was told, either.

She stepped into the room first and her gaze went straight to Gabriel, standing at the window, wearing jeans and a T-shirt. She'd never met a man who made those simple articles of clothing look so good.

"Gabriel Ortiz, it's good to finally meet you." Her father strode across the room, arm extended.

"Deputy Director." Gabriel shook his hand, expression slightly grim.

"Close the door, will you, Nikki?" her father asked.

Here it came. He wasn't a man with a lot of time on his hands, so she should have known he'd jump to whatever the purpose of this visit was.

She shut the door and slowly walked around the bed to join the two men. Her father had taken a seat on the rolling doctor's chair, leaving the two padded chairs for Gabriel and her. Nice. And by sitting, Gabriel had to follow suit to keep the playing field level.

"You aren't here just to check up on Nikki," Gabriel said. No question about it.

Her father paused before speaking.

"Not entirely." Her father never once glanced in her direction. It wasn't a slight, but right now Gabriel was the subject of whatever her father was up to, and she didn't like it. "I did of course want to know how she was, so I'm happy to kill two birds with one stone."

"What do you want?" Gabriel asked.

"Have you told him anything?" Now her father looked at her.

"No. Nothing," Nikki said without skipping a beat.

Gabriel's gaze switched between the two of them, unreadable.

"We're working on something. Nikki. Myself. Others. We're working on something that's going to do a lot of good for people. I can't get into specifics, but we could use people like you. People who want to do good things."

"What? You're offering me a job?" Gabriel frowned.

"Yes and no," Nikki said. She drew a deep breath.

"It's still ground-floor stage. You would be our first hire, so to speak," her father said.

"Why me?" Gabriel asked.

"You're one of the best covert agents the academy has turned out in a long time. You left and you're still helping people. We just want to let you do that on a larger scale. Can't say more, but there is more."

"Why now?"

"Seemed like the right opportunity at the right time."

"This would have nothing to do with my relationship with Nikki?" Gabriel inclined his head slightly toward her.

"It didn't hurt."

"So if we were to split, would the offer still be on the table?"

"That would be up to you and Nikki to sort out."

Nikki stared at Gabriel. Was that where this was going? Had something changed?

"And if I wanted to ask her to marry me?"

"I'd say don't ask her mother for advice on rings." Her father chuckled.

Okay, what the hell? First breakups, now wedding talk? Just where was he going with this?

"Is that a circumspect way of saying you wouldn't mind?"

"Depends. Are you asking for my permission?"

"I might."

"Then you'd better decide before you ask."

"What the hell?" Nikki blurted, but neither blinked at her. She was ready to bash them both over the head.

"I want to ask your daughter to marry me. Do you have a problem with that?" Gabriel spoke slowly, which was good, because she needed to replay those two sentences in her mind, over and over again.

"Not a problem at all." One side of her father's mouth hitched up.

He liked Gabriel.

And she wanted to strangle him.

But maybe she'd kiss him first.

Epilogue

Gabriel paced the length of Nikki's bedroom. The bathroom was too small and confining for him to wait in there, so he'd come out here to do his pacing.

"Anything?" he asked after his fifth pass.

"It's been thirty seconds."

"Longest two minutes of my life," he grumbled, and stalked back into the bathroom.

Nikki leaned against the vanity, staring at the white stick lying on the surface. Two weeks. They'd waited down to the day. She'd made him agree to not talk about it while he made his move up to DC and she started her evaluations following the Wilson case.

"What's that?" He leaned over and peered at the window on the test strip.

"It's a blue line." She blew out a breath.

Not pregnant.

"You sure?" He reached for the pregnancy test, but she slapped his hand away.

"The instructions said not to move it for two minutes after the results show up."

"You mean it could change?"

"I don't know. Will you calm down?" She shoved her hands through her hair.

He cupped her face and pressed his lips to hers. Gently. She was still healing, and he'd rather be shot than cause her a moment of pain.

She wrapped her arms around his waist and rested her cheek against his shoulder.

"What does it say?" she asked.

He peered at the test. "It's still a blue line."

"So we aren't pregnant," she said.

Gabriel couldn't deny the pang of disappointment. Sure, it wasn't good timing for a hundred different reasons, but he'd grown to want a child with Nikki.

"What do you think about that?" he asked. They'd agreed to stop all baby talk until they knew the results, and he wanted answers.

"I . . . don't know. I mean . . . I know it's for the best, but I'm a little sad, too." She pulled back and wrapped her arms around herself, staring at the pregnancy test. "Is something wrong with me?"

"Hey, don't start talking like that." He grasped her by the shoulders and pulled her in close again. "You said yourself that it wasn't good timing, that it was unlikely."

"I know, but now I'm . . . I don't know. I'll call my doctor tomorrow."

"And what?"

"And get birth control, for one thing." She gave him the stink eye. Despite his wanting her with an appetite that would never be sated, their sex life had remained tame due to their need for recovery. "They'll probably be able to tell me if I can even get pregnant."

"You will. When it's right, *mi cielo*." He kissed her brow, her nose, and her lips.

She smiled and his world was right. Coming back to DC

with her was the best decision he could have made. The crew understood. They were all invested in untangling what was going down in Miami, but it wasn't going to happen overnight. And they needed more than one set of eyes in DC. Besides, this way Gabriel could also check up on CJ.

"I love you." Nikki looped her arms around his hips, her fingers inching down over his pockets. Things were different between them now. They were good.

"Nice try." He slapped her bottom.

"What?" She gaped at him.

"There's nothing in my pockets except my wallet." To prove it, he slid the leather billfold out and laid it on the vanity.

"I wasn't—" She slapped her hand over her mouth before she admitted what she supposedly wasn't looking for.

What she didn't know was that the engagement ring she'd been so sneakily searching for was in his wallet. Waiting for the right time and place.

He grasped her wrist and pulled her hand away from her mouth.

"You weren't looking for—what?" He grinned, enjoying the way her cheeks went pink.

He loved teasing her, making her laugh, and even riling her up until she cursed at him. Everyone else got the picture-perfect agent, he got this side of her.

She crooked her finger at him before scampering out of the bathroom.

He followed her out through the bedroom and across the hall into her postage stamp of a home office.

"I did some digging. I've got new information for the crew. It's all here." She handed him a thumb drive.

"What is it?" He took it from her and turned it over.

"It's everything I could find on the Evers operation. Think it'll help Aiden and the others?"

"I do."

The others were going to shit their pants when he dropped this on them.

Their lives would never be normal. Gabriel was no longer part of the Classic Rides crew; that chapter of his life was over, but there was still a case to solve. He would wear more identities, but at his heart, he would always be hers. They would always be in danger. But they were together, and no alias had ever given him that. With Nikki, he could do anything, be anyone, go anywhere and still be happy. She was *mi cielo*.